"You're a gorgeous man.

With a kind heart. I'm sure I won't be the only woman in Royal who appreciates your sterling qualities."

"Aw, hell. You're making fun of me, aren't you?"

"Maybe a little." She smiled gently. "Six months ago your virtue might have been in danger. But now I have three babies to consider. Their welfare has to come before anything else in my life."

"Even romance?"

"Especially romance."

"Then I guess we've cleared the air."

"I guess we have."

"I should go," he said. But he didn't move.

Simone stood up, swaying a bit before she steadied herself with a hand on the back of the chair. "Yes, you should."

Squaring his shoulders, he nodded. The urge to kiss her was overpowering.

She kept a hand on the chair, either because she felt faint or because she intended to use it as a shield. Either way, it didn't matter. He wanted to taste her more than he wanted his next breath.

Trip
is part of the s

D0806770

4 1 0278597 1

TRIPLETS FOR THE TEXAN

BY
JANICE MAYNARD

First Published in Great Britain 2017
By Mills & Boon, an imprint of HarperCollins*Publishers*
1 London Bridge Street, London, SE1 9GF

© 2017 Harlequin Books S.A.

Special thanks and acknowledgement are given to Janice Maynard for her contribution to the Texas Cattleman's Club: Blackmail series.

ISBN: 978-0-263-92819-8

51-0517

USA TODAY bestselling author **Janice Maynard** loved books and writing even as a child. But it took multiple rejections before she sold her first manuscript. Since 2002, she has written over forty-five books and novellas. Janice lives in east Tennessee with her husband, Charles. They love hiking, traveling and spending time with family.

You can connect with Janice at:
www.janicemaynard.com,
Twitter.com/janicemaynard,
Facebook.com/ janicemaynardreaderpage,
Facebook.com/ janicesmaynard
and Instagram.com/janicemaynard.

For Charles Griemsman, editor extraordinaire.
Thanks for all your hard work and your
commitment to making stories shine.
The Texas Cattleman's Club
wouldn't be the same without you!

One

Royal, Texas, was a great place to call home. Running her own ad agency, being a member of the esteemed Texas Cattleman's Club and maintaining a hectic social life kept Simone Parker plenty busy. Busy enough not to worry about the ghosts of lost loves.

Today, her luck had run out. Five years. It had been five long years since she'd last laid eyes on Troy Hutchinson. Now here she sat in a freezing exam room at Royal Memorial, naked but for a thin paper hospital gown, and in walked the man who broke her heart. Pressing her knees together instinctively, she gripped the edge of the exam table and blurted out the first thing that came to her mind.

"Where's Dr. Markman?"

Hutch—almost nobody called him Troy—stared at her impassively. "He took a position in Houston. I'm the new head of the maternal-fetal medicine department."

Made sense. Royal's state-of-the-art hospital hired only the best.

It occurred to her that Hutch didn't look at all surprised to see her. But then again, he'd obviously glanced at her chart before entering the room. He was as gorgeous as ever—chocolate eyes, closely cropped black hair and mocha skin. The only thing missing was his killer smile.

Tall and lean, in his physical prime, the man was impressive even without the lab coat. Wearing it, he exuded authority and masculinity. Making Simone feel small and stupid.

Her stomach curled with nausea. Today's situation was volatile enough without having to confront old lovers. As if the term applied. She'd been a twenty-two-year-old virgin when she and Hutch first hooked up. She'd had only one relationship after that, and it had been brief and unexceptional.

For most of her life she'd chosen to hide behind her reputation as a shallow party girl. Even Hutch had believed it in the beginning. Until he'd realized he was the first. Then there had been hell to pay.

Her palms started to sweat. "You can't be my doctor."

"Of course not," he said. "Dr. Markman left rather abruptly. We've been in the process of notifying his patients. Somehow, your appointment fell through the cracks. Dr. Janine Fetter has agreed to take over your case…with your permission, of course."

"That's fine," Simone said impatiently. "But that doesn't explain why *you're* here."

A faint smile lightened his face. "Don't shoot the messenger. Scheduling should have postponed your ultrasound until next week. Dr. Fetter doesn't have any openings until then. She's not even here today."

Great, just great. Hutch knew every inch of her body. Even so, no way in heck was she going to calmly put her feet in those stirrups and let him examine her. That was too icky for words. "What are my options?"

"You can make an appointment for next week and go home…"

"Or?"

"Or if you don't want to wait, I can go over the ultrasound with you. But no exam," he said quickly.

"Ah." Simone had badgered the tech to explain all the grainy images on the screen, but the woman had been well trained. She'd done her job, escorted Simone to yet another exam room and left her to worry for forty-five minutes. Plenty of time for a single woman to regret the impulsive decision that had led her to this moment.

"So tell me," she snapped, her nerves getting the best of her. "I'm not pregnant, am I? Don't worry. I won't fall apart. I knew the odds when I went into this."

Pursuing fertility treatments and intrauterine insemination had been more involved than she had ever imagined. Even now, she wouldn't be entirely unhappy if it hadn't worked. Picking out a sperm donor and dealing with hormone shots had been stressful, expensive and time-consuming. It had also given her plenty of opportunity to rethink her hasty decision.

Her late grandfather had left instructions with the executors of his will that she would be entitled to half of his vast estate—five million dollars cash and the family homestead, worth infinitely more—if, and only if, she produced an heir to continue the family bloodline. With no plans to settle down anytime soon, she'd decided to go the route of single motherhood.

Trying to live up to the terms of her grandfather's will—without weighing the cost—was, in retrospect, probably a stupid decision.

She must have had gut-level doubts from the beginning, because she hadn't even told her two best friends, Naomi and Cecelia. Naomi had seemed distracted and tense ever since she got back from Europe, and Cecelia had been on cloud nine after reuniting with former flame Deacon Chase. So Simone had kept her plans to herself.

For the first time, Hutch's facade cracked. His jaw firmed, and his eyes were bleak. "No one told me you had gotten married, Simone. Though, knowing you, I'm not surprised you kept your maiden name. Don't you want the baby's father to be here when we talk about these results? Can you contact him? We could reschedule for later this afternoon."

She stared at Hutch. "Have you read through my file?"

"Not yet. But I will, of course. All I've seen is the ultrasound report. I only came on board officially yesterday. To be honest, I'm still a little jet-lagged."

And no wonder. He'd spent the past half decade in Sudan with Doctors Without Borders. The man was almost too good to be true, strong, sensitive and—when he unleashed that boy-next-door charm—virtually irresistible.

Though they had no longer been a couple when he left Royal, Texas, in the intervening months and years, she had worried about him. Malaria. Viral hemorrhagic fever. Political uprisings. He had thrust himself into a hotbed of danger and never looked back. Even without being there, Simone knew he had saved untold numbers of mothers and babies.

Hutch had completed not one but two stints in Sudan. When he hadn't returned after the first one, she knew for sure he was no longer interested in resurrecting their relationship—although that was possibly too mature a word for the affair. She and Hutch together had been like fireworks, burning hot and bright and beautiful, but over too soon.

While she mentally rehashed the painful past, Hutch waited patiently, his expression guarded. Having him eye her with the impassivity of a medical professional hurt. A lot.

Whipping up a batch of righteous indignation helped. It was none of Hutch's concern what she did with her life. "There is no father in the picture," she said bluntly. "Go ahead and tell me what you have to say."

For a split second, something flickered across his face. Shock? Probably. Relief? Unlikely.

"I'm sorry to hear that," he said, his tone so formal it

could have frozen the air itself. "Are you divorced? Widowed?"

"I don't think you're supposed to ask me that, Dr. Hutchinson." She was furious suddenly—at herself for making such a mess of things, at Hutch for having the audacity to come home looking wonderful and completely unapproachable, if a bit tired, and at life in general.

He swallowed. "My apologies. You're right. That was out of line."

Despite her best intentions, she couldn't stay mad. Not today. And besides, what did it matter if she told him? Not the whole truth, of course. But he had her file at his disposal. Sooner or later, he would know. She might as well put a good spin on it.

"I wanted to have a baby," she said bluntly. *Maybe for all the wrong reasons, but still...* "I chose to use an anonymous sperm donor, because I had no significant other in the picture. This baby will be mine and mine alone. There are plenty of single mothers out there doing very well. I have a good job, financial resources and plenty of friends. I'll be able to handle motherhood, Hutch. You don't have to look at me like that."

Her decisions about parenthood and her grandfather's bequest were her own. She didn't want to be judged, and in truth, the facts could very easily be misinterpreted, leaving her in a bad light.

It was a real worry, particularly since the mysterious Maverick had somehow found out about her fertility treatments and threatened to expose her secrets. She pushed that situation to the back of her mind. Dealing with Hutch was enough drama for one day.

He stared at her with such intensity she felt oddly faint. Her heart beat loudly in her ears. Hutch's expression was a mixture of incredulity, pity and disapproval. Or at least that was how she interpreted it. At one time, she could guess what he was thinking. That was long ago, though.

Tossing the manila folder on the counter beside the computer, he shoved his hands in his pockets. "I have no doubts about your ability to care for a baby," he said.

She frowned. "Then why all the mystery? Why do you look like you're about to deliver words of doom? Is it something else? A tumor? Some weird cancer? Am I dying? That would suck."

His lips twitched. "Not at all, Simone. You're having triplets."

Hutch cursed when Simone went milk pale and keeled over. He caught her before she hit the floor, but just barely. Hell, he knew better. It wasn't the kind of news one delivered with a baseball bat. As usual, though, she rattled him. Even now.

Cradling her in his arms, he turned back to the exam table. His instinct was to hold her until she woke up. But that was all kinds of unethical. Instead, he laid her gently on her back and reached into the cabinet for a soft, mesh-weave blanket. Covering her all the way up to her neck, he tried not to notice the way she smelled. He could have identified her scent with his eyes closed. A mix of floral and spicy that was uniquely Simone.

She roused slowly, those incredibly long lashes fluttering as she came back to him. "What happened?"

When she tried to rise up onto her elbows, he put a hand on her shoulder to keep her down. "Give yourself a minute to recover. You've had a shock."

Even befuddled and wrapped in a generic blanket, she was striking. Her blue eyes were electric, somewhere between royal and aquamarine. Her hair made as much of an impact her eyes. The smooth, silky fall was the black of a raven's wing…shot through with blue in the sunlight. He tried not to remember what it felt like to wrap his hands in all that thick, glorious hair. At one time, it had reached almost to her waist. The style was shorter now, but still a couple of inches below her shoulders.

Her gaze cleared gradually. "So I wasn't dreaming." The words were not really a question.

"No."

"I want to sit up."

He helped her, though it was difficult to touch her. She made him feel like a gawky adolescent. That was bloody uncomfortable for a man supposed to be in charge of Royal, Texas's world-class obstetrics department.

"I apologize for springing it on you, Simone. There's no easy way to drop that bomb. I have to tell you I'm surprised and concerned that you've chosen this option."

"I'm not getting any younger." The set of her jaw was mulish.

He remembered all too well what Simone was like when she made up her mind about something. "You're not even thirty. Couldn't you have waited and taken the traditional route?" he asked.

The wash of color that had returned to her face leached away again. Her eyes glittered with something that might have been pain or anger. "I tried that once or twice. I'm not a fan. Men complicate things."

The blunt retort was a direct shot at him. It found its mark. Clearly, Simone still blamed him for their breakup. He wanted to fight back, but it was pointless after all this time. His job wasn't to be her friend, or even her boyfriend. He was charged with overseeing her medical care.

"I suppose it's a moot point now," he said, feeling weary and discouraged. "Unless you've changed your mind. Do you want to terminate the pregnancy? If that's your decision, hospital staff would of course preserve your privacy."

Simone blinked. "Is that what *you* think I should do?"

He weighed his words carefully. "Having triplets is an enormous commitment, even for a two-parent family. You would be doing this alone."

She stared at him. Her restless fingers pleated the edges of the blanket. "I want these babies."

He cocked his head, trying to read her emotions. "You wanted *one* baby, Simone. I think you need to weigh the situation seriously. While it's still very early."

"There's nothing to consider. I made a choice. I have to live with the consequences."

"For the rest of your life."

Hot color streaked her cheekbones. "I know you think I'm flighty and impulsive and a lightweight. What you don't realize is that I've grown up a lot in the time you've been gone. I can do this."

"But why?" That's what confused him. It wasn't as if she was running out of time. Besides, she had never particularly struck him as the maternal type.

"My reasons are my business, Dr. Hutchinson. Am I free to go now?"

There were secrets in her eyes and in her heart. He knew it. The two of them might have been separated by time and distance for the past few years, but there had been a moment when he had known everything about her. Every thought. Every feeling. Every beat of her energetic, enthusiastic, passionate heart.

The Simone he knew jumped into life with both feet, usually via the deep end. She had her naysayers—Royal was a relatively small town with a long memory. Her youthful missteps had cost her. A reputation was a hard thing to shake. But he knew she had a good heart.

"Just hear me out. You should know, Simone, that a multiple pregnancy immediately puts you in the high-risk category. The hospital hired me for my expertise. I'll be overseeing your case indirectly. Dr. Fetter will alert me if any problems arise. Will that be a problem?"

Simone blinked. "Do you have any crackers?"

"Excuse me?" Had his hearing taken a hit in Sudan?

"I need saltines. I'm about to puke."

Oh, lord. "Hold on," he said. Opening the door to the hallway, he bellowed for a nurse. The poor woman must have sprinted, because she was back in two minutes with the crackers and a cup of ice chips.

He took them with muttered thanks, closed the door firmly and turned to Simone. She wasn't white anymore. More like a transparent shade of green. Grabbing a plastic basin from the cabinet, he put it in her lap and unwrapped the crackers. "Slowly," he said.

"Don't worry," she muttered. "I'm afraid to move."

"Poor baby." He'd seen pregnant women almost every day of his professional life, but none had ever touched him as deeply as this one. Without overthinking it, he put an arm behind her back to support her. "I'll hold the cracker," he said. "You nibble."

It was a measure of how miserable she was that she didn't fight him. No snappy comeback. No insistence she could feed herself. When she leaned into him, his heart actually skipped a beat. A huge neon sign flashed in his brain. *Warning! Warning!*

Even though he knew he couldn't get close to her again, his body betrayed him. She was so familiar, so delightfully feminine. Every caveman instinct he possessed told him to fight for her, to protect her. Women were tough, far tougher than men at times. Still, this Simone who had come to him today was at a low spot. He wanted to make it all right for her.

Yet he was the last person she needed. He'd suffered too much heartache, witnessed too much heartbreak to offer Simone anything resembling the love they had once shared.

She managed the first cracker and started on the second. In between bites, he offered the ice chips. Four crackers in each pack, eight in all. Eventually, she finished them.

"Thank you," she said. "I'm okay now."

It was patently untrue, but he took her words at face value. He handed her what was left of the cup of ice. "I have other patients to see," he said, wondering why the thought of leaving this room was so unappealing.

"I know," she said. "Go. I'm fine. I'm glad you didn't die in Africa."

He chuckled. "Is that all you have to say?"

"I don't want to add to your ego. I won't be surprised if the town makes you the patron saint of Royal. Saint Hutch. It has a ring to it, don't you think?"

"You're such a brat."

"Some things never change." Her teeth dug into her bottom lip.

Gradually, her color was returning to normal. The doctor in him approved. "That's not true, Simone. Neither of us is who we were five years ago. I know I'm not."

She tucked a wayward strand of hair behind her ear. "Is that a polite warning? You're telling me not to get any ideas?" Her sidelong glance held a touch of wry mischief.

Even now, she had the power to shock him. While he'd been willing to dance around their painful past, Simone plunged right into the murky depths. Maybe she knew him better than he realized.

"I wasn't, but I probably should have."

"You're not my doctor."

"No. Not technically." He paused, weighing his words. "Perhaps this is presumptuous on my part, but you opened this can of worms. I knew we would see each other again, Simone. It was inevitable if I came home. But…"

"But you've moved on."

"Yes. I have." He didn't tell her the rest. He couldn't.

Simone nodded. "I understand, Hutch. I think it's obvious I have my hands full, too. Maybe we can be friends, though."

"Maybe." He let the lie roll off his lips. As much as he wanted to help her, he couldn't get close. Not again. "Are you okay now? The nausea's better?"

She handed him the basin. "False alarm. You're good at this. Maybe you should be a doctor."

His smile was genuine. Simone had always been able to make him laugh, even when he took himself too seriously. He reached in his pocket for a business card and scrawled his cell number on the back. "I need you to promise," he said, handing it to her.

"Promise what?" She handled the little rectangle as if it were a poisonous snake.

"I want you to promise that you'll call me immediately if you have any problems."

"What about Dr. Fetter?"

He shoved his hands in the pockets of his lab coat. "She's a busy doctor with a lot of patients."

"And you're not?"

They stared at each other in silence. "Hell, Simone. You're not making this easy."

"I don't understand you."

"We share a past. I want to make sure you and these babies are okay."

"Saint Hutch."

If that's what she wanted to think, he might as well let her. It was far better than the truth. "I care about you," he said quietly. "I mean it. Any hour. Night or day. This isn't a typical pregnancy. I want to hear you say it."

She lifted one shoulder in an elegant gesture he remembered well. "Fine. I promise. Are you happy now?"

He hadn't been happy for a very long time. "It will do. I'll be in touch, Simone. Take care of yourself."

Two

After the run-in with Hutch, the actual appointment with Dr. Fetter a week later was anticlimactic. The rules for a multiple pregnancy were pretty much the same as any pregnancy. Take vitamins. Sleep and rest the appropriate amount. Exercise every day. Report any spotting or bleeding.

That last bit was scary. Simone stared at the obstetrician as the woman entered notes on a laptop. "How often does that happen? Bleeding, I mean."

Dr. Fetter looked up over the top of her glasses. "Ten to twenty percent of all pregnancies end in miscarriage, Simone. With multiples, the risk is higher. Nevertheless, you shouldn't waste time worrying about it. Your ultrasound looks good, and we'll monitor you closely, much more so than a typical pregnancy warrants."

"I see." It was easy for the doctor to say *don't worry*. She wasn't the one carrying three brand-new lives.

Soon after that sobering conversation, Simone was back outside staring around in a daze at the nicely landscaped grounds of the hospital. *Triplets.* No matter how many times she repeated the word in her head, it didn't seem real. She'd had daydreams about pushing a stylish stroller with a tiny infant dressed in pink or blue. It was hard to fathom the reality of taking three babies out on the town.

She sat in her car for the longest time, telling herself everything was going to be okay. Her initial motives in getting pregnant had been less than pure. Was the universe punishing her for playing around with motherhood?

Despite evidence to the contrary, she was stunned to realize that she *wanted* these babies desperately. Not one of them, or two…but all three. Placing her palm flat on her abdomen, she tried to imagine what she was going to look like in a few months. With triplets, she could be huge.

Oddly, the thought wasn't as alarming as it should have been. For a woman who wore haute couture as a matter of course and worked hard to keep her body in shape, the fact that she was able to imagine herself as big as a blimp without hyperventilating showed personal growth.

At least that's what she told herself.

It was getting late. She was supposed to be at Naomi's condo in less than an hour. Naomi and Cecelia were making their signature jalapeño and shredded beef pizza. Normally, Simone gobbled down at least three pieces. How was she going to make it through the evening when the thought of food made her want to barf?

As she drove to the other side of town, she practiced what she was going to say. *By the way, I haven't had sex in months, but I'm pregnant with triplets.* Or how about *I ran into Hutch last week. I don't think I ever got over him.*

Already she was reconsidering her decision to keep Naomi and Cecelia in the dark. This was too hard to do alone. She needed someone to talk to…someone who would have her back. If she couldn't confide in her two best friends, she couldn't confide in anybody. Naomi and Cecelia had been her closest companions and confidantes since grade school. Still, she wasn't ready to spill *all* her secrets at once. She needed time to wrap her head around things. It was happening too fast.

As Simone entered her code on a keypad and rolled

through the elegant gate, she noted the perfectly manicured grounds of the luxury condo complex. Naomi's privacy was protected here. Naomi Price was famous in Royal for any number of reasons. Her cable television show had been picked up nationally, so now she was dispensing style advice to women—and men—coast to coast.

Simone parked and walked up the path. When she rang the buzzer, Cecelia answered the door. "It's about time. Where have you been?"

Clearly, the question was rhetorical, because Cecelia disappeared into the kitchen, leaving Simone to put a hand over her mouth and gag at the smell of cooking meat. *Oh, lordy.* She fished a water bottle from the depths of her leather tote and took a cautious sip. If she wasn't ready to talk about the babies, she had to get her stomach under control. Otherwise, her secret wasn't going to be a secret for very long.

Gingerly, she rounded the corner and entered the kitchen. The room wasn't huge, but it was as stylish as the woman who hovered over the stove. Naomi had brown eyes and long copper-brown hair. She was charming and extremely pretty, but Simone knew her friend didn't understand how beautiful she was.

Cecelia, on the other hand, had bombshell looks and knew how to use them. Her platinum hair and long legs drew men in droves. Her company, To the Moon, produced high-end children's merchandise but had recently branched out to the adult furniture realm with the launch of Luna Fine Furnishings. Simone and her ad agency were currently producing a hard-hitting campaign designed to take Cecelia's company to the next level.

The other two women barely said hello at first. They were squabbling over the correct ratio of peppers to meat. At last, Naomi looked up. "Hey, hon. What's the matter with you? I've seen ghosts with more color."

That was the thing about good friends. They didn't sugarcoat things. "Just an upset stomach," Simone said. "I think I ate too much at lunch." Fortunately, meal prep took precedence and no one called her on the lie.

Normally, Simone would have offered to help, but right now she stayed as far away from the food as possible. When the large pizza was in the oven, the three women adjourned to the living room. Simone envied Naomi's innate sense of style. Her home was stunning but extremely comfortable.

Simone claimed a comfy chair and sat down gingerly. She'd always heard about morning sickness, but she had never imagined how wretched it could be. Tucking her legs beneath her, she tried to get comfortable.

Cecelia, on the other hand, hovered by the window. She was always a high-energy person. Today she practically vibrated with excitement.

Naomi took a sip of her Chardonnay and waved a hand. "What's up, Cecelia? You said we had to wait for Simone. She's here now. Don't keep us in suspense."

The tall blonde spun around, fumbled in her pocket and held out her hand. "Deacon proposed! And I'm pregnant."

After that dual announcement, much squealing ensued. Simone and Naomi hugged their friend and admired the ring. Deacon Chase was quite a catch. He'd lived in Europe for a decade, but had returned to Royal and purchased a beautiful country lodge on the outskirts of town. The gorgeous, self-made billionaire hotelier had confidence and charisma and a dimpled smile that broke hearts everywhere. As far as Simone was concerned, he was one of the few men alive who could handle Cecelia and not be intimidated by her looks and personality.

Clearly, now was not the time for Simone to share her own news. For one, she didn't want to steal Cecelia's thunder.

When the furor died down, they adjourned to the kitchen

and dug into the freshly baked pizza. Simone's stomach cooperated enough for her to get down most of one piece, though she surreptitiously removed the jalapeños and wrapped them in a paper napkin. No point in tempting fate.

"So who's your doctor?" Simone asked. *Please don't let it be Hutch.*

"I'm seeing Janine Fetter. She's not real chatty or friendly, but I don't need that in a doctor. I want someone I can trust to take care of me and my baby. Dr. Fetter fits the bill."

Naomi shook her head. "I still can't believe it. This means we'll have to plan a baby shower."

Cecelia laughed. "Give it time. I'm still in my first trimester. Plenty of opportunity for that. Deacon and I are going to keep the news to ourselves for a while, but he knew I would have to tell you two."

"Well, I should think so," Naomi said. "We've never kept secrets from each other."

Simone grimaced inwardly. The trio's tight friendship had backfired in Royal at times. Some people referred to them as the mean girls. The label wasn't fair. They weren't mean. But when three women were extremely successful, attractive and high-profile, there were bound to be those who took potshots. The criticism had sharpened after Naomi, Cecelia and Simone had been admitted into the Texas Cattleman's Club.

Some diehards still thought women should be kept out. And *somebody* had started the rumor that Naomi, Cecelia and Simone could be behind the malicious blackmail messages various residents of Royal had been receiving via social media.

It wasn't true. Even Cecelia had received one of the blackmailer's threats. Simone, too, though she hadn't told anyone.

Later that evening as Simone drove home, she struggled with feelings of envy. Cecelia had a baby on the way and a wedding to plan. That meant Cecelia's situation was cause for celebration. Simone, on the other hand, was pregnant with triplets whose biological father was an unknown sperm donor.

Lots of people used sperm donors in situations of infertility. But those were loving couples who made a joint decision and were excited about the chance to bring a child into their home.

Simone had done it selfishly because of her grandfather's stupid, archaic will. Blinking back tears, she clutched the steering wheel and apologized to the three tiny sparks of life in her womb. "I swear I'll be a good mom," she whispered. "I would take it all back if I could, but now you're on the way, and I want to keep you. You'll find out soon enough that grown-ups make mistakes. Me, in particular."

It would have been nice to have someone say, "There, there, Simone. Don't be so hard on yourself. Everything will work out for the best. You'll see." Unfortunately, unless she confided in Naomi and Cecelia, no one in Royal was likely to fulfill the role of pep squad. She'd have to be her own cheerleader. First order of business would be enjoying a relaxing evening at home.

Her house was welcoming and warm, but in a whole different way than Naomi's. After the ad agency landed its third big client, Simone had moved out of her bland apartment and purchased a five-acre estate in Pine Valley. The place was ridiculously large for one person, but she loved it.

At least she would have plenty of room for a live-in nanny. Or maybe two. *Triplets!* How would she ever manage?

When she made the turn from the main road onto her property, she noted with pride the way the flowering cherry trees lined the driveway. When the wind blew, tiny white petals fluttered down like snow. Spring in Royal, Texas, was her favorite time of year.

It was a surprise to see a black SUV parked on the curving flagstone apron at her front door. An even bigger shock was the man who stepped out to face her. Not bothering to put her small sports car in the garage, she slammed on the brakes and slid out from behind the wheel. "What are you doing here, Hutch?"

She hated the way her heart jumped when she saw him. Even without three babies on the way, she shouldn't get involved again. Given the current situation, it would be emotional suicide to think she had any kind of chance with the good doctor.

In his muscular arms he held a medium-sized box. "I brought you some books from my medical library. I remembered how you like to research things on your own, so I thought you could take a look at these. Plenty of stuff here about multiple births, both from a medical standpoint and from a practical parenting aspect."

"That's thoughtful of you," Simone said. "Do you offer this kind of service to all your patients?"

His lips quirked in a reluctant smile. "You're not my patient, remember?"

"True." She wasn't exactly sure what the protocol was here. In any case, she couldn't leave the man standing outside. "Would you like to come in for some iced tea or a cola?"

"Decaf coffee?" he asked hopefully.

"That, too."

"I'm in."

She unlocked the front door and tossed her keys on a table in the foyer. Hutch set the box on a chair and looked around with interest. "I like your house," he said. "It looks like you."

Simone made her way to the kitchen, painfully aware

that he followed closely at her heels. "How so?" She opened the refrigerator to cool her hot face and to hide for a moment. Her heart raced at a crazy tempo.

"Modern. Stylish. Simple. Sophisticated."

Wow. Was that really how he saw her? While she put the coffee on to brew, Hutch perched on a stool at the bar. "Thank you," she muttered. Was he thinking about all the money she had spent while he was caring for sick babies in terrible poverty? Was his compliment actually a veiled criticism?

Maybe she was reading too much into a casual comment.

"Where will you live now that you're back?" she asked. "Somewhere near the hospital?"

"Actually," he said with a weary grin, "I'm going to be your neighbor. I'll be closing on the brick colonial down the road soon."

"Oh." She knew the house well. It was less than half a mile from her place. Was that a coincidence?

Hutch shrugged. "I'm too old for bachelor digs. I wanted to put down roots."

"No more Doctors Without Borders?"

"I don't think so. It's a young man's game. I gave it more than five years of my life. It's the best thing I've ever done, but it was time to come home."

"I'm sure your parents are delighted." Hutch's mother and father were both lawyers. They had raised their son to believe he could be or do anything he wanted. Hutch had excelled all the way through school, despite the occasional run-ins with bullies.

"They were over the moon when they heard."

"Must be nice. My mom and dad drop by only when they want to lecture me about something. Of course, you probably remember that." Her parents had been none too thrilled about their only daughter dating someone they hadn't hand-picked for her. Neither Hutch nor Simone had let the veiled disapproval dissuade them.

Remembering the passionate affair and its inevitable end was something Simone managed to avoid. Mostly. But with Hutch in her kitchen, the memories came crashing back.

The two of them had met at a party at the Cattleman's Club. Simone had been barely twenty-two and ready to fall in love. The town had thought she was promiscuous—still did—but that was a facade she hid behind. If people wanted to look down their noses at her, she wasn't going to stop them.

Being introduced to Troy Hutchinson by a mutual acquaintance had been kismet. The moment she laid eyes on him, she knew he was the one. Though he was ridiculously handsome, it was his quiet, steady intelligence that drew her in. Hutch was no callow boy looking for an easy lay.

He had talked to her, listened to her opinions. Danced with her. Laughed at her jokes. And in a secluded corner outside the club, he had kissed her. Even now she could remember everything about that magical moment. The way he smelled of lime and starched cotton. The sensation of feeling small and protected, though she was more than capable of taking care of herself. He was taller than she was and extremely fit, which made sense, of course, for someone who had devoted himself to the pursuit of medicine.

"Simone? Hello in there…"

Suddenly he was standing in front of her, his smile quizzical. "You've been stirring that cup of coffee for a long time."

Heat flooded her cheeks. Did he know what she was thinking? Could he read her mind?

"Here," she said. "I fixed it the way you like it. Strong enough to peel paint and enough sugar to give you cavities."

He took the cup and sipped slowly, his eyes closing in

bliss. "Now *this* is good coffee. Might even compete with the real stuff in Africa."

"I'm sure not everything was great. As I recall, you were a meat-and-potatoes guy, too. Not much prime beef where you were, I'd say."

"You're right, of course. I lost twenty pounds after I arrived in Sudan and never quite gained it back."

"Let's take our drinks into the den." She grabbed a package of cookies out of the cabinet and led the way. Hutch chose a wing-backed chair near the dormant fireplace. Simone claimed one end of the sofa.

He sat back with a sigh, balancing his cup on his flat abdomen. "You've done well for yourself, Simone. I'm proud of you. Everyone in town sings your praises—well, your ad agency's praises," he clarified.

"That might be a stretch, but thanks. Hard work and a dollop of luck."

"I always knew you'd make your mark in Royal."

She frowned. Her ambition had been partly the cause of their breakup, but not from her perspective. She hadn't wanted to stand in the way of Hutch's dreams. When he'd offered to wait on Africa until her agency was established, she had insisted he should go. Hutch read that as a rejection. He thought she cared more about her business and money than about him. Stupid man.

Still, that was a long time ago.

For several long minutes they drank their coffee in silence. She was tired and queasy and sad. Seeing Hutch again was a painful reminder of how many times in her life she had made mistakes.

Would she ever learn?

At last, the silence became unbearable. She set her cup on a side table. "I think you should go now," she said. "I don't feel very well. I'd like to rest. And if I'm being honest, I'd rather not have people see your car in front of my house."

Three

Hutch grimaced. Her words stung, even though they gave him an easy out.

He had told himself he was indifferent to Simone now, but in his gut he knew the truth. The first moment he laid eyes on her in that exam room a week ago, he'd felt the same dizzying punch of desire he'd always experienced when he was with her.

Panic swept through him like a sickening deluge. He couldn't do that again. Not after what had happened in Sudan. It was better that Simone knew the score.

She lost patience with his lack of verbal response. "If you have something to say, say it. I've had a long, stressful day, and I want to take a bath and get into bed."

I'd like to join you... His subconscious was honest and uncomfortable.

The dark shadows beneath her beautiful eyes reminded him she was in a fragile state, both mentally and physically.

The fact that he wanted so badly to hold her told him he had to protect himself.

He stood and paced, his hands jammed in his pockets. "I understand why you want me to move my car. Now that I'm back in town and we're both still single, the gossip mill will undoubtedly have us hooking up any day now. People may even say your triplets are mine."

Simone swallowed visibly. "Gossip isn't reality."

"Maybe not. But I have to be up front with you. I'm not willing to get involved in a relationship."

She was pale and silent, her sapphire-eyed stare judging him. "I don't recall asking you to. But to clarify, is your distaste for romance because of our past?"

"Not entirely. I fell in love with a fellow doctor while I was in Sudan. Her name was Bethany."

For a split second, he could swear he saw anguish in Simone's eyes. But if it was there, she recovered quickly.

"You said was? Past tense?"

He nodded jerkily. "She died two years ago. Cut her foot on a rock. Doctors make the worst patients, you know. She didn't tell any of us how serious it was. Ended up with sepsis. I couldn't save her." Even now the memory sickened him.

Simone leaned forward. "I am so sorry, Hutch."

Her sympathy should have soothed him. Instead, it made him feel guilty. "I'll always be fond of you, Simone…and I'll care about you. But I need you to know that's all it will be."

She blinked. "I see."

"I suppose you think I'm assuming a hell of a lot to think you would even be interested after all this time."

"Not at all. You're a gorgeous man. With a kind heart. I'm sure I won't be the only woman in Royal who appreciates your sterling qualities."

"Aw, hell. You're making fun of me, aren't you?"

"Maybe a little." She smiled gently. "Six months ago your virtue might have been in danger. But now I have three babies to consider. Their welfare has to come before anything else in my life."

"Even romance?"

"Especially romance."

"Then I guess we've cleared the air."

"I guess we have."

"I should go," he said. But he didn't move.

Simone stood up, swaying a bit before she steadied herself with a hand on the back of the chair. "Yes, you should."

Squaring his shoulders, he nodded. The urge to kiss her was overpowering.

She kept a hand on the chair, either because she felt faint or because she intended to use it as a shield. Either way, it didn't matter. He wanted to taste her more than he wanted his next breath.

He put his hands on her shoulders, noting the tension there. She wasn't wearing shoes, so the difference in their heights was magnified. Winnowing his fingers through her hair, he sighed. "I should have come home a year ago. Then maybe I could have talked you out of this single-mom idea."

"Not your business, Doc."

It was as easy as falling into a dream. He had loved Bethany, deeply and truly. And grieved her passing. But this thing with Simone was something else. Did he dare explore the possibilities?

Slowly, he moved his lips over hers, waiting for the protest that never came. She tasted of coffee and wonderful familiarity. But not comfort. Never comfort. There was too much heat. Too much yearning. When she went up on her tiptoes and wrapped her arms around his neck, he groaned. Five years. Almost six. Gone in a flash.

He ran his hands over her back and landed on her bottom. She was thinner, but every bit as soft and appealing as she had ever been. Before he left for Sudan, when they were alone together, Simone had been unguarded…innocent. A far cry from the woman who tilted her chin and dared the world to disrespect her.

Every beat of his heart was magnified. He kissed the

sensitive spot behind her ear…nipped her earlobe with his teeth. Simone did nothing to stop him. In fact, she didn't even try to hide the fact that she wanted him. Temptation sank its teeth into his gut and didn't let go. He was hard as a pike. The sofa was close by. Damn. How could he still want her so badly? No. This had to stop. Now.

Dragging in great gulps of air, he broke free of the embrace, stumbled backward and wiped a hand over his mouth. "Does it make you happy to know I still want you?" he snarled. He felt like a fool.

Simone's expression was gaunt and defeated. "Not happy at all, Hutch. But message received. You have nothing to fear from me. I'd appreciate it if you would let yourself out."

She waited until she heard the front door slam before bursting into tears. Sliding down the wall and curling up in a knot of misery on the hallway floor, she cried ugly, wretched sobs that left her throat raw and her chest hollow.

She knew her hormones were all over the map, but it was more than that. Hutch might as well still be in Africa. The gulf between them was so deep and so wide, it was doubtful they could ever even manage to be friends. Yet the same incendiary attraction that had drawn them to each other in the beginning still existed.

The sensation of being wrapped in his strong arms…of feeling his steady heartbeat beneath her cheek…of knowing he wanted her as much as she wanted him brought back such crazy joy. Never in her life had she felt as happy or free as she had when she and Hutch were a couple.

What he said was true. If he had come home six months ago, she would never have embarked on this path of insanity. She'd been angry at her dead grandfather and determined to prove she was worthy of carrying on the family name. It had never been about the money, but more about legitimacy, a sense of belonging.

Now it was too late for second thoughts. The babies were a reality.

Stumbling to her bathroom, she washed her face and sprawled on the bed. She was hungry again, but it was a weird hunger. Beneath the pangs of an empty stomach rolled a sensation of nausea in the offing.

Finally, at midnight, she dragged herself out of bed and went to the kitchen in search of a snack. Milk seemed like a bad idea. Ditto for cheese or yogurt. Craving something salty, she found half a bag of stale, plain potato chips. She gobbled two handfuls and washed them down with ginger ale.

Her hunger appeased, she went back to bed only to jump up twenty minutes later and rush for the bathroom. She threw up violently, so hard that her ribs ached. Even rinsing out her mouth made her stomach heave.

Groaning, she found a damp cloth and pressed it to her forehead. The notion that she might have to endure weeks of this misery pointed out once again how foolish she had been. *I'm sorry*, she said silently to the three lives she carried.

No matter what sacrifices it demanded, she would make sure this was a healthy pregnancy.

The following morning was no better. Dry cereal and water came right back up as soon as they went down. Her hands began to cramp, signaling possible dehydration. Doggedly, she sipped from a water bottle and forced herself to put on the same dress pants from the day before but with a different top. She couldn't simply stay home because she felt bad. She had a business to run...a business that would soon support three tiny infants.

Driving was doable, but only because she never pushed the speedometer over thirty miles an hour. When she reached her office, the receptionist, Candace, gave her a wide-eyed stare. Simone didn't engage. She made a bee-line for her private suite, closed the door and put her head on the desk. The sharp corner of a business card poked her stomach through her pocket.

She pulled the rectangle out and laid it on the desk. Hutch. Dr. Hutch. Saint Hutch. It would be a cold day in hell before she called him for *anything*.

With nothing more than dogged determination and the inherent stubbornness that got her into trouble more often than not, she made it through an entire workday. The campaign for Luna Fine Furnishings, a subsidiary of Cecelia's company, To the Moon, was coming along nicely. Phase one had already been rolled out. In two weeks, an intensive social media blitz would back up the initial print ads and billboards.

The noon lunch hour came and went. Simone didn't even attempt to eat. At five o'clock, she closed her laptop, packed up her things and took a deep breath before heading out to her car. Once there, she had to spend another chunk of time convincing herself she could make the drive home. She was shaky, light-headed and so very sick.

She must have dozed when she got home, because suddenly it was seven o'clock. Naomi would bring her food if she called, but then Simone would have to explain what was going on. Even if it was time to share her secret with her friends, she'd rather do it with both women present.

Carryout pizza sounded revolting. Canvassing the pantry in her kitchen was an exercise in futility. She knew *how* to cook but seldom spared the time. Most days she had lunch with clients and grabbed a salad for dinner.

In the end, the only available choice was peanut butter. That was protein—right? Even her crackers were stale. But smeared with peanut butter, they were edible. At first, Simone thought she had landed on a miracle. The peanut butter was comfort food, its smell and taste appealing.

Sadly, no matter the enjoyment going down, everything she consumed came back up in a matter of minutes.

The night passed slowly. She alternated between lying on top of the covers covered in a cold sweat and hunching over the toilet. No matter how slowly she sipped water, it wouldn't stay down. Nor would anything else.

Once she almost fell, so dizzy the room spun around her. Finally, at 4:00 a.m., she collapsed into an exhausted slumber.

When her alarm went off, she muttered an incredulous protest. How did working mothers do this?

Dragging herself into the shower, she held on to the towel bar as she washed her hair. Blow-drying it took everything she had. At last she was dressed and ready to go. By now the thought of trying to eat was beyond her. Maybe she'd be able to attempt some lunch.

The ride to work was a blur. This time she barely noticed the receptionist's look of consternation. Simone's mouth was dry and fuzzy. How could she risk taking a drink when she might have to rush for the bathroom? No one in Royal knew she was pregnant. Well, aside from Hutch and Dr. Fetter. It was far too early to let that cat out of the bag.

As she sat in a stupor at her desk, the buzzer on her phone sounded. "Line two, Ms. Parker. It's your accountant."

Later, Simone couldn't remember the exact details of that conversation. For all she knew, she might have agreed to transfer her personal and business funds to illegal offshore accounts.

Thankfully, her two full-time employees—including her exceptional right hand, Tess—were out of town at a conference. The receptionist was fairly new and wouldn't have the temerity to invade her office uninvited.

So the hours passed.

At one, Simone knew she had to eat something. Her headache had reached monumental proportions. Maybe she would send Candace out to get chicken noodle soup. Not only would that guarantee Simone a few minutes of privacy to test her stomach with a sip of water, but the soup might actually be good for her.

She stood up on trembling legs. Rarely did she ask an employee to carry out a personal errand, but she was literally incapable of walking down the block. Carefully, she opened her door. "Candace, can you come in here?"

Candace looked up and blanched. Apparently Simone looked even worse than she felt. Her receptionist rushed into the office. "Can I help you, Ms. Parker?" she asked.

Simone nodded, wincing when the motion sent shock waves through her skull. "Would you mind grabbing me some chicken soup from the diner?"

"I'd be happy to," Candace said.

"Let me get my billfold."

"No worries. We can settle up later. Do you want something to drink? Lemonade? Iced tea?"

Oh, wow. Tea sounded wonderful. "Tea would be great." Her mouth was so dry. "Hurry, Candace. I don't think I can—" She stopped dead, nausea rising in her throat. "Oh, damn. I'm going to—"

It might have been hours or days later when she woke up completely. She had vague memories of an ambulance and several people in white coats. Now she was in her own bed.

When she shifted on the mattress, Hutch's voice sounded nearby. "Take it easy, Simone. You're going to be okay."

"My head hurts," she groaned, trying to recreate her spotty memory.

"No wonder." Hutch crouched beside her bed, his smile quizzical. "You whacked it pretty hard on the edge of your desk when you fainted. The ER doc put in three stitches, but there's no concussion."

Panicked, she tried to sit up. "The babies?"

"Steady, woman. They're fine."

"What happened to me?"

"Hyperemesis gravidarum."

"Oh, God. Is that as bad as it sounds?"

"Yes and no. You were badly dehydrated, Simone, and disoriented. One of the unlucky women who suffer from severe nausea and vomiting when pregnant. Women with multiples are more prone to it."

"Well, that's just peachy," she muttered.

"Dr. Fetter wanted to admit you, but you pitched a fit and demanded to go home. She only agreed because I promised to stay with you."

For the first time, Simone realized she was hooked up to an IV. "You did this?"

He looked at her strangely. "Yes. But if you've changed your mind, I'll take you back to the hospital."

Now that her head was clearer, she did remember most of what he was saying. It didn't paint her in a good light.

"How did you hear I had passed out? Why were you there with the EMTs? Candace doesn't even know you."

"She was trying to call 911 and saw my card on your desk."

"I knew I should have thrown that away."

Hutch had the audacity to laugh. When he did, she caught a glimpse of the carefree young doctor she had fallen in love with so many years ago. Heaven help her. With the shadows gone from his eyes—chased away by genuine humor—he was irresistible.

He fiddled with a setting on the monitor. "It will take at least twenty-four hours to get your electrolyte levels balanced again. After that, we'll have to see if you are able eat or drink at all. Otherwise, you'll have to get nutrition intravenously."

"How long will this last?"

"Well…" It was clear he didn't want to upset her.

"Go ahead, Hutch. I can handle it."

"Days. Weeks." He grimaced. "For some it's all the way till the end. But you're in the earliest moments of this pregnancy. Your body is adapting to the flood of hormones. With any luck, things will settle down soon."

"Thanks for the pep talk," she said drily. She watched as he moved around the bedroom. "You can't stay here. You have a job."

"I was going to talk to you about that. I have a friend, a nurse, who does in-home care. She's expensive, but it's cheaper than being hospitalized and a lot more comfortable."

"She would stay overnight?"

Hutch rubbed two fingers in the center of his forehead. "No. I would be here when I get off work in the evenings."

Simone closed her eyes and told herself not to get upset. That wouldn't be good for the babies. "You know that's impossible," she whispered.

He sat down on the edge of the bed and took her hand, the one with the needle taped into it. "My job is to protect high-risk infants. What happened to you is serious, but there's no reason to take up a hospital bed."

"What about staying away from each other?"

"You're all hooked up. How bad could we be?"

The droll comment startled a laugh from her when she could have sworn she didn't have it in her. "I have friends," she said. "And parents."

"Don't be coy, Simone. I happen to know that Cecelia is newly engaged and pregnant and Naomi flits all over the country. Your parents wouldn't begin to know how to be nurturing. I've met them, remember? I'm your best shot if you want to stay out of the hospital."

Well, damn. The idea of checking into a hospital for something like this gave her the hives. "You could teach me about the IV," she said, giving him a hopeful glance.

"Nice try, kiddo. Even Kate Middleton had to stay in the hospital a few nights when she struggled with this condition. Despite the fact that she had castles and servants at her disposal. Count yourself lucky that Dr. Fetter trusts me."

"She should. You're her boss."

"You know what I mean."

"I'm sorry Candace dragged you into this."

He leaned over and brushed a strand of hair from her cheek. "I'm not. You gave everyone a real scare. I'd just as soon be the one keeping an eye on you."

Four

Hutch kept his easy smile with effort. Never had he imagined seeing Simone in the state she'd been in when she collapsed. Severe dehydration could even affect the heart. When he'd first seen her, he had actually feared for her pregnancy.

Not only that, he had flashed back to losing Beth. Even though he didn't want a romantic relationship with Simone again, there was no way in hell he was going to let anything happen to her on his watch.

The stubborn woman had to have been in misery. Yet she'd been determined to power through on her own. She looked a little better now, but not much. He estimated that she had already lost six or seven pounds. Her cheekbones stood out sharply, as did her collarbone.

He touched the spot beneath her ear. "They put motion-sickness patches on you in the hospital. I'll change those out as necessary."

"Is it safe?" Her fingers moved restlessly, pleating the sheet.

He frowned. "A hell of a lot safer than collapsing from dehydration. You were in a bad way, Simone."

"I thought I could handle it."

"You hate depending on other people for help, don't you?"

"I don't like to take help from *you*." Tears welled in her beautiful eyes, making them sparkle.

He sat down again, telling himself he had to be the professional in this situation. "I owe you this much, don't you think?"

"For what?" She couldn't quite meet his eyes.

"For taking your advice and going to Africa." He couldn't help the fact that the words sounded accusatory. When it had become clear that he and Simone were crazy about each other, he had offered to linger in Royal for a few years until she got her ad agency off the ground. He'd assumed she would jump at the offer. Instead, she had broken up with him. She'd insisted she didn't want to stand in the way of his doing something so important.

Bitter and disillusioned, he had realized that Simone didn't love him the way he loved her. While he couldn't bear the thought of leaving her behind, she had cut him loose and bid him a cheerful farewell.

"I did the right thing," she said stubbornly. "You had a mission to fulfill."

"And what did *you* have, Simone?" Suddenly, he felt like a beast for harassing her. She looked fragile enough to shatter. "Forget I said that," he muttered. "I'm sorry. It's not important."

Without warning, a noise from the front of the house had his head jerking up. Surely no one would barge in uninvited. But he had forgotten about Naomi. The style guru/TV star was as much a force of nature as Simone, though in a different package.

Naomi burst into the bedroom, wild-eyed. She barely glanced at Hutch. "Good lord, Simone. What the heck is going on? I just saw you a few days ago. What happened?"

Hutch moved toward the door. "I'll leave you two ladies alone."

Simone held up the hand that wasn't tethered to an IV.

"No. Don't go, Hutch. You might as well both hear this at once."

Naomi turned to frown at him. "I didn't know you were back in town. Made yourself at home, didn't you? I fail to see why you're in this house. You hurt her enough the first time around. I'm here now. You can leave."

Simone tried to sit up. "Hush, Naomi. You don't know what you're talking about. Ignore her, Hutch. You know how dramatic she can be."

Naomi's teeth-clenched smile promised retribution. She sat down on the side of the bed, careful not to jostle Simone. "Fine. What don't I know?"

Hutch positioned himself at Simone's elbow. "You don't have to do this now, Simone. You're weak and sick." He worried about her state of mind.

She shot him a look that held a soupçon of her usual fire. "I'm not an invalid." Reaching for Naomi's hand, she twined their fingers. "Don't be mad. I didn't want to steal Cecelia's thunder the other night. I'm pregnant, too. And apparently not handling it nearly as well as our newly engaged friend."

The self-derision on her face hurt Hutch. "It's not a contest," he said.

Naomi gaped. "You're pregnant?" She glared at Hutch. He held up his hands. "Don't look at me."

"Then who?" Naomi seemed genuinely befuddled.

Maybe Simone had been telling the truth about not having a man in her life. That shouldn't have pleased him so much. Simone tried to sit up again, and again, he shook his head. "Too soon. Stay put."

"Fine. Anyone ever tell you you worry too much?" She transferred her attention to her shell-shocked friend. "I wanted to have a baby, Naomi. And I didn't want to wait. So I used a sperm donor."

"A sperm donor..." Naomi repeated the words slowly.

"Don't look so stunned," Simone pleaded. "It's a perfectly acceptable thing to do."

"But it's not something the Simone *I* know would do."

Hutch saw Simone's bottom lip tremble. "That's enough, Naomi," he said. "This has been a rough day for her."

"Sorry," she groaned. "What's the matter with her?"

"She's suffering from extreme morning sickness."

"I'm right here," Simone snapped. "And I don't know why they call it morning sickness. It lasts the whole damn day."

He and Naomi looked at each other, trying not to laugh. Hutch lifted a shoulder, edging toward the door. "I really do have some phone calls to make." He looked at Naomi. "Shout if you need me."

In the kitchen, he prowled restlessly. Neither of the phone calls was urgent, but he had needed some space to clear his head. He already regretted his impulsive decision to take on Simone's crisis. The odd thing was, *she* was the one who usually jumped without looking. There was a time when he had admired her joie de vivre and her impulsive spirit.

He'd been the older one, the stick-in-the-mud. He'd often wondered if that was why she broke up with him. Perhaps his overly conscientious approach to life had struck her as boring and pedantic.

It didn't matter now. If they hadn't had anything in common five years ago, that was even more true now. Hopefully, her nausea would soon settle down and he could go back to pretending she was just another pregnant woman.

Simone looked at Naomi. "Help me sit up, please."

Naomi frowned. "Hutch said that wasn't a good idea."

"Are you kidding me? Since when are you in the Troy Hutchinson fan club?"

"I didn't say I was a fan, but the man's a brilliant doctor, and you, my girl, look like something out of a zombie movie."

"Gee, thanks."

Despite her protests, Naomi stood up and grabbed extra pillows to put behind Simone. "Satisfied?"

Simone closed her eyes. "I'll be satisfied when I can eat a milk shake and a cheeseburger without puking."

"Can I get you anything?" Naomi hovered.

"No. Thank you." Unexpected tears stung her eyes. "I feel so stupid."

Naomi chuckled. "Well, you should. If anybody was going to knock you up, it should have been that Greek god doctor of yours."

"He's not my doctor," Simone said automatically. "And besides, we're not anything to each other."

"Which explains why I found him in bed with you."

"Don't be dramatic. He wasn't *in* my bed. He was *sitting* on my bed. There's a big difference."

"Not from where I'm standing."

"For God's sake, let it go, Naomi. Hutch and I were over a long time ago. And besides, even if I had the slightest interest in rekindling that flame—which I don't—what man wants to be father to some other guy's triplets?"

Naomi gaped. The look of total consternation on her face might have been funny if Simone hadn't felt so wretched. "Triplets?" she said, her eyes round.

"Um, yeah. I guess I forgot to mention that part. I'm having three babies. At least I hope so."

"What does that mean?"

"It's still early. Too early to know if all the fetuses are viable."

Naomi sprang to her feet and paced. "How can you be so damned calm? This is huge. What were you thinking, Simone? You own and manage a thriving ad agency. You have no husband. Why on earth would you do something so crazy?"

Sadly, Simone couldn't tell the whole truth. Not to Naomi or Cecelia, and certainly not to Hutch. "I wanted a baby," she said stubbornly. "By the time I got in the midst of everything, I began to have my doubts, but I didn't back out. I should have, I suppose."

"Ya think?" Naomi seemed more indignant than flat-out angry. Simone understood, really, she did. If the situations had been reversed, surely she would have expressed doubts about Naomi's decision.

"I screwed up, Naomi. I know that now. But I didn't know how sick I could get. And besides..."

"Besides, what?"

"I want them," Simone whispered. "The babies. All of them. Hutch said it wasn't too late from a medical standpoint to rethink my position, but I could never do that. I started this, and I'll finish it."

Naomi pursed her lips. "I hope it doesn't finish *you*."

Hutch returned in time to hear that last comment. He frowned when he saw Simone upright, but he didn't say anything.

Simone looked at him. "May I have a drink of water, please?"

"It's up to you. It would be good if you can manage it."

With both of them watching, Simone didn't want to make a scene, but she knew she couldn't avoid drinking indefinitely. There was a pitcher and disposable cups on the bedside table. Hutch poured one glass half-full and offered it to her. She took it from him, wincing. "Bottoms up."

With her two observers looking on eagle-eyed, she sipped tentatively. At first, the water tasted amazing. Her lips were partially chapped. The cool liquid felt wonderful in her parched throat. But moments later, her stomach cramped sharply. "Hutch!" She panicked.

He was there immediately, holding a small basin as the water came back up and she retched helplessly. Hutch held her hair. Naomi produced a damp cloth for her forehead. *Oh, God.* If she had ever felt so humiliated and miserable, she couldn't remember it.

Hutch didn't wait for permission. He removed the pillows and helped her lie flat again. "Okay now?" he asked.

She nodded, unable to look at either of them. "I'm sorry to drag you both into this."

Naomi forced a laugh that sounded almost natural. "C'mon, girl. We've been through a lot of rough patches together over the years. Cecelia and I will help. And you're not poor. That's a plus."

Even Hutch thought that was funny, though he quickly turned his chuckle into a cough. It was probably not acceptable bedside manner to make jokes at the patient's expense.

"Hilarious." Suddenly, it struck her. "Well, crud. I'll never fit into a slinky bridesmaid dress."

Even Naomi didn't have the chutzpah to pretend that wasn't true. But she tried to put a spin on it. "Maybe they'll elope. You never know."

Hutch spoke up, for the first time sounding more like a doctor than an interested party. "I'm glad you came by, Naomi. I'll keep you posted if anything changes. Simone needs to rest now."

Simone wanted to argue that he was being high-handed, but it was the truth. "I should tell Cecelia the news in person," she said.

"No worries." Naomi gathered up her car keys and cell phone. "I'll take care of it. She'll understand."

That wasn't the problem. *No one* was going to understand unless Simone's original motive was revealed. Then she was in big trouble. "Thank you, Naomi."

"Anything for a friend." With a wave and a smile, she was gone.

In the silence that followed Naomi's departure, Simone tried to pretend Hutch had left, as well. Unfortunately, he was impossible to ignore.

Simone loved her bedroom, as a rule. She had always found it soothing with its color scheme of pale lemon yellow and navy. It wasn't too girly.

Today, though, with Hutch in residence, the charming space felt claustrophobic. "How long do I have to have the IV?"

"Until you can take nourishment of some kind. I'll show you how to unhook and stop the monitor from beeping when you need to go to the bathroom. You'll have to promise me, though, that you'll hold on to something and sit down the moment you feel dizzy. Otherwise, I'm going in there with you."

"Over my dead body." Her whole body flushed.

He didn't bother arguing that one.

"You look tired," she said impulsively.

Hutch half turned, his striking face in profile. "It's been a tough day," he said.

"Surely not as tough as Sudan."

"Tough in a different way. You need to sleep now, Simone."

"It's only seven o'clock. Have you eaten?"

"I'll get something later."

"Go now," she urged. "I swear I won't move until you get back."

He shook his head, his expression wry. "I'm not sure I trust you. For the next seventy-two hours, you're my responsibility."

"What am I supposed to do if I can't eat or drink or get out of bed?"

"How about a movie?"

"Will you watch it with me?"

His dark gaze made her shiver, despite her weakened

state. He closed his eyes, took a deep breath and dropped his chin to his chest. After a moment, he lifted his shoulders and let them fall, then looked at her with a carefully blank expression. "If that's what you want. I'll go make myself a sandwich. Here's the remote. You pick something out and I'll be back shortly."

She channel surfed halfheartedly, feeling almost normal for the moment. The pregnancy didn't seem entirely real. Was that odd? Shouldn't she feel a rush of maternal devotion? She did have a connection already. She knew life was growing in her womb even now. But those little blips on the screen didn't have faces and personalities. What if they grew up to be like her?

Eventually, she found a Tom Hanks romantic comedy from the '80s in the on-demand section. That would do the trick. She and Hutch could make fun of the sappy dialogue. At least that's what she told herself. Never in a million years would she let him know how much she loved that story.

When he came back from the kitchen, he had his hands full. He stopped in the doorway as if expecting to find her flouting his orders. She smiled innocently. "I've been good as gold."

"That'll be the day."

Her bed was a king, so when Hutch parked himself on the opposite side, there was an entire stretch of mattress protecting her virtue. Not that it mattered. Who was she kidding? She'd seen herself in the mirror.

Hutch got comfortable and began to wolf down his meal. Suddenly he looked at her in dismay. "Will the smell bother you? I can eat in the kitchen."

"No. I'm fine. If you were eating Thai food, it might be different. That ham sandwich is nausea neutral."

She started the movie, trying not to notice the way Hutch seemed entirely comfortable in her bed. When they had been a couple, she had lived in an upscale apartment down-town, as had Hutch. They'd split their time between loca-tions, some nights in his bed, some nights in hers.

The sex had been incredible, but even more than that was the feeling of rightness... She didn't know how else to explain it. In the beginning, they had talked for hours. She learned that Hutch decided to go into medicine after an older cousin had a difficult pregnancy when he was in high school. The mother and baby both died. Thus, ma-ternal-fetal medicine became his focus when it was time to specialize.

Simone had been out of college barely a year when she met Hutch. She'd worked for a high-end clothing store as a buyer. Marketing was her passion, though, and she'd spent many hours telling Hutch about her intent to open an ad-vertising agency of her own.

Aside from that, they had, of course, talked about their families. Simone was an only child. Hutch had a younger brother who was studying abroad and hoped to go into the diplomatic corps.

Hutch's parents were warm and nurturing, whereas Simone's were strict and cold. Though it was a sad cliché, her father had wanted a boy. But complications during her mother's pregnancy meant no more children after Sim-one. No matter how hard Simone tried, she never seemed to measure up to a list of invisible standards.

Perhaps that was why she reveled in Hutch's attention. Not that she saw him as a father figure. Far from it. The age difference was too narrow for that. But when she spoke, he took her seriously. It was heady stuff.

In her peripheral vision, she could see that Hutch's atten-tion was focused on the television. Was he really engrossed in the movie? She doubted it. More likely, he was thinking about important doctor stuff.

Unlike Simone's endeavors, Hutch's work actually involved life-and-death situations. She teased him about being a saint, but she had never met another man who impressed her so deeply with his work ethic and his compassion.

If he had stayed, they might have ended up married, and Hutch's involvement with DWB might never have materialized. In Simone's twenty-eight years, many people in her life had characterized her as self-centered. Sadly, that had probably been true at one time. But at least she had the comfort of knowing that in this instance she had done the right thing.

She had loved Hutch madly, deeply, desperately...but she had let him go.

When the memories stung too sharply, she hit the mute button on the remote and silenced the TV. "I've seen this one a dozen times," she said. "What I'd really like is for you to tell me about Bethany. And about Sudan."

Five

Hutch froze. He'd been a million miles away. Simone's question caused him to flinch inwardly. Unfortunately, he couldn't think of an excuse to deflect it quickly enough.

"Why?" he asked bluntly.

Simone turned on her side and tucked her hands beneath her cheek. She was drowsy. He could hear it in her voice and see it in her eyes. "You were gone for a long time. Two tours of service. Why didn't you come home after the first one?"

It was a logical question. That had been the assumption all along. Still, when the time came, the thought of returning to Royal and confronting Simone had seemed far more dangerous than anything he would face abroad. So he had stayed.

A month later, he'd met Bethany.

Sensing that Simone wouldn't be dissuaded, he steeled himself for the pain and remorse that choked him when he allowed himself to remember. "I was introduced to Bethany just as I signed up for a second rotation. All the medical staff I had worked with were headed home. Bethany was one of the newbies."

"A nurse?"

"No. A doctor. A pediatrician. Bethany was the daughter of medical missionaries in Central America. She had never lived in the United States full-time until she went to college and med school. She adored children. Wanted five or six of her own one day. In the meantime, her goal was to save as many as she could in Sudan, specifically West Darfur, the state where we were stationed."

"Admirable."

"You would have liked her, I think. She was only five foot one, but somehow you never noticed that about her, because her personality was so compelling. She was passionate about her work and truly believed she was fulfilling her destiny."

"You said you fell in love," Simone prompted him with an expression that was difficult to read.

He stretched his arms over his head, feeling the fatigue of a long day. The last thing he wanted to do was rehash his past with Simone. Especially when it came to talking about another woman. But Simone was relentless when she wanted something.

"I fell in love," he said flatly. "It was slow. At first we were only friends. But I was lonely. I had been in Sudan for a long time."

"And Bethany?"

"I don't know what she saw in me," he said. "It certainly wasn't a romantic situation. Sometimes I think we were just two people doing the best we could."

Simone shifted restlessly. "You don't have to tell me any more, Hutch. She sounds like a lovely person. I'm sorry you lost her. Another day I'd like to hear about your work, but not tonight. I'm tired. I think I can sleep now."

He nodded. "I'll bunk on the sofa. I've programmed my cell number in your phone. Just buzz me when you need to get up."

"I have four perfectly lovely guest rooms, Hutch. You're way too big for the sofa."

He grimaced. "After the past five-plus years, I can sleep pretty much anywhere, trust me."

"But why would you?" Simone frowned.

It seemed cruel to be blunt when she was so sick, but it was better for him to draw the line in the sand. Better, and necessary. "You said it yourself, Simone—you know the way gossip spreads in Royal. It's important to me not to create the impression that I've moved in with you, even for the short-term."

"I see."

When her bottom lip trembled, he felt like a jerk and a bully. She looked small and defenseless in the big bed, though he knew that was only an illusion.

He sighed. "I don't want to hurt you." Hell, he didn't want to hurt himself.

She smiled, though her eyes glistened with tears. "I can handle honesty, Dr. Hutchinson. Let me get my stomach under control, and after that I doubt our paths will cross very often."

It didn't take a medical degree to know when a woman was hurt and fighting back. Rolling to his feet, he straightened the covers on his side of the bed. There was probably some kind of comment that would smooth this situation, but he hadn't a clue what it was.

"Do you want to try some water again?" he asked.

"Absolutely not." She shuddered.

"You'll have to eventually."

"Thanks, Dr. Obvious."

"I forgot what a smart mouth you have." His neck heated.

"And I forgot what a pompous, holier-than-thou hypocrite you are."

"Hypocrite? Seriously? How so?" His temper had a long, slow fuse. But Simone knew how to pour gasoline on any argument.

"You may be done with love and romance for now because Bethany broke your heart. I'll leave you to your crusty bachelorhood, believe me. But I wasn't the only one in the middle of that kiss the other day. I know when a man wants me."

"Damn it, Simone."

"Are you denying it?"

He'd taken an oath to heal and to protect. At the moment, he wanted to strangle his erstwhile patient. "Good night, brat. I'll be in to check on you several times, but use the phone if you need to. I'm close by."

She smirked at him. "Saint Hutch."

He didn't bother turning on lights in the house. During his rural rotations there had been many nights when he and his team only had enough fuel for two hours of lantern light. After that, he'd learned to maneuver in the dark under any circumstances.

He found a new toothbrush in one of the guest bathrooms. Since he always kept a change of clothes in the trunk of his car, he was able to put on a clean shirt and pants after a quick shower.

In the living room, he surveyed the sofa. Actually, it wasn't as small as Simone had intimated. If he bent his knees or propped his feet on the arm, he'd be fine. The couch was leather and cool to the touch. He settled down and pulled an afghan over his lower body.

Fatigue could be measured in degrees. There had been times in Sudan when he worked sixteen hours straight. In the blistering heat. On those nights, he had stumbled to bed and collapsed, asleep in seconds.

Now he was definitely tired. But it was different. Though his body wanted rest, his brain spun like a hamster wheel. Going nowhere.

Simone made him ache—not only physically, though that was certainly true, but emotionally, as well. If he could go back and undo the past, he would never have asked her to dance. That one misstep had led them down a narrow, treacherous road that petered out into nothing.

Time was supposed to heal all wounds. By rights, he should be able to look at his past and acknowledge that things had worked out for the best. But the opposite was true. He felt empty. Even in Africa, when he knew he was saving lives and improving the quality of other lives, he'd learned a painful truth. His being there had been a lie, in part.

Unlike Bethany, who had been so very confident and sure of herself and her life's goals, Hutch had gone to Sudan a broken man. He had utilized his training. He had contributed to the greater good. Still, it hadn't been enough.

He'd been adrift…lost. Losing Simone had made him doubt himself and his place in the world. Eventually, falling in love with Bethany had helped heal the rough places and ease his loneliness. But even before she died, he'd wondered fleetingly if he was using her as a stand-in for the woman he really wanted.

Closing his eyes, he practiced the relaxation techniques he'd used in med school. One muscle group at a time. He dozed on and off, never fully comatose. Many doctors were light sleepers, ready to spring into action when the situation demanded. Which reminded him of the real reason he was here.

He had set the alarm on his phone for three-hour intervals. At one o'clock, he walked quietly down the hall and peeked into the patient's room. If she was resting well, he didn't want to bother her. "Simone?" He whispered her name. She wouldn't hear him unless she was awake.

"Come on in." Her voice was soft, but alert.

"Why aren't you sleeping?"

"I did sleep. For a little while."

"And now?"

"I'm hungry."

"But still nauseated?"

"Oh, yeah…"

He hesitated. "Simone…"

"What?"

"I've seen acupressure really help in these situations. One of the doctors I worked with in West Darfur was Chinese. He taught me the technique, and I actually used it on half a dozen women in my care."

"Is there a downside?"

"I'd have to hold your hand for three minutes. Each one." A long silence ensued.

Finally, Simone spoke. "Sounds pretty risqué."

He choked out a laugh and sat on the end of the bed. Even at her lowest points, Simone was still able to manufacture humor. That ability boded well for a difficult pregnancy.

"Well," he said, "what do you think?"

"I'd dance with the devil if I thought it would make me feel better."

"Gee, thanks," he said drily. "Your enthusiasm is duly noted."

He stood up and moved closer. "We can do this with you sitting up or lying down, whichever feels the most comfortable." The bizarre situation somehow seemed more acceptable, because it was the middle of the night.

"I'll stay put," she said. "Don't want to make any sudden moves that might tip the balance."

It made more sense to sit on the bed, but instead he grabbed the small chair from the vanity and positioned it at Simone's elbow. He wanted the illusion of distance. For the same reason, he didn't turn on the lamp. The faint illumination from the night-light in the bathroom was all he needed.

Most of this procedure was by touch, anyway. He had

learned where to apply pressure. It wasn't an exact science, but he had practiced enough to feel comfortable doing it.

Now if he could be equally at ease with his beautiful guinea pig, he might come out of this next half hour unscathed. "Let's do the easiest one first," he said. Her left hand rested at the edge of the mattress. He picked up her arm, noting that her fingers were cold.

"Will it hurt?" she asked.

He had a hunch that the nervous question was more about him touching her than any real fear of acupressure. "It shouldn't. But if I press too hard, tell me."

Over the years, he had learned that speaking to a patient in steady, reassuring tones while in the midst of a difficult or painful procedure was helpful. In Simone's case, the distraction might prove useful for *both* of them.

Turning her hand palm up, he pressed his thumb to her soft skin. "The spot for this is P6," he said. "About three fingers above the crease of your wrist and in between two tendons." He applied pressure. "Okay so far?"

She nodded.

Three minutes was a hell of a long time when a man held a woman in a dark bedroom and knew every one of the reasons he couldn't or wouldn't let himself be drawn in again. He counted off the seconds in his head, trying to ignore the fact that she trembled.

After an eternity, he cleared his throat. "Other hand," he said.

He hoped this was going to help, because it was tearing him apart. Her hair fanned out across the pillow. The thin, silky nightgown she wore was cut low in the front. Though at first she clutched the sheet in a death grip, when she shifted slightly and gave him her right arm, he could see the shadow of her cleavage and the outline of her breasts.

God help him. He kept the pressure firm, resisting the urge to stroke upward to the crease of her elbow. Kissing her there had been a game he played in the past, a teasing caress she always swore tickled. But it also made her sigh and melt into his embrace.

"Hasn't it been long enough?"

Simone's timid question snapped him out of his reverie. He'd lost count of the seconds. "I think so," he muttered. He released her and sat back. "How do you feel?"

She rubbed her wrists together and flexed her fingers. "Better. I think. Is this honestly a valid treatment?"

"Been around for thousands of years."

"I hesitate to tempt fate, but I think I could eat something."

"Good. That's usually the case. The effects aren't permanent, of course, but you can take advantage in the interim. What can I get for you?"

"Let's start small. Dry toast with a tiny bit of apple jelly? Do you mind?"

"Of course not."

In the kitchen, he rested his forehead against the cool stainless steel of the refrigerator door. This wasn't going to work. He'd find someone else to help out, but it couldn't be him.

Desire was a steady ache in his gut. And it wasn't even entirely about sex. He wanted to crawl into that bed and hold her. Too many nights in the last few years he had summoned Simone's image to get through the hot, lonely hours. He'd missed home. He had missed his friends and colleagues. He had even missed the unpredictable Texas weather.

Now he had returned home, and almost everything was back to normal. Almost, but not quite.

On autopilot, he retrieved the bread and prepared a single piece of toast. Simone had to start slow. Her stomach had suffered significant trauma in the past few days.

In the end, he was gone maybe twenty minutes. When

he returned, she was sitting up. He frowned. "You should have let me help you."

Simone's smile was sunny. "I think I can eat," she said. "You're a miracle worker, Dr. Hutchinson."

"Don't get too excited," he cautioned. "The nausea will likely come back."

"I can handle that," she said. "At least if I can have some normalcy in between."

He offered her the small plate. "One bite at a time. We're in no rush."

She nodded. Carefully, she took one dainty bite. Clearly, she was so excited about eating that she had forgotten her state of dress. He tried not to stare. Instead, he prowled her bedroom, studying the things with which she had surrounded herself.

Between two large windows, a tall set of antique barrister bookshelves held a collection of travel books, popular novels and childhood favorites. In another corner, an overstuffed armchair and matching ottoman provided a cozy reading spot. Books were only one of many passions he and Simone had shared.

He remembered a summer picnic in the country long ago when they had laughed and enjoyed playful sex and finally rested in the shade of a giant oak. While he had drowsed with his head in Simone's lap, she had read aloud to him from a book of poetry. That might have been the moment he knew he was in love with her. She was so much more than a beautiful woman or a wealthy debutante or a Texas Cattleman's Club darling.

Simone Parker was a free spirit, a lover of life. She was warm and intelligent and effortlessly charming. Other men had looked at him with envious eyes when he and Simone were out together in public. She was the kind of woman some guys considered a trophy girlfriend.

To Hutch, she had simply been his life. When they met,

he'd been twenty-eight. Plenty old enough to have sown his proverbial wild oats. About the time he'd been rethinking his plans to head off to Africa, Simone had cut him loose. She'd insisted that he was a gifted doctor and that she wouldn't stand in his way.

"Hutch!"

Pushing the painful thoughts away, he spun around, alarmed. "What is it?"

Simone beamed. "I ate it. And I think it's going to stay down. Will you pour me some water?"

He did so immediately and handed her the glass. "Tiny sips," he cautioned.

She scrunched up her face as she drank the water one tablespoon at a time. "That's enough," she said finally.

"How do you feel?"

"Tired. Weird. But not pregnant. Is that bad?" She bit her bottom lip, a telltale sign she was agitated.

He took the glass and set it back on the table. "Of course not. It will be a long time before you start to show, especially because you've lost weight already. As far as actually feeling the babies kick, I'd guess that will be weeks from now. So it's no surprise you don't feel pregnant. That's why Mother Nature gives you three trimesters to get used to the idea."

"I suppose…"

"Can you go back to sleep now?"

She slid back down in the bed and straightened the covers. "I think so."

"And the nausea?"

"Hardly any right now. Thank you, Hutch."

He shrugged. "I'm glad the acupressure worked. Sometimes modern medicine looks for answers when they're right at hand."

"Right at hand." She giggled. "Dr. Hutch made a funny. Get it? You held my hands?"

"If I didn't know better, I'd think you'd been drinking," he said ruefully.

"I would never do anything so foolish. I'm just giddy with relief that you made the nausea go away, even for an hour. Are there other people in Royal who might know how to do what you did?"

The intent behind her question was obvious. Neither of them thought Hutch should be the one to help her through the terrible sickness produced by her pregnancy. Nevertheless, he spoke the truth. "I doubt it, Simone. Maybe in one of the big cities. But Royal is not exactly a hotbed of ancient Asian medical practice."

"I see."

It was impossible to miss the layers of frustration and unease she gave off. "We'll figure something out," he promised. "One day at a time."

She moved restlessly. "I shouldn't have let you kiss me the other day. That was wrong of me. I'm sorry."

"Forget about it. I could have stopped."

"Why didn't you?" she asked softly.

It was a very good question. One he had asked himself a dozen times since. He was a grown-ass man. He knew better than to show weakness to Simone.

"I guess part of me wanted to remember," he muttered. "But now all I want to do is forget."

Six

When Simone awoke next, she realized she had slept for six hours straight. Her head was clear, and although she did indeed feel sick again, it wasn't at the intense level she had experienced recently.

As she stretched and tried to convince herself she could get up and go to the bathroom without incident, a woman in navy scrubs peeked her head around the door. "Ms. Parker? Good, you're awake. I'm Barb Kellum. Dr. Hutchinson called me and said you needed some help."

"That would be great," Simone said. "I'd love to get a shower."

The nurse smiled. "First things first, young lady. Let's eat a bit of breakfast and go from there. I brought over some of my homemade chicken broth. Warmed it in the microwave. How does that sound?"

The nurse with the salt-and-pepper hair was midfifty-ish, tall and sturdily built. Her eyes were kind, but her tone of voice was more drill sergeant than nanny.

Simone smiled hesitantly. "I'll give it a try. But I make no promises."

While Simone sat up in bed, the nurse bustled about, straightening the covers and carefully placing a white wooden tray over Simone's lap. The serving piece must have come with Barb as well, because Simone had never seen it. Although the china, glass and silverware were arranged artistically, Simone's stomach rebelled at the aroma of the chicken broth.

Barbara picked up the bowl and held it under Simone's nose. "Don't let your brain overrule your stomach. You're hungry, even if you don't know it. Breathe in and tell yourself you're about to have a treat."

Amazingly, it worked. Mostly. Inhaling the scent of the thin soup sent a sharp hunger pang through Simone's stomach. She picked up the spoon and scooped up the first bite. "What if this doesn't work?"

Barbara pointed at the floor beside the bed. "Basin and plastic ready. Nothing to worry about."

It took half an hour, but Simone finished every spoonful. Afterward, she scooted down onto the mattress and lay there frozen, afraid to move. "How long before you think it's safe to get up?"

The nurse shook her head. "Sorry, love, but you can't play that game. It might help the nausea, but your muscles will start to atrophy if we don't keep you on your feet. Exercise can actually help nausea."

The following few hours were a lesson in patience. Barb unhooked the IV and hovered as Simone visited the bathroom. After that, the two of them managed a modified shower for Simone. She threw up twice in the process, but it wasn't as violent as the episodes earlier in the week.

Once she was clean and dry, she felt as weak as a baby.

Barb beamed at her. "I'd say we did well, Ms. Parker."

"Please call me Simone."

"And I answer to Barb. Now sit in that chair for half a shake while I remake the bed. Nothing feels better after a shower than clean sheets."

By the time Simone was tucked back into bed and the IV

was reattached, she felt embarrassingly exhausted. "How long do I have to be hooked up?"

Barbara checked her blood pressure and pulse before answering. "That all depends on how much you can eat on your own. I'll draw blood after lunch and send it off to the lab. Then again before dinner. Tomorrow, Dr. Hutchinson will read the results and assess how you're doing."

The nurse was right about clean sheets. Simone's eyes were heavy. "Is it okay if I nap?"

"Definitely. Later, we'll try a walk around the house. Don't worry, Ms. Parker. You'll survive this, I promise."

Simone dozed on and off during the next hour, watching the patterns of light and shadow on the ceiling. All her problems hovered just offstage, but for now, she was content to drift. She vaguely remembered Hutch checking on her a couple of times last night after the acupressure incident, but they hadn't spoken since. Beneath the sheet, she laced her fingers over her abdomen. Her stomach was flat and smooth, the muscles taut and firm. Though she had friends and acquaintances who had already become mothers, she had never thought much about the process. At least not until her grandfather died.

Suddenly, she realized she hadn't looked at her email in over forty-eight hours. Stealthily, not wanting to incur Barb's wrath, she reached into the bottom drawer of the bedside table and retrieved her laptop. Leaning on one elbow, she opened it up and turned it on. Fortunately, her battery charge was at 50 percent. She could do a few things quickly without asking for help.

Email was not a problem. She deleted the junk and replied to a couple of queries that needed an immediate answer. Then, with shaky fingers, she logged on to Facebook and checked the message box. A tiny numeral one appeared on the icon. Damn. Most of her friends texted her. The only recent Facebook message she had received was one from the mysterious Maverick. Maverick—the anonymous, eerie, dark presence who had threatened many of the citizens of Royal, one after another.

Simone's first message had appeared two weeks ago. Since nothing bad had happened in the interim, she'd hoped the blackmailer had moved on to someone else. Apparently not.

The message was brief and vindictive.

Simone Parker, you're a money-grubbing bitch. Enjoy life now, because soon everyone in town will know what you have done and why. Maverick.

She shut the computer quickly and tucked it under a pillow. This time, the nausea roiling in her belly had more to do with fear and disgust than it did with pregnancy. All she could think about was the look on Hutch's face if he ever learned the truth.

Unfortunately, Barb returned about that time and frowned. "You're flushed. What's wrong?"

Simone didn't bother answering. She was afraid she would cry. The thought that someone in Royal hated her enough to blackmail her was distressing. She wasn't a saint—far from it. But she tried to learn from her mistakes.

The nurse took her pulse and frowned. "You need to calm down, young lady. Stress isn't good for the babies. What brought this on?"

Simone scrambled for a convincing lie. "I have so much to do at work. Each day I get farther behind. I need to make plans...to decide how I'll manage three babies. It's a lot, you know."

Barb nodded sympathetically. "I understand, I do. But you can't climb a mountain in bare feet. Baby steps, remember. First we have to get you stabilized and healthy. Then you'll have plenty of time to plan for the future."

"Easy for you to say," Simone muttered in a whisper. Did no one understand what a colossal mess she had made of her life? It wasn't as if she could wave a magic wand and get a do-over.

Lunch was not as successful as breakfast. Two bites of lemon gelatin came right back up. But Simone waited an hour and tried again with better results. Afterward, Barb brought in her tray of torture implements. Having blood drawn was no fun, but Simone knew she had to get used to it.

Next was another nap, and after that, Barb came in to say it was time for a walk around the house. Simone leaned on the older woman unashamedly as they made a circuit from room to room. Clearly, this was necessary, because already her muscles were quivering.

Finally, she was allowed to collapse into bed again. Meanwhile, Barb changed out the IV bag, straightened the room and drew more blood. As she packed up the vials, she eyed Simone with an assessing gaze. "Will you be okay for the next few hours? I hate to leave you alone, but I promised a friend I'd sit with her mother at the nursing home this evening."

"I'll be fine," Simone said. "Dr. Hutchinson showed me how to unhook things so I can go the bathroom, and I'm feeling much stronger. Don't worry about me."

"There's more gelatin and broth in the fridge. And I brought you a fresh box of saltines this morning."

"You've been wonderful. Will you be here tomorrow?"

Barb nodded. "Dr. Hutchinson said at least three days."

"Okay then. I'll see you in the morning."

"Should I bring the meal before I go?"

"It's still early. I'd rather wait."

"All right then." She gave a little wave. "I'll let myself out."

With the nurse gone and Hutch still presumably at the

hospital, the house was desperately quiet. As the sunlight faded, Simone felt the weight of her situation drag her down. Whatever lay ahead, she would take care of these innocent babies. If she decided she was incapable of functioning as a single mother, she could give them up for adoption when they were born. There were likely dozens of couples in Royal with fertility issues who would be overjoyed at the chance to give three little babies a home.

The thought left Simone feeling hollow. Not only had she rushed into this situation with less than pure motives, she had given little or no thought to the future. Now that she was pregnant, the situation was painfully real.

At six thirty, she actually felt hungry…in a normal way. Hutch had said he'd be back, but who knew what kind of emergencies might have come up.

Mindful of her promises to Barb, she sat on the side of the bed for a full three minutes before attempting to get up. Unhooking the IV was not hard once she'd learned what to do. Walking slowly, she made her way to the kitchen and opened the refrigerator. After eating a few bites of the gelatin, she drank half a glass of ginger ale. The calories she had consumed today were helping. She felt steadier and stronger already.

Darkness closed in, and with it, her uneasiness returned. Hutch had given her his phone number. Should she simply text him and tell him not to come?

When she saw headlights flash as a car turned into her driveway, she scurried back to the bedroom, reattached the IV and settled into bed. She didn't want Hutch to think she was being reckless. It was important to her that he knew she was taking this pregnancy seriously.

When he finally appeared at her door, he looked tired, but wonderful.

"Hey there," he said, his lips curving in a half smile. "Barb said you had a pretty good day."

Simone nodded. "I'd give it a seven and a half. Thank you for suggesting her. She's very kind and competent."

"How's your stomach?" He sat on the foot of the bed and ran his hands over his face. He had obviously showered before leaving the hospital, because he smelled like the outdoors, all fresh and masculine.

She sat up and scooped her hair away from her face. Barb had taken the time to blow-dry it after Simone's shower. Now it fell straight and silky around her shoulders. "We're on speaking terms again. Barely."

"Good."

"Have *you* eaten?"

"I grabbed a burger in the cafeteria."

"That's not entirely healthy. Physician, heal thyself."

"You let me worry about me. What did you have for dinner?"

"Some gelatin. I was contemplating Barb's homemade chicken broth, but I'm feeling pretty normal at the moment, and I'd hate to tempt fate."

"You look better."

His steady regard made her blush. "Thank you."

"How 'bout I warm the broth and bring it to you?"

"Okay," she said reluctantly. "If you insist."

Hutch grinned. "I do."

While he was gone, she grabbed a small mirror out of her purse and examined her reflection. Other than having cheekbones that were too sharp, she didn't look half bad. Pinching her cheeks added color to her face.

Hutch must have found the bed tray in the kitchen. When he returned with her modest meal, he had poured a serving of broth into a crockery bowl and added a glass of ice water, along with some soda crackers.

Simone scooted up in bed. "Barb is a good cook."

"Her specialty is invalid food."

She wrinkled her nose. "That's a terrible way to describe it."

"Sorry."

The stilted conversation was awkward, to say the least. "You don't have to watch me eat, Hutch. And you don't need to spend the night. I'm much better. I appreciate all you've done."

He shrugged, his expression impassive. "One more night won't hurt. I'll have the results of your blood work in the morning. If everything looks sound, you can follow up next week with Dr. Fetter at a regular appointment."

"And you'll ride off into the sunset to rescue another damsel in distress."

His eyes narrowed. His jaw tightened. "Are you pissed that I went to Africa? Is that it, Simone? If you'll recall, I offered to stay here until you got your agency off the ground. But you were pretty emphatic that I should go. So don't blame me for the mess you've made of your life."

She swallowed hard. Already, her stomach cramped with nerves and nausea, and she hadn't even taken a bite yet. The old Hutch would never have been so blunt. There was a time he'd humored her every whim and thought her biting sarcasm was funny.

Not so much anymore.

She lifted her chin, striving for dignity. "You're right. I apologize. Now if you don't mind, I think I'll have a better chance of getting this to go down successfully if I don't have an audience. And to be clear, I don't blame you for anything. You're an easy target, and I'm at the end of my rope. But don't worry, Hutch. I'll be just fine."

Hutch cursed softly, striding rapidly out of the room. How was it possible for one small woman to make him feel like a complete and utter failure? No one in his entire adult life had caused him as many sleepless nights as Simone Parker. Not even Bethany.

He prowled the house, pacing from room to room, feeling his bitterness and frustration grow. Though he finally managed to sleep for a few hours, at 3:00 a.m. he was up again. In the darkest moments of the night, he at last admitted to himself why he was so angry.

In some foolish, illogical corner of his brain, he had entertained the hope that he and Simone might mend fences. Despite his utter despair at losing Bethany, seeing Simone that first day in the exam room at the hospital had given him hope.

But the feeling was a lie. He was a bloody idiot. He and Simone were no more compatible than they had ever been. She had a chip on her shoulder so big it was a wonder it didn't crush her. Surely she didn't expect him to sit at her feet like a puppy dog begging for scraps. Those babies she carried weren't his. She didn't want to be married. Not to him, not to anyone. With this unconventional pregnancy, she was thumbing her nose at the world.

He might not understand why, but he knew it was true.

At last, sheer exhaustion trumped his fury. He went to Simone's bedroom to check the IV, more for something to do than any real expectation that the bag was empty. Barb had changed it late that afternoon.

What he heard as he stood in the hallway put a knot in his chest.

Simone was crying...not just crying, but sobbing. Plucky, confident, decisive Simone sounded as if her heart was completely broken.

He backed away quietly, not wanting to embarrass her. Then he stopped. Not even the most coldhearted of bastards could leave her in that condition.

Though he suffered misgivings on a massive scale, he

padded over to the bed in his sock feet and crouched beside her. She lay on her back with one arm flung over her eyes.

"Simone," he whispered, not wanting to alarm her. "Stop crying, honey. It only makes things worse."

Without waiting for permission, he unhooked the IV, scooped her up and sat down with her in his lap. Leaning against the headboard, he stroked her hair. "Talk to me, little mama. Tell me what's going on in that head of yours."

Though she huffed and protested and struggled briefly, he felt the moment she went limp in his embrace. She burrowed into his chest like a frightened child. Tears wet his shirt. The sobs were less ferocious, but the crying didn't stop.

It worried him. Simone was not one to give up on any challenge. He'd never seen her like this. Gently, he held her close, telling himself the position was for her benefit. He didn't even flinch at the lie. That's how easy it was for his libido to seize the wheel.

Minutes ticked away on the clock. Simone was a welcome weight against his body. Though she was too thin, and arguably not at her best, to him, she was as stunningly beautiful as she had ever been. Imagining her round belly in the advanced stages of pregnancy flooded him with an entirely inappropriate rush of arousal.

At one time, he had envisioned that scenario with pride and anticipation. Now everything was wrong. And he felt powerless to make it right.

Seven

"Enough, Simone," he said firmly. "That's enough."

Gradually, she calmed. Except for the occasional tiny, hiccupping sob, the storm was over.

He played with her hair, plaiting it between his fingers. He didn't touch her breasts. He wanted to… God knows he wanted to. But that would be too much temptation. He wasn't prepared to throw all caution to the wind.

Pregnancy was the most natural thing in the world, and yet complicated. From teenagers who didn't mean to get pregnant to full-grown women who craved a child and couldn't conceive, the process was messy and fraught with pitfalls. He couldn't imagine the toll this was taking on Simone emotionally.

He smoothed his palm over her back. "Better now?" he asked.

She nodded, sitting up and sniffling. Her damp eyes were sapphires framed in coal-black lashes. "Hutch."

His name was a caress on her lips, a sweet, irresistible invitation. God help him. He slid his hands beneath her hair and steadied her head, tipping her mouth up for his kiss. He wanted her to stop him. He needed her to be alarmed and outraged. Instead, she leaned into him.

Their lips clung, mated. She tasted like toothpaste.

"Sweet Simone," he muttered, easing her onto her back. He moved half on top of her, his leg wedged between her thighs. She sighed and welcomed him, though her thin nightgown hampered her movements.

He kissed her forehead, her eyelids, her slender throat. Simone arched against him, her breathing ragged. When he made his way down to the place where the neckline of her gown covered her breasts, Simone stiffened for the first time.

Instinctively, he drew back. He was half out of his mind, but not so far gone he didn't know when a woman said no. Verbal or body language, it didn't matter.

She frowned. "Why did you stop?"

"I felt you tense up."

"Not because of you."

"Then why?"

"I don't want to hurt the babies."

He smiled, though it took an effort. "Nothing a man and a woman do in this situation is cause for alarm. I swear to you."

She kept one hand on his shoulder, the other free to comb through his hair. The feel of her fingertips on his scalp made him shiver. "Hutch?"

"Yes?"

"I guess it's obvious we both need this. But it won't mean anything beyond tonight. It can't."

"Is that an ultimatum?" Why couldn't the damn woman live in the moment? That was a lesson he had learned in Sudan when life was so very fragile and joy came only in fleeting snatches.

She rubbed her thumb across his cheekbone. "No ultimatum." She sighed.

"Do you want me?"

"So much it hurts. Is that normal?"

"Many pregnant women find themselves with increased libido."

Simone laughed at him. "You're funny when you get all serious and medical."

"Most people respect my position and my expertise."

"Most people haven't seen you naked."

His lips twisted in a wry grin. He would never develop too much of an inflated ego with Simone around. "Are you feeling ill? At all?"

She wrapped one slender, toned thigh around his leg. "I'm good to go."

Hutch knew he was making a mistake. Simone must have known it, too. But the heat and yearning between them was too powerful to ignore. "I've been tested recently," he said. "I'm clean."

"I'm in the clear also. And it's not like you're going to knock me up." The line should have been funny, but neither of them laughed.

Very deliberately—to give them both a chance to change their minds—he stood and stripped off his clothes. Simone tracked his every move. Afterward, he helped her sit up, and they both managed to raise her gown over her head. She wasn't wearing any underwear, so now she was completely nude.

He reclined beside her and put a tentative hand on her belly. "Odd, isn't it…that you can't really feel anything when so much is going on?"

She leaned against him, her hand on top of his. "I'm scared, Hutch."

"Of which part?" He kissed her softly, almost lightheaded because every bit of blood had rushed south to his sex.

"All of it. Labor. Delivery. Bringing home three newborns. Trying to breastfeed."

"Women have been doing this since the dawn of time.

You're smart and organized. I have no doubt you'll conquer motherhood like you do every other hurdle in your life."

"Make love to me, Hutch."

Her eyes were damp. She seemed more sad than amorous. But he couldn't tell her no. Not anymore.

Carefully, he spread her legs and tested her readiness with two fingers. Her sex was moist and swollen. "Simone," he groaned. He slid into her with one steady push. The sensation was indescribable. Pausing to let her adjust to his size, he rested his forehead on her shoulder. Her fingernails scored his back.

"More," she demanded. "More, Hutch."

He lost his mind. There was no other way to describe it. His fantasies from endless dark, hot, uncomfortable nights in West Darfur burst into life with a euphoric explosion that took him to the brink of a powerful orgasm in seconds. He could tell Simone wasn't far behind.

Deliberately, he reached between their sweat-slickened bodies and found the little spot that made her tumble over the edge. They clung to each other like survivors in the aftermath of a killer wave.

The room was dark and silent. At last, he pushed up onto one elbow and cupped her cheek with his hand. "Again?" he asked hoarsely.

"Yes," she whispered. "Again…"

Simone spent the waning hours of the night wrapped in Hutch's arms. He spooned her, her back pressed to his chest. Though she felt his sex flex against her bottom, stiff and ready, they didn't make love again.

It was the most restful sleep she'd experienced in the last two weeks. If she tried really hard, she could pretend the past five years never happened.

Toward morning, the nausea returned. Hutch held her hair and washed her face after she retched helplessly. He helped put her nightgown back on and sat with her, coaxing her bite by bite until she finished several crackers.

Then Barb arrived and Hutch transformed into Dr. Hutchinson. "I'll call with the lab results," he said, his expression distant and remote.

"Thank you," Simone said, her heart shredding in agony.

Barb bustled about, oblivious to the tension in the room.

Hutch nodded. "You ladies have a good day. I need to get to the hospital."

When Simone didn't reply, he spun on his heel and walked out.

After that, the day was an endurance test. Eat. Get sick. Eat again. But the episodes were coming further apart, and she was actually managing to keep food down long enough to reap the benefits.

When Hutch called the landline with Simone's test results, Barb answered and jotted down some numbers. She hung up the phone and gave Simone a thumbs-up. "Your electrolytes and other blood levels are right where they need to be, young lady. Let's take that needle out of your hand and allow you to get back to normal."

Barb stayed for the remainder of the day, but it was clear that Simone was learning to manage the nausea on her own. The efficient nurse said her goodbyes just before five o'clock, about the time Cecelia showed up with a huge pan of lasagna and a crusty loaf of French bread.

Cecelia blanched when Simone got teary-eyed. "What did I do?" she asked urgently. "Are you in pain?"

Simone hugged her tightly. "I'm just so glad to see you."

Her beautiful blonde friend carried everything through to the kitchen. "No garlic on the bread and no heavy spices in the lasagna. I'm determined to fatten you up. You look awful, hon."

Simone simply shook her head. Was there no one who would lie to her and tell her she looked great? "I feel like I could eat the whole pan. But I won't," she said hastily. "My poor stomach is barely speaking to me as it is."

Cecelia nodded. "It should keep in the fridge for several days. When will you be able to go back to work?"

"I know you're worried about your campaign, but I'm not going to drop the ball, I promise. I'm planning to go in tomorrow, even if I have to cut the day short."

The other woman raised one perfect eyebrow. "Please give me some credit. I'm not worried about the campaign, I'm worried about *you*, Simone. Would you mind telling me why in the world you had to get pregnant right now? It doesn't make sense."

"I thought Naomi filled you in." Simone perched on a stool at the granite counter. She didn't really want to go through the whole explanation again, especially when it wasn't all that believable the first time.

Cecelia waved a hand, the one not showcasing her amazing engagement ring. "Naomi tried to put a positive spin on it, but I wasn't buying it. Since when do *you* want to be a mother?"

Cecelia's skepticism stung. "Is that really so hard to imagine?"

"You've poured your heart and soul into the agency. You've dated one or two…not more than three guys since Hutch headed off to Africa. And never once have you given any indication that your biological clock is ticking any louder than mine or Naomi's. I know you, girl. Something strange is going on." Cecelia broke off a warm piece of bread, wrapped it in a paper napkin and handed it to Simone. "Tell Auntie Cee Cee what's up, or I'll be forced to resort to blackmail."

It was a poor choice of words. When Simone flinched, Cecelia frowned. "What did I say? You know I was only kidding. But seriously, Simone. Tell me what the heck is going on."

Sooner or later the truth would come out. Sooner or later Simone would have to confide in her two best friends. But she still felt raw and guilty about her decision. She needed time to come to terms with what she had done before she came clean completely.

"It's true," she muttered. "There's more to this than you know. I won't keep it a secret forever. But in the meantime, I need you to be my friend and tell me everything is going to work out fine."

"Is that because the gorgeous doctor is going to step in and make an honest woman out of you?"

"Don't even joke about that," Simone snapped. "Hutch doesn't deserve to be dragged into my mess."

"Well, maybe he'll at least stick around this time." Cecelia's dour comment made Simone want to rush to Hutch's defense. The man had simply followed his dreams and his calling. While she appreciated her friend's whole-hearted support, it really wasn't fair to paint Hutch as the villain.

"Let's eat," Simone said. "The lasagna smells amazing. And if you don't mind, let's not talk about Hutch or babies or my sordid secrets. Dr. Fetter says stress can make my nausea worse."

"Sordid?" Cecelia perked up. "I'm intrigued."

"You're also wildly happy, aren't you?" Simone said, trying to change the subject as she piled a small dollop of lasagna on her plate. "Deacon must be good for you. I'm pretty sure you're glowing."

Cecelia's smile was smug. "He's amazing. And we're both thrilled about the baby."

"I'm very happy for you."

Cecelia sobered for a moment. "Is it true you're having triplets?"

Simone nodded. "As long as nothing goes wrong. Sometimes one fetus doesn't develop. It's too soon to know."

"Would you be relieved if you only had one or two?"

Trust Cecelia to cut to the heart of the matter. "You'd think so, wouldn't you? Lord knows how I'll manage. But now that I know there are three, I want them all so badly. It doesn't make any sense. I can't really explain it. All I know is that I would be heartbroken if anything happened to even one of them. I feel like their mother already."

Cecelia leaned over to hug her. "I get it, hon. This whole pregnancy thing turns the world upside down." She hesitated, clearly looking for a tactful way to phrase her question. "So how does the good doctor figure into all of this? Naomi said he was here the other night when she came over."

"He's the new head of the maternal-fetal department at the hospital. Not *my* doctor," Simone said hastily. "I'm Dr. Fetter's patient. But I'm considered high-risk because of the multiples. Hutch oversees and keep tabs on all the cases."

"And does he make house calls to each of those pregnant women?"

"Of course not."

Cecelia rolled her eyes. "Fine. Live in the land of denial while you can."

Simone felt her face get hot. What would Cecelia and Naomi think if they knew about last night? "I doubt I'll see much of him. The only reason he was here is that I chose to have my IV at home instead of taking up a hospital bed. He wanted to make sure I was okay. That's all."

"Whatever you say, little chick. I won't harass you when you're so sick. Still, the day of reckoning will come. Don't think you can avoid this subject forever."

That was the problem, Simone thought bleakly. With this Maverick person threatening her, she was always going to have the sword of Damocles hanging over her head. Telling her parents was going to be bad. She knew she had to do it soon. If they got wind of her pregnancy any other way, they might pressure her into marrying the baby's father. How was she going to explain that the mystery man was no more to her than a control number on a test tube?

Cecelia waved a hand in front of Simone's face. "Hello, in there. Anybody home?"

Simone took a bite of lasagna and washed it down with tea. "Sorry. I was thinking."

"About what?" Cecelia said. Clearly, *her* pregnancy was going well. She ate an astonishing amount of lasagna with no consequences as far as Simone could see.

"I don't want to make a big deal about this pregnancy. Especially not this early, not when there's a chance I could miscarry."

"Lots of people wait until after the first trimester to make any kind of announcement."

"True. But you know how gossip flies in this town. The fact that I was taken from my office on a stretcher is not a secret."

"You'll figure something out," Cecelia said breezily. She grabbed her sweater and purse. "I've gotta run. I'm meeting Deacon for a late dessert."

"Oh, Cecelia. Why didn't you tell me? You should have dropped off the lasagna and had dinner with your brand-new fiancé."

Cecelia's grin was cheeky. "Don't be silly. That lucky man gets to eat dinner with me the rest of his life. He won't begrudge me one evening with a sick friend."

"I'm doing better, honestly."

"Good. 'Cause to tell you the truth, Naomi had me worried after she saw you the other night."

"Let her know I'm fine."

"I will." Cecelia hugged her. "I'll call you tomorrow.

Don't worry about the campaign. You're the most important thing to me. Love you, hon."

And with that, Simone's gorgeous friend blew out the door.

Simone stood at the living room window and watched the car fly down the driveway and onto the main road. Suddenly, she was aware of the crushing silence in the house. No Cecelia or Naomi. No Barb. No Hutch.

He had talked about staying three nights, but she was better now. All her tests had come back with good results. The nurse had removed the IV and packed up all the paraphernalia to take back to the hospital. There was absolutely no reason for Hutch to return.

Life was back to normal. Almost.

Telling herself she wasn't depressed, Simone took a shower and changed into an old pair of yoga pants and an oversize T-shirt. She'd spent far too much time in bed. She wanted to get outside and breathe the fresh spring air.

Not bothering to put on shoes, she opened the back door and made her way down the steps. Dr. Fetter had said moderate exercise was helpful, so Simone had no qualms about risking the babies. The healthier she was, the healthier they were.

Outside, she perked up instantly. Her gardener was a genius. Flowers and ornamental shrubs and fruit trees met and mingled in a display that was appealing without being too formal. In the center of it all lay a deep, verdant lawn. It reminded her of the quad at college where this time of year she and her friends would toss Frisbees and sunbathe and study when they absolutely had to...

All of that seemed like a lifetime ago.

The evening air was cooler than usual. She wrapped her arms around her waist and meandered aimlessly. There in the corner might be a good spot for a play structure. Swings and a slide and maybe even a tiny house with real windows and miniature furniture inside.

It was fun to daydream, because she wanted to be a good mother. She wanted her children to grow up feeling loved and supported. If she had a boy who aspired to be a ballet dancer or a girl who loved fire engines, she would nurture them and help them follow their dreams.

But what happened when the babies grew old enough to ask about their father? What would she say? Stricken by her own selfishness and shortsightedness, she fell to her knees and covered her face with her hands. The scope and ramifications of her mistake were crushing. How could she ever make this right?

She blamed the cry fest on hormones. The tears leaked between her fingers and spotted the front of her shirt. In the spacious yard surrounded by a tall privacy fence, she faced the enormity of what she had done. There was no one to see her break down…no one to witness the moment she hit bottom.

Later, she wasn't sure how long she'd been kneeling there in the grass. She only knew that her knees were sore and her skin covered in gooseflesh when a very familiar voice said her name.

"Simone?"

Eight

Hutch hadn't meant to come. He'd had a hell of a long day. He was exhausted, and he needed seven or eight straight hours of uninterrupted sleep.

Despite all that, here he was at Simone's house. Again.

He crouched beside her in the grass, touching her shoulder briefly. "What's wrong, Simone? Are you hurt?" Her hair shielded her expression.

She jumped to her feet and backed away from him, rubbing the tears from her face with two hands. Her smile didn't reach her eyes. "Hormones," she said lightly. "You should know all about that. Crazy pregnant women."

After last night, he'd wondered if Simone might want more from him than medical advice. Apparently not.

He took a moment to absorb the breath-stealing realization that she was not happy to see him. Her response was painful and unexpected. It was just as well. Hadn't he come tonight for the express purpose of telling her there was nothing between them? He wasn't prepared to risk his heart a third time. He had an important new job and little opportunity for a social life, much less a love affair.

"Barb told me you're improving slightly," he said.

"Yes. Especially in the evenings. Cecelia brought me lasagna. I managed some of that. And bread."

"Good." Fourteen hours ago they had been naked together in her bed. Now she could barely look at him. "I won't stay tonight," he said. It was a statement, but it came out sounding like a question. Would she ask him to change his mind?

"I know," she said, her gaze wary. "No need."

He cursed beneath his breath. She was far too pale. "Simone, I—"

She held up her hand. "I think we both know what last night was," she said. "Curiosity. Echoes of the past. Let's not beat ourselves up over it. Even if you wanted a repeat, I would have to say no. I need to start planning for my new family. If I hang around with you, the temptation will always be there to lean on you for help. I can't afford to do that."

"Everybody needs a hand at times."

"You know what I mean."

He did. All too well. She was putting up walls. Shutting him out.

He should be relieved. "If you go back to work, please pace yourself. Otherwise, you'll wind up in the same situation as before."

"I understand. You can trust me, Hutch. I want these babies to be safe and healthy. I won't be stupid, I promise."

He nodded. "I should go."

"One more thing." She seemed to hesitate, as if searching for the right words. "I appreciate all you've done for me, Hutch. Later on, when I'm stronger, I'd like to make dinner for you. No strings attached," she said quickly. "Just friends."

"Okay. But you know it's not necessary."

"I want to."

"Just let me know." For some reason, he couldn't get his feet to move. "You still have my card? My phone number?" There was so much they weren't saying.

"I do." She seemed lonely and forlorn.

"Good luck, Simone."

"Thank you."

Simone watched him walk around the side of the house and disappear. The hollow feeling in her chest would get better. It had to. She was done with tears for now.

As she headed back inside, she didn't feel sleepy yet. Watching television wasn't appealing. Instead, she decided to measure one of the guest rooms. Upstairs, she had three guest rooms. The main level of the house included her master suite and a fourth guest room. That might make the best nursery.

She made a few notes and pursed her lips. How did one handle triplets? Did all three babies share? Three cribs in one space? What if one kid woke up in the middle of the night and started crying? Wouldn't that bother the other two?

Abandoning her architectural conundrum, she went in search of the box of books Hutch had dropped by earlier in the week. She planned to start with something simple, perhaps one of the parenting guides. The medical books would be too scary. She didn't want to think about complications, even in a theoretical sense.

With a cup of decaf coffee and a cozy lap blanket, she curled up in her favorite chair in the bedroom and started to read. It wasn't only the advice about being a mom of multiples she needed, it was advice about *everything*. She felt woefully unprepared for motherhood.

At the end of a chapter, she closed the book and stared out the window. It was dark now, that time when problems grew bigger and optimism winnowed away. What would have happened if Hutch had come home a year sooner? Would she have pursued the same course? Her grandfather's death had rattled her...that and his will.

For now, the circumstances of the will were private, but Maverick seemed to know something about it. Perhaps she should go to the police. A cybercrimes expert might be able to use her laptop and trace the blackmailer's IP address.

Still, that would involve exposing her secrets, and she was scared. How would Hutch look at Simone if he learned the truth? It wasn't about the money, not really. She wanted to be recognized as a full-fledged member of the Parker family. Her father had made no secret of his disappointment that he had no son. Her grandfather had felt the same way about having only a granddaughter. Simone, as successful and ambitious as she was, was a poor substitute for two men who should have known better.

It was a skirmish she had fought her entire life. Unfortunately, in the heat of battle sometimes a person made mistakes. Simone's was a whopper. Only time would tell if she could survive the fallout.

The following morning, she made it to work more or less on time. She had set her alarm earlier than usual in order to give herself time to be sick. It was a ghastly way to start the day. Still, she counted it a victory that she had to dash to the bathroom only twice. Maybe she would be one of the lucky ones and this nausea business would eventually subside.

Her two key employees were back from the conference, so the three of them dug into the campaign for Cecelia's business. Candace must have given them some kind of report on her health, but Simone's associates were too professional and kind to grill her. Until she started showing, she hoped to be able to conceal her pregnancy and carry on as usual.

Unfortunately, even though the nausea was no longer as severe, her energy level was nonexistent. She had many, many months to go, but already these babies were impacting her life. It must have been sheer naïveté that made her think the adjustments would happen only *after* the birth.

For ten days, she had no contact with Hutch at all. Even when she visited Dr. Fetter's office at the hospital, there was no sign of the man who had returned from Africa...the man who recently shared her bed for one incredible night. Even at her lowest point, being intimate with Hutch again had made her feel like a desirable woman.

She told herself his absence from her life was for the best, and she almost believed it.

Fortunately, she was able to roll out the last of the campaign for Luna Fine Furnishings without incident and right on time. Cecelia was ecstatic. Deacon treated the three friends to dinner to celebrate. He probably enjoyed being out on the town with a trio of attractive women, but in truth, he had eyes only for Cecelia.

Simone laughed and talked during the meal, but it was hard to keep up a celebratory front. Though she was thrilled for Cecelia, it hurt to see the way Deacon looked at his bride-to-be. Simone had practically guaranteed that she would never have that kind of relationship. What kind of man would want to take on an instant family, including babies that weren't his?

She picked at her salmon, pushing the meal around on her plate so her friends would think she was eating. Unfortunately, no matter how hard she tried, she was still losing weight rather than gaining. Many pregnant women would love to have her problem, but it wasn't good for the babies.

April came to an end. May dawned with blue skies and balmy temperatures. Simone missed Hutch terribly. Knowing he was living in Royal was somehow worse than when he had been on the other side of the world.

Work became her salvation. She managed to keep her pregnancy under wraps from most of Royal, but she decided to tell her parents, come what may. She spent an uncomfortable afternoon at their house trying to explain convincingly why she'd taken the route she did.

She suspected that both her mother *and* her father knew she was going out of her way to fulfill the conditions of her grandfather's will, but they didn't press her. Perhaps her father was willing to overlook an indiscretion or poor judgment if he finally got the boy he'd always wanted.

What if all three babies were girls? What then? In that situation, Simone would have satisfied the letter of the law, but would her father still be disappointed? That would be hard to bear.

After the first few days of the month, spring began to feel like summer. The higher temperatures made Simone's nausea worse. She lived off decaf iced tea and fresh-squeezed lemonade. On the hottest days, even the mention of food was enough to make her ill.

Though she tried her best to eat, she wasn't keeping up. She grew weak and listless, and one morning she couldn't convince herself to crawl out of bed. Naomi was at a convention on the West Coast. Cecelia and Deacon had flown off to Bermuda for a quick holiday.

Simone was alone in her misery.

Around noon she knew she had to eat something. When she sat up on the side of the bed, the room spun around her. Hutch's number was programmed into her phone. All she had to do was call him.

Did he really care? Was it the doctor in him who had made the offer, or the lover? Had Simone alienated him? She never had issued the official thank-you dinner invitation, mostly because she hadn't been well enough to cook.

Stumbling to the kitchen, she held on to the walls for support. She felt terrible. This was more than simple nausea. She had a pain in her left side, and a terrible sense of foreboding. When the cramping started low in her abdomen, she panicked.

She had forgotten to bring her phone to the kitchen. It was an agonizing trip back to the bedroom to retrieve it. With fumbling fingers, she found Hutch's name and hit the call button.

One ring. Two. *Please, God, let him pick up.*

On the fourth ring, he answered. "Simone. It's nice to hear from you." Obviously the caller ID let him know it was her. The sound of his voice was enough to calm her a fraction.

"I'm sorry to bother you, Hutch. Can you stop by after work? I'm not feeling very well."

His voice sharpened. "Can you drive yourself to the hospital?"

"No…I…" Her throat clogged with tears. "Never mind," she whispered. "Never mind…"

Hutch heard a noise on the other end of the line as if the phone had been dropped. His heart plummeted to his stomach. He shoved the stack of charts he was holding into a nearby nurse's hands and grimaced. "I have to leave. Get Dr. Henry to cover my appointments. I'll let you know when I'll be back."

"Is everything okay, Doctor?"

"I don't know," he said grimly.

He jumped in his car and headed across town. On the way, he called Janine Fetter and explained the situation. Today was her day off. Fortunately, they were old friends. She agreed to meet him at Simone's house.

Hutch arrived first by minutes only. Simone always hid her extra key in the same place, even at a new address. He tipped over the flowerpot, retrieved the key and burst through the door, leaving it ajar for Janine.

The steps from the front door to Simone's bedroom seemed to happen in slow motion. He found her in a heap on the carpet, her face ashen. Her pulse was sluggish. She was clammy and barely responsive.

"Simone!" He said her name sharply, trying to cut through the fog.

Her eyelids fluttered. "Hutch? You came?"

"Of course I did," he said, cradling her in his arms. "Why are you so damned hardheaded?"

Janine arrived right about then and assessed the situation in a glance. Hutch didn't even care. The other doctor smiled at him gently. "Put her in bed and I'll examine her. You wait in the other room."

He bristled. "But I—"

She touched his arm lightly, with sympathy in her eyes. "I don't think you can be impartial about this one. Let me see what's going on. You need to take a few minutes to pull yourself together. Are the babies yours?"

The question caught him off guard. He wanted them to be. But they weren't. "Of course not," he muttered. "You know she had IUI with a sperm donor."

Janine shrugged. "I've seen doctors falsify charts for a friend. I'm not judging."

"Well, they're not mine," he growled. "You'll see that soon enough when you deliver them." Standing awkwardly, he carried Simone to the bed. "Do we need an ambulance?"

"What do you think?" Janine's grin was wry. He was acting like a total basket case.

"Sorry," he said. "She's stable. So, no."

"Go on, Hutch. Get yourself a stiff drink. I'll yell for you in a few minutes."

He paced from the bedroom down the hall to the kitchen. There he saw that Simone had tried to fix herself a sandwich. The jar of mustard was still open, and a grilled chicken breast languished on a plate.

The situation was unacceptable. He should have known from the beginning that she was going to need a babysitter. This kind of pregnancy was tricky. Simone was too inexperienced to know what she was facing.

It seemed like hours before Janine summoned him, but according to his watch, only twenty minutes had elapsed. He found Simone awake but chastened. Janine sat on the end of the bed. "I've given our patient a stern talking-to," she said.

"It's about time somebody did," he grumbled.

"I can't stay home for weeks and months," Simone wailed.

"Actually, you can." Janine's bark was worse than her bite, but the other doctor meant business. "Think about it, Simone. You're more fortunate than most. You own your own business. You have capable employees. Not only that, but you can keep tabs on things via your laptop. Now all we need is someone to play watchdog."

Hutch folded his arms across his chest. "That would be me," he said bluntly. At this point, he didn't care what Janine thought. Simone was still too damn pale. Her inky hair emphasized her pallor.

"No way," Simone said. She still had a bit of spunk left. "You have an important job."

"So I'll take some time off."

"You just got back from Africa," she cried. "You don't *have* any time off."

"Then I'll quit my job." His priorities were crystal clear. A sense of calm fatalism swept through him. He and Simone were bound by invisible threads. Maybe she didn't want him here, and maybe he shouldn't be here. But there it was. Some things defied explanation.

Janine watched both of them with speculation in her gaze. "Do you still want me to be her doctor?"

Hutch grimaced. "Of course." Then he looked at Simone. "Right?"

She glared at him. "Why ask now? It looks like you're prepared to take charge of my whole life."

Her sarcasm didn't faze him. "Damned straight."

Janine put her bag back together and checked Simone's pulse one more time. She smoothed a hand over Simone's flushed forehead. "Listen to the man. He may be arrogant, but he knows what he's doing. I'll feel a lot better knowing you're not living here on your own."

Simone's eyebrows shot to her hairline. "He can't move in here."

"Oh, yes, I can," Hutch said.

Janine grinned and stayed quiet.

The patient simmered. "What about gossip?" she said. Her gorgeous blue eyes were damp with tears.

Her vulnerability caught something in his chest and gave it a sharp squeeze. "I don't give a damn about gossip," he said. "What we do is our own business. My job is to take care of mothers and babies. For the foreseeable future, you're at the top of my list."

Janine nodded. "Sounds good to me. You have my number, Hutch. If you need me outside office hours, don't hesitate to call."

He kissed her cheek, overwhelmed with gratitude. "Thanks," he said gruffly.

Janine motioned toward the hall. Hutch followed her, closing the door most of the way so they wouldn't be overheard. "Honestly, how is she doing?" he asked.

"I'm concerned that Simone is still losing weight, by her own admission. Even in cases of hyperemesis, we need to see her belly growing. She's as tiny as the first day I examined her. Force-feed her if you have to...little bits around the clock. But if those babies are going to have a chance, we need to strengthen their mother."

Hutch nodded. "When is her next ultrasound scheduled?"

"Not for another month. But under the circumstances, I think I'll bump it up. I want to make sure things are progressing."

"And if they're not?"

Janine shrugged. "You know the statistics. Don't alarm her more than necessary. But make her eat."

"You can count on it."

"I'll let myself out," Janine said. "Unless you want me to stay while you run home to pack a bag."

"It can wait until tomorrow. I'm sure one of her friends will come over if I call."

"I'm guessing she's been putting on a brave front."

He grimaced. "That would be Simone. Never let them see you sweat."

"Or in this case, barf."

Hutch chuckled. "Thank you for coming."

She cocked her head and stared at him. "Are you sure you know what you're doing?"

Janine had known him a long time. And she knew the history. "Not at all," he said. "But I don't really have a choice."

Nine

Simone overheard the last thing Hutch said to Dr. Fetter, and it cut her to the bone. *I don't really have a choice.* He was stuck with Simone because of some kind of moral obligation. Saint Hutch.

She bit her lip to keep from crying when he came back into the room. He still wore his white coat with Dr. Troy Hutchinson neatly embroidered on the chest. "Why are you doing this?" she asked wearily. "We can get Barb."

"Barb is overbooked as it is. Besides, I know you, Simone. You wouldn't be comfortable with a stranger in your house."

"*You're* practically a stranger," she shot back. "You've been gone for almost six years. Neither of us is the same person we used to be."

He didn't let her bait him. "That's a good thing, isn't it? Surely we've both grown up by now. I hope I have."

When Simone closed her eyes and didn't answer, he knew she was trying to shut him out. It didn't matter. Whatever the current relationship between them, he was going to protect her and her babies, God willing.

Shrugging out of his lab coat, he unbuttoned his blue dress shirt and rolled up the sleeves. The house was hot. Simone could use some fresh air. But the heat and humidity outside would only make her feel worse. He found the thermostat and made the AC click on. Soon, cool air began to blow out of the vents.

When he returned to the bedroom, Simone still had her eyes closed. He didn't know if she was resting or pouting. Grinning inwardly, he sat down on the edge of the bed and stroked her arm. "What if I fix scrambled eggs and bacon? That used to be your favorite." On the weekends in the old days, they would often spend most of their time in bed. When they were sated and content, they ended up in the kitchen eating breakfast for dinner.

Simone opened one eye. "With cinnamon toast?"

"Whatever you want, brave girl. All you have to do is ask."

Finally, he coaxed a smile from her. "That would be lovely," she whispered.

"And you'll stay in bed in the meantime?"

She nodded. "I will."

Fortunately, he found the kitchen stocked with basics. Soon, he had bacon sizzling as he worked on the toast. The eggs turned out fluffy and perfect. He hoped having the comfort food on hand would coax Simone into eating something, at least.

When he carried the tray to the bedroom, he realized that she had dozed off again. He wondered if she'd had trouble sleeping at night, or if it was her weakness making her drowsy. He set the tray on the bedside table and touched her arm. "Wake up, sleepyhead. Dinner is served." He guessed she had missed lunch entirely.

Simone struggled to sit up in bed. "That was fast."

Once she was settled, he sat down beside her. "I'm going to feed you," he said.

"I'm not a baby."

"No, but you're not a hundred percent. We'll take this slow. If we need to stop, we will."

She was visibly hesitant, but she eyed the plate long-ingly. "I want to gobble it up," she said glumly. "But that would be a disaster."

"I'm sure your stomach has shrunk. You won't be able to eat a normal meal yet. We'll get there gradually over the next few weeks. What do you want first?"

She wrinkled her nose. "Eggs, I think. I need the pro-tein."

He offered her a forkful and nodded approvingly when she opened her mouth, chewed and swallowed. "So far, so good?"

Simone nodded. "You always were a better cook than me."

"Doesn't matter. You have other talents."

Her cheeks turned pink. She shot him a look from beneath her lashes, a look that made his blood run hot. "Naughty, naughty, Dr. Hutchinson. Are you trying to raise my blood pressure?"

"Whatever it takes, honey. Whatever it takes."

The gentle flirting reassured him. Simone looked a hell of a lot better now than when he'd first arrived and found her on the floor. He shuddered inwardly at the memory. If he had any say in the matter, she would never get to that point again.

His patient managed to eat half of the eggs, one piece of bacon and an entire slice of cinnamon toast. It was prob-ably too much, but he didn't have the heart to refuse her when she was clearly starving.

She wiped her mouth with a napkin. "That was wonder-ful, Hutch. It seems to help when I don't have to be the one to fix it. Yesterday, I took one look at a raw egg and had to dash to the bathroom."

"Understandable. Let me clean up the kitchen, and then I have an idea."

The chore didn't take long, but once again, Simone was

asleep when he returned. He decided to let her rest for a little bit. He needed to deal with a few urgent work situations if he was going to stay here semipermanently.

After half an hour of answering emails and texts, he was done, for the moment. Like Simone, part of his responsibilities could be dealt with remotely. His patient list was very small so far. Most of what he had been doing in these first few weeks was consulting on cases. Since he had access to the electronic records in his department, some things could go forward unchanged.

When he entered her bedroom this time, she was awake. Her color was better, and her eyes were brighter. "More dinner?" he asked.

"No. But so far, so good with what I ate."

"Excellent. I know you're exhausted, but what if we take one short stroll around the backyard? The exercise will do you good, and it will help you sleep more deeply. I'll be right beside you."

"Okay." She climbed out of bed on her own, waving him off when he tried to take her arm. "If this is going to work, you can't treat me like an invalid. I can go to the bathroom by myself."

He didn't like it, but he had to tread carefully with Simone. Her fierce independence was going to be at odds with his need to cosset her.

When they made it outdoors, the heat of the day had abated. The air was fresh and sweet. Simone's backyard was a rainbow of color, flowers blooming everywhere.

He put an arm around her waist. "Lean on me," he said. "And tell me if you need to stop."

They didn't speak as they made a lazy circuit of the premises. Simone's legs were shaky...that was easy to tell. But she powered on. By the time they made it back to the starting point, she was leaning on him heavily, and her breathing was rapid. He scooped her up in his arms and climbed the shallow steps.

"Good girl," he said softly. "I'm proud of you. Food and exercise. You'll make it yet."

"My hero," she smirked.

His lips twitching in amusement, he managed the knob and bumped the door open with his hip. "Do you want to go ahead and take a shower now? Or do you need to rest first?"

Simone looked up at him with big eyes. "Are you offering to join me, Doctor?"

"Do you need medical assistance?"

"I'm sure I do."

The little brat was taunting him, but there wasn't a chance in hell he was going to make love to her tonight. She knew the power she had over him, and she wasn't afraid to use it.

He deposited her on the bed and inspected the bathroom. If he put the tiny vanity stool in the shower, Simone wouldn't have to stand the whole time. "Okay," he said. "Let's do this."

She raised up on one elbow. "Don't you still keep a change of clothes in the car?"

Actually, he did, but he'd forgotten. Finding Simone semiconscious had thrown him off his game. "Why do you ask?"

"Well, if you're going to help me shower, you'll get soaked. You should go get what you need before we start."

"True."

She watched him intently.

"What are you thinking, Simone?" he asked. "I don't like that look."

"You know it makes sense for you to be naked, too."

Immediately and urgently, he was hard...painfully so. He schooled his expression not to reveal his physical turmoil. "I can take off my wet clothes when we're done. Stay put. I'll be back."

Outside, he put his hands on top of the car and banged his head softly against the metal door frame. He and Simone were playing a dangerous game of chicken, and he was losing. Grabbing the gym bag that held a clean pair of jeans, a knit shirt and underwear, he told himself he could be a gentleman.

Despite her propensity for suggestive repartee, Simone was in a fragile state. Even if she *wanted* to make love to him, she was in no condition to do so. He would help her with the shower and tuck her into bed. Period.

Their first argument was over who would undress her. She stood at the bathroom counter, eyes blazing. "I can take off my own clothes, Hutch."

"If you get dizzy and fall, you'll hit something hard and smash your skull. You don't want that to happen, do you?"

"What I want is for you to treat me like an adult. Take off your own clothes, big boy." No man with an ounce of testosterone could resist such an all-out dare. He wasn't a teenager. He could control himself.

They stripped down side by side. Hutch tried not to look in the mirror. It was bad enough seeing Simone in the flesh. He didn't need to be surrounded with multiple images.

When he saw her completely naked for the first time, he cursed. The one and only time they had made love since he came home from Sudan, the room had been mostly dark. Now, in the bright light from the bathroom fixture, he took note of each feminine detail.

She crossed her arms over her breasts. "What's wrong?"

"I can see every one of your ribs, damn it. I can't believe how much weight you've lost."

"It's a new technique. I call it the triplet diet."

Even now, she was a smart-ass. "That's not funny." He couldn't decide if he wanted to spank her or kiss her.

Ignoring the urge to do either, he stepped past her to turn on the water and adjust the faucet. When he was satisfied the temperature was just right, he put the small stool in the large granite shower stall and took Simone's arm. "In you go."

She sat down with a small sigh. Closing her eyes, she leaned her head against his hip. "Thank you, Hutch," she whispered. "For everything."

Tenderness came, overwhelming him and muting his physical need for her. "You're very welcome. Close your eyes and let me take care of you."

He started with shampoo, lathering Simone's long, dark tresses and rinsing with the handheld sprayer. Afterward, he grabbed the bottle of shower gel and soaped up a washcloth. Moving it over her shoulders and back, he made himself recite multiplication tables in his head to keep from going insane.

Her breasts were full and firm. When he soaped them lazily, the rosy nipples perked up. Eventually, he had washed everything he could reach. "Do you think you can stand for a minute?" he asked gruffly.

She nodded but didn't move.

"Do you want to do the rest yourself?"

Simone looked up at him with drowsy eyes. Her pupils were dilated; only a ring of deep azure remained. Her eyelashes were spiky and wet. "You're doing fine. Don't stop now." She put her hands on his forearms and drew herself upright.

Now her nose reached the center of his chest. He wanted to lift her and slide her down onto his rigid sex. He wanted to take her up against the wall of the shower and pound into her until the gnawing ache in his gut found release.

Instead, he did the honorable thing. He knelt and washed her feet and calves and thighs. Then, standing, with Simone embracing him, he rubbed between her legs.

Her breath caught audibly. "I want you," she whispered.

Hell. He shut his eyes and gritted his teeth. "We can't, sweet girl. Not today."

Their bodies were wet and slick and primed for action. But Simone was weak as a baby kitten. She fussed half-heartedly when he shut off the water and urged her out of the shower. As he dried her with a big fluffy towel, she murmured something he didn't quite catch. Afterward, he set her on the counter and grabbed another towel for himself.

Simone's back was to the mirror, her hair a tangled mess of black silk at her shoulders. "I'll have to dry your hair," he said. "It's too wet for you to get straight into bed."

He found a large-tooth comb and a hair dryer in one of the drawers. Simone seemed to be half asleep sitting up. Though he was clumsy at best, he managed to dry her hair until it was tangle-free.

She leaned into him. "You should do this for a living," she muttered, yawning.

"Only for you, kiddo." He picked her up and carried her to the bed. "Pajamas?"

Her smile was wicked. "Not tonight."

With shaking hands, he covered her all the way to the chin. "Go to sleep, Simone. I have some work to do, but I'll be in later. I'll take the other side of the bed."

"Will you be here when I wake up?" Her eyes had darkened, and for a moment, the impertinent facade slipped and he saw loneliness.

"I'm not going anywhere," he said firmly.

He pulled on the clean boxers and pants without the shirt. The house had cooled down some, but not enough. Or maybe he was the one who was overheated.

Firing up his laptop and dealing with a backlog of email occupied him for an hour. Simone had an exercise bike in the guest room, so he did ten miles there. After that, he prowled, trying to convince himself he could lie in that bed with Simone and not go stark, raving mad.

During the course of the evening he had managed to get his erection under control for brief periods of time. Still, every moment he allowed his attention to wander, his libido took over, telling him how damn good it would feel to be intimate with Simone again.

His head was messed up, no doubt about it. First, there was the ghost of Bethany. The guilt he felt about her death might be illogical, but it lingered. Then there was Simone's unorthodox pregnancy. She was hiding something.

There were any number of men in Royal who would have been happy to provide sperm the old-fashioned way. What reason had been compelling enough to send Simone down this path?

He prayed unashamedly for her three babies. If she lost any or all of them, it would destroy him. Even more harrowing was the prospect of losing Simone. Women still died in childbirth occasionally. It was rare, but it happened. She wasn't his to lose, but he was the one in her court for the moment.

Finally, at eleven, he decided he was tired enough to go to sleep, no matter the provocation. He moved through the house checking locks and turning off the lights. By now, he knew his way around the master bedroom. He brushed his teeth with the toothbrush from last time. Leaning his hands on the counter, he gave himself a pep talk.

"Don't be stupid, Hutch. She doesn't need any added stress, and you don't need the drama. She broke up with you the last time. Now she's in an even worse place to have a relationship with you. Get over it. Move on."

It was a good speech. Maybe even a great one. Despite that, when he stood beside the bed and studied the small lump under the covers, he rubbed his chest, trying to ease the ache there.

He'd always assumed he'd have a family one day, though not like this. Even if Simone had any residual feelings for him, he would have to wonder if she needed a father for her babies more than she needed a lover. It was a sobering thought.

Thankfully, he did sleep. And on his own side of the bed.

Once, toward dawn, he roused when Simone got up to go to the bathroom. He could see the outline of her nude body. "You okay?" he asked groggily.

"Yes."

She wasn't gone long. When she climbed back in bed, he could hear her breathing. "Hutch?" she said.

"Hmm?"

"Will you hold me?"

He inhaled sharply. "I don't think I can do that."

"Why not?"

Was she deliberately being obtuse, or did the woman truly not understand how badly he wanted her? "You're naked. I'm naked. Things will happen."

She chuckled. "Is that so terrible?"

Desperately, his better nature fought the good fight. "You're not one hundred percent."

"Then make love to what's left of me, please. And this time don't let go."

Simone knew she was being unfair. What was the penalty for tempting a saint? Eternal damnation? She had already tasted the depths of hell. When Hutch left for Sudan, she'd come close to falling apart completely. Only sheer force of will had enabled her to get out of bed and get dressed every day.

Eventually, the pain dulled. Work and friends and hobbies filled the hours. After a year, she dated again. Casually. Always, she wondered what would happen when Hutch came home. And then he didn't come home.

After the first three years, she had faced the bitter truth. By sending him off to fulfill his destiny, she had destroyed her chance at happiness with him. Even now, she was under no illusions. They had sexual attraction going for them, no question. But she was pregnant with another man's babies.

Lots of couples adopted children. This was different. Even if he could forgive her for the huge mistake she had made, surely he would want to father his own son or daughter.

What if she got pregnant again and it was as bad as this time? The thought of facing another nine months of misery was too wretched to contemplate. And four children? Simone didn't even know how to mother one or two or three, much less four.

The only thing left was hot sex with no strings attached. Even that would come to an end when she got embarrassingly huge.

With tears stinging her eyes, she met him in the middle of the mattress. "I'm not a very nice person," she whispered. "I should leave you alone."

He ran a hand down her flank, raising gooseflesh everywhere he touched. "I'm a big boy," he said. "I can handle it."

Ten

She reached for him in the dark, finding his erection and wrapping her hand around it. Hutch shuddered. She stroked him firmly, remembering instinctively what he liked. In the space of a hushed breath, the years melted away and the two of them were the same young, wildly infatuated couple they had once been.

Her body wasn't cooperating. She felt weak and barely able to move. Still, she wanted Hutch desperately. With the empathy that marked everything he did, he held her close and winnowed his fingers though her hair. "You're not up to this, Simone. Admit it."

His body was warm and hard and masculine against hers. The light fuzz of hair on his broad chest tickled her breasts and reminded her that he was a man in his prime. The stark contrast of tough male to soft female sent a shiver of delight down her spine. Having him wrap his muscular arms around her in a firm hug made her feel secure and cherished. He was right. She didn't have the energy for sex. Yet everything she knew told her to bind Hutch any way she could. She didn't want to lose him again. And she didn't want only his tender care. She wanted his love.

Dear God. The truth left her breathless. She still loved Troy Hutchinson. Illogically. Inescapably. Which meant she was destined for even greater heartbreak than before. The yawning hole in her chest was terrifying. She couldn't survive a second time. Especially not with babies in the mix.

As she lay there trembling, her change in mood must have alerted Hutch that something was wrong. He eased her onto her back and reclined on one elbow. Placing his hand, palm flat, on her stomach, he sighed. "Talk to me, honey. I'm not a mind reader."

"I shouldn't have gotten pregnant." She wanted to tell him the truth. She wanted to tell him why. But she was afraid he would look at her in disgust and disappointment.

"Your timing could have been better, that's true. But there's nothing wrong with wanting to become a mother."

Except that Simone had taken something so sacred and wonderful and used it for her own ends. "Are you still in love with Bethany?" She blurted it out, her pain and confusion erasing all sense of boundaries.

Hutch went still. He removed his hand. "Bethany has nothing to do with you and me," he said, the words flat.

"You didn't answer my question, Hutch." Why was she torturing herself? "Do you still love her?"

She heard him curse beneath his breath. His reaction was so out of character it shocked her.

"I will always love Bethany," he said. "She was selfless and pure in her devotion to the hurt and needy. She gave her life doing the things she considered essential for the good of humanity. She made me a better doctor...a better man. So, yes, Simone. I love Bethany. But she's gone, and I'm still here. If that's a problem, tell me now."

Her throat was so tight she could barely breathe, much less speak. Why had she wanted so badly to know the truth? Now she would never be able to forget what he'd said.

She touched his arm. "I'm sorry. You're right. She has nothing to do with us." Moving carefully, she climbed on top of him and buried her face in the curve of his neck. He was still hard and ready.

Hutch didn't need any further invitation. He lifted her hips and joined their bodies with a firm thrust. She cried out, the small sound muffled against his shoulder. He made love to her with such tenderness she wanted to weep. He was a doctor, yes. So he had taken an oath to do no harm. But this was more than that. He was coaxing her into trusting him, one heartbeat at a time.

What he couldn't know was that she would trust him with her life…and the lives of her babies. That wasn't the issue at all. The problem was the way she had let herself get twisted in knots over her grandfather's will and her feelings of not being able to measure up to her family's expectations.

It was too late now.

Hutch was hot, his taut body damp. He held her hips in a grip that might bruise, though she didn't think he realized it. "Are you okay?" He ground out the words between clenched teeth.

She cupped his cheek with her hand, feeling the stubble on his face and chin. "I'm glad you came home, Hutch. I missed you." It wasn't an answer to his question. She wasn't okay…not at all. How could she tell him that she had been missing a part of herself for five long years?

At twenty-two, twenty-three, she hadn't understood how rare it was to find someone like Hutch. It shamed her to realize that if the situation arose now, she would beg him not to leave. In her youthful naïveté, she had assumed one of two things—either Hutch would come home after two and a half years and they would pick up where they left off, or she would eventually find someone else to love.

Neither scenario had been the case.

He rolled suddenly, taking her with him. She wrapped her legs around his waist and twined her arms around his neck. Hutch was wild now, his thrusts uncontrolled, his passion barely in check.

"Simone… Ah, hell…" He came with a groan that sounded more like pain than pleasure.

She wasn't even close. As much as she craved his touch, she was unable to summon the energy to climax. It was enough to know he wanted her.

In the aftermath, he moved them onto their sides and held her gently, stroking her hair and feathering kisses over her eyelids and cheekbones.

"I remembered this," he said quietly. "In Sudan. When things got bad. Sometimes we lost babies who should have lived. Mothers, too. It ate me up inside. When I couldn't sleep at night, I would imagine you in bed with me. It helped. It anchored me."

"But you didn't come home the first time." She heard the note of accusation in her own voice. "That sounded angry," she added quickly. "And I wasn't. I'm not." What she had been was devastated.

He sighed, his breath stirring the hair at her temple. "I was going to," he said. "I had every intention of coming back to Royal when my first tour was over. But…"

"But what?"

"You and I had ended things on a difficult note. I wasn't sure there was any reason to come home. And the need in West Darfur was overwhelming. You were so damn young when we broke up. It occurred to me that I was probably someone to experiment with…someone unsuitable you could toss in your parents' faces to prove you were a grown woman."

Simone flinched, incredibly hurt. "It wasn't that. It was never that, Hutch. I adored you."

"But not enough to beg me to stay."

"That's not fair."

"I knew you were ambitious. I knew you wanted to be

successful. You had life in the palm of your hand. It's not surprising that my life and yours didn't mesh."

"I was trying to do the right thing," she said bitterly. "For once in my life, I was being unselfish." *And look where it got me...*

He sighed. "Why don't we agree to let the past stay in the past? Neither of us handled the relationship well."

"And now?"

"What do you mean?" His question held a tinge of wariness.

"Are we handling *this* well?"

"How the hell should I know? I'm an obstetrician, not a shrink."

Simone was shocked when he rolled away from her and left the bed. "Where are you going? It's still dark out."

"I need to clear my head," he said gruffly. "Go back to sleep."

Hutch didn't wait to see if she obeyed his command. Her scent was on his skin. The sound of her voice echoed in his head. His heart pounded as adrenaline surged through his veins. He either wanted to run or to fight or to climb back into his lover's bed and stake a claim.

It was easy to pretend that Simone was the same woman he'd left behind. Easy, for now. When her pregnancy began to show, all bets were off. Every time he looked at her, he would be reminded that she had made a choice to be a single mom. It still made no sense. Simone was the quintessential career woman. Not only that, she was far too young to worry about her biological clock.

He let himself out of the house quietly and prowled the backyard. At this hour, the air was cool and sweet. Janine Fetter was no gossip, but sooner or later, word would filter around town. Simone Parker was pregnant. And Troy Hutchinson was living in her house.

Did he care? That was the million-dollar question. People would make assumptions about Simone's pregnancy. It was only natural. Undoubtedly, some folks around Royal would believe he had returned from Africa so that he and Simone could pick up where they left off.

If anybody did the math, they would know he wasn't the father of her triplets. But was anybody going to be following their situation that closely?

For one brief moment, he considered offering Simone a version of what they'd had in the past. Not his heart. That wasn't up for grabs. Something else instead. She was going to need help. He liked having regular sex with someone he cared about.

There were worse reasons to hook up.

Still, there was no rush. He was here to make sure she took care of herself. In the meantime, he could decide if they were actually compatible. Simone liked to jump in the deep end without pondering the consequences. He was a planner, a cautious man who preferred to calculate the risks.

Maybe it would work. Maybe it wouldn't. He had time to decide.

After that first night, their time together fell into a routine of sorts. The mornings were hardest for Simone. He was a decent cook, so he tempted her with light fare, anything he thought she would enjoy and be able to keep down.

Gradually, her color improved and she became stronger—strong enough to want to go back to work.

They argued ten times a day, it seemed. Him pointing out that she had a long way to go in this pregnancy, Simone insisting he was a worrywart. In the end, they compromised.

He'd been sleeping under her roof for seven nights when Simone revealed the real reason she was desperate to get back to work. While Hutch made grilled cheese sandwiches and tomato soup for both of them, Simone sat at the kitchen counter with her laptop and fretted.

"I'm in charge of this upcoming charity event," she said, waving her hands. "It was my idea. I can't let the preparations slide anymore or we'll never be ready."

He listened with half an ear, wondering if the rough weather that buffeted the windows would turn into a tornado watch. He'd been in Sudan when a killer storm leveled big chunks of Royal a few years ago. People were still antsy whenever the skies turned dark.

Simone tossed a paper wad at him. "Pay attention, Hutch. I'm trying to explain."

He shrugged with an unrepentant grin. Now that Simone was feeling slightly better, she talked his ear off. "I'm sorry," he said. "Go ahead. I'm listening. What's it called again?"

"Nothing yet," she grumbled. "That's part of the problem. The invitations need to go out by Monday, and I have everything ready but the name."

Royal's hardworking charity organization, Homes and Hearts, was slated to be the beneficiary of Simone's latest PR idea. When she fell ill recently, she'd been in the midst of planning a grand masquerade ball to raise money to build more houses for the homeless.

Instead of hosting at the Cattleman's Club, Simone and Cecelia had cooked up the idea of christening the grand ballroom at Deacon Chase's new five-star resort, The Bellamy. He and Shane Delgado had been inspired by the Biltmore House in Asheville, North Carolina, though their architectural baby here in Royal was hipper and more modern. Sitting amid fifty-plus acres of lush gardens, The Bellamy was lavish and expensive.

Simone had declared it the perfect location.

"How about Masks for Mortar?" he said. "Has a ring to it, don't you think?"

Simone squealed and jumped off the stool, rounding the

island to hug him enthusiastically. "That's perfect, Hutch. Let me insert that line in the file, and I'll get it off to the printer."

"Don't you need somebody else's approval? I don't want to be responsible if the idea bombs." He was only half kidding.

"It's exactly right," she insisted.

While she futzed with her email, he shoved a plate under her nose. "Here's your lunch, Simone."

She nodded absently. "Put it right there. I'll try a few bites."

Leaning over the counter, he closed her laptop. "Eat now. Doctor's orders."

He wasn't going to budge on this one. It pleased him to see her so happy, but she could easily get into trouble again if she didn't make sure to nibble when her stomach was actually cooperating.

She made a face at him. "Dictator."

"Shrew." He grinned. Gradually, they were becoming less cautious with each other. It was a good sign, but he was pretty sure the détente was only temporary.

For one thing, Simone never talked about the babies. She let Hutch check her blood pressure twice a day, and she ate as much as she was able to. Other than that, there was no outward indication that anything was going on beneath the surface.

One afternoon a week or so later, she seemed moodier than usual.

He tugged the end of her ponytail. "What's bugging you?"

"I'm almost three months along. When will I feel them move?"

Suddenly, he realized she was still fretting about the pregnancy. "Well…" He hesitated, trying to speak the truth without offering false promises. "Every day that passes brings you one day closer to a successful outcome. In a normal pregnancy, you'd likely start to notice the baby moving at five months."

"But with triplets?"

"Could be sooner. Could be later."

"And for that sound medical judgment you went to med school…"

Her snarkiness amused him. "Things are going well," he said gently.

Simone bit her bottom lip. "Dr. Fetter wants me to come in for the ultrasound tomorrow."

"I know."

"What if…"

He put his hand over her mouth and kissed her nose. "The ultrasound will make you feel better."

"Or maybe not," she mumbled against his fingers.

"Are we having the glass half-empty, half-full conversation?"

Her blue eyes glistened with tears. Like bluebonnets in the rain. He knew he was in trouble when he realized he was waxing poetic, even in his head.

Simone wriggled until he released her. She wrapped her arms around her waist. "You don't understand. As long as I'm standing here with you in this kitchen, those three babies are alive and developing normally. I don't want to go to the hospital and find out differently."

He wondered if any of the other people in her life knew that beneath Simone's facade of bravado and confidence lurked a sensitive, vulnerable woman. "I'll go with you," he said. "It will be fine. And if it's not, you can lean on me."

"I have to do this alone," she insisted, her chin set in stubborn mode.

"No, you don't. That's ridiculous."

"I'm serious, Hutch. It's one thing for you to stay here and make sure I eat. It's a whole other ball game for you to parade up to that hospital with me when everybody in the building knows who you are. I can't deal with that, too. You can drive me there if you insist, but I want you to drop me off at the door and leave."

His temper started to boil. "You're being absurd."

"Don't patronize me," she snapped. The tears spilled over now. "Leave me alone," she cried. "I'm going to my room."

He told himself pregnant women were at the mercy of roller-coaster hormones. Simone needed her space.

It made sense. The artificial situation in which they found themselves was beginning to fray at the seams. After the first night of his stay, he hadn't made love to her at all. He'd wanted to, God knew, but he had felt the need to back up and reassess. He'd been sleeping in the guest room ever since. Alone.

If Simone really cared about him as more than a doctor and a friend, she would make the first move. But she hadn't.

A crack of thunder right over the house made him jump. He was horny and frustrated and angry at himself for getting involved with a woman who had far too many issues at play.

The fact that she didn't want him in the room when she had the ultrasound done was a red flag. He wanted to protect her and keep her from any kind of pain, physical or mental.

What Simone wanted was a mystery.

Her sandwich and soup sat uneaten on the counter. He zapped the plate in the microwave and carried it down the hall as a peace offering.

He found the bedroom door ajar. Simone sat in the middle of the carpet with a strange look on her face. He set the tray on the dresser and squatted beside her. "Is this some new yoga pose I don't know about?" he asked lightly.

She raised the hem of her shirt, took his hand and placed it flat on her belly. "I have a baby bump, Hutch. I really do!"

Eleven

She actually did. Only someone who had studied her body as much as he had would have been able to tell, but it was legit. He stroked her stomach. "You do, indeed. A real baby bump. Congratulations."

Simone rested her head against his knee. "I know it sounds stupid, but I was afraid nothing was there."

"And you were deathly ill because…" He raised an eyebrow.

"I said it didn't make sense."

Being so close to her after a week of strained celibacy filled his body with a fine tension. He rose to his feet. "You still haven't eaten lunch. I hate to beat a dead horse, but I'm not willing to see you back in the shape you were in before." He reached out a hand to help her to her feet.

"I'll eat, I swear. But Hutch…" She looked up at him, her eyes sparkling.

"What?"

"I'm feeling lots better."

The look on her face spelled trouble for him. Especially because he hadn't decided what he wanted from her or what Simone needed from him. "I'm glad," he said, pretending to misunderstand her artless invitation.

"Are you going to make me beg?" She wrapped her

arms around his waist and rested her cheek right over his heart—or what was left of it.

He'd spent hours wondering why this woman still had the power to move him. It was more than the past they shared, though that was part of it. It was also more than the fact that he felt protective of her as a mother-to-be in the midst of a high-risk pregnancy.

Even now, he was afraid to name the emotion that made him hold her close. He wouldn't cheapen it by calling it lust. But he couldn't say it was love. He'd loved two women in his life, and both relationships had ended badly. Maybe he was using Simone. Maybe she was using him. In the end, what did it matter? They were emotionally and physically entangled, for better or for worse.

"I assume you're talking about sex?"

She leaned back and scowled at him. "Don't be so stuffy, Doctor."

"You still haven't eaten your lunch." Though he tried to stave off the inevitable, he was hard and ready. And he was pretty sure Simone knew it.

"Bring me the damned sandwich," she said.

"And the soup."

"Oh. My. Gosh. You're going to drive me insane."

He scooped her up in his arms and dumped her on the bed. "I'd say that's a two-way street." He liked carrying her. Some people thought doctors had a God complex. Hutch didn't. At least, he didn't think so. However, he *would* cop to being an inveterate caretaker. It was in his blood.

When he grabbed the food and turned back around, he stumbled. Simone had stripped off her top and bra and was starting in on the rest of her clothes. "You said you would eat," he pointed out. It was hard to speak because his throat was so dry.

She crooked a finger. "I didn't say when."

Even a highly trained medical professional had his limits. He abandoned the meal tray so quickly it was a wonder he didn't spill tomato soup all over Simone's beautiful carpet. "Damn it, woman. Move over."

Simone was giddy. For the first time in days she felt almost like herself. Even more important, she saw tangible proof of her pregnancy. The change in her belly was infinitesimal, but it was real. Without Hutch's careful attention, she might have become so ill that she miscarried. Instead, he had watched over her day and night, despite the fact that she was pregnant under the worst of circumstances.

Her heart overflowed. Everything that had drawn her to him six years ago was still there: his patience, his sense of humor, his deep commitment to his calling. In some ways, *she* was the one who was different. And in the midst of that fresh perspective, she found herself falling more deeply in love with him than ever before.

In the years Hutch had been gone, Simone had grown and matured. Even in her misguided attempt to become a mother, she had found new meaning in her life. The babies she carried were a sacred responsibility.

If she could have her way, she would kneel beside the bed and propose to Hutch. *Marry me. Make a family with me.* But that would be so unfair. So she did the next best thing. She gave herself to him and demanded nothing in return.

She hadn't truly understood what it cost him to stay out of her bed the past few days. Not until now. He was flushed and desperate, his body pinning hers to the bed as his teeth raked the curve of her neck. His intensity didn't frighten her. She understood it in the marrow of her bones.

No force on earth could have kept them apart.

He handled her roughly, with little foreplay. They kissed wildly. She wrestled with him and taunted him, for nothing more than the pleasure of being subdued. He manacled her wrists in one big hand and tried to mount her. She eluded him but didn't get far. They rolled from one side of the mattress to the other, kicking the sheets aside in their frenzy. Hutch muttered her name along with a few choice expletives.

Laughing out loud, she bit his earlobe. "I love you this way," she whispered. "Take what you want. Make me submit. Do it, Hutch."

When he moved between her thighs and thrust all the way in with one deep push, she cried out. "Don't stop. Don't stop."

He took her at her word. She had waved a red flag in front of the bull, and now he was crazed. He rode her hard. Never had she seen him so greedy, so dangerously male. Maybe she had wanted to make him snap. Maybe she reveled in his physical need for her.

Even so, his total absorption was shocking. And thrilling.

Her climax hit hard. Hutch groaned, his face buried in her hair. She clenched him with her inner muscles, wresting from each of them the last ripples of pleasurable sensation. Then he shuddered, his body went rigid and he slumped on top of her.

Time ceased to have meaning. The Grecian shades at her bedroom windows were open, letting the harsh midday sun flood the room. Hutch might have been asleep. She wasn't sure. She didn't know whether to let out an exultant sigh or to burst into tears.

When he didn't move, she surmised that he really was out cold. It was no wonder. He'd spent the last week wandering the halls at night, making sure she was okay. The man had to be exhausted.

Silently, she eased out from under him and went to the bathroom to clean up. Afterward, she put her clothes back on and examined the cold sandwich and soup. The simple meal was a truce flag of sorts. Wrinkling her nose, she made herself eat three-fourths of it.

Perhaps it would have made more sense to go back to the kitchen and heat it up, but she wanted to be around when Hutch roused. She wasn't about to climb back into bed to eat. Though there were two chairs in the bedroom, she didn't like the idea of balancing the tray on her lap. In the end, she sat on the floor, legs crossed, and leaned back against the dresser.

He opened his eyes without drama. One minute he was dead to the world—the next he was completely alert.

"Did you eat?" he asked.

She shook her head at his single-mindedness and held out her hand, indicating what little was left of the meal. "As promised."

Hutch nodded. "Good." Without fanfare, he climbed out of bed, picked up his clothes and disappeared into the bathroom.

She was rapidly discovering that sex in the daytime was far different than sex at night. There was literally nowhere to hide. Not that Hutch had any apparent qualms about his nudity. Fortunately, she was completely clothed.

The urge to escape was humiliating, but she gave in to it, anyway. It was *her* house, her bedroom. Why did she feel the need to disappear?

In the kitchen, she rinsed her lunch dishes and put them in the dishwasher. Hutch still hadn't made an appearance. Chewing her lip, she sat down in front of her laptop. Remembering how he had shut it without her permission should have made her angry. Instead, it made her sad.

Deep in her heart she wanted Hutch to be her date at the masquerade ball. Assuming, of course, she was well enough to attend when the time came. Unfortunately, she sensed that the two of them were fast approaching a showdown. They couldn't go on as they were.

After giving the mock-up of the invitation one last edit, she hit Send. The card stock and envelopes had been selected days ago. The printer already had a list of the recipients and would take care of the mailing. After that, it was only a matter of how many invitees would RSVP with a yes.

Cecelia and Naomi were supposed to drop by tomorrow afternoon to finalize decorating plans, not only for the tables, but for the ballroom as a whole. Deacon had given them carte blanche to spend whatever necessary to make this a night Royal would never forget.

With that one pressing chore completed, Simone pulled up the Neiman Marcus website. She visited the flagship store in Dallas a couple of times a year, but hadn't been recently. Fortunately, even though she had been too sick to travel, her personal shopper several hundred miles away had dropped images of four exclusive ball gowns into Simone's shopping cart.

She clicked on them one at a time. Buying this kind of dress while pregnant might ordinarily have been a risky roll of the dice. But she had lost so much weight, she knew she would still be able to get into her regular size.

With the prospect of a late-stage pregnancy in her future, it seemed only natural to want to look her best on the special night that was rapidly approaching. Two of the dresses were black, another white and the last one was a vibrant red. Although the guests would be asked to wear masks, the evening was formal. No Tin Man and Dorothy or Darth Vader costumes for this crowd.

Royal's elite would be out in full force wearing tuxedos and couture fashion. Both of the black dresses on her computer screen were beautiful and undeniably suitable for the occasion. But she didn't feel a strong connection to either one. The white dress was sexy, but a little too bridal for an unwed mother-to-be.

That left only the red. With Simone's jet-black hair, the

vivid color would be dramatic in the extreme, and the style of the dress was perfect. The halter neckline would leave her shoulders bare. The back would plunge to the base of her spine. Though there were no adornments at all, the fabric was a slubbed-silk blend that would hopefully move and sway as she walked.

Only by trying them on could she decide for sure. She selected the red dress and added one of the black ones in case her first choice didn't work. With overnight express shipping, she would still have plenty of time to shop for other options if neither of these fit well.

She was reaching for her credit card in her purse when Hutch startled her.

"Retail therapy?" he asked casually, dropping a kiss on top of her head.

"How do you do that?" she said.

"Do what?"

"Walk like a ghost."

He shrugged. "Lots of night rounds. We learned not to wake the patients unless absolutely necessary."

"Ah."

He sat at the opposite side of the counter and stared at her. "We need to talk."

She nodded glumly. "I know."

"I would like to go with you to the ultrasound tomorrow."

That wasn't what Simone had expected him to say. She shook her head. "I've already explained why that's not a good idea."

"And I've already told you I want to be there."

"Please don't make this difficult."

His gaze narrowed. "You're the one who's throwing up barriers. Are you saying it's okay for us to sleep together but not to be seen in public?"

"Not at the hospital," she muttered. She was still holding

out hope that Hutch would be her date for the masquerade ball, although to be fair, they would all be wearing masks, so even then no one had to know Hutch and Simone were a couple. Sort of... Who was she kidding? The man had a serious presence and would be recognized—mask or no mask.

Usually in the wake of sexual satisfaction, men were relaxed and mellow. Hutch was livid. His jaw was carved from stone, and his brown eyes burned. "Okay then." He reached for his own laptop, unplugged it and tucked it into the sleek leather briefcase monogrammed with his initials.

Simone frowned. "What are you doing?"

"I'm leaving." He never even looked at her as he calmly gathered his pens and billfold and hospital ID.

Panic made her stomach cramp. "Why?"

"Don't be naive, Simone."

"Tell me," she said, distraught. "The ultrasound is no big deal."

"I'm a doctor," he said, the words colder than any she had ever heard him utter. "Of course it's a big deal. But this is about more than ultrasounds, isn't it? You're making sure that no one but Janine knows we have any kind of connection. I was prepared to be a friend to you and these babies, but you don't need any more friends, do you, Simone?"

She grabbed his arm as he started to walk out of the room. "I don't want you to go," she said. Her heart cracked along fault lines years in the making.

He shrugged her off. "You're eating a suitable amount now. The nausea has subsided to manageable levels. There is absolutely no reason for me to remain. Or am I wrong?"

His gaze was impassive. Yet beneath his icy calm, she understood that he was daring her to do something. Anything.

The trouble was, she had no clue how he felt about her. Could she bear to have a relationship with him knowing the sainted Bethany would always be a ghost in their bed? And even if she could make peace with being second best, would Hutch ever want to be more than her friend? Was he interested in any kind of permanent role as stepparent?

Why would he be? He had the world at his feet.

During a split second when time stood still, mocking her indecision, she imagined and discarded half a dozen scenarios for her future. In none of them was there any real possibility that Hutch would be included.

So she tamped down her terror and her desperation and lifted her chin. "No," she said quietly. "No reason at all."

She had honestly thought she couldn't sink any lower than the miserable days of severe nausea and collapse. But it turned out she was wrong. Watching a stern-faced Troy Hutchinson walk out of her house without a backward glance sent a knife through her chest.

The pain was so intense, she thought she might pass out. She clung to the counter, her breathing shallow and rapid, and tried to stop shaking. Life was so unfair. Why had Troy come back to her at such an inauspicious moment? Why did she still love him when he had left his heart in Africa?

Why had she ever thought her grandfather's will was such a big deal?

In the space of a few weeks, all of her priorities had changed. It was a sobering realization to understand that every single one of her heartaches and heartbreaks was of her own creation.

She wasn't able to sleep in her bed that night. Instead, she went to the guest room and curled up in a ball where Troy had lain. The sheets still smelled like him. She cried for an hour and then made herself stop. It was no longer possible to be the same self-centered, ego-driven woman she had once been.

By this time next year, she would have three infants living under her roof. Hutch or no Hutch, that was her reality. It would have been easy to blame the babies for her situation. Without them, perhaps she and Hutch might have found their way back together for good.

Even reeling from the afternoon's trauma, she had to face the truth. Hutch was gone. The babies were here to stay. And she was their mama. Bless their hearts. Already, she knew they deserved better.

Somehow, she would pick herself up and go on. Somehow...but not tonight. Tonight, she would grieve, and if she was lucky, perhaps she wouldn't dream about the good doctor at all.

Twelve

When morning came, she tried to avoid looking in the mirror. She knew she was haggard and pale. At least she was strong enough to drive. Her stomach was a little queasy, but that had more to do with heartbreak and a sleepless night than her pregnancy.

She showered and styled her hair on autopilot. Choosing something to wear, once a pivotal point in her daily routine as a young twentysomething, now barely merited a moment's thought. The only reason she cared at all was that she didn't want anyone to feel sorry for her.

With that in mind, she chose a sunshine-yellow dress, sleeveless with white trim, and paired it with cork-heeled sandals. Normally, she used foundation only for special occasions. She'd been blessed with good skin.

Today, though, she needed help covering up the deep shadows beneath her dull eyes. Mascara and brightly colored lip gloss gave her a semblance of health, but if anyone looked closely enough, they wouldn't be fooled.

Frankly, she was terrified. She knew the ultrasound itself was painless, but what the test would reveal was a mystery. If she had asked either Naomi or Cecelia, both would have volunteered to come with her. Was it pride or a need to lick her wounds that kept her from contacting her two best friends?

She would see them later today. If the news she received at the hospital was bad, she wouldn't be able to hide her grief. Maybe that was for the best. They were the only people who would be able to help, the only ones who knew her inside and out.

Much like before, the ultrasound tech was professional but frustratingly uncommunicative when it came to explaining the images on the screen. Simone lay on the table with her eyes closed and prayed.

At last it was over. She dressed again in her cheerful outfit and managed a smile when the tech escorted her to an exam room. Then came the usual pokes and prods. Her blood pressure was a tad low. The scale showed she had lost ten pounds since her last visit. The nurse's expression of consternation was quickly masked, but Simone knew she should be gaining.

The last hurdle was waiting for Dr. Fetter. There was no need for a pelvic exam today. The only reason Simone had come to the hospital was to discuss the ultrasound. So she clasped her hands in her lap and waited.

Twenty-seven-and-a-half minutes. Could have been worse. Janine Fetter burst through the door with a quick apology. "I've got two babies in progress, one about to deliver three weeks early. But we have a few hours yet. Let's take a look at these pictures so you can be on your way."

The other woman opened Simone's record on the laptop. The tech had already uploaded the images. The doctor studied them for interminable minutes, flipping from screen to screen, and finally looked up with a smile. "Congratulations, Simone. As far as I can tell, you have three extremely healthy fetuses. Barring any unforeseen circumstances, I think we're past the immediate danger point."

"But what about all the weight I've lost?" Simone asked, afraid to give in to relief too fast.

Dr. Fetter stood up and tucked her reading glasses in the pocket of her lab coat. "That's the wonderful thing about babies. They've been taking all the nutrition they need. You're the one who's fragile right now, not them. Since your nausea is easing to a great degree, I'm confident we'll see your weight bounce back in the coming weeks."

"Oh…"

The doctor cocked her head. "Simone?"

"Yes, ma'am?"

"You can drop the *ma'am*. I'm not that old."

"Sorry."

"My job is to take care of you and your babies, not to pry into your personal business. But…" She trailed off with a wince.

"But what? Go ahead. Say what you're thinking."

"I don't think you understand what you're facing."

The doctor's lack of faith hurt. "I'm doing my best," Simone said stiffly.

"It's not that. I'm talking about *after* the pregnancy. Having triplets is not a solo event. It requires coordinated teamwork. For quite some time."

"Naomi and Cecelia have promised to help me."

"That's lovely, and I'm sure they mean well, but neither of them knows babies, do they?"

"No. Isn't it a kind of learn-as-you-go thing?"

"Yes and no. Giving birth to triplets means having your life scheduled beyond belief. It means *at least* three adults holding, feeding and diapering three babies around the clock until they begin sleeping through the night. Are your parents physically capable of helping you?"

Simone shook her head. "Physically, maybe, but not emotionally. They won't be the warm, fuzzy kind of grandparents."

"Pardon me for asking, but what about Dr. Hutchinson?"

Simone froze inside. "What about him?"

The doctor clearly tried to choose her words with care. "If there is something between you—if he is willing to help—I think it would be in your best interests to let him."

"And that doesn't strike you as a poor bargain for Hutch?"

"Troy Hutchinson is a grown man. I'm sure he can make those decisions for himself."

Simone left the hospital in a daze. She was thrilled her pregnancy was not in danger. Even so, the confirmation that she would be giving birth to three babies was shockingly real.

She returned home just as Naomi and Cecelia pulled into her circular driveway. Hugging them both, she blinked away stupid tears. "Thanks for coming. I really want to finish all the details for the masquerade ball. The nausea is better for the moment, but it might come back again. I want all my ducks in a row before that happens."

"*If* it happens," Naomi insisted as she gathered up a stack of file folders and followed the other two up the steps.

Cecelia nodded. "Think positive."

Simone didn't shoot back with a sarcastic retort. Naomi was entitled to her optimism. After all, she was the only one not slated to be a parent in the near future. Cecelia, on the other hand, should know better. Even though she seemed to be sailing through her own pregnancy, surely she didn't think the rigors of childbirth and motherhood could be withstood using perky catchphrases.

Suddenly, the truth dawned on Simone. Cecelia wouldn't be any help at all with the triplets. She and Deacon would have their own bundle of joy. How had Simone ignored that glaring reality? Maybe because Cecelia seemed so normal.

Not to mention the fact that the three friends had barely seen each other in the past few weeks.

As the other two women spread all their work on the dining room table, Simone grabbed a handful of plain crackers. "You want anything?" she asked.

Naomi shook her head. "I'm good."

Cecelia declined, as well. "Let's get started," she said. "We have a lot to do."

Planning an event of this magnitude was fun but challenging. Cecelia had struggled at length with color-coded spreadsheets to work out the placement of tables in the large room. The final information would be transferred onto diagrams so the volunteers and hotel staff would have something to work from during decorating and setting the tables.

Naomi, a gifted amateur artist, had sketched out three different themes and color palettes for the event as a whole. "I like the silver and navy," she said. "But do we need an accent color?"

Simone and Cecelia studied the other two contenders. Cecelia pointed at the brightest of the lot. "These colors are great, but they remind me more of a beachy summer event."

"I agree," Simone said. "And I think the burgundy and gray is *too* dark."

Naomi nodded. "So we're going with the silver and navy?"

Cecelia nodded. "I do like it the best. We could always add some pops of crimson."

"Perfect," Naomi said.

Simone jotted notes in her phone. Pregnancy brain must be a real condition, because she was already having trouble remembering things. She hoped one of the dresses she had ordered would fit. With the color scheme they had selected, the red would work nicely.

After an hour, most of the urgent decisions had been made. Naomi yawned, still in the midst of jet lag. Cecelia excused herself to call Deacon about something. Simone nibbled the end of her fingernail.

"Naomi," she said quietly.

"Hmm…" Her friend blinked and sat up straight. "Sorry. I should have flown home yesterday. Early-morning flights are a killer."

"Do you still think me getting pregnant is a terrible idea?"

Naomi lifted an eyebrow. "Does it matter? That horse is out of the barn, if you'll pardon the expression."

"Well, duh. But yes, it does matter."

"Why?"

Simone jumped to her feet and took a glass out of the cabinet, keeping her back to Naomi so the other woman couldn't see her face. "I know you won't lie to me."

"Damn." Naomi sighed. "Nothing like being boxed into a corner. Look at me when I say this."

"That bad, is it?" Simone managed a smile.

Naomi drummed her fingers on the countertop. "I don't understand why you did it. I don't know how in the world you're going to manage. I'm worried about the risks of childbirth and a complicated pregnancy. I'm feeling like an outsider while you and Cecelia are in some special club I can't understand. I'm confused about why Troy Hutchinson is hanging around. I know I want to help you, but my on-camera schedule is not very flexible right now. The whole situation seems like a recipe for disaster."

"Wow…" A tear rolled down Simone's cheek.

"Let me finish." Naomi stood up and wrapped her arms around Simone. "I know you, Simone. I know your generous heart and your loyalty. I've seen you make big mistakes, but I've always noted how hard you work to overcome them. If you want babies, then by damn, I'm going to play the auntie role to the hilt. And if anybody in Royal has the guts to criticize you, they'll have to answer to me."

Simone sniffed. "I think I got snot on your shirt."

"No worries."

"It's a designer piece, isn't it?"

Naomi gave her one last hug and released her. "Gucci. But my dry cleaner is a miracle worker."

Cecelia returned right about then, all starry-eyed from her conversation with her fiancé. She stared at the two in the kitchen. "What did I miss?"

"Not a thing," Naomi said. "Simone was being stupid, but I straightened her out."

Cecelia sniffed. "You shouldn't be unkind to a pregnant woman. We need to be cossetted."

Simone shook her head ruefully. Cecelia—blonde, tall and gorgeous on any given day—was absolutely radiant right now. "I'm fine. Believe me."

Naomi changed the subject. "Have either of you heard any more about the mysterious Maverick?"

Simone felt her face freeze. She knew she should disclose the contents of her own threatening email, but she was afraid. "The rumor in town is that he or she has gone underground. Things have been suspiciously quiet."

Cecelia huffed. "Good riddance, I say. After the pain he caused me and some of the other members of the TCC, he should be prepared for backlash."

After that, the conversation drifted back to the upcoming masquerade ball. Simone ordered pizza for the three of them. When it arrived, they all sat in the backyard to enjoy the evening.

By eight o'clock Simone was drooping. "I hate to run you off, but I have an old-lady bedtime right now." The fatigue came in waves, threatening to squash her beneath its weight.

They walked back through the house and out onto the front porch. After exchanging hugs, Naomi slid behind the wheel of her car. She had picked up Cecelia on the way. "Call us if you need anything."

Cecelia nodded. "I don't like you being here alone. What happened to the yummy Dr. Hutchinson?"

"He has a job, you know." Simone managed a cheery smile. "I'm doing lots better. Don't worry about me."

As the car drove away, she bit her lip, hard enough to remind herself that she was a proud, strong, independent woman. She didn't need Naomi or Cecelia or even Hutch to hold her hand for the next six months.

After turning off the lights and locking up the house, she took a shower and curled up in her bed with the TV remote. She was too restless to read.

Hutch was gone. She might as well get used to it.

The trouble was, everywhere she looked, she saw him. Laughing at her in the kitchen…caring for her in the bedroom when she was too sick to stand…holding her up as he coaxed her through laps around the backyard.

The man was a healer. Looking after the needy was what made him tick. She couldn't and shouldn't read too much into the fact that he had made himself available as her round-the-clock personal physician.

Really personal. She moved restlessly in the bed. It was humiliating to realize that despite his disdain and their argument and his icy exit, she still wanted him.

Glancing at the clock, she saw that it was only nine forty-five. Earlier, she'd been exhausted. Now, with yearning and arousal pulsing through her veins, she had no desire to sleep. At all. With a mutter of ridicule for her own foolishness, she climbed out of bed. After putting on old jeans and a soft cotton sweater in blue and gray stripes, she shoved her feet into espadrilles and tossed her hair up in a ponytail.

She didn't have a clue about the location of Hutch's temporary apartment. But she did know which house he had bought. It was the only one for sale in her neighborhood. Suddenly, her curiosity overcame her good sense.

The pizza she had eaten earlier rolled suspiciously in her stomach, but she ignored it. She was on an investigative mission. Soon, Hutch was going to be living very close to her. What if he brought beautiful women home with him? What if Simone saw them arriving and departing in a steady stream? How was she going to handle that?

The For Sale sign was still up in the front yard, but the Realtor had tacked a Sold banner diagonally across the original notice. Simone parked in the driveway and got out. The landscaping looked scruffy. Nothing a master gardener couldn't take care of in a week or two.

Unlike Simone's more modern home, this was one of the last original structures on the street. It probably dated back to the earliest days of Royal. She remembered that the previous owner, or maybe the one before him, had gutted the inside and created a more open floor plan.

Of course, the front door was locked. Someone had left a single light burning somewhere down the hall. She had to be content with peering through a window. The hardwood floors gleamed. In the front foyer, a set of stairs led upward to the second floor. Did Hutch have plans to settle down and fill his new home with children and a wife?

A wide porch ran all the way around the main floor of the house. It would be perfect for swings and flowerpots and maybe even a hammock on the side facing away from the street. She sat on the back steps and propped her hands behind her. The night breeze picked up, raising gooseflesh on her arms beneath the light sweater.

Hutch had clearly come home to Royal planning to stay. He'd been awarded a prestigious job, and he had family nearby. Everything he could possibly want, Royal had to offer.

It would be up to Simone to learn how to be friendly

without betraying her secret. Hutch could never know she still loved him.

Moodily, she kicked at a cricket that hopped around her shoe. "Go away," she said. "I don't like pests."

"I hope that doesn't mean me."

The deep voice startled her. She jumped to her feet, and as she did so, her toe caught the edge of the top step. She pitched forward in slow motion, striking her knee hard on the wooden floor of the porch.

Hutch reached for her, but she went all the way down in an ungainly heap. Pain shot from her shin to her toe.

"Did you hit your head?" he asked urgently, squatting beside her as she struggled to sit up.

"No."

"Are you sure?"

She gaped at him. "Seriously? You don't even think I'm capable of assessing my own injuries?"

"Do you have a medical degree?" he asked mildly.

Refusing to admit that her leg hurt like hell, she shook her head. "No, Doctor, I don't. I can tell you with confidence, though, I'm fine."

He helped her to her feet. "What are you doing at my house?"

That was a tricky question. He didn't sound mad, but he didn't come across as friendly, either.

"I couldn't sleep."

"So you thought breaking and entering was the way to go?"

Thirteen

Hutch was stunned at how glad he was to see her. The last twenty-four hours had been rough. He'd been forced to rethink his whole life's plan. And all because of an impetuous, contrary, completely frustrating woman who was pregnant with another man's babies.

Simone's grin was sheepish. "I was curious about your house."

"Would you like a tour?"

"Of course."

He unlocked the front door, feeling the same rush of satisfaction that had overwhelmed him when he signed his name on the sheaf of closing papers. This old house welcomed him. Though he wasn't a whimsical man, he had a healthy respect for the past. He liked feeling a part of something bigger than he was.

He led Simone from room to room, standing back and observing as she got to know his home.

In the dining room, she ran her hand along the chair rail. "It's beautiful, Hutch. The whole place. I can imagine Christmas dinners in this room."

The dining room was larger than most. It included a working fireplace that would be expensive to insure and maintain, but Hutch looked forward to using it the following winter. "I have some painting to do. And a few small repairs. Hopefully, I'll be able to move in a couple of weeks from now."

She stood at the window, looking out into the dark with her back to him. "Why such a big place, Hutch?"

The silence lasted for half a dozen beats. "The usual reasons. I want to have a family someday…a boring, normal life."

She glanced at him over her shoulder. "You'll never be boring, trust me. Arrogant, maybe. Bossy, infuriating and egotistical. But not boring."

"Careful, Simone. Too many compliments and I'll begin to think you might actually like me."

She whirled around. "Those *weren't* compliments, Dr. Hutchinson."

He chuckled. "Come on. I'll show you the kitchen." Actually, it was the kitchen that had sold him on the house. All the modern conveniences were included, but the hardwood floor remained, as well as the antique oak cabinets. During past renovations, granite countertops had been chosen to complement the color of the wood. Cream appliances, clearly special ordered, finished the cozy look.

Simone put her hands to her cheeks. "Oh, Hutch. This is gorgeous."

Her reaction pleased him more than it should. "I'm glad you like it. My parents raised me to appreciate the old with the new. I made an offer on this place the first time I saw it. I knew it was the one for me."

Without overthinking it, he put his hands on Simone's waist and lifted her to sit on the countertop. "I owe you an apology," he said.

"For what?" Her gaze was wary.

"For thinking it was my right to go with you to the ultrasound. You're a grown woman. Those babies you carry are your responsibility. I was out of line." He had realized his mistake after storming out of Simone's house. As much as he hated to admit it, she had been right to go alone.

"It went well," Simone said, her soft smile radiant. "Dr. Fetter says I have three viable fetuses. Three babies, Hutch. Can you imagine? Not one, but three. I don't know whether to be terrified or ecstatic."

"A little of both would be in order." He kissed her forehead. "I have a question to ask you."

Her eyes widened. "What is it?"

"Would you allow me the honor of escorting you to the masquerade ball?" He'd been thinking about it on and off. He realized there was no other man he'd want to see by her side. Even the thought of it left a bad taste in his mouth. In his gut, he knew he was cruising for a fall, yet he was helpless to stop himself.

Knowing the right thing and doing it were two entirely different realities.

Simone nodded slowly. "I like that idea. In fact, I was going to ask *you*, but you beat me to it." She hooked two fingers in the open neckline of his collar and pulled. "Let's seal the deal."

One thing he'd always loved about Simone was her confidence when it came to sex. She had a healthy self-image, and she didn't play coy games. "I could be persuaded," he muttered. Already, his body responded to her invitation. He was pretty sure all she had in mind was a kiss. Still, he was good at persuasion.

With a deep sigh that encompassed relief and inevitability, he slid his hands beneath her hair and cupped her face. "You are so damned beautiful, Simone Parker. I think pregnancy becomes you."

It was the hint of vulnerability in her blue eyes that did him in. It always had. He kissed her slowly, taking his time, demanding a response and receiving more than he asked in return.

Her arms wrapped around his neck in a stranglehold. "Let's declare a truce," she pleaded in between frantic kisses. "Until after the babies are born."

"On what grounds?" He nipped her bottom lip with his teeth. She had put him through hell over the years. It was only reasonable that he made her work for this.

"Neighbors. Friendship. Old times."

"I could live with that. Lift your hips, woman."

When she obeyed instantly, dangerous lust roared through his veins. He ripped her jeans down her legs and tossed them aside. Her white cotton undies struck him as ridiculously erotic. Pressing two fingertips to her center, he caressed her through the layer of fabric.

Simone gasped, arching her back. He lifted her sweater but didn't take the time to remove it completely. Then he went still. "You're not wearing a bra."

As statements went, that one was sophomoric at best. But his brain had gone all fuzzy. "You're not wearing a bra," he repeated, dumbfounded.

Simone cocked her head and gave him an impertinent smile. "It's late. I was all alone. I had no idea the master of the house was planning to seduce me."

"I wasn't planning *anything*," he insisted. "But when a man finds a gift on his porch, he isn't dumb enough to throw it away." Deliberately taking his time, he lowered the zipper on his pants.

Simone shivered. "Are there any beds upstairs?"

"Not even a measly cot. Don't worry, little mama. We'll make do."

"Hurry," she said.

When the tail of his shirt caught in his zipper, Simone laughed. "For a doctor, you're awfully clumsy."

She was taunting him deliberately. It was an old game they played, one guaranteed to drive him insane. At last he managed to free his erection. He was burning up, but a shiver snaked its way down his spine as he looked at his very first houseguest.

"We can do this," he muttered. Somehow.

Simone scooted closer to the edge of the counter. "That refrigerator seems awfully sturdy."

"Good point." He lifted her into his arms and groaned when she wrapped her legs around his waist and her arms around his neck.

"You won't be able to do this too much longer," Simone said.

"Couples can have sex until very late in the pregnancy." He was counting on it.

"I was talking about carrying me, silly man. But I like where you're headed."

Where he was headed was to a padded room if he didn't get inside her soon. "Hold on," he muttered. He pushed her up against the refrigerator and grinned when the cold metal against her bum made her squeak. "I hope you're not attached to this underwear." Panting from exertion, he kept one arm around his prize and used his free hand to shove aside the narrow strip of fabric that was the only thing standing in his way.

When he joined their bodies, Simone moaned and buried her face in his neck. "Oh, Hutch."

He loved the way she said his name, her bedroom voice drowsy with pleasure. Simone could be a firecracker, a sharp-edged combatant. But when he had her like this, she was an entirely different person.

"Hold on, darlin'," he said, barely able to form a coherent sentence. The position taxed his strength, but it also gave him a jolt of satisfaction. Slowly, steadily, he thrust upward, taking her again and again until there was nothing left to take.

In this position, Simone was helpless. He was the aggressor. If there had been anything on top of the fridge, it would have crashed to the floor. He thrust wildly, coming in a climax so powerful it blurred his vision.

Through it all, Simone clung to him and never let go.

At last, the storm passed. He thought he heard and felt her orgasm. He hoped so. In his own delirium, he hadn't been the most considerate of lovers.

He eased her to her feet and steadied her when her legs wobbled. The water had been turned on, so the kitchen tap worked. There was nothing in the house, though. No paper napkins, no cloth towels.

Simone wrinkled her nose. "I should go home now. I need a shower. And it's late."

He nodded. "You want some company?"

She looked up at him, smaller and less combative than in many of their confrontations. Her smile bloomed, her blue eyes clear and happy. "What a lovely idea, Dr. Hutchinson."

That first evening set the tone for days that followed. He and Simone, by unspoken agreement, tabled their arguments and their differences. Often, he slept at her place. Other nights he worked at his own home, unpacking boxes until his eyes crossed with exhaustion. Simone tried to help, but he'd been forced to exile her when he found her lifting a container of heavy glassware in the kitchen. She'd pouted at him, but she hadn't gotten mad.

They were living in a fantasy world, totally ignoring the fact that Simone's life was about to change radically. Not to mention his.

Once the triplets were born, he wouldn't see much of Simone anymore. She would have her hands full caring for three small infants.

The thought of losing her again made his stomach clench. He reminded himself that he hadn't been home from Sudan long. Royal had dozens of available women, one of whom might even be his soul mate if he believed in such a thing. He was a man in his prime. During med school, he hadn't sown many wild oats. He'd been focused on getting through and excelling. It was what his parents expected and what Hutch wanted.

Now was the perfect time in his life to see who was out there for him. Not that he was foolish enough to think that there was another woman who could set his blood on fire like Simone did—but a man could hope.

Fortunately, Simone was incredibly busy getting things ready for the masquerade ball. He didn't have to worry about neglecting her when things got crazy at the hospital. The advent of the full moon meant a rush of babies being born. Though he hadn't picked up many patients of his own yet, he'd been called in on several high-risk cases.

A breech birth. One drug-addicted newborn. A seven-month infant delivered prematurely as a result of a car accident. Thankfully, in that situation, mother and baby had stabilized, but it was touch and go for a while.

There were seventy-two straight hours where Hutch didn't make it home at all. He snatched a few hours of sleep in the doctors' lounge, but it was fragmented rest and unsatisfying. He lived off hospital food and bottled water. The only way he knew time had passed was that he changed into clean scrubs twice a day.

Several times he thought about texting Simone, but each moment he pulled out his phone, he ended up being summoned to one labor room or another.

His week went from bad to worse on Wednesday. A young woman, barely six months pregnant and a recent transplant to Royal, came in through the ER. Her vitals were all over the map and the monitors showed fetal distress. It took hours, but finally a team nailed down the cause. The woman was diagnosed with a previously undetected and very rare blood abnormality. She was hemorrhaging internally.

Despite every attempt to save them, the mother and baby both died.

Unfortunately, Hutch's on-call rotation ended on that note. What he desperately wanted was to stay at the hospital and lose himself in work, trying to get those images out of his head. But that choice would endanger the patients in his care because of his extreme exhaustion.

Instead, he would do the mature, responsible thing. He would go home and sleep.

Simone bounced from day to day on a bubble of pure happiness. All of her problems were still out there on the horizon, but for now, life was good.

The masquerade party appeared destined to be a smashing success. Over 95 percent of the invitees had responded with an enthusiastic yes.

Thanks to Simone and her staff, the event received unprecedented saturation in both traditional print media and radio as well as blogs, email blasts and social media. Naomi and Cecelia had coordinated an entire crew of volunteers to help transform the ballroom. Tomorrow, the actual decorations would start going up.

Every day, Simone tried on the red dress, almost superstitiously afraid to leave anything to chance. She'd heard some pregnant women say they'd had to resort to maternity clothes overnight. One day they were fine with their jeans unzipped, the next, nothing fit.

She didn't want that to happen to her.

Knowing that Hutch would be her date for the party was both exciting and alarming. Even with Hutch wearing a mask, everyone would know who he was. Then the speculation would begin.

It probably already had, but this would be the first and likely only time she and Hutch would make an official appearance as a couple. Simone was pregnant. Hutch was back from Africa. Lots of people would make educated guesses.

She hadn't heard a word from him in almost four days. Fortunately, she wasn't the kind of woman who needed constant attention from a man. Still, when he neither texted nor called, she began to wonder if she had done something to upset him.

Though she was feeling markedly more like herself, Dr. Fetter had been insistent that Simone not overdo it. Thus, even though Thursday would be the last full workday before the party, Simone closed the office at five sharp on Wednesday and drove herself home.

Now that she felt like eating again—at least most of the time—she was actually hungry. Would Hutch be up for dinner at a quiet restaurant? Honestly, that sounded wonderful to Simone. This pregnancy was taking more of a toll on her body than she had anticipated. Her usual fount of energy was nowhere to be seen. Unwinding with Hutch and a nice, juicy steak might perk her up.

On a whim, she texted him before getting in the shower. By the time she was clean and dry and dressed, he still hadn't answered. Frowning, she tried to recall his schedule. She was almost certain he'd said he'd be off on Thursday *and* Friday, which meant that his shift should have ended this afternoon.

Maybe she would pick up carryout Chinese and go over to his house. If he was tired, too, he might welcome the food and the company. At one time, she would have been reluctant to invade his privacy. They'd been on good terms lately, though.

She sent him another text.

Still, he did not answer.

Bit by bit, her confidence eroded. She and Hutch were temporary. They both acknowledged that. What if Hutch had met someone else? What if he regretted his offer to escort her to the masquerade ball?

Maybe he and the mystery woman were over at his house now christening Hutch's new bed. He'd been sleeping on a mattress on the floor, but she had met the furniture delivery truck day before yesterday and opened Hutch's house so the men could set up the massive cherry king-size bed in the master suite.

Even with misgivings swirling in her stomach, she grabbed her keys and climbed into the car. Unfortunately, the Chinese restaurant was in the wrong direction, but the detour gave her more time to think. The order took no time at all. When she arrived at Hutch's place, the house was dark, and his car was in the driveway.

Now, she began to get worried. What if he were ill?

That was dumb. The man was a doctor. He was more than capable of taking care of himself.

Again, she wondered if his sudden absence from her life was because he had realized he was wasting his time. The man had a strongly developed moral conscience. Perhaps it had finally occurred to him that Simone was not meant to be a part of his life.

Leaving the food in her car for the moment, she got out and walked up the front steps. Testing the door gingerly, she found it locked.

Maybe he had come home and gone to bed early. At six forty-five? Not likely. Then what was the explanation for the fact that the house was in total darkness? Again, her mind went to the other-woman theory. If Hutch had brought someone home with him, they could be upstairs.

With her chest tight, she took a deep breath and let it out. Hutch would never sleep with two women at the same time. If he met someone else, he would do the honorable thing and tell Simone face-to-face.

Even so, she had a bad feeling about this. Something

was definitely amiss. Had the blackmailer chosen now as the time to reveal Simone's secret? Was Hutch pondering how to boot her out of his life?

She had to *make* herself walk around the porch. The easy thing would be to run away. But she had to be sure Hutch was okay.

The end of her search was anticlimactic. She found him sitting on the top step, slumped over, his elbows on his knees, his head in his hand.

"Hutch?" She crouched beside him, alarmed. Something in his body language kept her from touching him. "Why didn't you answer my texts?"

"Go home, Simone."

She froze. His voice was monotone, gruff and raspy. "Have I done something to offend you, Hutch? Talk to me. I can't fix it if you don't let me know what it is."

He stood up, forcing her to do the same. His eyes were the dull brown of fallen leaves in the late fall. Yet somehow, a tiny flame in them seared her. His body language spoke volumes. "For God's sake, Simone. The whole damn world doesn't revolve around you. Not everything I do or don't do is about *you*. Grow up, damn it. I don't need you hovering every minute of every day."

Fourteen

Simone gaped at him, her heart imploding in shock and bitter hurt. Never, even in their most painful days before he left for Sudan, had Hutch lashed out like this. He'd always possessed a maturity beyond his years. Hutch was never cruel.

Apparently, people changed.

She could do nothing about the tears that spilled down her cheeks. Stepping back awkwardly, unconsciously putting distance between herself and the furious, aggressive male, she held out a hand. "I shouldn't have come. My mistake."

Hutch only stared at her.

Everything crumbled in slow motion. The faux happiness that had helped her ignore their problems was a sham. She'd been living in a dream world.

One last time, she tried to get through to him. "I brought dinner. Chinese. Your favorite. I'll grab it from the car."

"I'm not hungry. And I'm not in the mood for company."

"I see." She didn't. Not at all. But she wasn't stupid. "Okay, then." Embarrassed, humiliated, hurt and angry, she gave him a curt nod. Without another word, she fled.

It took her three tries to put the car into gear. She was crying so hard, she couldn't see. At the end of Hutch's driveway, she stopped. She shouldn't operate a vehicle in her condition. Resting her head on the steering wheel, she wept.

Hutch had taken a bad day and made it worse. In the midst of his burning guilt and regret over what had happened at the hospital, he had added the poisonous taste of shame. The memory of Simone's face galvanized him into action.

Racing around the side of the house, he inhaled sharply when he saw her car still parked in his driveway. He jerked open the driver's-side door and felt like the lowest kind of scum when he realized she was crying too hard to make the short trip home.

"Oh, hell," he groaned. "Come here, baby. I'm a bastard. Let me hold you."

He scooped her out of the car without a struggle. Bumping the door closed with his hip, he strode back to the house.

Inside, he wasted no time. He carried her up the stairs and sat down with her on his bed. "I'm sorry, Simone. My bad temper had nothing to do with you. Please forgive me."

She had cried so hard her face was blotchy and red. And she couldn't stop. He held her tightly, unable to stem the flow of tears.

It was a hell of a time to figure out he was still in love with her.

The bolt of truth was a knife to his gut. Was this something new, or had his feelings for Simone lain dormant all those years in Sudan? Maybe deep down, his guilt over Bethany's death wasn't so much about not being able to save her as it was knowing he had never loved her the way he should have.

Bethany had given her heart and her trust to him. Had he unwittingly offered her far less in return?

He stroked Simone's hair. "Hush now. You'll make yourself sick again."

It took a long time, but finally, Simone wore herself out.

He wiped her face with the tail of his shirt. To explain would be to dump some of his anguish on her, but how else could he account for being so deliberately cruel? "I lost a mother and a baby today," he muttered. It embarrassed him that his voice broke on the word *baby*.

Simone struggled to sit up. She stared at him with big, wet eyes. "Oh, Hutch. What happened?"

He gave her an abbreviated version. "I don't think the patient ever really had a chance, but we tried. God, we tried. I kept seeing the nurses' faces. It's hard, you know. We're supposed to maintain that professional distance…so we can do what we have to do. Loss of life in any circumstance is difficult beyond words. This…this was devastating."

"The baby couldn't be saved?"

"No. She looked perfect. Tiny, but perfect. Still, it was far too soon. Sometimes, even with all our sophisticated equipment and technology, we can't overcome that. We save dozens of preemies, often against large odds. Today we lost. She lived for an hour."

Simone—generous, openhearted Simone—wrapped her arms around him and held him so tightly he could barely breathe. Or maybe that was his reaction to knowing he had the love of his life in his arms.

She shuddered. "I can't even imagine what it was like for all of you. I couldn't do what you do. How does anyone bear it?"

He *knew* what she was thinking. "You don't have to worry about your pregnancy, Simone. The woman today had a serious medical condition. You're healthy and strong and perfectly normal."

"I don't think anyone's ever called me normal." Her

smile was wry, her face still damp as she pulled back and stared at him.

He wanted to ease her down on the bed and make love to her to erase the memories of the day. But he felt raw and unsteady and light-headed. It was a time for caution. Simone didn't deserve to be used as tranquilizer. He needed to take stock of what was happening.

Carefully, he released her and stood up. "Did you mention something about food?" he asked, trying to lighten the mood.

Simone's face was hard to read. She rose as well, her posture defensive, arms wrapped tightly around her waist. And no wonder. He'd treated her like dirt. She shrugged. "It's hot outside. I don't know if we should risk it. Food poisoning is not fun."

He winced. "True." And in Simone's condition, it could be lethal. "What if we drive through somewhere and grab a milk shake and fries?"

She raised an eyebrow. "For a doctor, you don't seem to have a grasp of good nutrition."

He knew she was teasing him. "After today, I think we could both use some junk food, don't you? How about it?"

Simone hesitated. "I need to get home," she said.

"You're mad."

"No." She shook her head vehemently. "I forgive you. But the next two days are going to be tough. Dr. Fetter says I need to pace myself."

"Of course." He didn't want to eat alone. He sure as hell didn't want to sleep alone. But his outburst on the back porch had changed something. Maybe Simone was rethinking her relationship with him.

The awkward conversation ended there. Simone headed downstairs with him on her heels. Once she climbed into her car and started the engine, he leaned down, one hand on top of the car. "Are you sure you're okay to drive?"

Simone nodded. "I'm good."

He winced, remembering what else he had to tell her. "I'd hoped to do something fun with you tomorrow, but my dad needs me to help him in the garden. The man does love his fresh produce, but he overplanted his year."

"No worries, Hutch." Her gaze was guarded. "I'm going to be working flat out, too. I'll see you Friday evening."

"What time do you want me to pick you up?"

"Five thirty will work. I have to be there early. I could drive my own car, though," she said. "No need for you to hang around."

"I could help."

She pursed her lips. "Maybe. What if I let you know tomorrow?"

"I'm picking you up, Simone. End of discussion." His temper started a slow boil. Something had shifted. Was it the things he had said to her earlier? Had he damaged a relationship already on shaky ground? Or was something else going on?

"Fine." Simone revved the engine. "Good night, Hutch."

He was forced to step back or risk having her run over his foot. After his recent behavior, he couldn't blame her.

Simone refused to think about Dr. Troy Hutchinson. He could hurt her only if she allowed it. The new lives growing in her womb were all she needed. Even if Hutch wanted to hang around after the babies came, she wouldn't have time for him.

Tonight had exposed a valuable truth. Hutch didn't love her. It hurt to admit it. It hurt like hell. But she was better off accepting reality.

She didn't hold his bad temper against him. Anyone in a similar situation would be raw and grief stricken and likely to lash out. No, that wasn't the root of her sadness. What pained her was that Hutch, in his hour of need, hadn't turned to Simone for help and comfort. If she dug deep to the heart of their relationship, she saw the chasm between what she wanted and what he was willing to give her.

Friendship? Yes. They had mended fences over their earlier breakup and moved on. Sex? The sex was amazing... hot, intense and deeply satisfying. She and Hutch had no problems in the bedroom.

She could even see that the two of them had established a tentative relationship of trust. Certainly, she trusted him to look after her physical well-being. Not only that, but Hutch had been very honest with her about Bethany. There were very few secrets between them.

Though in Simone's case, the one she had omitted was gigantic.

Tonight's drama with Hutch had stolen her appetite, replacing it with the now-familiar nausea. Nursing a cup of hot tea, she curled up in the comfy chair in her bedroom and opened her laptop.

For some reason, she had never deleted the message from the mysterious Maverick. The cryptic note was evidence, in any case. Maybe he or she was not a threat anymore. Word of her pregnancy was slowly beginning to spread. The cat was out of the bag. Perhaps Maverick had wanted to extort money from her to keep her pregnancy quiet.

When she opened Facebook, she saw that she had received a new message. She clicked on it and read, "Your day of reckoning is near. Maverick."

That was odd. And menacing. She placed a hand on her stomach, instinctively alarmed. It was one thing to fear for her own safety. Now she carried the responsibility for three tiny humans.

The only secret she had kept from Hutch and her friends...from everyone, in fact, was private. This Maverick person would have no reason to know what Simone had done...or at least *why* she had done it.

She hated feeling helpless. Even more, she hated feeling powerless to track down the subpar person who held grudges against so many of Royal's upstanding citizens. She sure as heck wasn't going to engage in an online conversation with Maverick. The best thing to do was to go about her business, pretending that everything was normal.

Thursday morning dawned bright and clear and sunny. After a restless sleep, Simone was grateful for weather that lifted her spirits. Sometime around three the night before, she had turned on the light and made a list. She was a mother-to-be with a successful business to run.

This thing with Hutch, well, it was fun, but it was also painful. After tomorrow night, it was probably best if she put an end to it. At least that way, she would be the one calling the shots and not Hutch.

Beneath her surface calm, her heart was breaking. She wanted it all. The babies. The company she had built from the ground up. The respect of her parents. And last but not least, she wanted the man she had loved since she was twenty-two years old.

Fifty percent wasn't a bad average. In baseball, it was extraordinary. Too bad she had never been good at sports.

After showering and drying her hair, she put on a new black knit dress and topped it with a cheery hot-pink cardigan. The knit fabric and empire waistline were designed to grow along with her belly. Today, it simply looked liked a casual outfit suited to a pleasant spring day.

She had called Tess and told her she was coming in a little late. Tess was brilliant. Simone had hired the younger woman straight out of business school with a freshly minted MBA. At no time had Tess ever let her down or not been able to handle the work. Simone was counting on that.

When she made it in to her office, she asked Tess to come in and close the door. Tess might have been alarmed, but she didn't show it. "What's up, boss?"

Simone had insisted that Tess call her by her first name. But Tess had just as insistently refused. Simone eyed the girl on the other side of the desk. From her magenta-accented pixie cut to her triple-pierced right ear, Tess was an original.

For some reason, Simone was having a hard time getting this conversation off the ground. "Tess," she said, "are you happy working with me?"

Tess nodded. "Of course."

"And do you have plans to move up the ladder? To go somewhere else? Dallas, maybe? Or Houston?"

"None." A tiny frown appeared between Tess's brows. "Are you trying to get rid of me?"

"Not at all. Quite the opposite."

"I'm confused."

Simone realized she wasn't handling this well. "I suppose you know I'm pregnant."

Tess grimaced. "Yes, ma'am."

"What you may not know is that I'm having triplets."

"Good God." Tess's eyes rounded. "I hope it's not contagious." She shuddered. "I'm not antibaby, but three?"

"Yeah," Simone said wryly. "It's a lot to take in. But on the other hand, it's a done deal, so I'm trying to make plans."

"No offense, boss, but I'm not really a fan of little kids. They scare me. Probably comes from my dad dropping me on my head when I was six months old. I think it warped me."

Tess was talking a mile a minute, clearly rattled.

Simone sighed. "Stand down, Tess. I'm not asking you to babysit. I want to know if you're willing to be top dog of this company for a year. I'd still be involved in all major decisions, but you would be in charge. What do you think?"

"Where will you be?"

"At home. I'll have help with the triplets…out of necessity. There's no way I can do it alone. But I'll be their mother. Even saying that out loud sounds strange. I want these babies, Tess. I'm going to give this motherhood thing a hundred percent of my time when they're born, at least for a year. After that, if we've managed some kind of routine, I may consider day care. But that's a long time off, so I can't think about that now."

"You're awfully brave."

"Not brave. Just determined. If you need time to think about this, I understand."

"I don't have to think about it," Tess said with a huge grin. "I'm honored. And pumped. You can count on me, boss."

"When we get around to this new arrangement, do you think you could call me Simone?"

Tess shrugged sheepishly. "Maybe. I'll try."

"Good. And, Tess?"

"Yes, ma'am?"

"This is between you and me for the next few months. I don't want anyone to know I'm thinking about taking a sabbatical. It's my business."

"I get it." She mimed sealing her lips. "Your secrets will go to my grave."

"Thank you." Simone shooed her out and tackled the stack of paperwork overflowing her inbox. Between snail mail and email, she never caught up. The business was growing undeniably. Soon, she might have to consider adding another employee. But then again, with Simone gone for a year, they might lose ground. It would be a game of wait and see.

For the second day in a row, she closed the office at five. As someone accustomed to keeping late hours when in the midst of a project, it was not her usual behavior. She liked to think motherhood was going to be good for her. Keeping a healthier lifestyle…all of that.

She didn't call Hutch that evening. Or text him.

He didn't contact her, either. Maybe they were both ready to admit their relationship was never going to blossom into something permanent. Simone had known that from the beginning. Getting pregnant with an unknown man's sperm had erased virtually every chance she had to get married. No one she knew would be willing to take on a young mom with three babies, even if that man was madly in love with her.

Hutch wasn't madly in love. She didn't deceive herself there. He liked her. He enjoyed having regular sex. Neither of those things guaranteed a happily-ever-after. As she let herself into the house, she told herself she could handle this baby thing with or without Hutch.

Though she cooked oatmeal for dinner, she was barely able to eat half. Afterward, she read and watched TV until ten o'clock. Like a high school girl in the throes of a crush, she picked up her phone every ten seconds to check for messages.

The screen remained blank.

Uncertainty was painful and demoralizing. She was even more resolved to end things with Hutch after the ball. Never mind that her heart raced in panic at the thought. The two of them had enjoyed reuniting. Nothing that came afterward pointed to a rosy future. Even Hutch himself had never made any pretense of wanting to be a father to her babies. He was too honest to lead her astray.

More honest than she deserved.

When she finally turned out the light and curled up in a ball underneath the covers, her heart raced. Tomorrow night was big. Huge, in fact. A good turnout meant significant sums of money for the charity.

Unfortunately, all she cared about at the moment was seeing Hutch again and, hopefully, dancing the night away. Even if the bliss would only be temporary.

Fifteen

Hutch had some big decisions to make. He knew it, but he couldn't quite wrap his head around what that would mean. Everyone thought he was so smart, so damned wise. The truth was, he was as clueless as the next guy.

It felt odd to put on a tux again. He'd been forced to buy a new one for the masquerade ball. His time in Africa had made him leaner, harder. Living life on the edge of civilization had taught him how to survive without many of the comforts of home. His physical stamina was greater than it had ever been.

He looked at himself in the mirror and straightened his bow tie with a grimace. All he had ever wanted in life was to make his parents proud of him. On a whim, he grabbed his keys and headed out to the car. It was too early to pick up Simone, but he had a sudden urge to see his father.

Both his parents were sitting outside on the porch enjoying a cold beer when Hutch arrived. His mother was her usual stately, put-together self. His dad was scruffy today. Apparently, he'd worked in the garden again.

Hutch took a wicker chair and sat across from them.

His mother cocked her head. "Did I forget it's my birthday? You look very handsome this evening, Hutch."

The senior Hutchinson nodded. "You clean up real nice. But I'm guessing you didn't come to pull more weeds."

"Should I leave you two boys alone?" his mother asked.

"No, ma'am." Hutch might be closing in on his midthirties, but his mother still ruled their family with an iron fist. "I want you both to hear this."

"So serious," she said, smiling. But he noted a trace of anxiety in her brown eyes that were so like his.

His father frowned. "Spit it out, son. Bad news never gets any better in the waiting."

"Who said I have bad news?" Hutch ran a hand over his head, aware that he was starting to sweat.

His mother leaned forward and patted his knee. "You look as somber as a judge. Tell us, son."

Hutch rubbed his damp palms on his pants legs. "Do you remember Simone Parker?"

Both of the older adults flinched. "We do," his father said. "Your grandmother never got over the way she treated you. Thank God she's passed on. I have a feeling she wouldn't like what you're about to tell us."

"You raised me to believe that people deserve second chances."

"Yes, we did," his mother said. "But that woman was wrong for you in many ways."

Hutch bristled. "Like what? I thought you were glad she convinced me to go to Sudan."

His dad drained his beer and set the bottle on the floor. "We were. We still are. Those years will make a huge difference in how you practice medicine. But this Simone... well, she's..." He trailed off.

"She's selfish and shallow," his mother said sharply. "She has a reputation around town as a bit of a snob. Only child. Wealthy parents."

"I'm an only child," Hutch pointed out mildly, though he felt anything but calm. "I'm surprised to hear both of you speak so negatively. Simone might have been a little self-centered in her youth, but she's changed."

His father shrugged. "If you've come to ask for our blessing, I don't think we can offer it. But you're a grown man and long past needing our approval. Give it some time, boy. Sleep with her, but don't marry her."

Hutch's mother punched her husband in the arm…hard. "Don't talk like that, Edward Hutchinson. What's gotten into you?"

"You don't like her, either."

"I don't know her," she conceded.

Hutch stood up. He wasn't sure what he had expected from his parents. Maybe he just wanted someone to tell him that what he was contemplating wouldn't make a damn fool out of him. "I haven't made any big decisions, so you can quit having heart attacks. I suppose I was hoping you'd tell me that true love lasts."

"Well, of course it does," his father said. "The trick is to marry the right person in the first place."

Hutch was not in a good frame of mind to go to a party. He was horny and agitated and completely confused. Just when he thought he had things figured out, something happened. Either Simone pulled back, or he did. And now his parents, thanks to him, had weighed in on the situation. With a big ol' negative.

He parked in Simone's driveway and stared up at the house. The structure was attractive and neatly kept. Exactly like its owner. The golden brick with the mahogany shutters at the windows was modern and, at the same time, classic.

Fumbling to slide his phone into his pocket, he told himself that tonight was not the time for grand gestures. Tonight was mostly business for Simone. He was only her escort, not her boyfriend. In fact, this wasn't some romantic date where the two of them would be all alone.

Two-thirds or more of Royal's movers and shakers would be out in force tonight. Maybe they would come to show off their jewels and their trophy wives. Perhaps they really cared about the charity. Either way, the word of the evening was *money*...and lots of it.

Simone answered the door as soon as he knocked. He took a step backward, feeling a mule kick to the chest. She looked incredible.

"Hi, Hutch," she said breathlessly. "Come on in. I'm almost ready. A phone call slowed me down."

She was fluttering, nervous, her eyes not quite meeting his.

Without overthinking it, Hutch captured her wrist and gently reeled her in. "You look stunning, Simone." He kissed her softly, keeping a tight check on his caveman instincts. Her lips were soft beneath his. Her hands landed on his shoulders. For a few breath-stealing moments, he lost himself in the kiss. He wanted to carry her up the stairs and lock the door.

His heart pounded, his entire body hard as iron. He wanted to take and take and take. The prospect of sharing her with hundreds of other people tonight was unappealing at best.

She wore a red dress designed to make a statement. Simone Parker was *in* the building. In his arms she felt fragile and small, though he knew she was anything but. Simone was smart and strong and determined. Having triplets would be extremely challenging, but he had no doubts about her ability to cope.

In the end, he had to force himself to release her and step back. Her silky black hair fell in soft waves about her shoulders. Her sapphire eyes, framed in dark lashes, sparkled.

Her grin was self-conscious. "I really do have to finish getting ready."

He waved a hand. "Go. I'll entertain myself down here."

He glanced at his watch. "You'd better hurry, though, if we're supposed to be getting there early."

Simone rolled her eyes. "I'm not the one who started that kiss."

She disappeared before he could retaliate. With a smile on his face, he prowled the downstairs restlessly. Anticipation flooded his veins. He and Simone had things to discuss. Big things. Life-changing things. Maybe this time, they could rewrite the ending.

After the talk with Tess, Simone had begun to feel as if she finally had a handle on the mess that was her life. Seeing Hutch at her door just now in black tie knocked the wind out of her. He was so handsome, so brilliant, so unbelievably sexy. Why would a man like that want to tie himself to a woman like Simone? Nevertheless, she was going to give it a shot.

She had built her business on taking calculated risks. Hutch cared about her. The fact that he wanted her physically was irrefutable. The only question that remained was how he would respond if Simone asked for more.

Earlier, she had decided to break things off with Hutch, but that was the coward's way out. Tonight, after the ball, she was going to lay her cards on the table. Love was a hard thing to offer outright, but maybe she owed him that. Above all, she was going to confess the truth. It would put her in a bad light, no doubt about it. Still, there was no hope for a future with Hutch unless she was completely honest.

After tweaking her hair one last time and applying a bold lipstick to match her dress, she eyed her reflection in the long mirror on the back of her closet door. Not too shabby. She placed her hand, palm flat, against her belly. Feeling the tiny bulge filled her with wonder and humility.

Despite everything she had done wrong in her life, here was a chance for a new start. More than anything else, she wanted to be a good mother to these three babies. Unlike her own upbringing, she was determined to be a hands-on parent. Though she would have to have help, professional or otherwise, she was going to be *present*.

A quick glance at the clock told her there was no time left to linger. Lifting her skirt in one hand, she made her way carefully down the stairs. Hutch stood at the bottom, waiting. She held up a hand. "No more kissing. I'm camera ready, as Naomi would say."

His smile was wicked. "I can wait. Maybe." He ran his thumb over her cheekbone. "Let's just say I'm really looking forward to removing that dress in a few hours."

"Hutch!" She gaped at him.

He shrugged. "If you don't want me to open the gift, you shouldn't wrap it so nicely."

They made it to the hotel in record time. Because they were early, traffic wasn't bad yet. In the parking lot, Simone handed Hutch the rectangular box that had come in the mail. "These are our masks. Will you hang on to them for the moment?"

He grimaced, exhibiting the usual male reluctance for such things. "Sure."

The following hour was taken up with a variety of last-minute responsibilities. While Hutch cooled his heels in the bar, Simone met with Naomi and Cecelia for one final, excited rundown. Everything had fallen into place perfectly.

At last, it was time to find Hutch and start enjoying the more personal portion of the evening. He had returned to the car in search of fresh air and his business card wallet. After a quick text to ascertain his whereabouts, she joined him there, relishing the moment of privacy inside the vehicle to catch her breath and collect her thoughts before the event began in earnest. "I missed you, my handsome doctor."

As masquerade parties went, this one was going to be

ultrasophisticated, no costumes or elaborate ensembles allowed. The men had been instructed to wear traditional tuxes. With so many of them in the room, anonymity would be upheld. The women, on the other hand, had been asked to choose a color. The masks for the female guests would complement their gowns. Simone's mask was scarlet trimmed with delicate black lace.

Her heart beat faster when Hutch put on his black mask. It made him look remote and dangerous. "Will you help me with mine?" she said. "So I won't mess up my hair?"

Hutch took the mask from her trembling fingers and carefully fitted it over her head, smoothing any strands of hair that were pushed out of place. Then he bared the side of her neck and pressed a kiss just below her ear. "I could eat you alive," he muttered.

His hot breath against her skin and the subtle rake of his teeth against her sensitive flesh flooded her body with heat and yearning. "I could say the same to you," she whispered. "I used to think your white lab coat was the sexiest piece of clothing you owned. But tonight you're seriously hot. I'll have my hands full keeping other women from stealing you away."

He cupped his hand around her breast, using his thumb to tease the nipple that beaded beneath the fabric. "Does that mean you want me all to yourself?"

Simone shuddered. Arousal stole through her veins and made her reckless. "I dare anyone to lay a hand on you, Troy Hutchinson. For tonight, you're mine."

He groaned, resting his forehead against hers. "What are we doing, damn it? I can't walk in there with an erection. Hell, Simone, you make me crazy."

For once, he didn't sound too happy about that. She sat back in her seat and tried to steady her breathing. "I'll go in alone," she said. "You can follow when you're ready."

Beneath the mask, his jaw was like iron. "I'm ready

now," he growled, deliberately misunderstanding her suggestion. The words were forced beneath clenched teeth.

Helpless to stem the tide of insanity that had overtaken them, she touched him lightly through his trousers. His erection was as hard as his jaw. "Oh, Hutch," she said. "What I wouldn't give to walk away from all of this. I don't know if I can wait."

"Maybe you don't have to." He leaned over her. The windows of his black SUV were tinted. No one was around to notice when he slid a hand beneath her skirt and ran his fingers from her ankle up her thigh to the edge of her satiny underpants.

"Um, Hutch…" She gripped the door handle with her right hand.

"Relax, Simone."

That was easy for him to say. Her entire body clenched in anticipation of what he was about to do. When he pressed two fingers against the very heart of her yearning, she gasped. Carefully, he pleasured her.

She should have made him stop. Cecelia and Naomi were expecting her inside. But none of that mattered. Hutch took her somewhere dark and visceral and so compelling, she lost everything except the feel of his hands on her body.

When she came, her fingernails left marks in the leather seat. Chest heaving, she opened one eye. "You're some kind of sorcerer," she said.

His grin was a slash of white teeth beneath his mask. "All the better to seduce you, my dear."

Heart pounding still, she hesitated. This was where her lack of experience failed her. "Do you want me to…"

"No." He said the word forcefully, though his body spoke otherwise. "When I have you in bed tonight, and I'm deep inside you with you crying out my name, *then* I'll get what I'm waiting for…but not before."

Simone nodded, unable to find the words to tell him

what she felt. With all her heart, she wanted to believe Hutch would forgive her when she told him the truth. Honestly, she wanted to tell him now and get it over with… end the suspense. That wasn't an option, though. She had a party to execute.

They barely spoke after that. Hutch brooded, gaze trained out his window as Simone fussed with her hair and makeup. When she was reasonably certain she was back to normal, she picked up her small clutch purse. "I'm ready."

The Bellamy was magnificent. From the vast, sophisticated lobby, down the wide hallways covered in luxurious Oriental rugs, to the entranceway into the ballroom, the place was awash in flowers and tiny white lights and golden gauze bows. Pale orchids in cream and lavender emitted a subtle fragrance. Cecelia's touch was on every bit of design and decor in the building. This new hotel was destined to become a centerpiece of Royal's social scene.

Hutch was deeply grateful he was wearing a mask. He felt raw and gutted. If he hadn't known he was in love with Simone before, he knew it tonight. She was incandescent. Pregnancy gave her a glow of contentment. His physical need for her was only outweighed by a gut-deep certainty that she was the only woman who could make him whole.

After his stunt in the car, which slowed Simone and him down, a crowd of guests already gathered in the lobby and moved toward the ballroom.

The Bellamy had hired ample staff for the big evening. In addition to its own roster of chefs and waiters, tonight's event demanded even more. Every guest would be expecting perfection.

Even with attendees wearing masks, it was easy to pick out a few here and there. He was almost certain he identified Harper Lake with one of the Tate brothers, though he couldn't tell the twins apart. Clay Everett limped in with his gorgeous secretary. That might raise a few eyebrows.

Thirty minutes after the official starting time of the masquerade ball, the room was packed. Old friends and new. Octogenarians whose history went way back in Royal. Young, hip entrepreneurs who had made their mark in re-shaping the town. Everything in between.

After twenty minutes of mingling and chatting, Simone was flushed and sparkling with excitement. "Let's dance," she said.

"I thought you'd never ask."

Hutch led her onto the floor and tucked her against his chest. With Simone wearing heels, they could have kissed easily. He inhaled sharply, dizzy from the scent of delicate perfume and warm female skin.

He held her firmly, confidently. As they twirled around the room, he saw people watching them. All male eyes were on Simone. She would stand out in any crowd with her dark hair and sexy dress. His arms tightened around her. No man in the room was good enough for her, not even him.

Over the past few weeks, Simone had told him stories about the headaches involved in planning tonight's event. The committee had squabbled over which band to hire. A few people wanted a modern, trendy group. But in the end, given the stately atmosphere of the hotel and the knowledge that the crowd would include a variety of ages, the decision was made to go with a small orchestra. The playlist included songs from all decades, primarily the kind of romantic pieces that encouraged slow dancing cheek to cheek.

Hutch thought it was a brilliant strategy. When a man dressed up in a monkey suit and took a woman out on the town, he wanted to be able to hold her. Vertical foreplay. That's what it was. And he couldn't wait to get Simone horizontal.

Occasionally, the band would break into a fast, snappy

number so the folks who really knew how to dance had a chance to shine out on the floor. Simone was a good dancer, and Hutch was decent…but she begged off because of the babies. Her lengthy illness had sapped her stamina. Now she appeared to be slowing down. Instinctively, he wrapped his arms around her.

"I'm dying of thirst," she said, leaning into him. "And I wouldn't mind sampling that menu I've spent weeks planning."

Sixteen

Hutch steered a path to the buffet with Simone in tow. The spread was amazing, even by Royal's standards. Prime rib, of course. After all, this was cattle country. But also chicken kebabs skewered with vegetables, crab puffs and enormous prawns iced down in a magnificent crystal bowl. Not to mention all the usual accoutrements.

"Well," he said. "Anything you want me to avoid?" He was keenly aware that even the sight of certain foods was enough to set off Simone's nausea. This was her special night. He didn't want to take any chances.

She leaned her head against his shoulder momentarily. "That's sweet of you, Hutch. I think I'm okay, though. I won't attempt the caviar, but everything else looks good to me right now."

They filled their plates to overflowing and sought out a table for two in a distant corner. Large potted plants provided cover for discreet trysts. "Was this your idea?" he asked as he held out her chair and helped her get seated. They were sheltered, although not completely private, of course.

She popped a carrot stick in her mouth and grinned. "Romance is alive and well in Royal…didn't you know?"

"I'll grab us a couple of drinks."

"Plain tap water, please."

When he returned moments later, Simone sat with her chin on her hand staring at a large stuffed mushroom with a frown. He handed a glass. "What's wrong?"

She shrugged. "I don't know about this one."

"Then for God's sake, don't take any chances," he said. He filched the mushroom and popped it into his mouth. Fortunately, the rest of her choices were winners.

The food was excellent, but he knew he was in trouble when just watching her eat made him hard again. Soft lips. Small white teeth. Lord help him. Simone was oblivious to his mood, her gaze tracking various couples on the dance floor. She named them off one by one.

"How do you do that?" he asked. "Isn't the whole point of a masquerade ball anonymity? I know I've been away a long time, but I only managed to spot a few people I could identify for sure."

"I cheated," she confessed. "I was the one who processed all the names and built the spreadsheet. Even with everyone wearing masks, I think I could name most of them."

"My hat's off to you. I'm guessing a few of those couples who responded were a surprise?"

"Oh, yes. Definitely. I *would* tell you, but then I'd have to kill you."

"Isn't that taking secret identities a step too far, Mata Hari?"

"You could always try to torture it out of me."

Her big blue eyes were wide and innocent. When she stuck out her tongue to catch a bit of cocktail sauce at the corner of her mouth, he sighed. "You're messing with me, aren't you?"

"Would *I* do that?"

"In a heartbeat."

He reached across the table and took her hands in his. "You think you're safe from retaliation because we're in a public place, but fair warning, my sweet. I could toss you over my shoulder, walk out of here to the front desk and get a room."

"You wouldn't…" She eyed him askance.

"Try me."

"Okay, Hutch," she said, her tone placating. "I'll behave from here on out. No flirting. No innuendo. No dancing."

"I didn't say no dancing. A man has to take what crumbs he can get."

She cocked her head. "I'm confused. Are you a barbarian laying down the law or a puppy begging for scraps?"

He stroked the backs of her hands with his thumbs. "What do you think?"

For a long second, their gazes locked. Her eyes were nothing so simple as blue. They were dark at the outer rim, like midnight, but lighter near the pupil. He was mesmerized studying them.

"Hutch?"

He heard her say his name, but he was lost in a fantasy where she was stark naked on his bed. "Hmm?"

"We probably should get back out there since we've finished eating. After all, I'm one of the ones in charge."

"Yes…" He whispered the word, still caught up in a vision he hoped like hell would come true in only a few hours.

Suddenly, his dream woman stood up. "Hurry," she said, excitement in her voice. "I think Deacon is about to make an announcement."

Hutch followed her, disgruntled. They found a spot near the front. The stage was set up just behind the orchestra. Deacon Chase stood at the microphone with a genial smile on his face and a raised hand. When the crowd at last fell silent, he spoke.

"First of all, friends and neighbors, Shane Delgado and I would like to welcome you to The Bellamy. This hotel and all it encompasses is a dream come true for us. We're delighted to have all of you here tonight. I hope you'll spend a lot of time at The Bellamy in the years to come, not only overnight for special occasions, but also dining with us on a regular basis at either the Silver Saddle or the Glass House. Our new spa, Pure, is open to the public. All you need to do is make a reservation." He paused and cleared his throat. "I know everyone is eager to get back to the dancing, but I hope you'll grant me a moment of personal privilege."

He held out his hand, and to Hutch's surprise, Simone's friend Cecelia took the stage. Deacon introduced her with a broad smile. "If you think we have a beautifully appointed hotel, this is the woman who gets the credit. I'm forever in her debt for helping us make The Bellamy a reality. Even more than that, I am beyond happy that she has agreed to be my wife."

The room erupted in shouts and cheers. Shocked, Hutch looked sideways at Simone. "Did you know about this?"

She nodded, beaming. "He gave her the ring several weeks ago, but they only told close friends and family before tonight. I guess this makes it official. Look how sweet they are together."

He did look, and Simone was right. Judging from the expressions on their faces, Cecelia and Deacon were ridiculously happy with their new status. Hutch continued to brood while Simone joined the crowd of friends who wanted to congratulate the bride-to-be and her groom.

Deacon Chase had chosen well. As far as Hutch could tell, the billionaire hotelier and the gorgeous platinum blonde had a lot in common. Case in point—the two of them, along with Delgado, had turned a dream into a reality. Deacon built hotels. Cecelia had the know-how to furnish them.

What did Hutch and Simone have in common? Not one damn thing.

Suddenly, his bow tie choked him, and the room was

far too hot. His heart beat out an unfamiliar cadence in his chest. Working his way over to Simone, he reached out and tapped her on the arm. The crowd was so noisy, he had to bend down so she could hear him.

"I'm going outside for some fresh air," he said. "Stay here and enjoy your friends."

Big blue eyes searched his face. "Are you okay?"

He dredged up a smile and brushed the back of his hand across her cheek. "Never better," he lied. "I'll be back shortly."

"How will you find me?"

Was she serious? "Honey, that red dress stands out in a crowd. Don't worry. I won't leave without you."

Desperately, he plowed his way to the other side of the room. Had the fire marshal okayed this crowd? Hell, the marshal had probably been invited for that very reason.

Outside, he jerked his bow tie off and stuffed it in his pocket. After that, he took a deep, cleansing breath and leaned against a marble statue of Pan in a clump of daisies. He wished he smoked. Since he didn't and never had, the next best thing was walking. He'd read the press packet about the new hotel. The grounds included several miles of wooded trails.

He didn't care where he went at this point. It wasn't like he could get lost. This was Royal, not the middle of a wilderness.

The night was perfect…too perfect. He walked with his head down, trying not to notice the moonlight or the sweet scent of flowers in the air. If he proposed to Simone and she accepted, there would be no going back. He wouldn't be able to return to Sudan to escape her hold on him.

Could he and would he be able to love three babies who weren't his biological offspring? That seemed the least of his worries at this point. He adored children. He always had.

Besides, the triplets carried half of their mother's DNA. If he loved Simone, he would love her babies, too.

But what if he proposed and she said no? Why had he purchased a house so near hers? He had to drive by Simone's house every day on the way to work. That would be unbearable if they broke up for a second time.

He'd never been good at games of chance. Knowing the odds were stacked against him meant he'd never had any real trouble staying away from gambling. He liked being in control.

Yet here he was, contemplating a course that was neither certain nor even advisable. On paper it seemed absurd. His parents clearly agreed. Why would he risk so much when he had no idea if Simone cared for him at all?

Again, he visited the possibility that she was using him. With triplets on the way, she might think she needed a second parent in the house above all else. Such a rationale made her seem cold and calculating. The Simone he knew was neither of those things.

When he regained a modicum of control over his emotions, he put on the bow tie again. It was time for him to go back inside to smile and to dance and to do whatever it took to make it through the remainder of the ball. After that, he'd get his reward. One whole night in Simone's bed. Or his. He wasn't too picky about locale.

As he turned around to head back the way he had come, a large man about Hutch's height stepped out of the shadows and blocked the path. Hutch froze, sensing danger. But the man was in formal attire and wore one of the masquerade masks. Surely this wasn't some gate-crasher come late to wreck the party.

"What can I do for you, sir?"

The man straightened. He was big and broad, but even in the moonlight Hutch could see that his face was gaunt. "It's what I can do for you, Dr. Hutchinson."

"Who are you? How do you know my name?"

"You can call me Maverick. It doesn't matter how I know your name. I'm here to give you fair warning about the woman in the red dress."

Hutch frowned. "Simone?"

"Of course, Simone. Who else? You don't have a clue what she's really up to, do you?"

"This conversation is over." Hutch was furious and perturbed underneath that. Why did the stranger even care? Hutch went to brush past him, but the old guy put a beefy hand smack in the middle of Hutch's chest. "Don't run off, young man. I'm here to save you from yourself."

"It sounds to me like you're here to bad-mouth Simone. And I don't care to listen anymore."

The man got up in his face. "That little slut in the red dress got pregnant on purpose so she could inherit half of her grandfather's estate. Did your precious Simone ever bother to tell you *that* twist in the story?"

"You're lying," Hutch said. Fury blurred his vision. He wanted to drag the man into the moonlight and see his face. With the mask and the shadows, he hadn't a clue who he was.

"It's no lie. You ask her. And ask her if she knows Maverick. I think you'll be unpleasantly surprised."

"Go to hell." Hutch shoved past him, determined to walk away without indulging in a fistfight. He knew how to fell an assailant, but he'd rather not in this setting.

The other man was older, but bulkier. Hutch never even saw the blow coming. It caught him in the temple. Something sharp, a ring perhaps, cut into his skin. Then he fell hard and hit his head.

Simone began to worry when Hutch didn't come back after half an hour. Fifteen minutes after that she decided to go in search of him. She didn't bother with looking inside the hotel. He had professed a need for fresh air.

Outside, she inhaled deeply, happy to be away from the crush of the party. It was, by every measure, a grand success. She and Naomi and Cecelia could be justifiably proud of what they had managed to pull off. The money raised for Homes and Hearts would be enough to build modest homes for three needy families.

Even knowing that her event was a smashing victory wasn't enough to erase her unease. She walked away from the building toward the parking area. "Hutch!" she called out, her voice fraught with worry. She noticed that the space in and around the cars had been landscaped beautifully. Plenty of places to hide if a person or a couple didn't want to be discovered.

"Hutch!" She stood by his car now, only a little relieved to see it was still there. At least he hadn't left the premises.

Still no answer. She followed a series of small signposts leading back into the trees. For a moment, she stood, irresolute. Normally, she would take more care with her personal safety. This was private property, though. She had seen at least a dozen uniformed security guards mingling with the crowd and monitoring the entrances and exits. No one was out here trying to mug unwary party guests.

At least she hoped not.

She continued to walk, half a mile at least. Her shoes were not meant for traipsing about in the woods. When the pain of a blister became too much to handle, she stopped and took off her expensive footwear. Chances were, the heels were a loss. When she looked back, she could see the hotel in the distance all lit up like a fairy-tale castle. "Hutch!"

A faint groan was her only answer. She almost tripped over him. "Hutch!" She knelt urgently, reassured in part when she heard him breathing. "Hutch, it's Simone. Wake up." Frustrated and scared, she removed his mask and her own. This was no time for pretense.

She had no water, no rag to put water *on*. No way to sponge his face and wake him up. Nevertheless, she got one arm around his shoulders and held him against her breast. "Hutch. Can you hear me? It's Simone. What happened to you?" Even in the shadowy woods, she could see something dark against his temple. When she tested it with a fingertip, she got woozy. Blood. Definitely blood.

Gently, she ran her fingers over his scalp and discovered a second injury, this one an enormous knot. He must have hit his head when he fell. But that didn't explain the wound at his temple.

Why hadn't she brought someone with her? This was the worst rescue attempt in the history of rescue attempts. She wished she remembered her first-aid training.

It seemed as if she held him forever, but in reality only five or ten minutes elapsed. She stroked his forehead carefully, speaking to him in a jumble of whispered words. Fear unlike any she had ever known paralyzed her. She couldn't lose Hutch. Not again. Not forever.

Part of her wanted to run for help. The other part was desperately afraid to leave him here alone in the dark. So she stayed…and she prayed.

At last, Hutch regained consciousness. Slowly, he stirred. She felt him stiffen as he realized where he was. With her help, he sat all the way up, putting his head in his hands, groaning and cursing beneath his breath.

"Tell me how this happened," she pleaded. "Who did this to you?"

"Would you believe I ran into a door?"

"That's not funny. Let me help you up."

He batted her hand away. "I can do it."

It took him two tries, but he managed. His truculent independence was a good thing, because Simone had no idea how she would have managed to stand with a two-hundred-pound man draped across her shoulder.

When he swayed, she reached for him. Again, he eluded her touch. Instead, he leaned on the nearest tree.

"Are you able to walk?" she asked calmly. Something bad had happened. She knew it in her gut. Something beyond Hutch's head wounds. His body language screamed at her to stay away.

He nodded. "I can do it."

They were farther from the hotel than Simone first realized. Hutch made it a quarter of a mile or so before he had to sit down and rest.

"This is stupid," she said. "You stay here. I'll go get help."

"No!" He shouted the word and then cursed again as his outburst clearly caused him agony.

"You might have a concussion."

"I'm a doctor. I don't need *you* to practice medicine."

Now she was certain something was wrong. The disdain in his voice, edged with fury, was a far cry from the Hutch who had wanted to make love to her in a tucked-away corner.

Her heart sank. She waited in silence until he was able to stand again. This time she knew better than to offer help.

They made it only as far as the parking lot. Beneath a streetlight, she caught her first glimpse of the wound at his temple. It was an angry red knot, sliced clean through with a cut that oozed significant amounts of blood.

"Tell me what happened, Hutch. Who did this to you?"

He leaned against his own vehicle. She saw his chest rise and fall as he struggled to speak. "Does the name Maverick mean anything to you, Simone?"

Seventeen

Dread made her blood run cold. Her voice froze in her throat.

Hutch's gaze was bitter. "I see that it does. Your face gives you away."

Hot tears burned her eyes, but she didn't let them fall. "Maverick is the stranger who has been sending mysterious, threatening messages to people in Royal. I got two of his nasty notes, but so have others."

"I don't really care about anyone else but you, Simone. Why would an anonymous blackmailer have anything to hold over *your* head?" The words were icy and clipped. It appeared that Hutch was prepared to be judge and jury.

"How do you even know about this?"

Hutch shrugged, wincing as he did so. "I ran into him on the trail. He confronted me. We argued. I tried to leave. He punched me."

"You need X-rays, Hutch. Please go to the hospital."

"First things first, Simone. Tell me… Is it fair to say that you got pregnant only to satisfy the terms of your grandfather's will?"

Hutch watched her face. Every drop of color washed away. Her eyes welled with tears. He had his answer. "My

God," he said. "It's true." His heart shattered into sharp pieces that stabbed his chest. "You wanted money, so you decided to have a baby. Do you have any idea how incredibly selfish and immoral that is? I've spent my entire career protecting mothers and babies. What you did is unconscionable."

She stood proud and tall as he annihilated her. "I made a foolish mistake. I admit that. But it wasn't really about the money, I swear."

"Of course it wasn't," he sneered.

"I'm telling you the truth," she cried. "Let's go back inside so you can sit down. I'll explain everything."

He shook his head violently, almost welcoming the pain. "I don't need to hear your explanations. I see it all now. That's the real reason you sent me off to Africa, isn't it, Simone? You thought you were dating an up-and-coming surgeon, but then you found out I was more interested in offering my services to the poor than building a mansion in Royal and inviting you to be lady of the manor."

"Tonight isn't a good time to discuss this," she said quietly. "Come back inside with me. I'll get some ice for your head."

When she tried to take his arm, he jerked away. He saw the agony in her eyes, but he didn't care. He didn't care about anything at this moment. "I'm sure there are a number of people at the ball who will be glad to take you home, Simone. You and I are done here. In fact, we're done permanently."

"Hutch, please..." Tears spilled down her cheeks. "You're twisting the facts and coming up with the wrong answers. This isn't as bad as it seems."

He opened the car door and managed not to groan when he slid behind the wheel. "I don't want to hear it, Simone. Goodbye." Barely allowing her time to jump out of the way, he put the car in gear and screeched out of the parking lot.

Though he was cautious getting out of town, when he made it to the interstate, he pressed down on the accelerator and tried to outrun his demons.

Thank God he hadn't told her he loved her. That would have been the final indignity. He felt like a credulous fool. Hell, he *was* a fool. He had let hot sex blind him to Simone's real nature. She was a user and a manipulator.

He drove on into the night with no particular destination in mind. At last, though, his massive headache forced him to pull off and find a motel room for the night. The clerk gaped at him—he must have looked like something out of a horror movie—but handed over the key without protest.

Hutch parked in front of the door to 11C. He had no suitcase, no shaving kit, nothing. What did it matter?

Before he could collapse onto the bed, he had one phone call to make. He was scheduled to work Saturday and Sunday. Fortunately, he was able to get in touch with his second in command, who agreed to switch shifts for a couple of days.

That left Hutch totally unencumbered for the next forty-eight hours. He stumbled into the bathroom, took a quick shower and carefully washed the wound on his head. Then he went back into the other room, pulled back the hideous bedspread and fell facedown on the mattress.

The following morning, he awoke with the hangover from hell. Then he realized he hadn't been drinking. After that, he remembered that Simone was gone. He felt empty inside. Though he was hungry, no amount of food could fix what was wrong with him.

Even so, he couldn't sit around in his tux all weekend. He downed some acetaminophen and made it out to the car on shaky legs. Fortunately, there was a diner nearby... the ubiquitous staple of rural Texas. The waitress took one look at his face and didn't bother with chitchat.

After a hearty meal of bacon, eggs and toast, Hutch felt marginally better. Next on his list was a stop at a discount store. There he found a pair of jeans that fit his long, lanky body. He grabbed a couple of plain knit shirts, some underwear and socks, and cheap sneakers.

Back at the motel, he took another shower. It was hot as hell outside. Afterward, he put on his new duds and stretched out on the bed to watch TV. He rarely had time in his life for something so mindless and sedentary. Every day was filled with work and more work and, recently, Simone.

For the first time, he allowed himself to remember what had happened. There was plenty to be pissed about. The worst was that she had lied to him. By omission, but still. She told him she got pregnant because she wanted to be a mother.

Maybe that part was true, but it wasn't the whole truth. The real truth was money. Lots of it. People would do almost anything for money.

Eventually, his anger was replaced by a dull acceptance. Maybe he wasn't supposed to get married and have a family of his own. Maybe he was supposed to devote his life to helping other people have healthy babies.

By Sunday morning, both bumps on his head were healing nicely. In addition to his new clothes, he had bought a handheld mirror so he could look at the knot on the back of his skull. That was a mistake, because suddenly the memory of Simone stroking his brow and running her fingers over his head came back with a vengeance.

He had to check out of the room by eleven. After that task was accomplished, he sat in his car and clenched the steering wheel with two hands. One thing was certain. He was not returning to Royal in order to worm his way back into Simone's good graces. He probably wasn't even in love with her, not really. He'd been dazzled by good sex and his need to watch over triplets who needed him.

Slowly, he cruised the small town, which was little more than a wide space in the road. They had a fast-food place but little else. The only meal he had eaten was breakfast yesterday. His stomach had been rolling and pitching too much to think about food again. Now, though, he was hungry.

In the drive-through he ordered a double cheeseburger with fries and a Coke. His whole life was in ruins. Why not indulge in junk food, as well?

The calorie-laden meal filled the hole in his stomach. Unfortunately, the aching maw in his chest was not so easily appeased. It hurt. His whole body hurt. So be it.

He turned the vehicle around and headed for Royal. Monday morning would come bright and early. He'd taken far too much advantage of his flexible schedule lately. If he kept this up, the hospital board would decide they had made a mistake in hiring him.

Hutch was good at medicine. He was lousy at love. It made sense to concentrate on the one aspect of his life that had never disappointed him.

When he finally made it back to Royal, darkness had fallen. He deliberately avoided looking at Simone's house when he was forced to pass by it on the way to his. At home, he walked from room to room, pacing aimlessly. In the back bedroom there were still a few boxes he hadn't unpacked yet. Maybe he would list the place this week and move across town.

If he were honest, though, he didn't want to give Simone the satisfaction of knowing she had that kind of power over him. He'd been taken in by a pro, but he didn't have to let it happen again.

Monday morning, he showed up for work clean shaven and bright eyed. He'd slept reasonably well from sheer exhaustion. Despite that, the pain in his chest and his gut remained. Doggedly, he concentrated on the cases at hand. His own personal trauma would not be allowed to interfere with the quality of his performance.

The day lasted a thousand hours. It was all he could do to dispel the images of Simone from his mind. She was what she was. He needed to cut his losses and move on.

He was thirty minutes from finishing his shift when he ran into Janine.

She frowned at him. "You look like hell. Are you ill? Go home, Hutch. Get some rest."

"I'm not sick," he said. "Just tired. I was about to leave."

"I know you're glad Simone is doing better," she said.

Hutch went still. "Oh?"

Janine frowned. "I assumed you've been with her since she got out of the hospital. Isn't that why you look like you're running on four hours' sleep?"

"I haven't seen Simone recently," he said carefully. "What's wrong with her?"

The other doctor stared at him. "She collapsed at the party Friday night. One of the guests found her in the parking lot. No one could find you, so they called an ambulance."

Hutch felt his bones turn to water. "An ambulance?"

"Her blood pressure skyrocketed. She had some kind of panic attack. Because she was already weak from the battle with nausea, we had to give her IV fluids again. Simone told me you were meeting her at her house. That was the only reason I released her when I did."

"I wasn't there," Hutch said slowly. His heart slugged in his chest. "But I'm headed there now. Thank you, Janine."

This couldn't be happening again. Another woman he cared about slipping away, and him powerless to save her. Simone wasn't perfect. If he took a mental step backward, though, he could admit that the love she had demonstrated for her babies was real and fierce.

Maybe he had made too much of her original motives. God knows, he had screwed up at several major points in his own life. Was it fair to judge Simone for *her* missteps, when his had been equally egregious?

The truth dawned slowly, in tandem with incredulity. The reason he'd been so angry with her at the party was because he loved her. Her betrayal had cut straight through to his heart, leaving him bleeding in more ways than one.

He drove like a madman, half expecting to find Simone unconscious or worse. When she answered the door at his first knock, the moment was anticlimactic at best.

"Why did you lie to your doctor?" he demanded, going on the attack.

Simone gazed at him with blank eyes. "What are you doing here, Hutch?" She didn't back up, and she sure as hell didn't invite him in.

Suddenly, everything coalesced into one shining bubble of certainty. "We need to talk." He said the words quietly, trying not to spook her.

"I don't think so." She tried to shut the door, but he stuck his foot in the opening.

"Please, Simone. Let me speak my piece. Then if you want, I'll leave."

She lifted one shoulder in a careless shrug. "Whatever."

He closed the door behind him and followed her to the den. Simone chose a straight-back chair. Hutch decided to stand. "I'm in love with you," he said bluntly.

Her eyelids flickered, but the look on her face didn't change. "I see."

"I don't care if those babies aren't my biological children. I want to be their daddy."

"That's not going to happen." At last a spark of blue in those lovely eyes gave him hope. He couldn't get through to frozen Simone. Angry Simone was another story.

He ran a hand over the back of his neck. "I've done a

lot of thinking in the last seventy-two hours. I was a fool to think your motives for carrying those babies were anything but pure. It was a knee-jerk reaction. You'll never know how sorry I am for not trusting you."

"And that's supposed to make me feel better? You shut me out, Hutch, and not for the first time." Her anger made him wince.

"I know. My only excuse is that your Maverick guy got inside my head. As far as your inheritance goes, who am I to judge? Money isn't a bad thing in and of itself."

"Just people like me…" Her facade cracked. For a moment, he saw how deeply he had hurt her.

"Oh, God, Simone." He knelt at her feet. "I was an ass. I lost you once. I won't lose you again. I love you, and I'm pretty sure you love me, too. Marry me, sweetheart. Let's make a family together. Forgive me, little mama."

She lifted a hand to touch the scab at his temple. "People would talk."

"Let them. Nothing matters except you and me and those precious babies. I won't give up on us. I won't. This is too important."

Simone eluded his hold and stood, fleeing to the other side of the room. She had her back to him, so he couldn't read her expression. "There's something else you should know," she said.

His chest tightened. "Oh?"

After a long silence, she turned around. "You wouldn't be marrying an heiress."

"I don't understand."

"As soon as I deliver these babies, I receive five million dollars. That was the deal. I could only inherit my share of the estate if I produced an heir of my own. Otherwise, all of it went to my father. But my lawyer has drawn up papers to put three million in trust, one million for each of the children when they turn twenty-five."

"Two million is still a lot of money."

"That's how much I'm donating to Homes and Hearts. I didn't want to keep any of it. Not after the way you looked at me Friday night. I need you to understand why I did what I did."

"You don't have to explain. You're entitled to your own choices."

Her short laugh held little humor. "Don't you mean my own mistakes? Here's the thing, Hutch. I've been jockeying for my father's attention my whole life. He and my grandfather made no secret of the fact that I was a disappointment. They wanted a boy, another Parker male to carry on the family tradition. When I heard the terms of the will, I was hurt. And angry. I've never been good enough, you know?"

"Simone—"

She held up a hand, cutting him short. "I don't want you feeling sorry for me. It is what it is. But I'm keeping the land. Those acres of Texas are my birthright. Generations of Parkers have lived there and ranched and farmed and done whatever they had to do to survive. I won't apologize for wanting that legacy, not only for me, but for my children."

He exhaled, his shoulders tight. "Are you done?"

"What else is there to say?"

"You could tell me you love me." He managed to say the words jokingly, but the fear he had ruined something precious choked him. Simone's silence was frankly terrifying. "I'll grovel if need be, my sweet firecracker."

He saw the muscles in her throat work as she swallowed. "You'll want children of your own."

It wasn't a question. He frowned. "I think it would be more correct to say I will want *more* children of my own. I already cherish those three little lives you're carrying. I don't care if their biological father is blond and blue-eyed. We live in a global world. I grew up understanding that many people drew lines to shut me out. I want to make a family with you, of children who never have to know those limits. We'll build our lives around love, Simone. You and I were both made to feel less at times, but that's over. Tell me you believe that. Tell me you love me. Tell me I didn't destroy our second chance."

His life hung in the balance.

Tears rolled down cheeks that were too pale. She came to him at last, sliding her arms around his waist and resting her cheek over his heart. "I do love you, Hutch. I never stopped. And, yes…I want to marry you and make a family together."

"Thank God." He held her tightly, his own eyes damp. "I adore you. I swear you won't regret this."

After long, aching moments, Simone pulled back and looked up at him. "I'm sorry these babies aren't yours," she said, regret shadowing her gaze. "I'm so very sorry."

He shook his head, feeling everything in his world settle into his place. "That's where you're wrong, my love. Those babies *are* mine, in every way that counts. I love them, and I love you. Now hush, and let me kiss you."

Simone smiled at him tremulously. "Only a kiss?"

"Oh, no," he said, scooping her into his arms. "We have a lot of makeup sex coming our way."

His bride-to-be gave him a wicked grin, looking more like herself at last. "Then let's get started, Dr. Hutchinson. I've been waiting a long time for this."

He strode down the hall and up the stairs with his precious burden. "So have I, sweet Simone. So have I…"

* * * * *

September 2017: TAKING HOME THE TYCOON
by USA TODAY bestselling author Catherine Mann.

October 2017: BILLIONAIRE'S BABY BIND
by USA TODAY bestselling author Katherine Garbera.

November 2017: THE TEXAN TAKES A WIFE
by USA TODAY bestselling author Charlene Sands.

December 2017: BEST MAN UNDER THE MISTLETOE
by USA TODAY bestselling author Kathie DeNosky.

* * *

If you're on Twitter, tell us what you think of
Mills & Boon Desire! #MillsandBoonDesire

"I get to kiss you on two occasions."

Kisses. Just kisses. But when had they ever been able to stop at just kisses?

She should protest. End this now.

Instead, Lydia breathed in the feel of having Ian this close to her. So close she caught a hint of his sandalwood aftershave that had occasionally clung to her skin after a night in his bed.

"When would those kisses happen?" Her eyes tracked his. "On what occasions?"

"Once on our wedding day. And once to seal the deal."

"As in…now?" She would not lick her lips even though her mouth went chalk-dry at the thought.

"Right now." His hand found the center of her back, his palm an electric warmth through the mesh fabric of her cover-up. "Do we have a deal, Lydia? One year together and I'll honor all of your terms."

Bad idea. Bad idea. Her brain chanted it as if to urge the words out of her mouth.

She nodded her assent.

* * *

The Magnate's Marriage Merger
is part of the McNeill Magnates trilogy: Those
McNeill men just have a way with women.

THE MAGNATE'S
MARRIAGE MERGER

BY
JOANNE ROCK

MILLS & BOON

First Published in Great Britain 2017
By Mills & Boon, an imprint of HarperCollins*Publishers*
1 London Bridge Street, London, SE1 9GF

© 2017 Joanne Rock

ISBN: 978-0-263-92819-8

51-0517

Our policy is to use papers that are natural, renewable and recyclable products and made from wood grown in sustainable forests. The logging and manufacturing processes conform to the legal environmental regulations of the country of origin.

Printed and bound in Spain
by CPI, Barcelona

Four-time RITA® Award nominee **Joanne Rock** has penned over seventy stories for Mills & Boon. An optimist by nature and a perpetual seeker of silver linings, Joanne finds romance fits her life outlook perfectly—love is worth fighting for. A former Golden Heart® Award recipient, she has won numerous awards for her stories. Learn more about Joanne's imaginative Muse by visiting her website, www.joannerock.com, or following @joannerock6 on Twitter.

For Heather Kerzner,
who inspires everyone she knows.
I miss seeing you in person, my friend,
but I smile to think of all the people you meet
who benefit from having you in their lives.
Thank you for being a bright light!

One

"You found her?" Ensconced in his office at the McNeill Resorts headquarters in New York's Financial District, Ian McNeill glanced up from the file folder on his desk at the private investigator standing before him.

Ian had been back stateside for less than twenty-four hours when he'd gotten the message that the PI he'd hired two months ago had news for him. Ian's older brother, Quinn, had asked for his help to locate an anonymous Manhattan matchmaker who'd tried to pair their younger brother, Cameron, with a renowned ballerina. While that sounded harmless enough on the surface, the potential "bride" had had no knowledge she was supposed to meet Cameron, and it had caused a public scandal.

Bad enough in itself.

Except then the next day, the matchmaker responsible had closed up shop. Ian discovered within the week that the woman had been using a fake name and an assistant as a front to do most of her work. But despite a few leads, he hadn't had any luck finding the woman.

Until now.

"That's her." The investigator, Bentley, pointed to the closed file folder on Ian's desk. The guy was a former college roommate and someone he trusted. Bentley's specialty was digital forensics, but he took the occasional job outside the office if the case was interesting enough or, as in Ian's case, if the work was for a friend. With his clean-shaven face, wire-rimmed glasses and a faded pair of camo pants, Bentley looked more like a teenage gamer geek than a successful entrepreneur. "It's no wonder she used an alias for her matchmaking business. She's certainly well-known in Manhattan by her real name."

Ian slid the file closer, tapping a finger on the cover.

"The New York tabloids sold plenty of papers trying to guess her identity last winter after she paired up one of the Brooklyn Nets with that fashion blogger," Bentley explained. The mystery matchmaker had been responsible for a string of high-profile matches between celebrity clients and wealthy movers and shakers, and her success under an assumed name had the New York social scene all trying to guess who she was.

Curious, Ian leaned back in the cherry-red leather executive chair, manila folder in hand. The late-morning sun slanted in through the huge windows with a view of the river. Taking a deep breath, he flipped open the file to the papers inside.

Only to see an eight-by-ten glossy photo of his ex-lover's face on the top page.

Lydia Whitney smiled back at him with that Mona Lisa grin he'd fallen hard for a year ago—before she'd disappeared from his life after a huge argument.

Ian's blood chilled.

He sat up straight and waved the photo at his friend.

"What kind of sick joke is this?" He hadn't told Bentley about his brief affair with Lydia, but the guy specialized in unearthing digital trails. He must have stumbled across some link between them in his investigation.

"What do you mean?" Bentley frowned. Shifting positions, he leaned forward to peer at the folder as if to double-check what Ian was looking at. He shoved the wire-rimmed glasses up into his shaggy dark hair. "That's her. Lydia Whitney. She's the illegitimate daughter of that billionaire art collector and the sexpot nurse he hired before he died. Lydia's mother sued the family for years for part of the inheritance."

Tension kinked Ian's shoulders. A tic started below his right eye.

"I know who she is." *Damn. It.* Just looking at the picture of Lydia—the Cupid's bow mouth, the dimples, the pin-straight dark hair that shone like a silk sheet flowing over one shoulder—brought the past roaring back to life. The best weeks of his entire life had been spent with those jade-green eyes staring back into his. "I'm asking why the hell there's a photo of her here."

"Ian." Bentley straightened. When his glasses shifted

on his head, he raked them off and jammed them in the front pocket of his olive-green work shirt. "You asked me to find the matchmaker who used the name of Mallory West. The woman who hid behind an alias when she worked for Mates, Manhattan's elite dating service. That's her."

The news sank into Ian's brain slowly. Or maybe it was Bentley's expression that made him take a second look at the file in his lap. His former college roommate was a literal guy, and he wasn't prone to pulling pranks. And he appeared serious about this.

Gaze falling back on Lydia's flawless skin, Ian flipped past the photo to see what else the file contained. The first sheet was a timeline of the events of last February when "Mallory West" had paired Cameron McNeill with ballerina Sofia Koslov. There were notes about Mallory's assistant, Kinley, who'd admitted that Mallory was an alias but refused to identify her boss. Then there were pages of notes about Kinley's whereabouts, including photos of Kinley meeting with Lydia at various places on the Upper East Side—where Ian knew Lydia lived.

"Lydia Whitney is the mystery matchmaker?" As he said the words aloud, they made a kind of poetic sense.

Lydia had ended the most passionate affair of his life when she'd discovered Ian's photo and profile were on a dating website while they were seeing each other. He'd understood her anger, but mistakenly assumed she would listen to his very reasonable explanation. He had not posted the profile or created the account. He'd given cursory permission to his grandfather's personal aide to do so after a heated argument with the old man, but had heard no more about it after that day.

Grandpa Malcolm McNeill was so determined his grandsons should marry that he'd since written the condition into his will. None of his grandsons would inherit their one-third share of the global corporation he'd built until they'd been married for at least twelve months. That stipulation had come last winter, prompting Cameron to find a bride with a matchmaker, leading to the fiasco with Sofia Koslov. But the pressure to wed had started long before that. And it had resulted in Ian's offhanded agreement to allow his profile to be listed on a dating website.

But Lydia didn't care about his explanation. She'd been furious and had cut off all contact, accusing him of betrayal. What if she'd gone into the matchmaking business—at the very same agency his grandfather had used—to spite Ian? In the months after that, Ian had indeed received some odd suggestions for dates that he'd ignored. Could Lydia have been behind those, too? Anger rolled hot through his veins. Along with it, another kind of heat flared, as well.

"I was surprised, too," Bentley observed, moving closer to the window overlooking the river and Battery Park. "I thought Mallory West would be someone with more Park Avenue pedigree. An older, well-accepted socialite with more connections among her clientele." The investigator rested a shoulder on the window frame near Ian's bookcase full of travel guides.

It didn't matter that he could get maps of every country on his phone when he traveled for work. Ian liked seeing the big picture of a foldout map, orienting himself on the plane ride to wherever it was he headed to oversee renovations or development work on resorts all over the globe.

"She used to work as an interior designer," Ian observed lightly, tossing aside the file before he gave any more away about the relationship he hadn't shared with anyone. "Do you know if she still does?"

He needed to think through his response to this problem. He had planned to hand over Mallory West's real identity to Vitaly Koslov—the ballerina's father—who had every intention of suing the matchmaker for dragging his daughter through unsavory headlines last winter. But now that Lydia was the mystery matchmaker? Ian needed to investigate this more himself.

"Yes. Throughout the year she worked as a matchmaker, she continued to take jobs decorating. Since she walked away from the dating service, she is back to working more hours at the design business, but she still volunteers a lot of her time with the single mothers' network I mentioned in the notes."

"Single mothers?" Frowning, Ian opened the file again and riffled through it.

"Moms' Connection. She gives a lot of money to the diaper and food banks." Straightening, Bentley backed up a step. "Anyway, mystery solved, and I've got an appointment in midtown I can't miss. Are we good here?"

"Sure. I'll have my assistant send the payment." Setting aside the file, Ian shoved to his feet and extended a hand to his friend. "I appreciate the time you put into this."

Bentley bumped his fist. "Not a problem. I'd forgo the payment if you could get me a meeting with your brother Cameron."

"Cam?" Ian frowned, thinking his friend must have confused his brothers. "Quinn's the hedge fund manager. Were you thinking of doing some investing?"

"No. It's Cameron I'd like to meet with. Word is, he's working on a new video game and I've got some ideas to speed graphics. I'd prefer to work with an independent—"

"Done." Ian wasn't ready to dive into a discussion full of technojargon, but he knew his younger brother would speak Bentley's language. Cameron was the family tech guy since he owned a video game business in addition to his role in McNeill Resorts. "I'll put him in touch with you."

Seeing his friend out the door, Ian returned to the photo of Lydia Whitney he'd left on the window ledge. He felt the kick-to-the-chest sensation all over again. He needed to see her in person to get to the bottom of this. He'd thought they were finished forever when she broke things off last spring. But clearly, there was unfinished business between them.

Pivoting on the heel of one Italian leather loafer, Ian pressed the intercom button on his phone to page his assistant. In seconds, Mrs. Trager appeared in his doorway, tablet in hand.

"Yes, Mr. McNeill?" The older woman was efficient and deferential in a public setting, but she'd been with him long enough that she didn't pull punches when they worked together privately.

"I need to find a consulting gig, and I'm willing to take a pay cut to secure the right one. It doesn't matter where it is in the world, as long as you can get me onto a project where Lydia Whitney is providing the design services."

Despite the highly unusual request, Mrs. Trager didn't even blink as she tapped buttons on the digital tablet. "I just read in an architectural trade that Ms. Whitney recently committed to Singer Associates for a hotel renovation on South Beach."

"Good." He knew Jeremy Singer well. The guy only bought highly specialized properties that he liked to turn into foodie havens. "I'll call Jeremy myself. Once I speak to him, I'll let you know how soon I'll need a flight."

"Very good." His assistant tucked the tablet under one arm. "I forwarded you an article about the property."

"Thank you." Settling back into the chair behind his oversize desk while Mrs. Trager closed the door behind her, Ian had a plan already taking shape.

He had met Lydia on a shared job site a little over a year ago. Working closely together to develop a unique property had meant they spent long hours in each other's company. Once Lydia realized who she'd be working with, she might very well try to detach herself from the Singer project, but she was too much of a professional to simply walk off a job site.

Which gave Ian at least a few days to figure out what in the hell was going on with Lydia Whitney.

She'd taken some anonymous revenge against him,

it seemed, and he had every intention of calling her on it. But first things first, he needed to slip back into her world in a way that wouldn't send her running. Once he had her in his sights, he would figure out how to exact a payback of his own.

He'd never considered himself the kind of man who could blackmail a woman into his bed. But with the surge of anger still fresh in his veins at this betrayal Ian planned to keep all his options open.

Tilting her head back, Lydia Whitney savored the Miami sun. The weather was still beautiful at eight o'clock in the morning before the real heat and humidity set in. Seated at her outdoor table at the News Café on Ocean Drive, she had a breeze off the water and a perfect cup of coffee to start her day before her first meeting for the new interior design job on South Beach.

The swish of the ocean waves rolling onto the shore, along with the rustle of palm fronds, was a persistent white noise. Foot traffic on both sides of Ocean Drive was brisk even though June was a quieter time for the tourist area. The tables near her were both empty, so she felt no need to rush through her coffee or her splurge breakfast of almond brioche French toast. No one was waiting for her table. She could linger over her newspaper, catching up on the Manhattan social scene.

Perhaps, if she was a more dedicated interior designer, she'd be studying the other recent hotel renovations on South Beach so she could ensure she approached her new job with a singular, distinctive style. But she didn't work like that, preferring to let her muse make up her own mind once she saw the plans and the proposed space.

Instead, Lydia read the social pages with the same avid interest that other women devoted to watching the *Real Housewives* series. She soaked in all the names and places, checking to see who was newly single or newly engaged. It was all highly relevant because, in her secret second job, Lydia still did some moonlighting as a matchmaker to Manhattan's most eligible bachelors and bachelorettes. It was a job she couldn't seem to give up, no matter that she'd had to leave the high-end dating service that had allowed her to work under the alias of "Mallory West."

There'd been a bit of a scandal last winter, forcing Lydia to leave town and take a brief hiatus from matchmaking. Her life had been too full of scandals to allow for another, so she'd buried herself in design work for the next few months, ignoring the tabloid speculation about the true identity of Mallory West. But she'd missed the high drama and the lucrative second income of the matchmaking work, especially since she donated 100 percent of those profits to a charity dear to her heart.

"More coffee, miss?" A slim blonde waitress in a black tee and cargo shorts paused by her table, juggling an armful of menus and a coffeepot.

"No, thank you." Lydia switched off the screen on her tablet by habit, accustomed to protecting her privacy at all times. "I'm almost finished anytime you want to bring the check." She should be early for her first meeting, even if she hadn't done a lot of design homework to prep for it.

Singer Associates, the firm that had hired her to overhaul the interior of the landmark Foxfire Hotel, had been good to her over the years. The firm had hired her for the job where she'd met Ian McNeill, she recalled. Perhaps that had been the only time where a Singer Associates job had a snag attached, since her disastrous affair with Ian had broken her heart in more ways than one.

But that certainly hadn't been Jeremy Singer's fault.

Stuffing in one last bite of the almond brioche French toast, Lydia promised herself to arrive earlier for breakfast tomorrow so she could people watch on Ocean Drive. Most of her potential matchmaking clientele fled to the Hamptons or Europe this time of year, not Miami. But there were always interesting international travelers in South Beach, no matter the season. Not to mention the fresh-faced models who were a dime a dozen on this stretch of beach. And wealthy men were always interested in models and actresses. It couldn't hurt to keep her ears and eyes open for prospects as long as she was in town.

Retrieving her leather tote from the chair beside her, Lydia paid her bill and dialed her assistant back in New York as she walked south on Ocean Drive toward the Foxfire Hotel.

Traffic crawled by as tourists snapped photos of the historic art deco buildings in the area. The cotton candy colors of the stucco walls wouldn't work as well anywhere but at the beach. Here, the pinks and yellows blended with the colorful sunrises and sunsets, while the strong, geometric lines balanced the soft colors. The Foxfire Hotel had lost some of its early grandeur in misguided attempts to update the property, with subsequent owners covering up the decorative spandrels and fluting around doors and windows. Her contract with Singer Associates—the new owner—had assured her those details would be recovered and honored wherever possible.

"Good morning, Lydia." Her assistant, Kinley, answered the call with her usual morning enthusiasm. The younger woman was at her desk shortly after dawn, a feat made easier by the fact that she sublet rooms in Lydia's Manhattan apartment for a nominal fee. "Did you need anything for your morning meeting?"

"No. I'm all set, thanks. But it occurred to me that I could collect some contacts while I'm down here for our second business." Pausing outside the Foxfire, she knew Kinley would understand her meaning and her desire to be discreet. "I wondered if you could see who we know is in South Beach this month and maybe wrangle some fun party invites for me?"

"Are we ready to dive back into the dating world?" Kinley asked. In the background, Lydia heard her turn down the brain-tuning music that her assistant used while she was working.

"I think we've lain low for long enough." Lydia had quit working with the bigger dating agency when Kinley had paired a prominent client with a ballerina who was unaware she'd landed on a list of potential brides.

The snafu hadn't been Kinley's fault; it was caused

by the ballerina's matchmaker, who'd listed her client in the wrong database. The incident had made the New York social pages, implicating "Mallory West" as potentially responsible. Instead of drawing attention to herself and her business, Lydia had simply withdrawn from the matchmaking world, mostly because the prominent client had actually been Ian McNeill's younger brother, Cameron. Lydia hadn't wanted to draw the attention of her former lover just when she'd finally been starting to heal from their breakup.

And from the loss of the pregnancy she'd never told him about. The punch to her gut still happened when she thought about it. But the ache had dulled to a more manageably sized hurt.

"Music to my ears." Kinley's grin was obvious in her tone of voice. "I've been keeping our files up-to-date for just this moment so we'd be ready to go when you gave the okay."

"Excellent. Look for some South Beach parties then." She checked her watch. "I'll touch base with you after the meeting."

"Got it. Good luck." Kinley disconnected the call.

Lydia entered the building, her eyes struggling to adjust to the sudden darkness. The hotel had been closed since the property had changed hands, and was a construction site. Lights were on in the lobby, but some remodeling efforts were already underway with the space torn down to the studs.

"Right this way, ma'am." An older man dressed in crisp blue jeans and wearing a yellow construction hat gestured her toward the back of the lobby where plywood had been laid over the sawdust on the floor. "You must be here for the new owner's meeting." At her nod, he extended a hand. "I'm Rick, the foreman."

She quickened her step, approaching to shake his hand and blinking at the bright white light dangling from an orange electric cord thrown over a nearby exposed rafter.

"Nice to meet you." She'd learned early in her career to make friends with the site supervisor wherever possible since that person usually had a better handle on the job than whatever upper level manager was put on the project.

"We've got you set up at a table in the courtyard." He gestured to two glass doors in the back leading to a broad space of smooth pavers and manicured landscaping open to natural sunlight. "Just through there."

"Great." She straightened the strap on her leather tote and smoothed a hand over her turquoise sheath dress. She wished she'd found a restroom before she left the News Café so she could have touched up her lipstick and checked her hair; she hadn't expected the conditions at the Foxfire to still be so rough. "It's a beautiful day to enjoy the outdoors."

"For another hour, maybe." Rick chuckled to himself. "You New Yorkers all like the heat until you're here for a few days in the summer."

Yes, well. There might be a smidge of truth to that. She'd probably be melting this afternoon. Thanking him, Lydia pushed through the glass door on the right, her eye already picking out a wicker chair off to one side of a large wrought iron table. She was glad to be early so she could pull over the wicker seat and save herself from sitting on wrought iron for however long this meeting lasted.

A small water feature burbled quietly in the open-air courtyard, sending up a soft spray of mist as it tumbled over smooth rocks and landed in a scenic pool surrounded by exotic plantings. Dwarf palms mingled with a few taller species that attracted a pair of squawking green parrots. High up, at the top of the building, a retractable canopy over part of the space dimmed the sun a bit without blocking it completely.

"Lydia." She turned her head sharply to one side to find the source of the familiar baritone.

She hadn't heard that voice in over a year. It couldn't be...

"Ian?" She felt that breathless punch to her gut again, harder than it had been this morning when she'd thought of her lost pregnancy.

Ian McNeill stood in the far corner of the room beside a Mexican-style tea cart laden with silver ice buckets and cold, bottled drinks, his strong arms crossed over his chest. His slightly bronzed skin that hinted at his Brazilian mother's heritage made his blue eyes all the more striking. His dark hair was short at the sides and longer on top, still damp from a morning shower. He was impeccably groomed in his crisp dark suit, gray shirt and blue tie.

Ian McNeill. The lover who'd broken her heart. The man who'd kept his profile on a matchmaker's site while he dated her, prompting her to go into the matchmaking business just so she could try her hand at sending horrible dating prospects his way. She'd outgrown the foolish need for vengeance after she'd lost their baby. So it had been an accident when she'd paired Ian's brother with that famous ballerina.

How much did Ian know about any of that?

"Nice to see you, Lydia," he said smoothly, approaching her with the languid grace of a lifelong athlete. "A real pleasure to be working with you again."

His eyes held hers captive for a long moment while she debated what he meant by "pleasure." The word choice hadn't been an accident. Ian was the most methodical man she'd ever met.

"I didn't know—" She faltered, trying to make sense of how she could have taken a job where Ian McNeill played any role. "That is, Jeremy Singer never told me—"

"He and I agreed to exchange peer review services on a couple of random properties—a recent idea we had to keep our project managers on their toes and revitalize the work environment." Ian brought a bottled water to the table and set it down before tugging over the wicker chair for her. "I was pleased to hear you were in line for this job, especially since you and I work so well together."

He held the chair for her. Waiting.

Her heart thrummed a crazy beat in her chest. She could not take a job where she'd be working under Ian. *Oh, God.*

She couldn't even think about being *under Ian* without heat clawing its way up her face.

And, of course, those blue eyes of his didn't miss

her blush. He seemed to track its progress avidly as the heat flooded up her neck and spilled onto her cheeks, pounding with a heartbeat all its own.

When the barest hint of a smile curved his full, sculpted lips, Lydia knew he wasn't here by accident. It had all been by design. She wasn't sure how she knew. But something in Ian's expression assured her it was true.

She opened her mouth to argue. To tell him they wouldn't be working together under any conditions. But just then the glass doors opened again and the job engineer strode into the room with Rick, the foreman she'd met briefly. Behind them, two other women she didn't know appeared deep in conversation about the history of the Foxfire, comparing notes about the size of the original starburst sign that hung on the front facade.

Lydia's gaze flicked to Ian, but the opportunity to tell him what she thought about his maneuvering was lost. She'd have to get through this meeting and speak to Jeremy Singer herself since she couldn't afford to walk off a job.

But there was no way she could work with the man who'd betrayed her.

Even if he affected her now as much as ever.

Two

Doing his damnedest not to be distracted by the sight of Lydia's long legs as she sat on the opposite side of the room, Ian paid close attention in the Foxfire meeting, appreciating the favor Jeremy Singer had done by letting Ian step in at the last minute. Having worked with the resort developer on a handful of other projects over the years, Ian understood the man's style and expectations, so he would offer whatever insights he could on the job site. Since launching his own resort development company on a smaller, more exacting scale than his grandfather's global McNeill Resorts Corporation, Ian wasn't normally in the business of overseeing other people's buildings when he was in a position to design his own. Yet he did enjoy having a hand in specialty public spaces like the foodie-centered resort Singer planned for the revamped Foxfire.

One of the drawbacks of running his own business was less day-to-day focus on his clients' concerns, building restrictions and the inevitable permit night-mares. Being on-site now and again gave him renewed awareness of the obstacles in his work. So this brief stint at one of Jeremy Singer's buildings was no hardship.

And the payoff promised to be far greater than the sacrifice of his time.

Ian's gaze slid to Lydia's profile as the meeting broke up. She remained in her seat on the opposite side of the room, speaking to a woman in charge of indoor air quality on the job site. The room was full of people who would only play a limited role in the renovation, but Ian had wanted to attend the meeting and get up to speed as quickly as possible. The enclosed courtyard was crowded, too, ensuring Lydia couldn't walk out the door before he caught up with her.

Her turquoise dress skimmed her slight curves and was accented by a belt with a thin tortoiseshell buckle emphasizing a trim waist. The hem ended just above her knee, showcasing her legs in high-heeled gold sandals. Her straight dark hair slid over one arm as she turned, still in conversation with the other woman, her dimple flashing once as they continued their animated talk. Clearly, the two of them knew each other, but then again, they moved in a small world of elite professionals.

Would Lydia try to leave without speaking to him privately? He didn't think so. She was not a woman to mince words. And while he'd caught her off guard—clearly—by showing up here without her knowledge, she'd had two hours during the meeting to consider her course of action. She would confront him directly.

The idea tantalized far more than it should have. She'd walked away from him. Worse, she'd meddled in his affairs without his knowledge. Even that, he might have forgiven. But how could she extend her vengeance to his family? She'd matched his brother Cameron to an oblivious stranger. The meeting—and Cameron's impulsive proposal in the middle of a private airport—had been caught on film by a dance magazine that was doing a special on the ballerina and would-be bride. The episode put their older brother, Quinn, in the awkward position of trying to smooth things over in the media to placate the woman's furious and embarrassed father.

Lydia had been responsible for all of that, and Ian wasn't about to forget it. Even if things had worked out in the end when Quinn fell hard for the ballerina himself. The two were now engaged. Happy.

Ian exchanged pleasantries with the site manager as the rest of the group filed out through the glass doors and back into the main building, leaving him and Lydia alone in the interior courtyard. A water feature gurgled in the space as yet untouched by the remodel.

The babble of water over a short rock wall softened the impact of the sudden silence. Shoving to his feet, Ian stalked around the wrought iron table to where Lydia sat, gathering her things and tucking a silver pen into the sleeve inside her leather tote bag.

"I need to speak with you privately," she informed him, slinging the tote onto one shoulder as she met his gaze.

He'd forgotten how green her eyes were. He remembered staring into those jade depths while the two of them stood in a languid pool off the Pacific on a beach in Rangiroa, just north of Tahiti. He'd thought then that her eyes matched the color of the water—not really emerald green or aqua that day, but a brilliant green.

He'd thought a whole lot of foolish things then, though. A mistake he would not be repeating.

"I figured you might." He inclined his head. "My car is outside."

For the briefest moment, she nipped her lower lip. *Uncertain? Or unwilling?*

Or tempted? Ah...

"We might as well work while we talk," he explained. He didn't want her to think he planned to cart her off and ravish her at the first opportunity, the way he once would have after a tedious two-hour meeting. "Traffic should be reasonable at this hour. We can drive over to Singer's inspiration hotels and take a look around."

"Of course." She pivoted on her heel and preceded him toward the exit. "Thank you."

His eyes dipped to the gentle sway of her hips in the turquoise silk, the hint of thigh visible in the short slit at the back of her skirt. He didn't recognize the dress, but the thighs were a different story. He and Lydia had been crazy about each other, tearing one another's clothes off at the slightest opportunity. One time, they'd barely made it to an outdoor shower stall on their way up to his villa from the beach.

Now her hair had grown longer, reaching to the middle of her back. Last year, it had been cut in a razor-sharp line across the middle of her shoulder blades. Today, it draped lower, the ends trimmed in a V that seemed to point to the sweet curve of her lovely ass.

He reached around her to open the door for her, leading them into the Miami sun, grown considerably warmer over the last two hours. Once outside, he flicked open the top button on his shirt beneath his tie, knowing full well this noontime excursion wasn't going to be all about work and knowing with even more certainty that his rising temperature had more to do with the woman in step beside him than the sun above him.

"This way." He pointed toward the valet at the next hotel over, grateful the attendant behind the small stand noticed Ian and sent one of the younger workers into the parking garage with a set of keys.

No doubt his rented convertible BMW would be driven out soon enough. He ushered Lydia to one side of the street while they waited, his hand brushing the small of her back just long enough to feel the gentle glide of silk on his fingertips and the warmth of her body underneath.

The South Beach scenery—palm trees, exotic cars, brilliant blue water and beach bodies parading to and from the shore on the other side of the street—was nothing to him. Lydia had his undivided attention.

"You just happened to be in Miami?" She turned on him suddenly, the frustration that had been banked earlier finding fresh heat now that they were alone. "On a job that has nothing to do with McNeill Resorts or your personal development company?"

He caught a hint of her fragrance, something tropical that stood out from the scent of the hibiscus hedge behind her.

"I am here to see you." He saw no need to hide his intentions. "Although even I didn't realize until recently how much unfinished business remained between us."

"So pick up the phone." She bit out the words with careful articulation, though her voice remained quiet. "There was no need to fly fifteen hundred miles to ambush me on my project."

"*Our* project," he reminded her, letting the "ambush" remark slide. "And I saw no sense in calling you when you purposely went into hiding after we left Rangiroa." He'd been furious that she'd blocked him in every way possible, giving him no access to her unless he wanted to be truly obnoxious about seeing her. He refused to be that guy who wouldn't give up on a woman who wanted nothing to do with him.

"You knew how I felt about public scandals." She hugged her arms around herself for a moment, eliciting an unwelcome twinge of empathy from him.

With a very famous father and a mother who was unrepentant about going after his billions, Lydia had received way too much media attention as a child and straight through her teen years. Her parents were the kind of media spectacle that the tabloids cashed in on again and again. In Lydia's eyes, all her mother had done was to destroy Lydia's relationships with her father's family.

"You had no reason to believe I would ever make our affair public." He spotted the silver Z4 rolling out of the parking garage and pointed out the vehicle to her. "You know me better than that."

"I only thought I knew you, Ian."

She didn't need to say any more than that for him to hear the damning accusation behind the words as they headed toward the car.

Tipping the valet service, Ian grudgingly allowed one of the other attendants to close Lydia's door behind her, not surprised the thin veneer of civility between them was already wearing thin. He'd cared deeply about her and he was sure she'd once felt the same about him. The raw hurt of tearing things apart had left them both full of resentments, it seemed.

Indulging those bitter emotions wasn't going to get him what he wanted, however. His objective remained to find out what she was doing messing with his life and his family's welfare through her so-called match-making efforts.

"Do you mind having the top down?" he asked. They'd shared a Jeep with no top to roam around the French Polynesian island a year ago, but the stiff-shouldered woman in his passenger seat today bore little resemblance to the laughing, tanned lover of those days.

"It's fine." She reached into the leather tote at her feet and retrieved a dark elastic hair band that she used to twist her hair into a tail and then a loop so the pieces were all tucked away somehow. "Maybe having some fresh air blowing around this conversation will help us keep our tempers."

He pulled out of the hotel parking area and onto Ocean Drive.

"Either that or the Miami heat will only fire things up more." The question was would it result in hot frustration? Or hotter lust?

Seeing her arranging her long, dark hair had already affected him, and he knew his brain had stored away the image to return to later.

In slow motion.

"I prefer to think optimistically." She leaned back in her seat as he slowly drove north through heavy traffic that still didn't come close to the gridlock that plagued this city in the evenings. "So where are we going?" She swiveled in her seat. "There are more of the traditional art deco buildings to the south of us, I think."

"That may be, but I've got a spot in mind that will give us the lay of the land first." He needed to get her alone. Somewhere private where he could focus his full attention on the conversation.

"The lay of the land?" She shielded her eyes and peered ahead of them. "Florida isn't exactly famous for its high ground."

"That's what penthouses are for." He steered into the right lane where the street began to widen even as the traffic didn't seem to lessen.

"A penthouse?" She shifted to face him in her seat, her eyes narrowing. "You can't be serious."

"You'll like this, trust me."

"Not *your* penthouse?" she pressed.

Was that a hint of nervousness in her voice? Either she didn't trust him or she didn't trust herself. He tucked that intriguing thought away.

"I took the penthouse suite at the Setai." He pointed to the luxury hotel looming just ahead of them. "It comes with access to a private rooftop pool. We can speak up there and take in the whole art deco district at the same time."

"You're in the penthouse at the Setai?" She turned her attention to the front of the hotel as he steered the BMW toward the waiting valet. "One of the ten most expensive suites in the known world?"

"Is it?" He didn't usually indulge in that kind of extravagance when he traveled, but then, this wasn't his usual brand of business trip. "Then it's a property that will appeal to the designer in you."

He wondered if she would have agreed if it weren't for the private valet and concierge service already giving them the red carpet treatment as the car pulled up. Lydia's attention was on the attendant who opened her door. Another attendant offered to help with her tote as he discreetly asked what she might require.

That alone made the suite pay for itself, because in the end, Lydia got on the private elevator with Ian and headed to the fortieth floor where they could be alone.

Lydia, you have lost your mind.

She'd been so distracted by the gracious service as she entered the famous hotel that she'd somehow ended up speeding her way toward Ian McNeill's private penthouse suite. She wished it was as simple as the designer in her taking a professional interest in a world-class luxury space, the way Ian had suggested. But she feared that it was more complex than that. Ian had swept her right back into his world today, imposing his will on her work environment, and then staking a claim on her private time, too.

Yes, she'd wanted to speak to him privately. But damn it, that didn't necessitate a trip to a hotel suite with a one-night price tag as high—higher—than what many people paid for an automobile.

"Ian." She took a deep breath before turning to face him.

Just then, the elevator doors swished open, revealing the most gorgeous, Asian-inspired decor imaginable, framed by views of the sparkling sapphire Atlantic out of window after window.

"Wow." Her words dried up.

As a student of architectural design, she did indeed find a lot to savor about the rooms, the layout and the exquisite care taken to render every surface beautiful. She'd read about this suite before in an effort to keep up-to-date on the world's premiere properties, so she'd seen photos of the Steinway in the foyer and—oddly—recalled reading about the absolute black granite in the shower. She guessed the penthouse was close to ten thousand square feet with the double living rooms, a full dining room for ten people and multiple bedrooms. As she walked around the space in admiring silence, her eyes lit on the private terrace overlooking the beach below.

Ian had gotten ahead of her somehow. No doubt she'd been lost in her own thoughts as she'd circled the living areas of the penthouse. But she spotted him in the lounge area of the terrace, speaking to waitstaff who'd set up silver trays in a serving area under a small cabana. White silk had been woven and draped through a pergola, creating a wide swath of shade over the seating.

In all of this exotic, breathtaking space, Ian himself still seemed to be the most appealing focal point. In his crisp blue suit custom-tailored to his athletic frame, he drew the eye like nothing else. His whole family was far too attractive, truth be told. She'd seen photos of his Brazilian mother, who'd left Ian's daredevil father long ago. They'd made a glamorous couple together. Liam McNeill had the dark hair and striking blue eyes of his Scots roots, resulting in three sons who all followed a Gerard Butler mold, although Ian had a darker complexion than the others.

If the gene pool hadn't been kind enough there, Ian was also relentlessly athletic. He'd sailed, surfed and swum regularly while they worked on the hotel property in French Polynesia, and the results of his efforts were obvious even when he was wearing a suit. When he was naked…

Blinking away that thought, she forced her feet forward, refocusing her gaze on the glass half wall surrounding the huge terrace forty stories up. She breathed in the salty scent of the sea that wafted on the breeze while Ian excused the servers.

Soon, she felt his presence beside her more than she heard him. He moved quietly, a man in tune with his surroundings and comfortable enough in his own skin that he never needed to make a noisy entrance. Damn, but she didn't want to remember things that she'd liked about him.

"You were right," she admitted, relaxing slightly as she stared out at the limitless blue of the ocean. "In bringing me here, I mean. It's stunning. Although calling this space a penthouse hardly does justice to how special it is."

"I enjoyed seeing your reaction to it." Out of the corner of her eye, she saw Ian's posture ease. One elbow came up beside hers on the half wall as he joined her at the railing. "Being on the design end of so many projects—and experiencing all the headaches that entails—makes it easy to forget why we enjoy what we do. Then, you see a place like this where they got everything right. It's a reminder that not every project is about a bottom line."

She hesitated. "Yes. Except how many people will ever get to enjoy it?"

"Not enough," he agreed easily. "But if we're inspired, we'll do a better job with properties like Foxfire. And that's an attainable vacation for a lot of people." Turning from the view, he gestured toward the cabana where the food trays waited.

A few minutes later, she had settled herself on a long, U-shaped couch that wrapped around a granite coffee table under the shade of white silk, a plate of fresh fruit and cheese balanced on one knee. Ian poured them each a glass of prosecco even though she'd already helped herself to a bottle of water.

She'd forgotten how extravagantly he lived. While her father had been extremely wealthy, her mother hadn't always been. After suing Lydia's father's estate, she'd eventually taken great joy in overspending once her settlement came through, but by then, Lydia had moved on to her own life. Her father had left her a small amount that she had put toward the purchase of her Manhattan apartment, but his legally recognized children had inherited his true wealth. Besides, Lydia had spent her childhood perpetually worried that her mother would squander their every last cent on frivolous things, so Lydia maintained a practical outlook on finances, careful never to live above her means.

Still, who wouldn't enjoy a day like this?

"You mentioned you wanted to speak to me privately after today's meeting," Ian reminded her as he handed her the sparkling prosecco in a cut crystal glass. A single strawberry rested at the bottom. "Why?"

"Isn't it obvious?" She sipped at the bubbles and set the drink aside. "Ian, I can't work with you on this project."

He'd removed his jacket to expose the gray silk shirt beneath. His muscles stretched the fabric as he moved, reminding her of the honed body beneath.

"You're a professional. I'm a professional. I think we can put aside personal differences for the sake of the project." His expression gave away nothing.

Old hurts threatened to rise to the surface, but she kept a tight rein on those feelings.

"Don't you think you're diminishing what we once meant to each other to call our breakup a 'personal difference'?" Her chest squeezed at all that she'd lost afterward.

One eyebrow lifted as he met her gaze. "No more than you diminished what we meant to one another by playing matchmaker for me afterward, Mallory West."

Three

He knew.

Lydia felt her skin chill despite the bright South Beach sun warming the thin canopy of silk overhead. For a long moment, she only heard the swoosh of waves far below the rooftop terrace, the cry of a few circling gulls and her own pounding heart.

"That's what this is about?" she managed finally, shoving off the deep couch cushions to pace the lounge area near the hot tub. "You found a way to play a role in the same design project as me so you could confront me with this?"

"You don't deny it then?"

"I played a childish game of revenge after we broke up, Ian. You caught me. But it hardly did any damage when you never actually went on a date with any of those women." She'd started her matchmaking career out of spite. She wasn't proud of it, but she had been in a very dark place emotionally.

"No. But I also didn't post my profile on that match-making site, as I tried to tell you from the start. My grandfather's assistant ran the photo and the profile after Grandad twisted my arm about marriage." Ian unfolded himself from his place on the couch to stand, though he did not approach her. "So my grandfather personally reviewed your suggestions that I date…those women." His jaw flexed with annoyance.

She'd sent ridiculous dating suggestions to the man-ager of Ian's profile. She'd been furious to discover he had an active profile on a popular dating website while she'd been falling in love with him. And his refusal to understand why she was upset, his infuriatingly calm insistence that it meant *nothing*, had shredded her.

She'd been tired and overly emotional at the time, but she'd credited it to her broken heart and deep feel-ings for him. Only a week later, she'd discovered she was pregnant.

"I was hurt by your cavalier dismissal of my con-cerns." She moved toward the glass half wall, taking comfort from the sight of the ocean and the relentless roll of incoming waves. "It was petty of me."

"My grandfather was the one who was disappointed." Ian stalked closer, his broad shoulders blocking her view of the water. "But your temporary anger with me doesn't explain why you deceived my younger brother into thinking he was meeting a potential bride, only to have the woman turn out to be completely unaware of his existence." Cool fire flashed in Ian's eyes as he studied her. "It's one thing to lash out at me. But my family?" He shook his head slowly. "No."

"That was an accident." Her temples throbbed with the start of a tension headache as this meeting quickly spiraled out of control. "A genuine accident. Although it didn't help that Cameron signed a waiver saying he didn't care if the matches had been vetted—"

"He clicked a button online to agree to that. Hardly the same as signing something."

"But my assistant explained to him—"

"An assistant who impersonated you, by the way."

Which was something Lydia regretted tremendously. But she'd handed off Cameron McNeill as a client because she hadn't been ready to face Ian's brother with her emotions still raw where Ian was concerned. By the time she'd realized the error in Cameron's match, it was too late to fix it. Jumping in to deal with the aftermath would have meant facing Ian in person—and she hadn't been ready for that at a time when she'd only just started to recover emotionally from the miscarriage.

"I am sorry about that." She pivoted to face him head-on. "I really weighed the options for getting involved after I realized what had happened. But would you really have wanted me to step in when Quinn and Sofia had already announced an engagement? I didn't want to undermine whatever was happening between them by drawing even more attention to the mismatch with Cameron." She'd followed the courtship of Sofia Koslov and Quinn McNeill closely and it had been obvious to her from the photos of them together that they were crazy about each other. "And yes, I was trying to protect my identity. My work had become very important to me by then."

"Very important or very lucrative?"

"Both." She refused to be cowed by him. Straightening to her full height she narrowed her gaze. "I put one hundred percent of the profits after expenses from matchmaking toward a very worthy cause."

"Moms' Connection."

His quick reply unsettled her. How much did he know about her life in the past year? Her shoulders tensed even tighter.

"How did you know that?"

He rested an elbow on the railing, relaxing his posture.

"That's actually one of your less well-guarded secrets. I hired a friend to learn the identity of Mallory West in the hope of sparing Cameron any further embarrassment." Ian shrugged a shoulder. "And to spare Sophia Koslov further embarrassment, since Cameron's potential bride turned out to be the love of Quinn's life."

"I read about that. I'm glad that some good came out of the situation." She hesitated a moment before deciding to press on. "You hired someone to find me?"

What else did he know about the last year of her life? Worry knotted her gut, but she had to hope that the confidentiality of her medical records had withstood his investigation.

"I wasn't expecting to find *you*, Lydia. I hired someone to track Mallory West." His words were clipped. "I can't begin to describe my surprise at discovering you'd had a hand in my affairs ever since you broke things off with me last summer."

"You gave me no choice," she reminded him, remembering the sting of seeing his smiling, handsome face on a friend's page of potential matches on the Mates International dating site. "You not only betrayed me, you did so publicly. If we'd been dating in Manhattan instead of Rangiroa, I can only imagine the fallout." She needed to leave now. To escape whatever dark plans he had in mind by following her to South Beach and insinuating himself back into her life. "But thankfully, that wasn't the case and the rumors of our affair died quickly enough."

Pivoting on her heel, she retrieved her tote bag, prepared to request an Uber.

"I just have one question." Ian followed her across the private terrace, his arms folded over his broad chest as he walked.

"I'm listening." She found her phone and clutched it in one hand.

"Why do all the profits go to a charity benefiting single mothers?"

It was on the tip of her tongue to lie. To tell him that it was a way to help women like her mother, who'd allowed being a single parent to turn her into a bitter person.

But she knew that he wouldn't believe her. He knew her better than that, understood the complex and difficult relationship she had with her mom.

"I met a few women who worked with the group." That was true. Still, her mouth went dry and the heat was beginning to get to her. This whole day was getting to her.

No. Ian McNeill was getting to her.

Those intensely blue eyes seemed to probe all her secrets, seeing right through her.

"How? Where?" he pressed, even as he gestured her toward a seat on the couch again.

He lowered himself to sit beside her as she wondered how much he already knew. She didn't want to equivocate if his personal investigation had already revealed the truth.

"At a support group for single mothers." Her eyes met his. Held. "I attended a few meetings in the weeks after our affair." She had been so touched by those women. So helped by their unwavering support. She took a deep breath. "That was before I lost the pregnancy and... our child."

Ian felt like he'd stepped into the elevator shaft and fallen straight down all forty stories.

"What?" He thought he'd been shocked to discover Lydia was the woman behind Mallory West. Yet the blow he'd felt then was nothing compared to *this*. "You were pregnant when you ended things between us?"

She'd been so fierce and definite. So unwilling to listen to any explanation even though Ian hadn't done a damn thing to post that stupid profile. And all the time she'd been carrying his child? A new anger surged—putting all the other frustrations on the back burner.

How could she hide that from him?

"I didn't realize it at the time. But yes." Lydia unclenched her hand where she'd been holding her cell phone. Setting it carefully aside on the table beside their untouched lunch, she shifted her tote to the outdoor carpet at her feet. She seemed unsure where to look, her eyes darting around the terrace without landing on any one thing. "I realized later that the pregnancy hormones were probably part of the reason why I reacted so strongly to finding your profile online. But it never crossed my mind that I could be pregnant for another week, and then—"

"We were so careful." His mind went back to those long, sultry nights with her. Lydia all wrapped around him in that villa with no walls where they could look straight out into the Pacific Ocean, the sea breezes cooling their damp bodies after their lovemaking. "Every time we were careful."

"There were a couple of nights we went in the water," she reminded him, nibbling on her lower lip. "The hot tub once. And the ocean…remember?"

Her green eyes brought him right back to one of those moments when he'd been looking into them as a rainfall shower sprayed over them in the outdoor Jacuzzi. Her delicate hands had smoothed over his shoulders, nails biting gently into his skin as he moved deeper inside her.

"Yes." His voice was hoarse with how damn well he remembered. "I recall."

She pursed her lips. "Maybe one of those times. I don't know. But I can tell you that I tested positive when it occurred to me I might be pregnant and then—"

"I had a right to know." That part was only just beginning to really take hold in his brain, firing him up even more. "When you first found out, you should have told me."

"Because things had ended so happily between us?" she retorted, her brow furrowed. "Ian, you didn't even deny that you were going to date other people. You said your family wanted you to find a wife."

"That could have been you." He articulated the words clearly, restraining himself when he wanted to roar them for all of South Beach to hear. "And I didn't deny your ludicrous accusation about dating other people because I had no intention of dating anyone but you."

Hell, he'd fallen in love with her. He'd been ready to propose, thought they knew everything about each other there could be to know. And it had insulted him in the very fiber of his being that a woman he cared about so much could think so poorly of him that he would advertise himself for dates with other women. Clearly, they hadn't known each other as well as he thought. He'd been too damn impulsive and mistook intense—very intense—passion for love.

Later, he'd forgotten about his grandfather's plan, pure and simple, because he'd been caught up in his work and in Lydia. Plus, they'd been a million miles from home and the pressure of the McNeill world.

She went so quiet that he wondered what she was thinking. Instead of asking, he helped himself to a swig of the prosecco they'd left out on the table, trying to settle his own thoughts.

"As I said, I was probably operating under the influence of pregnancy hormones. I've spoken to a lot of other mothers since then, and they say it's a powerful chemical change." She surprised him with her practical admission, especially after the matchmaking games she'd played last summer.

Maybe time had softened her initial anger with him. Or showed her that he might not be fully to blame for his grandfather's matchmaking transgression.

"Setting aside the fact that you never informed me about our child—" he took a deep breath as he willed himself to set it aside, too "—can you tell me what happened? Why do the doctors think you miscarried?"

He had a million other questions. How far along had she been? Had she ever considered reaching out to him before she'd lost the baby? What if the pregnancy had gone to full term? Would she have ever contacted him?

That last question, and the possibility that the answer was no, burned right through him.

"The cause was undetermined. My doctor assured me miscarriages happen in ten to twenty-five percent of pregnancies for women in their child-bearing years, so it's not that unusual." She laid a hand across her abdomen as she spoke. An unconscious gesture? "The most common cause is a chromosome abnormality, but there's no reason to believe it would happen to me again."

Hearing the vulnerability in her voice, seeing it for himself in her eyes, made some of the resentment ease away.

"I'm sorry I wasn't there with you." He reached to take her hand resting beside him on the couch.

Her skin felt cool to the touch despite the heat. She

stared down at his fingers clasping hers, but didn't move away from the connection.

"I didn't handle it well." She retrieved her bottle of water and took a long drink. "It might have been hormones, but the sadness was overwhelming. But I spent a lot of time with the mothers' group I told you about. Being with them helped me to heal."

A row of misters clicked on nearby to provide water to the exotic flowers tucked in a planter by the doors to his suite. The cool spray glanced over their skin before the water evaporated in the Miami sun glinting off white stone walls all around the rooftop terrace.

"That's why you support this group now—Moms' Connection." He tried to fit the pieces together in his mind to figure out what she'd been through in the past year.

"Yes. I met some incredibly strong women who inspired me. Seeing their efforts to help other single mothers made me realize how petty it was for me to meddle in the matches that were being sent to you." She hesitated. "I started to put more effort into really matching up people and I discovered I was good at it."

Sliding her hand from his grip, she smoothed it along the hem of her dress, straightening the fabric.

"So you kept at it and used the funds to help the group that helped you." His vision of her shifted slightly, coming into sharper focus. "And what happened with Sofia Koslov and my brother was, as you say, a genuine accident."

"Yes. I shouldn't have taken your brother on as a client, but by that time, Kinley was filling in for me often.

I was away for several weeks last winter doing a job for a singer who moved to Las Vegas for an extended contract and wanted me to design her new home." Lydia picked one red strawberry from a plate on the table. "But the profits from the matchmaking work were doing a lot of good for the mothers' organization by then. I didn't want to let my support of a good cause lapse. I still don't."

She bit into the strawberry, her lips molding to the red fruit in a way that made his mouth go dry.

"You must be aware that Sofia Koslov's father is an extremely wealthy and powerful man. He allowed my family to investigate the matter of Mallory West's identity since she's now engaged to Quinn, but when he finds out who you are, he has every intention of suing." Ian hadn't told a soul about discovering that Lydia was behind the debacle.

He hadn't even told his two brothers, which didn't sit particularly well with him. But he'd been handed an opportunity to bargain with this woman and he wasn't about to lose it.

Initially, he'd entertained fantasies about leveraging his position for revenge. But now he knew that his relationship with Lydia was far more complex than that. There was still an undeniable spark between them—and a connection that went deeper than just the attraction. Otherwise, the news of her losing a pregnancy wouldn't have affected him like a sledgehammer to his chest.

Which meant he was going to be bargaining for something more than sensual revenge.

"I had hoped now that Sofia is marrying your brother

later this month, her father wouldn't want to draw public attention to the matchmaking mishap." The worry in Lydia's eyes was unmistakable as the ocean breeze tousled her dark hair where it rested on her shoulders.

Ian buried any concern he might have had about her feelings. She certainly hadn't taken his into account when she hid the news of his child from him.

"Vitaly Koslov strikes me as a man who does not forget a slight to his family." Ian respected that. He wasn't inclined to let a slight to his go unchecked either. "But I have a suggestion that might help you avoid a civil suit and restore your matchmaking business."

"You do?" The hope that sparked in her gaze ignited a response in him.

This was a good plan. And it was going to solve problems for them both.

"You are aware that, due to familial pressure, I am in the market for a wife?" The terms of his grandfather's will had caused him no end of grief in his relationship with Lydia, after all. "Last summer, my grandfather had already started to apply pressure to wed, but this winter, he created legally binding terms in a rewritten will. In order to retain family control of my grandfather's legacy, my brothers and I each need to marry for at least twelve months."

"But you already have your own successful business—"

"Keeping McNeill Resorts in the family is about legacy, not finances." He wouldn't allow his third of the company to go to strangers. Cameron and Quinn felt the same about the family empire.

"I can help you find someone, if you'd like a private consultation." Her words were stiff and formal.

Did she honestly not guess his intent? Or was she bracing for the inevitable?

"That's kind of you. But I'm perfectly capable of choosing a temporary wife for myself."

"You're taking over that task from your grandfather?" She arched an eyebrow at him, challenging.

With just one fiery look, she reminded him how good it was going to be when he touched her again.

And he would touch her again. Soon.

"Definitely. My search just ended, Lydia." He allowed himself the pleasure of skimming a knuckle down her bare arm. "You will solve both our problems if you agree to be my wife for the next twelve months."

Four

"He proposed to you?" Lydia's assistant, Kinley, squealed in Lydia's ear late that night during a conference call to catch up on business back in New York.

With her feet tucked beneath her on the sofa while she ate her room service salad, Lydia shifted her laptop on the coffee table to reduce the glare from the reading lamp. Kinley's hazel eyes were huge, her face comically close to her webcam as she gestured for Lydia to hurry up with her story.

"Yes." Stabbing a cherry tomato with her fork, Lydia tried to ignore the butterflies in her stomach that the memory invited. Why on earth would she feel flattered to be part of Ian's scheme to use her in order to deceive his grandfather? But the fluttery feeling in her belly had been undeniable—both when Ian suggested marriage, and now as she related the story to Kinley. "He means it strictly as a business arrangement."

Although when he'd asked her, he'd been trailing the back of one knuckle down her cheek, making her think about how good they were together and what the man's touch could do to her. So she hadn't said no as quickly as she would have wished.

"And he would protect you from scandal if it comes to a lawsuit over the match between his brother and Sofia Koslov?"

Lydia watched her assistant on the computer screen. Back in New York, Kinley's pen hovered over a crossword puzzle in the newspaper, a habit she'd developed once she started skimming the social pages for any interesting leads in the matchmaking world.

"He made it clear he would keep my name out of the headlines and negotiate with Vitaly Koslov if there are legal repercussions." The Ukrainian entrepreneur was the founder of the mega-successful start-up, Safe Sale, and was worth billions. Lydia had read all about him after the bad press she'd received for the misfire with his daughter's matchmaking experience.

And Ian would swoop in and save her. Just like she'd once dreamed a romantic hero would do for the woman he loved, back when she still believed in happily-ever-afters. Foolish, foolish visions for her to indulge when she'd grown up with the most cynical of parents whose relationship was a continual power struggle.

"So what did you say?" Kinley pressed, tapping her pen impatiently against the newspaper.

"I turned him down in no uncertain terms, at which

point he reminded me that if I wanted Mallory's identity kept secret, I should give his offer more careful consideration." Remembering that thinly veiled taunt still made her fume hours afterward. At the time, she'd been too angry to trust herself to speak.

She'd called the elevator and let the Setai's attentive concierge put her in a car the hotel offered her as Ian's guest. No doubt, they would have escorted her all over town if she wished—a reminder of how far apart their lifestyles had always been. For all that her father had been a wealthy man, Lydia worked hard to pay her own bills, refusing to fall into her mother's role of bilking others in order to lead an extravagant lifestyle.

"I'll admit it's not exactly the proposal every girl dreams of." Kinley began tapping the pen against her cheek, her lips pursed thoughtfully. "But still. Ian McNeill?" She whistled softly. "A woman could do worse for herself."

"Marriage isn't a competitive sport." Lydia twirled the hotel bathrobe tie around her finger, agitated at how the day had unfolded—start to finish. "I'm not trying to find the richest or most prestigious partner."

"I was thinking more along the lines of the best looking." Kinley grinned shamelessly. "He's seriously hot." She ran her finger over the screen of her phone before flipping it toward the camera to show Lydia a photo of the man himself. "C'mon, Lydia. You can't deny that he's super yummy."

Those blue eyes were magnetic. No doubt.

But the picture wasn't nearly as appealing as the temptation she'd faced today when he stroked a hand along her cheek or told her he wished he'd been there with her when she lost their baby. Those moments had rattled her resolve far more than the vision of his strong shoulders or disarming smile.

Perhaps the idea of a temporary marriage to Ian wouldn't sting so much if she hadn't once let herself imagine a very real marriage with him. Sure, they'd only dated for six weeks, but it had been an intense affair that dominated both their lives. Things had escalated fast.

"That's hardly a good reason to enter into a complicated relationship." If anything, the sensual pull she felt for him was a strike against the idea. She was so drawn to him that it would be easy to let herself confuse attraction for caring again.

And *that* she could not allow.

"Hmm...twelve months of having the world at your feet and a gorgeous, well-respected billionaire to fend off your enemies and keep you safe?" Kinley shook her head, her expression serious for the first time all evening. "I will go out on a limb and say there's more at work here than you're telling me."

Caught.

Lydia shot her an apologetic smile. "Ancient history better forgotten than relived." She took a deep breath. Lydia had resolved to move on after she shared this crazy turn to her day with Kinley. Now it was time to live up to her promise. "But on to more important things. Did you find some parties I should be attending to meet potential clients or possible matches for our current clients?"

She wanted to spend her time helping the cause dear to her heart by raising money for women who really needed it. That meant no more wallowing in regrets over how things had turned out between her and Ian. She'd find some other way to protect her business, even if he revealed her identity as Mallory West to the powerful Vitaly Koslov.

"I did. I'm emailing you a list as soon as I lock down a few more contacts for you. I want to be sure you don't have any trouble getting into any of the events. There are a few European royals in town this month, so invitations are in high demand." She paused. "Although I'm sure Ian McNeill would get the red carpet treatment at all of these places."

Thinking back to that over-the-top penthouse suite at the Setai, Lydia didn't doubt it. He moved in the circles Lydia's mother had never managed to penetrate. And although there'd been a time when Lydia didn't care about acceptance into that kind of elite, she'd begun to see the benefits if only for the sake of Moms' Connection.

"I'm sure he does. But since he won't be attending any of these functions with me, I will wait for you to work your magic on my behalf. Just do whatever you can with my father's name." She refused to feel guilty about that since her father had been a committed philanthropist. He would have applauded Lydia's efforts, she felt certain.

Not for the first time, she wished she'd had more time with him growing up, but she'd been her mother's bargaining chip from the day of her birth, withheld from her dad whenever her mother was unhappy with him.

Which meant she didn't see him often. And when she did, her mother was close at hand, making sure to take her share of the billionaire's attention.

Finishing up her business with Kinley, Lydia ended the video call and closed her laptop. She was staying at the Calypso Hotel close to the Foxfire, in a small room with an ocean view. The suite needed updating desperately, but as she padded across the black-and-white tile floor to the sliding glass door overlooking the water, she admired the same view that Ian had in his gargantuan spread just twenty blocks away. Her surroundings indoors might pale in comparison, but with the ocean waves lapping the shore below, providing a soothing music despite the stressful day, she too could enjoy the most priceless kind of beauty.

Breathing in the soft, salty air, she tried to let the Atlantic work its magic. But deep down, she knew she hadn't escaped Ian McNeill's marriage offer simply by walking out of his suite. He'd allowed her to leave, no doubt so she could mull over the idea—rage against it—and slowly realize how thoroughly he had her back against the wall.

Revealing her as the woman behind Mallory West threatened to derail all her hard work with Moms' Connection, turning her life back into another scandal-ridden media circus when she'd worked so hard to put the antics of her mother behind her. Furthermore, even if she managed to keep the matchmaking business afloat and somehow turn a profit in spite of all the media attention, she would have Vitaly Koslov to contend with, a powerful business mogul with the power to bankrupt her on every front.

Right now, she could afford to live in Manhattan and run a business she enjoyed. Losing a civil suit to Koslov might ruin her financially for years to come. All she had to do to avoid those consequences was put herself in Ian McNeill's hands for one year. She simply had to wed the man who'd left her heart with the deepest scars.

Just seeing him for one day had threatened to rip those old wounds open again. She couldn't possibly go through with it.

So, turning to enter her hotel room and slip between the sheets for the night, Lydia knew she'd have to refuse him when he asked her again. Because not for a moment did she think he'd dropped the idea of a temporary union between them.

Ian McNeill wasn't a man to take marriage lightly. Even the cold-blooded, contractual kind.

Nodding a greeting to the desk attendant at the Calypso Hotel shortly before dawn, Ian checked his watch as he took up a spot near the main elevators. It was one of South Beach's aging art deco–era properties. Standing on the huge tile inlay featuring a gold starburst design, Ian pulled his phone from his pocket to check his stocks for the day, but in reality all he could think about was Lydia.

It was a risk to surprise her. But when she'd ended their conversation prematurely the day before, she must have known he would find a time to renew their discussion. Sooner rather than later.

She was a woman of habit and that would serve him well now. He hoped. He remembered how much she had enjoyed swimming first thing in the morning when they were working together in the islands of Tahiti. He'd accused her of being a mermaid with her daily need to return to the sea, but even when he'd been bleary-eyed from working late the night before, he never missed a chance to swim with her. For safety purposes, he'd told her, and not just because he enjoyed the occasional chance to slide a hand beneath her bikini top or wind the wet rope of her hair around his hand and angle her sea-salty lips for his kiss.

When the elevator sounded its dull chime, he slowly looked up. The doors opened and Lydia strode into view. His gaze fell on her long, shapely legs, the hem of her black mesh tunic revealing a hint of thigh.

"Ian?" Her voice tugged his attention higher, pulling his focus to her green eyes and creamy skin devoid of makeup.

With her hair scraped back into a ponytail, she looked every inch the part of his earthy, warmhearted lover from last summer. He had to remember that she hadn't been the woman he thought, that he'd been wrong about her, or he might have swept her up into his arms and ridden the elevator back up to her hotel room to remind her how good they were together in at least one respect.

Sex. Raw, sensual, mind-blowing sex.

His pulse ramped up at the steamy memories, so much so that he had to shut down those thoughts and focus on the present or his plan would be doomed before he even started.

"Hope you don't mind if I join you." Ian tucked his phone back into the pocket of the cargo shorts he'd slid on over his swim trunks.

She halted in front of him abruptly. Then, eyes sliding to the desk attendant, she stepped closer. Probably she did it to minimize the chance of being overheard.

Ian liked the opportunity to breathe in the scent of her—the lavender fragrance of the detergent she washed her clothes in and a subtle perfume more complex than that.

"What on earth are you doing here?" She glanced over her shoulder. "You realize most of the consultants working on the Foxfire are staying in this hotel? What will they say if someone sees us together at this hour?"

"They'll think we had a whole lot more fun last night than they did."

Last night, he'd paced the floor of his penthouse suite for far too long, thinking through every aspect of a contract marriage and what details he should include in the paperwork.

In the end, she would sign. But she wasn't going to like him forcing her hand, and that bothered him more than it should have.

"And that doesn't concern you? I happen to enjoy a hard-earned reputation as a professional." Her clipped words and the high color in her cheeks told him he'd gotten under her skin in record time.

"If you don't want anyone to see us together, we might as well hit the beach. Take refuge in the water." His hand itched to touch her. To rest on the small of her back and steer her out the door, across the street and onto the soft sand. But he had to be careful not to push or she could dig her heels in about his suggestion and delay the whole thing.

Now that he'd made up his mind and seen the benefits of a union between the two of them, he couldn't think of one damn reason why he should delay.

After narrowing her green eyes at him for an instant, she pivoted on her wedge sandals and strode toward the exit.

He caught up to her in two long steps, holding the door wide for her before as they headed out onto Ocean Drive, which was strangely quiet in the predawn dark. There were more joggers on the beach than bathers; a few runners kicked up sand as they pounded past them.

"It'll be quieter down here." He pointed out a stretch of the shore where no beach loungers had been set up yet, a spot free from any hotel guests.

In fact, he'd claimed the location for them earlier when he'd ordered a cabana and sunrise breakfast. Lydia apparently didn't notice his preparations, however, instead appearing too absorbed in her frustrated march toward the water, her feet churning through the sand at breakneck pace.

The horizon was starting to smudge from inky black to purple as she reached the shoreline and kicked off her shoes. Then she yanked the black mesh cover-up off and over her head. Mesmerized by her silhouette as his eyes adjusted to the light, Ian watched as she ran into the surf and made a shallow dive under an oncoming wave.

He retrieved her clothes and put them in the cabana where he removed his own shorts and tee, stacking them off to one side out of the way of a server still setting up a tea cart full of trays for their breakfast.

Then Ian sprinted into the ocean after Lydia, seized with memories of other times they'd done this. They'd had plenty of games they played in the water, from him grabbing an ankle and tracing the long line of her leg up to the juncture of her thighs to races of every kind. He didn't think she'd appreciate the former, so he settled for the latter, pacing her as she executed perfect butterfly strokes through the salty water.

With the horizon turning lavender now, he could see her better. Her creamy skin glinted in the soft light each time her arm broke the surface. Only when they were far from the shore did she stop short to tread water.

"You're insane," she accused softly, even though she seemed significantly calmer than when she'd been on her march toward the water. With her dark hair plastered to her head and the long ponytail floating around her shoulders, she looked so beautiful and so damn familiar that it hurt.

"To swim in a dark ocean before the sun rises? Or to brave your wrath and swim beside you when I know you're angry?"

Her huff of frustration rippled the water in front of her. "To propose marriage when we have so much… unhappy history. So much frustration between us. It's crazy and you know it." She swatted aside a drifting clump of seaweed.

"I'm a practical man, Lydia. And by now, I'm sure you've had enough time to realize how practical my suggestion is." He'd wanted her to have cooling off time yesterday, but he guessed she'd been awake as long as he had last night, thinking about the possibilities.

"Practical?" She rose up on her toes to move out of the way of a swell coming toward them. "Ian, we aren't some royal couple needing to secure the family line or keep the castle in the clan. Marriage isn't supposed to be a line item in a business deal."

"And it won't be." He took her hand before the next swell rolled over them. "Come this way so you can touch the bottom."

Even that simple touch—his grip wrapped around her fingers in the cool water—sent a flash of undeniable heat through him. Judging from how fast she pulled back, he would guess she felt it, too.

"I'm fine," she argued despite the goose bumps along her arm.

"You're cold." He pointed to the shore where their server had left a small hurricane lamp burning on the table. "You see the cabana? I ordered some breakfast for us. Let's dry off and talk about this reasonably before the next wave drags you under."

"We're having breakfast there?" She shook her head slowly, but began swimming toward shore. "I have the feeling you could have had the free buffet at the Setai."

He laughed.

"Maybe so. But my hotel lacks your company. A situation I hope to change once you agree to my proposal."

She stopped swimming. But they were so close to the shore now, they were able to stand and walk side by side the rest of the way. She'd stopped arguing, which he took as a positive sign. So he kept his peace for now, shortening his stride to stay beside her as they moved closer and closer to their destination. The all-white tent was closed on three sides but open to the water, the domed roof making it look like something out of *Arabian Nights*.

She nibbled her bottom lip, then released it slowly before shooting a sideways glance his way. "You're really serious about this."

"You doubted it?" He passed her a towel from the stack an attendant left near their clothes.

"Not really." She squeezed the water out of her long ponytail and let it drip onto the sand. "I guess I hoped maybe you were just trying to scare me with the threat of Koslov's lawsuit. Make me regret what I'd done by interfering in your romantic life with the matches I suggested."

She'd sent him suggestions for dates with a reality TV star renowned for her diva-ish behavior and an ex-girlfriend she knew he disliked for using his name to get ahead in her career for long after they'd broken up.

"No." Moving to the sideboard where the food had been set up, he poured them both coffee. "Although I won't deny I let myself imagine all kinds of inventive sensual blackmail once I found out you were the woman behind Mallory West."

She clutched the towel tighter to her lovely body as he set the mugs on the bistro-size table. When she said nothing, he waited another moment to continue, letting his words sink in. He wasn't going to pretend that he wasn't attracted.

Or that he wouldn't act on it.

"But after we had the chance to speak yesterday, I realized you were under an incredible amount of stress at that time, and I regret not being there for you." It made his chest go tight thinking about her alone and losing their child. *Their child.* He had to swallow down the lump in his throat before he could continue. "No matter what else happened between us, you should have known you could contact me."

He hadn't forgiven her for keeping the baby a secret in the first place, but he hated that she'd been through that by herself.

She sank into her chair at the table, stirring sugar into the coffee he'd placed in front of her. She made no protest when he set a plate of food before her, the stoneware loaded down with fruits and cheeses he knew she liked. The scent of eggs and bacon wafted from the warming trays as he prepared a plate for himself and a smaller, second one for her.

"So you didn't suggest marriage as a punishment." She gave him a lopsided smile and slid her arms into the black mesh bathing suit cover-up.

"Far from it." He pulled on his linen button-down shirt and took the seat across from her, letting his knee brush hers under the table and seeing the jolt of awareness in her eyes. "I think a marriage between us could have all kinds of added benefits."

Five

A shock of heat radiated out from that one spot where their legs brushed, seizing Lydia's attention faster than any words. How easy it would be to heed that impulse, to fall under the spell of simmering attraction until she was powerless to resist it. Of course, it didn't help that she remembered so many other times when she'd allowed this very sensation to carry her away, pulling her into his arms to answer the hunger only he could fill.

Urging herself to be stronger than that, she shifted her legs away from him under the table, crossing one knee over the other to put herself farther out of his reach.

"I'm not sure it's fair of you to resort to underhanded tactics to convince me we should try this crazy scheme of yours." Taking a sip of her coffee, she focused on the pink sun rising past the horizon, bathing them both in warm light.

The beach was still quiet at this early hour with a smattering of tourists more focused on the famed nightlife than the joys of the early morning. About twenty yards away, a fisherman cast a line and waited to see what was biting, his chair half in the surf. A few interested birds stalked him, sensing the possibility of an easy meal.

"Underhanded?" Ian straightened, as if rearing back from an undeserved slight. But then a smile curved his sculpted lips, sliding right past her boundaries. "Under the table, maybe. But hardly underhanded."

"You know what I mean." She stabbed a half strawberry with her fork and ignored all the nerve endings urging her to listen to him, to let him woo her back where her body would love to be. "If we can't hash out terms logically, it's not a good idea to start wielding seduction as a weapon."

"Lydia," he began, his tone gently chiding. "Seduction was a very rewarding part of our relationship. I'd never want it to be anything but a pleasure."

He didn't move any closer as he spoke, but somehow the air thickened around them as if he'd grazed against her again. Hearing the word *pleasure* on his lips wasn't good for her defenses.

"Then let's keep it out of the negotiations." She spoke through gritted teeth, she realized, and forced herself to take a breath.

"Of course." He finished his eggs and moved his plate aside, leaning his elbows on the table.

The breeze off the water blew through his dark wavy hair, which was beginning to dry. He was impossibly handsome with his deeply bronzed skin and blue eyes.

"Good." Relaxing a little, she hoped she could still reason with him. "Then we can discuss alternatives to the marriage plan."

"The only alternative is me revealing Mallory West's identity to the world, Vitaly Koslov included." Ian lifted the coffee carafe to pour her more.

Her stomach cramped. He was perfectly serious. Ian might be the peacemaker within the McNeill family, brokering middle ground between his conservative older brother and his playboy, techno-genius younger sibling, but that didn't mean Ian himself ever gave ground. More often than not, the other McNeills let themselves be guided by Ian's position.

"That will ruin any hope of resurrecting my matchmaking career. Aside from the personal loss, I would be saddened by the missed opportunity for the world of good it's doing for so many people," she reminded him, unable to enjoy the fresh fruit on her plate when her nerves were wound tight. She didn't want to lose her ability to give back to Moms' Connection and the women who'd helped her through the darkest time of her life.

He shrugged with a pragmatic air. "Sometimes we make sacrifices for the things that are most important to us."

How could he be so cavalier about love? "And you don't care if I look at marriage to you as sacrificing myself?" Maybe she'd hoped some small part of him still cared about what they had meant to each other once.

"We are both offering something to get what we want." He tapped the table as if jabbing home his point. "I prefer to focus on the positives."

"Like you getting around your grandfather's terms for the will?"

"Precisely." He reached to take her fork from her plate and spear a grape. He then lifted it, offering it to her. "And you avoid a civil suit while growing your business." He paused, fork hovering in midair. "Among other benefits."

That damnable heat returned to her skin. How could she have forgotten how easily he tampered with her ability to think clearly?

"So you mentioned. But I'm not going to suddenly take up where we left off just because we sign on for a year together." She withdrew the fork from his fingers and set it down again, unwilling to play romantic games with him. "Not that I'm seriously considering this idea at all, Ian. If anything, I'm still trying to figure out how to get out of my contract with Singer Associates so I can leave South Beach and the Foxfire project altogether."

"I would never expect you to pick up where we left off a year ago." His gaze was steady and direct. He appeared sincere. "I know the heat is still there, but it would be up to you if we did anything about it—plain and simple."

Her heart beat faster just talking about it. How would she ever find enough strength to resist the man day in and day out for a whole year if she were to actually consider going through with this?

She really didn't want to lose her matchmaking business because the proceeds did so much good for the charity she cared about. Confused and flustered, she stood abruptly.

"I can't do this again." She shook her head, wishing she could shake off the old feelings crowding out reasonable thought. "The first time hurt too much."

Retrieving her towel, she wanted to retreat before she did something foolish. Like throw her arms around his neck and press herself against him, or drag him deeper into the cabana and peel off his clothes.

"Please." Ian stood with her, a hand darting out to capture hers, linking their fingers with an ease from their past relationship. "My grandfather had a heart attack last winter after the debacle of Cameron proposing to Sofia."

Ian's touch curved around her elbow, gentle but firm.

"I'm sorry. I didn't know."

"It happened while he traveled abroad. In China, in fact. That helped us to keep it quiet."

She softened a little, knowing how much Malcolm McNeill meant to all of his grandsons. She recalled how Ian had told her about his fond memories of the older man throughout his childhood.

With the sun just above the horizon now, pink and orange light spilled over them, a spotlight just for them. Ian's fingers caressed the back of her arm lightly and she could feel her resistance ebbing away with the tide.

"Will he be okay?" She read between the lines. If something happened to Malcolm McNeill and Ian had not fulfilled the terms of the trust, the family would lose control of McNeill Resorts.

"We hope so. He had a pacemaker put in and his doctors say he's doing well. But Gramps wouldn't let us take him to see his physician in the States yet until he's certain he can control any rumors spreading about his health."

They stood just inside the cabana's shelter, her bare toes curling in the sand as Ian's fingers stroked lightly over the back of her arm. She wasn't even sure he was aware that he was doing it. His gaze turned sober, his shoulders tense with concern.

"He wants to protect the integrity of the business." She understood the older man's reasons. Even the strongest companies could experience a downturn over rumors about a change in leadership.

"Yes." Ian's touch stilled as he met her gaze. "Even at the expense of his health. But you see why I am all the more concerned about protecting his legacy? Not for me, but for him?"

She understood about wanting approval. She'd craved it her whole life from her father and then, after his death, from her half siblings and the family she'd never gotten to know. But that had eluded her. Ian didn't have those kinds of concern, though. He knew his grandfather loved him.

"If keeping the company in the family was that important to him, don't you think he would alter the terms of the will?" She tipped her face to the sea breeze off the water, feeling off-kilter over having an intimate conversation with Ian at such close range. "Maybe your grandfather is more concerned with your happiness. I can't imagine he'd want you to marry someone just for the sake of keeping the business in the family."

"Malcolm McNeill was raised in a different time. He doesn't see the problem with choosing a bride for practical purposes." Ian released her but didn't move away, which in essence blocked her from leaving the cabana. "So I'm trying to see his reasoning in those terms. You and I make sense together, Lydia. We can help each other."

This would be so much easier if she didn't keep mixing up the past and the present, seeing her former lover in Ian instead of the hard, pragmatic man she knew him to be. Even last year, he'd put his grandfather's wishes before hers, so why should it surprise her that he would marry for the sake of his family? Yet no matter how hard she tried, she saw the man who made love to her in a waterfall at dawn. A man who'd shown her a level of pleasure in bed she'd never imagined possible.

A man who'd held her heart in his strong palm.

"I can't help you." Her words were soft, fragile things, not nearly as fierce as she would have liked.

"What could I do to make you say yes?" He corralled a flyaway strand of hair and smoothed it behind her ear. "Just name it."

He was offering her the chance to keep her matchmaking business and protect her identity from another scandal. He'd keep Vitaly Koslov at bay and give her a kind of respectability she'd never known as the daughter of a notorious tabloid diva. All of which would be very beneficial.

Now, he was even allowing her to dictate her terms.

She couldn't deny she was tempted. Especially now that she knew his motive wasn't payback for the matches she'd sent him last fall. She believed he was truly worried about his grandfather's health and fulfilling one of the old man's wishes.

"Separate rooms." The words came tumbling from her mouth before she'd really thought through all the ways this could go wrong. "Help with my matchmaking business if I need it." She remembered what Kinley had said about the McNeill family's access to A-list events that would be difficult to get into otherwise.

"I don't know a lot about matchmaking," he admitted. "I would have thought you and I were going to be great together."

Her heart squeezed tight, remembering that she'd thought the same thing until she'd discovered he was only using their relationship to fill the time until he found the right woman to marry. Now it seemed Ian didn't mind compromising his standards for a wife when he was in a hurry.

"Not that kind of help. I mean it might aid my work if I could use the McNeill name to meet more potential clients."

"Done." Ian didn't hesitate. "It's a deal then?"

A deal? For real? She must have lost her mind for considering this. But it was only for twelve months, right?

"I would have one other condition." She swallowed hard, needing to be forthright with him if she was going to go through with this.

He stayed silent, which somehow swayed her more than a million words.

She found herself speaking slowly, weighing each

thought, almost like dipping her toe in to test the waters. "I would expect you to honor what you said earlier about not using seduction as a weapon." Her voice did that high, breathy thing again, and she swallowed hard to make it go away. "While I acknowledge there is a pull between us, Ian, I need you to promise me you won't take advantage of that."

"On one condition." His voice lowered. His forehead tipped closer to hers.

Her heart pounded like it wanted to leap free of her chest.

"What?" She should have spelled out that he couldn't even get this close to her.

What had she been thinking?

"I get to kiss you on two occasions."

Kisses. Just kisses. But when had they ever been able to stop at just kisses?

She should protest. End this now. Let Vitaly Koslov sue her into bankruptcy for embarrassing his ballerina daughter by sending her a marriage-minded suitor to propose to her in front of the press.

Instead, Lydia breathed in the feel of having Ian this close to her. So close she caught a hint of his sandalwood aftershave that had occasionally clung to her skin after a night in his bed.

"When would those kisses happen?" Her eyes tracked his. "On what occasions?"

"Once on our wedding day. And once to seal the deal."

"As in...now?" She would not lick her lips even though her mouth went chalk-dry at the thought.

"Right now." His hand found the center of her back, his palm an electric warmth through the mesh fabric of her cover-up. "Do we have a deal, Lydia? One year together and I'll honor all of your terms."

Bad idea, bad idea, her brain chanted, as if to urge the words out of her mouth. But she could not forsake the women—the mothers—who needed her help. And selfishly, she could not put herself through another scandal.

She nodded her assent.

A wicked, masculine smile curved his lips.

"I'm so glad to hear it." His blue eyes glowed with a new heat in that moment of victory right before he lowered his mouth to hers.

If one kiss was all he got until their vows, Ian planned to make it count.

His hands cupped her waist just above the gentle curve of her hips. Her skin was warm through the thin mesh cover-up. She pressed closer, or maybe he did, the space between them shrinking until her breasts teased against his chest, the soft swell of sweet feminine flesh making him ache for a better feel of her.

Hunger for her roared down Ian's spine the moment their lips touched. The electric connection they'd always had sparked to flame, singeing his insides with a need to have her. Here. Now. He could lower the curtains on the cabana for privacy and ease her beautiful body down to the table. With no effort at all he could sweep aside that scrap of fabric that counted as a swimsuit and be deep inside her. He knew her body so well.

Felt the answering heat in the breathless way she kissed him back, her fingernails clutching lightly at his shirt to keep him close.

Even now, she fit her body to his, her hips arching into him. Or maybe her legs felt as weak beneath her as his did and she was simply melting against him.

Yes.

He reached behind her, just above her head, to release the tie holding back one side of the cabana's front curtain. The fabric fell in a rush, cloaking them in shadows. Lydia levered back, blinking up at the change in the light. She focused on the fallen length of white fabric.

"What are you doing?" Her lips trembled. "Why?"

He couldn't take his eyes off her mouth.

"Giving us more privacy." He kissed her again, feeding on the plump softness until her lips parted.

He turned them both, pinning her to him with one hand at the small of her back while he flicked free the other side of the cabana curtain, letting it tumble to the ground and shield them completely from view of anyone else on the beach.

"A kiss." Her words whispered over his mouth in a soft sigh. "We said one kiss."

"We did." He bent to taste the skin just below her ear, feeling her pulse beat fast. "And see how well that turned out for both of us?"

"Ian." She fisted her hands tighter in his shirt for a moment, then edged back from him.

Wide-eyed in the newly dim interior of the closed cabana, she gazed up at him while the white curtains shifted gently in the breeze off the water. He listened to the waves roll in to keep his focus off the way she looked with her cover-up sliding off one shoulder and her lips swollen from his kiss.

He needed to be patient. To not push for more. It would be better when she came to him because she was ready to pick up where they left off. But damn. Keeping his hands off her right now when the air between them pulsed with want and heat proved a staggering test of restraint.

"Yes?" He wanted to trace the fullness of her lower lip. Memorize the feel of her.

"How fast is this going to happen? A marriage, I mean?"

She was talking about marriage? A surge of triumph pumped through him. This deal was all but done.

He held back his victory shout and kept his voice level. "I hope you're asking because you're looking forward to that next kiss as much as I am."

"I'm wondering how to handle us being on the same job in the same city. If we're supposed to look like a couple, and if that's okay while we're working together." She straightened her cover-up and took a step back from him.

He tugged the privacy curtain back into place on one side of the cabana, giving up on the idea of resurrecting their relationship with impromptu sex on the breakfast table.

Patience.

"I'll find a justice of the peace and see how quickly we can put in the paperwork." He would rest easier when he knew he was on track to meet the terms of his grandfather's will. The sooner they got married, the sooner that would happen.

His brother Quinn and his ballerina fiancée were due to wed in two weeks. With any luck, Ian would already be wed to Lydia by then. Not that they needed to announce it until afterward.

"And you think we can stay on this job together as a couple, no emotions, no sex involved?" She seemed worried about that and he wondered why.

He'd never imagined her as overly concerned with finances. She was donating 100 percent of the money she made in her matchmaking business, after all. His friend Bentley's report had confirmed as much.

But then again, if she was so financially stable, he had to wonder about her accommodations at the old, worn-down Calypso Hotel.

"I will honor your wishes every step of the way. But to be certain, I'll speak to Jeremy today. And in the meantime, I have several vacant bedrooms at the suite at the Setai. I'll ask the concierge service to move your things." He sent out two text messages to arrange for her clothes to be delivered to the penthouse.

She'd said separate rooms. But she could hardly quibble when his suite was bigger than most private homes.

"There's one other thing. About the terms I mentioned?" She followed him out of the cabana across the sand, back toward his car. "I'd like to use your name to get into a party later this week. I think I'll get in more easily as your guest."

"I'll put you in touch with my assistant if we need an invitation. I'll go with you and we can debut our romantic relationship publicly." He withdrew his phone and sent a message to Mrs. Trager.

She paused near the Calypso.

"I'm parked this way." He pointed toward his vehicle in a spot up the street.

"But I should at least go shower and change."

"You can do both those things at my suite. For all we know we'll be able to marry by this afternoon." He took her hand and led her forward when she hesitated. "We might as well stick together."

"I can't believe we're really going through with this." She matched her steps to his, heading toward the BMW convertible. "Should we sign an agreement of some sort? I'd feel better if we had things in writing."

"Of course." He would ensure their terms were spelled out clearly. Put her at ease with the plan so she could relax and enjoy the benefits of marriage.

Because the next time they kissed, he planned to take his time reminding her how very rewarding the next twelve months together could be.

Six

Three whirlwind days later, shortly before noon, Lydia stood in front of a Dade County justice of the peace and signed the documents to become Ian's wife.

Privately, they'd already signed the papers spelling out the terms for separation in one year. She'd had a trusted attorney look over it to be sure she understood all aspects of the document and agreed the settlement was fair. Ian had added numerous financial benefits that she'd had stricken from the agreement since she wasn't marrying him for a cash prize, for crying out loud. They'd argued about it more than once, but in the end, he'd capitulated when she'd flat-out refused to sign under those terms.

Now, signing her name beside Ian's in the public register, Lydia clutched her flowers tighter as the simple ceremony got underway. They hadn't even forewarned their families. But though there was no fanfare, she wore an ivory silk cocktail dress that Ian had ordered for the occasion. He'd insisted it was his tailor's idea since her dress matched the accessories on his charcoal silk suit. And she had to admit the lines of the sheath gown with its wide-set straps and square neck were pretty without shouting "bridal" when they'd walked into the courthouse.

So she watched the petals of the peach-colored lilies tremble in her bouquet while the justice of the peace made their temporary marriage official. She'd barely had time to think since agreeing to all this, from moving into the luxury penthouse suite of Ian's hotel to explaining her upcoming nuptials to Kinley and doing her job for the Foxfire after Ian had officially disclosed their relationship to Jeremy Singer. Since that last heated kiss on the beach, Ian hadn't pressed for further physical intimacy, which didn't surprise her since they'd agreed she would set the pace.

And yet, had he thought about those electric moments in the cabana as often as she had? Knowing that another kiss awaited them today—their wedding day— only added to the butterflies in her stomach as the judge made their marriage official. This time, however, things wouldn't spiral out of control the way they had at the beach. For one thing, she was prepared this time.

For another, there were witnesses, for crying out loud. Strangers, perhaps, but legal witnesses nevertheless.

As Lydia peered up into Ian's blue eyes and the rest

of the world seemed to disappear, she acknowledged that he had the power to make her completely forget herself. It was why she'd need to be very careful during the next twelve months or she would lose her heart to him all over again. Because no matter how much her body responded to the chemistry they generated, her head understood that Ian would always put the McNeills—the family and the business bearing their name—before her.

Ian was impeccably dressed in a custom-tailored H. Huntsman two-button gray silk suit, a white shirt with an ivory silk tie and a pocket square that took the outfit to another level of formal. She had to admit his tailor was correct in suggesting the outfits—their wedding photo snapped by the secretary out front was bound to be beautiful. For a wistful moment, Lydia wished she had Kinley with her to share what was normally a momentous occasion in a woman's life. But in the end, she'd thought it was best to simply keep the nuptials quiet until the marriage was a *fait accompli* since Lydia's mother would have been the first to insinuate herself into the media coverage.

"And now for the presentation of the rings," the justice of the peace announced, startling Lydia from her reverie and inducing a moment of panic.

Ian had said he'd take care of that. Had he remembered?

But he was already producing platinum bands. One was plain and masculine with some kind of etching. The other had a square yellow diamond in a cushion-cut setting that made her gasp out loud. The clerk continued, prompting them to repeat after him the standard vows from the simplest ceremony offered. Lydia repeated the words, hoping she wasn't making a colossal mistake, as she slid Ian's ring onto his finger and accepted the gorgeous canary sparkler on her own hand.

"I now declare you man and wife," the justice of the peace intoned, closing the black leather book he read from and shuffling it to one side of the polished oak desk behind him. "You may kiss your bride."

Lydia couldn't have said which idea provided the greater shock to her system. That she was now Ian's wife? Or that his lips were about to covers hers again?

She saw the glow of possessive fire in her groom's eyes—or maybe she just felt the answering fire in her blood. Either way, her heart rate increased to double-time and the silk bodice of her gown seemed to shrink, cutting off her air as she held her breath for a suspended moment.

When Ian dipped closer, however, he merely brushed his lips along her cheek and whispered in her ear.

"I'm banking the real kiss for later," he promised, the deep timbre of his voice smoking over her skin and calling to mind heated scenarios she felt sure no proper bride would be dreaming about at the altar.

Or, in this case, at the courthouse desk.

Off-kilter from that whispered vow and her new marital status, Lydia smiled woodenly for another photo as Ian finished their business and took copies of their paperwork. They didn't speak again until they left the courtroom and their words wouldn't be overheard.

"Congratulations, Mrs. McNeill," Ian told her as he

took her hand and led her from the building out into the heat of a Miami afternoon.

They'd traveled inland and north of the city for the courthouse visit, but Lydia hadn't paid much attention to their surroundings that morning when they'd parked the car. She'd been too nervous. Now she felt even more on edge thinking about Ian's plan to bank that kiss.

She lowered her nose to the bouquet of lilies and roses and inhaled the fresh fragrance to soothe her nerves.

"Congratulations to us both. We've fooled the world into thinking we are in love for the sake of our personal objectives." She hadn't meant to taint the day with the bitterness she felt since it would be easier to simply coast along like none of this was getting to her.

But something about the dress and the beautiful diamond now on her hand—all the trappings of a real wedding—had gotten under her skin.

"We've merely set aside our differences to help one another." He waved over a dark luxury SUV that was not the vehicle they'd arrived in. "Let's celebrate the occasion, shall we?"

Lydia's silk kitten heels skidded on the pavement as she halted. Ian slowed his step to take her elbow. Steady her.

"What do you mean?" She kept her eye on the SUV as it pulled up to the curb beside them, the tinted windows dark enough to prevent her from seeing inside. "I have an online meeting with an overseas supplier this afternoon."

She needed to regain her equilibrium. Work would help with that.

"I remember." Ian gave a nod toward the SUV and at his signal, a liveried driver stepped from the vehicle. "I've got a conference room prepared for you. I was hoping to sit in on some of it since I think this group has some architectural salvage pieces that could be incorporated into the courtyard design."

The driver opened the rear door of the SUV, revealing champagne-colored bucket seats as a blast of air-conditioning cooled Lydia's skin. A passing vehicle honked its horn at them as someone shouted "Congratulations, newlyweds!"

"You see?" Ian's hand slid around her waist to nudge her gently forward. "Everyone else wants us to seize the day. You can work for two hours while we are in the air and by the time you're done we'll be almost ready to land. Tonight, we can toast our marriage while the sun sets over the Pacific."

She didn't budge. The last time she'd been in the Pacific with him, she'd ended up pregnant.

"You know I wouldn't want to go back there—"

"Of course." He shook his head, lowering his voice for her ears only. "I wouldn't take you to Rangiroa. But we can be in Costa Rica in a couple of hours. We could have a decadent dinner overlooking the water, then return in the morning."

Lydia wondered far more about what could happen in the time *between* that decadent dinner and the flight home in the morning. Yet she was relieved to know Ian hadn't tried to resurrect the magic of last spring in the Polynesian islands when she'd fallen head over heels. Too many memories in that part of the world.

"I was not expecting anything like this. I don't have anything packed." She should probably have just said no outright. But the gesture was thoughtful even if it was more over-the-top than something she would have chosen.

"Taken care of. And if we are going to spend a year in close proximity, I think it would benefit us to try and find our footing as friends." He nodded at the driver again, chasing the attendant back to the front of the vehicle without a word.

"Friends." She tested the idea, unable to imagine such a tepid term for the relationship they'd once shared. But since that was in the past, perhaps he had a point. "This seems highly romantic for friendship."

"We just wed, Lydia. The illusion of a quick honeymoon will only cement our story for the rest of the world—our families included."

"So it's also for show." She nodded thoughtfully. She knew Ian would honor their agreement. There would be separate rooms. He would let her make the next move. She trusted in this implicitly because she knew his sense of honor.

It was that damnable kiss that had her rattled.

"And I think you'll enjoy being out of town when the news breaks about our nuptials," he reminded her.

Oddly, that won her over more than anything else he might have said. The thought of being in the papers—for any reason—made her skin crawl after growing up with her attention-seeking mother. As a bonus, she would have every reason in the world to ignore calls from her mom about her marriage for a little while longer.

"Deal." Lydia slid onto her seat inside the SUV and told herself the time together could be put to good use anyhow. She would speak to him about setting boundaries and house rules for living together over the next year once they settled into dinner.

Or, better yet, she would keep that topic for their *after*-dinner conversation. Because as the SUV whisked them away toward the nearest private airport, she knew she needed to figure out a way to fill that mysterious void of time between their meal and the return flight home.

Ian might be entitled to one more kiss, but she planned to make certain it didn't lead to a wedding night.

"I thought you weren't concerned with the terms of Gramps's will." Cameron McNeill scolded during a teleconference Ian was holding on board the chartered Gulfstream currently flying Lydia and him to Costa Rica for the night.

Ian had been sitting in the jet's small conference room with Lydia when his phone went berserk with repeated texts from both his brothers. Excusing himself from the online meeting with the overseas supplier to let Lydia handle it, Ian had taken a seat in the lounge and put his feet up before he dialed Quinn's office in New York, hoping to speak to his older—more cool-headed—sibling first.

But apparently Quinn only found out about the secret wedding because Cameron had barged into his office with an eight-by-ten printer blow-up of the photo taken at the Dade County clerk's office. Who leaked the information was anyone's guess since neither Ian nor Lydia was particularly well-known outside their social and professional circles, but clearly someone had keyed in on the McNeill name and publicized Ian's hasty marriage. The article Cameron had found was on a New York gossip blog, but the story was making the rounds in other places, fueled in part—Ian would guess—by how knockout beautiful Lydia looked in that ivory gown. She had a Mona Lisa smile in the photo, but there was something unmistakably mischievous in her bright green eyes.

No wonder the tabloids couldn't post the story fast enough.

"I didn't marry her just because of the will," Ian argued. "We had a prior relationship. Although I will admit, our grandfather's heart attack gave his terms a new sense of urgency."

Both his brothers were in Quinn's office in the Financial District back in New York. Quinn rested one hip on the window seat with a view of midtown behind him while Cameron paced the large office with the restless energy of a caged animal. Tall and rangy, he almost didn't fit in the frame captured by the webcam as he stalked back and forth in front of the antique bookshelves. Ian adjusted the angle on the fold-down screen above his seat to cut the glare from a nearby window as the plane began its descent.

He'd far rather be staring at his bride right now, but Lydia sat behind a partition in a separate section of the plane intended for teleconferencing on a big screen.

"You both told me Gramps was bluffing," Cameron reminded them. "You said he would back off on this. And now Ian tied the knot in secret and Quinn's getting married in two weeks." Cameron flung himself into the leather chair behind Quinn's oversize desk, wheeling the seat back a few feet. "I'm beginning to think it's you two who are bluffing."

"Our point, Cameron," Quinn interjected, loosening his gray silk tie, "was that you shouldn't marry for Gramps's sake. If you meet the right woman, that's one thing." He turned toward the camera—and Ian. "And I'm assuming this was a serious relationship for Ian to make him think of marrying."

Talking down Cameron's bluster was far easier than working his way around Quinn's canny gaze. The oldest of the three, Quinn had taken on the parenting role early when their mother divorced their father and the three McNeill sons split the year between the two of them. In Rio, with their mother, they were well supervised. The rest of the time, if their thrill-seeking, globe-trotting father, Liam, was in charge, Quinn proved a more reliable guardian for the three of them.

"Of course." Ian's reasons for marrying Lydia were complex enough that he wasn't entirely certain he could pick through them all himself. But he regretted walking out of her life without a fight last spring. He should have stayed. Should have been there for her when she miscarried their child. Now? He might have torched the old feelings for her, but he could damn well build on what they'd had before. He was comfortable with a marriage built on a legal foundation. He understood the terms and knew what was expected—unlike last time when he'd fallen too far too fast.

When both Quinn and Cameron stared at him expectantly, Ian realized he needed to offer up some kind of explanation. Not easy to do when he'd agreed not to reveal the secret of Mallory West.

"Lydia and I met last year when I was supervising the hotel project in Rangiroa." He clicked on his seat belt when he heard the chime overhead from the pilot and saw the sign go on. His gaze went to the conference room door, but it was still closed so Lydia must be buckling in for the descent in there. "We had a strong connection, but we wanted to see if it was because we met in a tropical paradise or if the bond could withstand the real world. Turns out, we're very good for each other."

Quinn frowned. Cameron's eyes widened.

"You dated for a year without telling anyone about her?" Cam asked, spearing his fingers through his dark hair.

"No." Ian should have thought through his response more before having this conversation but he wanted it done, and after the constant texts, he'd realized the McNeills weren't going to let a secret wedding stand without an inquisition. "We had our ups and downs, but we reconnected on the South Beach project and felt drawn to be together. We agreed we didn't want to detract from Quinn and Sofia's wedding so we thought we'd marry quietly. It didn't occur to me that filing for a license would flag any media interest."

"Wrong on that count, dude." Cameron reached for

the eight-by-ten photo of the courthouse wedding and waved it. "This sucker was making the rounds half an hour after you did the deal."

Ian gritted his teeth. "Quinn, please extend my apologies to Sofia if my awkward timing for the marriage upset her. We hoped to wait until after your wedding to announce ours. But if that's all, gentleman, I'm about ten minutes away from touching down in Costa Rica for my honeymoon."

"Sofia doesn't mind sharing the spotlight as a bride, only as a ballerina." The grin on Quinn's face was a new expression that they'd only started to see when the New York City Ballet dancer had entered his life.

Sometimes it still took Ian a second to reconcile that expression with his ever-serious older brother. He envied their complete devotion to one another. A kind of happiness Ian knew he'd never find in his temporary contract marriage.

There would be other rewards, however. For both of them.

Cameron elbowed Quinn. "Tell him why we really called, man."

Instantly on alert, Ian straightened, the fine leather in the chair squeaking as he moved.

"Is it Gramps? Is he okay?" He'd been worried about Malcolm McNeill's transition from Shanghai to New York, a trip that had been delayed twice because of his doctor's concerns and the need to travel with good medical equipment.

"He's fine," Quinn assured him. "But he contacted

us today after your wedding photo circulated online. He wants to meet with all of us."

Ian's gut knotted. Tightened. "Of course. How soon?"

"No immediate rush. He wouldn't want to disrupt the honeymoon." Quinn rose from his spot at the window ledge and flipped a page on the desk calendar. "Three days from now, maybe? I'll be in New York then and so will Cam, right?" He glanced up at their youngest brother.

"Sure thing," Cam answered as the plane broke through the cloud cover and the Costa Rican mountains became visible in a wavy carpet of dark green below.

"I'll be there." Ian's honeymoon would be over by then. "Any idea what he wants?"

"No." Quinn shook his head, brow furrowed. "But I would bring Lydia with you. She's part of the family now."

Ian nodded as he disconnected the call, hating the hollow feeling in his chest. He'd had good reasons for this marriage, but they weren't anything his grandfather was going to understand or approve. Even now, his new wife tended to business just on the other side of that partition. He couldn't hear her conversation, but he knew she would be bargaining for the best price on the decor and artwork she hoped to secure for the Foxfire. But soon, they would be alone and they could figure out what this marriage meant for their future.

His arrangement with Lydia was strictly between the two of them. She understood what was at stake and so did he. No complicated emotions meant they wouldn't crash and burn like they had last year. As for her other terms?

A McNeill knew that everything was open for negotiation. And he still had one kiss to bargain with.

Seven

*M*rs. *Lydia McNeill.*

Seated inside her dressing room at their private villa in Costa Rica late that afternoon, Lydia read the engraved luggage tag on the buttery leather suitcase tucked under a bamboo shelf of the walk-in closet off the bathroom of her suite.

None of this felt real. Not the suite at the Honeymoon House. Not the flight on a Gulfstream jet that she'd boarded with only a few minutes' notice. And certainly not her new name.

Her eyes wandered over the wardrobe selections some unnamed staffer of Ian's had chosen for her. There was a silk tropical print maxi dress with coral-colored hibiscus flowers on a white background. A teal-colored pair of gauzy palazzo pants with a white sequined crepe halter top. A silver evening gown that looked like something a fairy princess would wear with gossamer-thin layers of vaguely iridescent fabric. Designer everything, of course. There were other clothes stacked neatly on the bamboo shelves, as well. Italian-made underthings. A nightgown so soft and sheer it was perfect for a bride with its combination of innocence and sensuality.

Except she wasn't a bride in the real sense. And she would not be putting that gorgeous nightdress on her body tonight.

"Lydia?" Ian called from the other side of the bathroom door. "Can I get you anything?"

Her stomach did a fluttery flip at the sound of his voice so close in this piece of paradise. No doubt he wanted to make sure the clothes fit before the dinner they would share on the open-air patio. He'd seemed pleased to show her their accommodations for the night, stressing the way the separate bedrooms fit her requirements but also gave them a chance to celebrate a new peace between them.

Except she didn't feel one bit peaceful about this marriage. If anything, the tropical retreat on the country's western coast only emphasized all the ways today fell short of what she'd once hoped to share with him. If not for the need to hide the true identity of Mallory West, she never would have said yes to this arrangement. But she needed to protect her matchmaking business and the important income it gave to a cause that meant so much to her, to women who inspired her with their strength and determination to be good mothers no matter what obstacles life handed them. Her mother had afforded parenthood by making herself and her daughter tabloid spectacles. Worse, she'd put her energy into fueling that drama rather than showing up at science fairs or even Lydia's high school graduation, which had unfortunately coincided with a face-lift.

Small wonder Lydia felt called to champion single moms who genuinely adored motherhood.

"No. I'll be out in a moment," she called, forcing herself to her feet. The dressing area was as luxe as some women's living rooms with a comfortable leather chair, plenty of mirrors and soft ambient lighting. But she could hardly afford to languish here, staring at her married name on a luggage tag.

Pulling on the silk maxi dress, Lydia let the fabric fall over the soft, imported lace slip that was too beautiful not to wear. She'd never spend her hard-earned dollars as a decorator on something so extravagant, but a woman would have to be blind not to appreciate the careful stitchwork that went into such a delicate design.

"There's no rush. The sun set won't set for another half hour," he called. After a moment, Lydia could hear the sound of his footsteps as he retreated deeper into the resort villa.

Leaving her to remember how many sunsets they'd watched together last spring when they'd been falling in love.

Twelve.

She'd marked them on a calendar, because that was the kind of silly nonsense young women indulged in when they fell in love. They drew hearts around meaningful days in a date book and scribbled effusive prose punctuated with too many exclamation marks in diaries. Lydia had been guilty on all counts.

Emerging from the dressing area, she stepped into her bedroom where she'd left all the windows open to the fresh air. A white-faced capuchin monkey sat on the low stone wall behind her hammock, munching on a piece of mango. Beyond the terrace, she could see the path down to the ocean, hear the gentle rush of waves to the sand.

Any other time, she would have loved an impromptu trip like this to an exotic destination. Travel was her favorite thing about her job since she couldn't afford it otherwise. But tonight, she was getting ready to face her new husband over the dinner table, and that made her too nervous to fully enjoy the surroundings.

"Wish me luck," she called to the monkey before it hopped off the wall and into the pink glow of the coming sunset.

Then, leaving her bedroom, she climbed the stairs to the third story of their private villa and the open-air deck where a local restaurant had set up the catered meal.

"You look incredible." Ian greeted her near the outdoor stairs, offering his arm to escort her past the lone table in the middle of the wooden deck overlooking the ocean. "I hope you found the clothing options as appealing as I do."

His blue eyes never left hers as he spoke, yet her whole body responded to his words, a tingling sensation skipping along her skin. She couldn't help but notice how handsome he looked in a dark suit with a white linen shirt open at the neck. Formal, but with a touch of the reprobate about him.

And now he was her husband.

"Thank you." Clearing her throat, she thought it better not to linger on how well Ian McNeill wore a suit. "The whole place is beautiful." She gestured to the view overlooking the water, the elegant table for two set with a crisp white cloth and laden with silver dishes, bright tropical flowers in vases and seven wax tapers flickering in a candelabra. "I thought it was nice of your local chef to text us his menu suggestions beforehand."

She'd received a message from the chef on the plane, offering a selection of dishes made from the freshest ingredients his culinary staff obtained that morning.

"Were you brave enough to order the grilled octopus he recommended?" Ian teased, drawing her to the edge of the deck to watch the pink sun slip lower on the horizon. His hand lingered at her waist even after they reached the wooden railing, his fingers separated from her skin by the thinnest silk.

Her heartbeat sped faster and she concentrated on the fragrant angel's trumpet flowers spilling over the railing at their feet, sending their heady perfume into the air to mingle with the salty brine of the ocean. Monkeys and birds called to one another as they hastened to their homes before dark fell. Better to think about monkeys and birds than the way Ian's touch affected her.

"I went with the Thai coconut shrimp and pineapple. The preparation sounded suitably tropical." The breeze blew a strand of hair across her chin.

Before she could fix it, Ian reached to skim it aside and tuck it behind one ear, his touch slow and warm. Deliberate.

Oh. So. Inviting.

"There's fresh mango salsa if you're ready for hors d'oeuvres." His voice rumbled low, vibrating along her sensitive skin. "Are you hungry, Lydia?"

Her gaze flashed up to his. Did he know how hard she struggled with the temptation he presented? Was he teasing her again?

But his blue eyes appeared concerned, not intent on seduction. Perhaps she shouldn't rush to judge him.

"I wouldn't mind a drink while the sun sets." Her mouth was dry and her heart felt more than a little bruised to undergo the trappings of marriage without the feelings that should go along with it. "Maybe we should have our toast now."

"Certainly." He excused himself to pour the champagne from a bucket chilling on a stand near their table. "I hope you don't mind, but we'll be serving ourselves tonight. The honeymoon suite service is...discreet in that way."

"Of course." She tensed, crossing her arms. "That way, if we decide we have to tear each other's clothes off before dessert, we'll have complete privacy to do so."

Ian finished pouring the champagne, but she could see his shoulders stiffen underneath the impeccably tailored suit jacket.

"I guess we would. But since you've been very clear about your expectations in this marriage, I realize that's not going to happen tonight." He stalked toward her, a champagne flute in each hand. "And that's another reason I thought it would be best for the waitstaff not to be around. I want to protect your privacy and respect your wishes about all things."

Somehow that consideration made her heart beat faster still. The sea breeze tickled the silk of her dress against her thighs and toyed with the spaghetti straps on her shoulders, a phantom lover's touch. She needed a dose of reality back in this faux honeymoon.

"You say that." She tugged the flute from his hands with a bit more force than necessary, her emotions getting the better of her as a few bubbles slid over the side of the glass. "And yet you persist in pretending that this is a real marriage with a flight to Costa Rica and a sunset meal in a villa called the Honeymoon House. I can't help but feel the weight of very different expectations."

"Lydia." He set his glass on the railing then guided hers there, too. "We need to present the world with a believable marriage or our agreement isn't worth anything." He folded both of her hands in his, turning her to face him. "I spoke to my brothers on the flight here and they informed me that news of our nuptials has already been leaked. Believe me when I tell you, the world is watching what happens next."

"Leaked?" She tried to imagine how that could happen. "Why? Who would care about our marriage?" Panic tightened in her chest as she thought of all the horrible ways the tabloids could ratchet up interest in a story. She'd been the object of media interest far too often in her life. "What are they saying?"

"Only that we married. Someone in the district court

offices must have leaked the news directly since my brothers had a copy of the wedding photo within thirty minutes of the ceremony."

"If they aren't saying anything ugly yet, they will soon." She needed to sit. Or maybe walk. She didn't know what she needed, but she felt all the makings of a full-blown panic attack coming on. "Excuse me."

Pulling away from his touch, she paced the deck.

"There is nothing ugly to say," Ian assured her, watching her progress but not following her, which she appreciated.

"Then they make something up. That's how the tabloids sell their sordid work." She recalled old headlines from her past—stories about her mother. Stories about her. "Did you know there was a whole year where the media sold papers on the idea that my mother was part of a religious cult that cast a spell on my father?" They'd taken a laughable photo of her mother in a Halloween costume and used it for weeks on end. "Then, there was a whole other year where they used zoom lenses to snap photos of her stomach to analyze it for a baby bump. And one extremely hellish year when *I* was photographed and accused of having a baby bump. At sixteen."

She didn't mention the stories that suggested her mother had pimped her out to rich men for a fat payday. Or the fact that she'd been treated for an eating disorder after being accused of looking pregnant as a vulnerable teenager.

Feeling a wealth of old resentment threaten to wash over her like a rogue wave, Lydia took the wooden stairs leading away from the third-floor deck all the way down to the beach. Vaguely, she heard Ian call out to her, and his footsteps as he followed her. She didn't stop, though. She couldn't get enough air into her lungs no matter how deeply she breathed. Kicking off her jeweled sandals, she let her toes sink into the powdery sand as she hurried down to the water's edge.

By the time Ian reached her side, she had the hem of her long silk maxi dress in one hand, the fabric hiked up to her knees so she could stand in the rolling surf. The warm water soothed her, lapping gently along her calves and beading up on her skin slick with the coconut oil lotion supplied as a resort amenity. Somehow the feel of the water against her skin took her heart rate down a notch, and she tipped her face into the soft sea breeze.

Ian removed his socks and shoes at the water's edge, preparing to join her. She thought about telling him not to bother—that she was okay—but then she wondered why she needed to pretend she was fine when she so often wasn't.

She'd denied herself comfort in life many times out of the need to look like she had her life together and a deep-seated desire to avoid scandal. But no matter what she did, she was a favorite target of the tabloid media. She could live the most pristine, blameless life possible and they'd still find some way to make a tawdry tale out of her.

And right now, as she watched Ian stride toward her with his broad shoulders that looked like they could take on the problems of the world, she had to wonder why she kept denying herself pleasure for the sake of a good reputation she would never achieve.

Ian McNeill was her husband. He was the most generous, amazing lover she'd ever had. And he'd made it very clear that he still wanted her.

As long as she could separate pleasure from a deep emotional commitment, couldn't she at least indulge herself for a little while?

Ian had almost reached Lydia's side when she sent him a look that sizzled over him like a lover's tongue.

The sensation was so tangible he had to halt his forward progress through the shallow surf. No way had he read her expression correctly. He was mixing up his own emotions with hers—seeing what he wanted to see in her bright green eyes. His heart slugged harder in his chest, urging him toward her, while he fought the need with all his might.

She'd just shared some hurtful memories he never knew about, so no way in hell was she thinking what he was thinking.

Get it together.

"Lydia." He forced an even tone into his voice, reminding himself that good men didn't confuse compassion with sex. "I'm so sorry you went through that as a teen."

He reached for her, cupping her cheek in one hand even as he maintained a bit of space between them. Her eyes slid closed at his touch, her cheek tilting into his palm in a way that urged him to give more physical comfort.

Reigniting the war within.

Gritting his teeth against all the ways he wanted to surround her body with his—protect her, pleasure her—Ian shifted closer to slide an arm around her waist. He drew her against him, fitting her to his side, resting his cheek on top of her silky hair. The scent of coconut drifted up from her skin. His mouth watered.

"I promise you," he assured her, stroking along the soft skin of her upper arm while he stared out to sea, "if anyone dares to initiate a story about you that isn't true, I will sue their company into bankruptcy."

"They will say I married you for money." She pulled back to look him in the eye. "The same way my mother pursued my father."

"We both know nothing could be further from the truth." He'd tried to include a financial settlement in their contract, but she'd refused. Had she done so because she anticipated that kind of negative press?

"Your family will have their doubts about my intentions in this marriage. As will all of Manhattan. I received a famously small settlement from my father upon his death." She knotted the silk of her skirt at one knee so she didn't need to hold on to the fabric to keep it out of the water. "There will be questions about my motives for marrying you and the press speculation will only fuel the fire."

He'd seen that trick with a skirt hem in Rangiroa a few times, and he liked this side of her that was a little messier.

"My family has faith in my judgment." He'd already

told them to stand down where she was concerned. "And that means they will trust you."

When she didn't answer right away, he noticed that she was staring out at the horizon where the sun was sliding the rest of the way into the sea. She'd told him once that she liked to make a wish on it before it disappeared.

"I wish *you* could trust me to make you happy for the next twelve months." He got the words out just before the final glowing orange arc vanished.

The sky glowed pink and purple in the aftermath, the ocean reflecting the colors in watery ripples while a heron and a pair of white ibis flew overhead.

"I don't think that's such a good thing to wish for." She turned to face him, her exposed skin reflecting the sunset hues.

"No?"

"No," she told him flatly. "Investing too much in this marriage will only make things all the more complicated when our year together is done." She folded her arms across her chest and stared down into the water where they stood. "We both need to remember this is a business arrangement. Nothing more."

"One thing doesn't have to preclude the other, does it?" He turned his attention to her arm, where the strap of her dress flirted with the edge of her shoulder. "We can be happy and respect the business arrangement, too."

Maybe this time together would help cure him of his preoccupation with her. He'd barely dated since they'd split.

"I've been thinking about that." She glanced down at the water where the gentle swell of the tide lapped at her ankles. She lifted one foot and skimmed it over the surface in a slow arc in front of her. "About the benefits of marriage."

His throat dried up. He stayed very still to keep from touching her the way he wanted to, convincing her with his hands and his mouth how *beneficial* this relationship could be for both of them. He'd promised her she could set the pace with any kind of physical relationship and he wouldn't earn her trust anytime soon if he took that power out of her hands.

But the temptation to draw her into the water—into his arms—was so strong he could barely breathe.

"Like Costa Rican vacations?" He tried for a light tone but failed, his whole body fueled with a biological imperative to take his bride to his bed.

"This is definitely a treat." She quit her game of drawing her toes through the water, turning to face him in air that felt suddenly too still. "But I was thinking more along the lines of how—" she bit her lip for a second before pressing on "—*satisfying* we both found our previous relationship."

Blood pounded through his temples for a split second before surging south.

"Meaning you're reconsidering the idea of separate bedrooms?" He kept his eyes on hers in the growing dimness despite the flickering tiki torches dotting the sand near Honeymoon House. "We need to be very clear about this point, Lydia, since it's your move next."

During the heavy beat of silence that followed, an

owl hooted from a tree nearby. In the distance, Ian spied a party boat on the waves, the music cranked high as the vessel sped through the dark water.

"It occurs to me that no matter how hard I've tried to live beyond reproach, I'm always going to be a target for the tabloids. In their eyes, my mother was a gold digger who duped my father into getting her pregnant. And I'm the bait she used to ensure she got her payoff." Lydia shrugged and the spaghetti strap that had been teetering on the edge of her shoulder gave up the ghost, sliding down her arm. "Why should I create some exaggerated facade of respectability when I'll forever be a tabloid story waiting to happen?"

He dragged his gaze from her bare shoulder and the delicate curve of her neck. "You make it sound like being with me compromises your reputation."

"No. I only mean that I have to stop worrying about what other people think of me and find what happiness I can. Because no matter what I do or how careful I am, I will be a magnet for rumors."

He sifted through her words. Put them in the context of the one question that burned brightest in his brain as the stars began to dot the sky above them.

"You want to find happiness." This seemed highly relevant. "And you agree that there were *satisfying* aspects of our relationship before things fell apart." Heat burned over him despite the fact that he stood ankle-deep in the Pacific. He wanted a taste of her more than he wanted his next breath as the tropical air blanketed his skin with sultry touches.

"Correct." She kept her arms clenched around herself, but there was no mistaking the challenging tilt of her chin. The throaty edge in her voice.

He waded an inch closer. Their bodies weren't touching. But the water swirled between them in circles that seemed to connect them anyway.

"Can I assume that you're open to revisiting those satisfying aspects?" He wouldn't have to use his kiss as a bargaining tool to woo her into his bed tonight.

"I'm starting to think it would be foolish to deny ourselves." Her words were breathless, a barely there sound that caressed his ears.

"I couldn't agree more." He waited for her touch. Watched for it.

Even the cries of birds and monkeys seemed to quiet in the still moment of her decision.

"It's my wedding night," she informed him, her voice picking up strength and volume. "I don't need to sleep alone."

"Not when I want you in my bed for days on end," he assured her, only too happy to describe exactly how thoroughly he would pleasure her if given the opportunity to touch her tonight. "Although I will be very disappointed if we are sleeping."

Despite the growing dark, he could see the convulsive movement of her throat as she swallowed. Licked her lips.

"Ian?"

"Mmm?"

"I think I'd like that kiss now."

Eight

A year ago, they would have fallen on each other with the ravenous hunger of lovers who need to be touching all the time.

Truth be told, she was so ready for his kiss, she felt more than a little ravenous now as they stood in the surf outside Honeymoon House.

But their relationship was much different now. Careful. Tenuous. And—she still couldn't believe it—they were married. Maybe that's why Ian took his time closing the distance between them. Instead of taking her in his arms, he stroked along her bare shoulder where one strap of her gown had fallen away. She hadn't realized how cool her skin was from standing in the water until she felt the warmth of his hand when he made contact. His callus-roughened palms reminded her he wasn't the kind of developer who simply drew plans, although he was talented enough to design his own buildings.

No. She'd seen Ian McNeill clamber up ladders and take a crowbar to stubborn wall supports himself, never afraid of getting his hands dirty on a job site. She liked that his millions hadn't robbed him of the ability to walk among the workmen or appreciate the less glamorous aspects of actual physical construction.

"Are you cold?" he asked, perhaps feeling the difference in their skin temperatures, and yet still he didn't kiss her in spite of her request. He held back, even as the fire in his eyes broadcast how much he wanted her.

"I'm not chilly at all. Thank you, though." She was plenty hot on the inside; in fact, she was anticipating that kiss, aching for him to take her lips. To take her. "I like being outside." She could breathe deeply out here without feeling suffocated by all the expectations weighing her down back home. Without the scandal rocking her world again.

"You're trembling," he observed softly, his other hand coming between them to skim a knuckle along her lower lip, drawing out the moment.

Lydia nipped it to put an end to that line of conversation since she was overwhelmed by her feelings for him. *Sensual feelings*, she told herself. *Nothing deeper*. The trembling didn't have a thing to do with romantic notions about the relationship she was undertaking again.

Finally—*thank goodness*—Ian cupped her face and tipped her chin up, perhaps to see her better in the moonlight. The glow of the tiki torches on the beach and dotting the railing of the deck on the third floor of

Honeymoon House didn't give off enough light to see each other well now that the sun had set.

The look in his eyes sent of a flash fire along her skin. Brooding and intense, he stared at her as if she were a complicated puzzle he'd rather devour than solve. So when his kiss came, she was surprised by its devastating gentleness. His soft, full lips covered hers, coaxing them apart to taste and explore.

Sighing into him, she gave herself up to the wholly masculine feel of his strong arms wrapped around her. The hint of sandalwood on his skin unleashed a torrent of fiery memories. Stripping each other's clothes off in a hotel dining room because they couldn't wait to get to the bedroom. Ian slipping her swimsuit aside to pleasure her behind an island waterfall where no one could see them. Her hoarse shouts of fulfillment when he'd demonstrated a deftness with his tongue that had been her undoing, not just once, but many, many times.

Past and present mingling, Lydia pressed her body to all that hard, masculine heat, wanting to lose herself in him. In pleasure. No holding back. She wanted those memories to be reality now. The good memories. Not the aftermath of lies and deceit.

She worked the buttons of his linen dress shirt, hastily unfastening each one to splay greedy hands over his sculpted chest and abs. The moonlight shone down on his bronzed skin, making her greedy to see more of him. All of him.

"I want to take you inside." He captured her questing fingers, stilling her hungry explorations before he kissed the fingertips, one at a time. "I need to see you."

With a jerky nod, she agreed, even though she could have gladly pulled *An Affair to Remember* moment and wrestled him to the beach to make love in the surf.

Together, they hurried out of the water. He scooped up both pairs of shoes and set them on the first stair leading to the villa. She followed him barefoot up the wooden steps and onto the cool stone patio of the first floor. Here, the light from the small gas torches set at intervals in the stone railing cast plenty of light on them as he led her toward the outdoor shower.

And while she would have also pulled her dress off then and there, Ian turned on the shower spray at foot level just long enough to rinse the beach sand from their toes. She unfastened the knot she'd put in her dress hem to hold it up, letting the silk fall back around her calves while he shut off the nozzle.

She eyed his strong back as he straightened, the ripple of muscles evident through the thin, pale linen of his shirt.

"Damn, Lydia, you're killing me when you look at me like that."

Ian tugged her closer with one hand. Caught openly ogling him, she felt her cheeks heat and was glad for the rosy glow of the torchlight.

"I'm sure I don't know what you mean," she told him archly, turning to head up the stairs since both bedrooms were situated on the second floor.

"What I'd like to know—" he palmed the small of her back, shadowing her movements as his voice overwhelmed her senses "—is what you're thinking about when you look at me that way."

"Probably something really benign," she lied, teasing him only because she knew there would be an end to both their torments soon. "Like what you'll think of the outdoor rugs I chose for the Foxfire courtyard."

She paused in the hallway between the two bedrooms, unsure which way to go. The villa was exposed to the Costa Rican elements on three sides and they'd left all the retractable windows open to savor the mild weather. She could see into his bedroom where a king-size platform bed covered in a black duvet and batik-patterned pillows was illuminated only by the flickering outdoor torches of the master suite's deck.

"Rugs? Not even close," he taunted lightly as he steered her toward his bedroom and the small shelter it offered from the thick, jungle-like branches that brushed against the open half walls. "I'll bet you were thinking about how much you wanted our clothes off."

He turned her to face him and her heart raced a crazy staccato beat as her gaze fell to his bare chest where she'd already undone half the buttons on his shirt.

"If we're being totally honest—" she hooked her finger into the gap of the soft linen and wrangled another button free, her knuckle grazing the warmth of those beautifully chiseled abs "—I was far more fixated on getting your clothes off than my own."

"That can be arranged." He stood in shadow, his back to the glow of torchlight while he shrugged out of the shirt, letting the expensive material float to the floor behind him. "I'll gladly do what it takes to put that gleam in your eyes again."

He tipped her face up and their gazes collided. Her

breathing hitched and her skin tingled everywhere. She was seized with the need to kiss and touch him. To follow all the pent-up emotions their reunion had stirred, leaving her aching for him for days on end.

"There it is." He ran his hands down her shoulders, dragging the only remaining strap of her dress off so the bodice slid loose to sag against her breasts. His eyes remained on hers, however. "There's that look I like. When you watched me walking into the surf tonight, you were staring at me with that expression in your eyes. It was all I could do not to haul you into bed like a caveman."

He turned her inside out with just his words while the heady scent of angel's trumpet and jasmine drifted on the warm breeze.

"I do that to you?" She leaned forward to press a kiss to his chest, savoring the smooth warmth of one pectoral. "I wish I'd known I had that power."

"Lydia." He skimmed a hand down her hair. Stroking. Petting. "You distract me too much already. If I told you everything you do that drives me crazy with wanting you, I'd never get anything done."

Through the veil of her hair, he toyed with the zipper at the back of her dress, flicking at the toggle and tracing the path it would take if he pulled it down. She thought she'd come out of her skin faster than she'd get out of her clothes, the slower pace making her flesh feel too tight and sensitive.

"You say that." She pressed another kiss to his chest, letting her tongue flick along the silken heat of smooth pectoral there. Then, gathering her courage, she arched up on her toes to speak softly in his ear. "But if I was anywhere near as irresistible as you claim, I'd be underneath you already."

With both her hands on his chest now, Lydia could feel the hard shudder go through him. Only then did she understand the restraint he was exercising.

"Is that what you think?" His hands pressed harder against her, molding her to him before he found that zipper again and started to ease it downward. "Because I was doing everything in my power to make tonight different than any time we've been together before. To give us a fresh start."

Her heart turned over in her chest even though she'd told herself a hundred times she wasn't going to let her emotions get all tangled up in this like last time. She couldn't go through that heartbreak again. Right now, she wanted to lose herself in pleasure, not think about a fresh start.

And yet...

How unexpectedly thoughtful of him to want to make tonight a new beginning. To make it different from their past together. She wanted to tell him that was unnecessary, but with the silk dress gliding lower and lower on her body, she found it difficult to argue with him. The sound of the sea rolling in provided a soothing music in harmony with the rustle of palm fronds, drowning out everything else as she shimmied the rest of the way out of her dress. The silk pooled at her feet, leaving her clad in the beautiful imported lace lingerie she thought he'd never see tonight.

"You're my wife now," he reminded her, backing her

toward the bed while his blue eyes moved languidly over her body. They were both more visible now as they neared the bedside sconce. "Not just my lover. We should make tonight the start of something new. Different."

"I like that idea." She was breathless. So turned on she could hardly find enough air to speak. Underneath the coral-colored lace, her breasts tightened to impossibly taut peaks. "A new start, that is."

She remembered—vaguely—that she wanted their relationship to be different than before. So a do-over was a good thing. She could protect her heart from all the ways this marriage could hurt her before they said goodbye. But right now, she mostly wanted Ian McNeill all over her. Inside her.

He lowered her to the bed, her body meeting the soft duvet while Ian loomed over her, shirtless and golden in the torchlight. He unfastened his belt. She held her breath.

"But, Ian?" She chewed her lip as he freed himself from his trousers, her eyes sliding to the gray silk boxers that couldn't conceal how much he wanted her.

"Yes, wife?" He bent over her on the bed, brushing a kiss over one hip, his lips working a decadent magic on her skin.

"We don't need to make *everything* different than it was before." She remembered multiple orgasms—the first of her life. And then there was the tireless lovemaking that woke her in the middle of the night and left her sleeping more deeply—happily—than ever before.

She felt his lips smile against her hip while he kissed

her there, and then licked a path along the hem of her lace underwear.

Her eyes might have crossed before she closed them, giving herself over to him.

"No?" He kissed. Licked. Kissed again.

Behind her eyelids, she was already seeing stars just thinking about what he might do next. Her body tensed with anticipation.

"No. Some things were really quite perfect." She debated shouldering her way out of the strapless lace bra top holding her in, the fabric like a straitjacket when she wanted to feel nothing but Ian's body against hers.

Her breath came in short pants. She licked her lips. Wriggled her hips. Arched her spine to get closer to him because she needed him. Now.

"Perfect." He repeated the word in a whisper over her skin, trailing a kiss into the indent of her waist as he covered her with his body.

Finally. Finally.

A moan of satisfaction hummed through her as the hard length of him pressed at the juncture of her thighs. She dragged him down to kiss her. She nipped his lower lip, unable to stay still beneath him. She couldn't get close enough, her breasts flattening against the hard wall of his chest in a delicious caress that left her wanting more.

The humid air hung heavy on her skin and his too, a salty ocean tang that made the night feel all the more exotic but familiar, as well. Like the past, but different.

When his mouth closed on her breast through the soft lace, she twined her fingers in his hair. Held him close and clung to the sensations he loosed in her with each flick of his tongue. He unfastened the series of hooks at the front until she could sidle free of the confining fabric. She slid one leg around his, wanting him everywhere.

He must have guessed, or else he was as caught up as she was, because he skimmed a touch between her thighs, teasing over the damp lace until she shuddered with the small convulsions that were a precursor to all the pleasure that was to come. She remembered this wildness, the heated, primal joining that had overwhelmed her in the past.

As Ian tugged aside the thin scrap of panties to find her slick core, Lydia forgot everything but the way he made her feel. Mindless. Sensual. Wanted.

With each stroke of his fingers, each press of his palm against her, the tension in her body coiled more tightly. He wound her up, taking her higher. She gripped his shoulders. Breathed his name.

And flew apart in a wave of orgasms that washed over and over her. It was even more amazing than she remembered. A blissful retreat from the world to a place where only pleasure remained. She reeled with the aftershocks for long moments knowing the night was only beginning.

Soon, he would be deep inside her. Joined with her physically to make their marriage legal. Binding.

As he poised above her, his body taut with a hunger he hadn't appeased yet, Lydia had just enough wits about her to wonder how she'd ever survive the onslaught of pleasure while guarding her heart. She

walked an emotional tightrope tonight and—possibly—
for many nights to come.

Heaven help her, she couldn't stop if she tried.

Ian needed her with a fierceness that defied logic.

Beads of sweat popped up along his brow. He ground
his teeth together against the ache of it all. He'd waited
this long to take her. He could wait another minute to
chase the sudden shadows from her gaze.

"Look at me," he commanded, unable to soften the
edge in his voice. Instead, he simply lowered the volume.

His gaze met hers. There were definitely shadows
there. The light was dim, but he knew the nuances of
those green eyes. Time hadn't dimmed his memory of
this woman's moods.

"I want you," she said simply. Urgently.

Was she running from her shadows by losing herself
in this night with him? He was too amped up to figure
out what might have upset her, but he knew she wanted
him, too. She couldn't hide that.

"That's going to happen soon," he promised, already
clutching a condom in one hand. "But I never gave you
the proper kiss to commemorate the day."

Her eyebrows lifted.

"There were kisses," she argued, lifting her neck to
plant another on his cheek, to one side of his mouth. "I
was there for a lot of highly memorable kisses just now."

"Not a 'you may kiss the bride' kind of kiss." He let
go of the foil wrapper, setting it beside the pillow near
her head, where dark hair spilled in every direction.

She was so damn beautiful.

"I'm not sure how that kind is any different." Frowning, she seemed appropriately distracted from whatever had bothered her a moment ago.

And that made holding back worth it, even if he throbbed as though a vise were clamped around him.

"I put it off before because I wanted to get it right." He wanted her to be happy on her wedding day, and he wanted to be the one to banish those shadows in her eyes. Call him old-fashioned, but even if it was a temporary marriage, Lydia was now his wife. She deserved something to mark that occasion—something more than the courthouse visit. "It didn't seem like the kind of kiss to share in front of strangers."

Her eyes locked on his. Curiosity mixed with desire. And he was damn glad he'd taken this moment to remind them both what it meant to be together tonight. Digging under the covers, he found her left hand and held it, running his finger over the platinum band and square-shaped diamond there. He twisted it gently—back and forth a few degrees in either direction before resetting it right where it had been. Resting it there anew.

Then, his gaze lowering to her lips, he kissed her. Savored her. He felt the tension ease out of her as her arms went around him. She returned the kiss with a sweetness that almost made him forget everything else that had passed between them.

And before he let himself think about that, he retrieved the condom and rolled it into place. Never breaking the kiss, he made room for himself between her thighs and pressed deep inside her. Her fingernails scored his chest, scratching lightly as he found a rhythm that pleased them both. Heat flared all over, building gain until it roared up his spine with new urgency. He'd put this off too long. Forced himself to wait and wait. So now when the pressure built, it powered through him with an undeniable force.

He wrapped Lydia in his arms, rolled her on top of him so he could watch her. She bit her lip, her dark hair spilling over her shoulders as she moved in time with him, her narrow hips rocking in time with his.

He remembered so much about her and he used it to his advantage now, recalling exactly where to touch her to send her spiraling into ecstasy. He reached between them, fingering his way to where she was slick with heat. She arched back, still for a moment, before she collapsed over him, her body convulsing all around him. The soft, feminine pulses were his undoing, the feel of her pleasure spiking his own.

Their shouts mingled with the night birds and howler monkeys, a wild coming together that pounded through both of them. When the spasms slowed and stopped, Ian turned her in his arms so they lay side by side, breathing the same humid air of the Costa Rican jungle while the bamboo fan blades turned languidly overhead.

Their marriage was real now. The words they'd spoken in front of the county clerk were only a precursor to this, the ultimate bond that made it legitimate. He had been prepared to wait to consummate the marriage until she was ready, but maybe Lydia had seen that their union could have as many benefits as they allowed themselves.

Tonight might be a shadow of what a real marriage between them could have been like. But he could take a whole lot of pleasure from more nights like this. Whatever had driven her into his arms tonight, Ian wasn't about to argue.

Nine

Seated at the polished stone patio table across from Ian two hours later, Lydia decided she preferred dining while dressed in one of the T-shirts and boxer shorts he'd packed for their trip. Wrapped in a cotton throw blanket that she'd found on the back of the couch, she tucked sock-clad feet beneath her while Ian filled their water glasses from the pewter pitcher, still cold all these hours after they should have eaten.

But the caterers had left several covered trays of food with small candles burning in the stands below them on the buffet, while other dishes had been placed on ice, so everything she'd put on her plate remained delicious. She helped herself to another bite of the baked pineapple that was so good she couldn't wait to recreate it at home. Or maybe everything simply tasted better after multiple orgasms. She didn't think she could shake the pleasurable feeling in her veins if she tried.

Even knowing her marriage was utterly unorthodox and it wouldn't last beyond this time next year, Lydia was determined to savor the joy of the night. There would be worries enough when they returned to the real world.

For now, eating cold lobster at midnight overlooking the Pacific with a fascinating, handsome dinner companion, she couldn't muster the energy to worry just yet. The heady scent of flowers wafted on the sea breeze, and she reveled in how her cooling skin was still warm from a shared shower with Ian.

She flushed just thinking about the things he'd done to her under the shower spray. But better to think about that than the moments when he'd toyed with her wedding ring and kissed her as though she would be his bride forever.

"More wine?" he offered, lifting the decanter of pinot grigio.

With his jaw shadowed by stubble and his dress shirt unbuttoned to his waist, Ian still managed to look completely at home at the formal dining table, his blue eyes hooded from the glow of the candelabra that had remained burning thanks to the glass globes around the tapers.

"No, thank you." She took another drink from her water glass. "Being in Miami and now here, I'm thirstier than usual from the heat."

Or else she was thirstier than usual from the unaccustomed physical activity. Sweet, merciful heaven, but the man could do incredible things to her.

"Do you usually stay in Manhattan over the summer?" he asked as he bit into a slice of fresh mango. It was an innocuous question but one that reminded her of the differences in their worlds.

"Unless a client hires me for a job outside the city, I'm always in Manhattan." She shifted the cotton throw on her shoulders and tucked closer to the table. "I can't afford to get used to the McNeill lifestyle."

All around the deck, tiki torches still burned. The animal life had quieted some so she could hear the roll of waves onto the beach below along with the ever-present swish of palm fronds in the breeze.

Ian frowned. "We have a house in the Hamptons. You could go there on the weekends if you'd like to escape the heat."

"That's just what I mean." She remembered how many times her mother had dragged her to Newport in the summer, couch-surfing with any potential acquaintance while she tried to wrangle an invitation from Lydia's father to stay at the Whitney mansion. "I don't want to get in the habit of living beyond my means."

He wiped his hands on a linen napkin and set it aside, then moved to take the seat next to her at the round table. Just his physical nearness affected her, spiking her heart rate the same way it had every single time he got close to her. It had been this way last year when she'd fallen for him. It had stayed that way even when she'd been angry with him and told him they were finished. Right to the last minute when he'd walked out of her hotel room in Rangiroa, she'd felt the hum of response to his nearness.

"Lydia, we'll be sharing my home in New York. You need to be comfortable there." He took her hand, threading his fingers through hers. "Our marriage needs to be believable."

She stared down at their interlocked hands, wondering what was for show now. His touch? His kiss? She needed to remember that they had a relationship based on mutual needs. Ian's legal need to keep the family business in family hands, and her need to protect the secret of Mallory West so she could continue her more lucrative side business of matchmaking to help struggling mothers. Simple.

And yet it would be so easy to let the chemistry she shared with this man distract her from her goals.

"I don't need to start spending weekends in the Hamptons to have people believe our marriage is real." She plucked a plump berry from a bowl of fresh fruit and took a bite. "Even if we were wildly in love and planning our forever, I wouldn't suddenly quit my job and give up my work with Moms' Connection."

"But you can expand your role there now." He leaned back in his seat, keeping her hand in his and resting their joined palms on his knee while the candelabra candles burned down a little more, dripping wax on the linen tablecloth. "Maybe chair your own fund-raiser for the group when we return to New York."

The possibility shimmered like a beautiful mirage. Help her favorite cause? Aid the women who had given so much to her those weeks when she'd been thinking she would be a single mother to Ian's child? She could do so much good there.

Except that it wouldn't last. Her time as a New York socialite would be short-lived.

"That's what I mean, Ian. In twelve months' time, I won't have the kind of social standing needed to chair Manhattan charity events. If anything, my reputation might very well be in a worse state than ever, and that's saying something considering my past."

"Then take a one-year position on their board. Do what you can to further their goals in that time. All I'm saying is, it would be good to get involved at the level people would expect of my wife." He turned her shoulders toward him so she faced him head-on. "You might as well work with a group you support anyhow."

"Thank you." She couldn't deny the idea intrigued her. "It's generous of you to suggest."

He shrugged like it wasn't a big deal to write a substantial check to a group that struggled for every dime. "You'd be doing the legwork, not me. Besides, I'd like to find ways for you to be happy over the next year." A wicked grin slid over his face. "Outside of bed, I mean. Because that much I believe we have covered."

He drew her forward, his eyes intent on hers before he closed them at the last moment. He nipped her lower lip, and then soothed the spot with his tongue, sending a shiver of pleasure all over her body.

He hadn't been kidding about making her happy in bed. Ian McNeill had that power locked down.

"What about when we go back to the real world?" she asked, her eyes fluttering open. "I'm concerned you may have underestimated the level of interest the press will take in this marriage. Not to mention the interest my mother will have."

"We'll deal with that as it comes," he said firmly. "For now, if you're finished with dinner, I'd like my dessert."

The heated look in his eyes turned her blood molten.

"What about mine?" She pushed the words past lips gone dry.

"You'll get yours, Lydia McNeill," he whispered in her ear before licking along the lobe, his hand already seeking the hem of the T-shirt she wore and tucking underneath it. "That much I promise you."

An hour later—after much taste-testing of the dessert menu and his wife—Ian counted himself a lucky man. The marriage might be fake, but Ian was confident he was having as rewarding a honeymoon as any groom on the planet.

He sure as hell had a hotter wife than anyone else.

He had convinced Lydia to join him in the oversize hot tub off the master suite, another space that was mostly open to the elements. The sinks and bathroom had been situated on an interior wall, but the shower and hot tub could be partially exposed to the villa's private patch of forest on the steep mountainside that led down to the beach. With no other accommodations for miles, the Honeymoon House was the perfect blend of seclusion and luxury, with services available from the local resort.

Ian had shut down all the outdoor torches now that

it was well past midnight. The house was quite dark except for the moonlight spilling across the hot tub's surface and the spa light underwater.

He watched as Lydia stripped off her T-shirt. His T-shirt, actually. He liked seeing her in his clothes. And he really, really liked seeing her out of them. He couldn't take his eyes off her now as she looked back over one shoulder before slipping a thumb into the band of the boxer shorts she'd folded over and tucked to fit her slender frame.

It didn't matter that the shadows were thick around them. He could see the shape of her hips as she wriggled free of the cotton. And, damn, he could see her even better as she faced the tub and hurried—naked—into the bubbling water.

Her high, firm breasts hid just beneath the surface. For a moment he wondered why he'd suggested this since what he really wanted was to bury himself inside her all over again and the hot tub was only going to slow him down. But then, this was her honeymoon, too. And he wanted to make sure he made their time here unforgettable for her.

She was already worried about returning to the real world and facing their families, which reminded him what a good, generous woman she was. He didn't want her to worry about any of that when he could take care of everything. She was his to protect now. He planned to erase all those concerns tonight before they slept.

"It's your turn," she called from the water, her glossy, dark hair spilling around her like a mermaid in the clear bubbles.

"Just admiring the view." He stripped off his shirt that he had hadn't even bothered to button, tossing it onto the wood planks of the deck.

"So am I." She leaned back against one of the neck rests of the molded spa. "Feel free to take your time."

"You saying things like that makes it all the tougher to take my time. I hope you know that." He eased his shorts off, his body ready to go again from just looking at her.

Though her playful words only amped him up more.

"Maybe I like cracking that legendary McNeill control." She watched him as he stepped down into the tub beside her. Her pale skin was a liquid shadow in the water.

"Legendary?" He gathered up the hair floating around her and laid it over her shoulder. "You overestimate me."

"Do I? I've heard you're as coolheaded in the boardroom as you are on the job site—never rattled, utterly restrained, and it's impossible to guess what you're thinking."

Is that how she saw him?

He studied her pretty face washed clean of any makeup, her lips still deeply pink without any added color. Her eyelashes were dark and spiky from the water. And she studied him as thoroughly as he did her. It amazed him they didn't understand each other better.

"I'm actually more of the negotiator of the family. The link between my two brothers, who make a habit of taking the opposite views on just about everything." If he and Lydia were going to spend this year together, it might help if they knew each other better outside the bedroom. "Far from being the guy with legendary control, I'm the one most likely to do the compromising."

She arched her eyebrows and smiled. "Ian McNeill? Compromise? I can think of a whole host of independent contractors working on the luxury hotel in Rangiroa who would have been astounded to hear it. For that matter, most of my colleagues at work on the Foxfire are already nervous about the possibility of budget overruns."

"That's not necessarily a bad thing." He wondered if she was overstating the case. "I respect deadlines and budget constraints. I expect the people who work with me to follow suit."

"And they rush to do just that. All I'm saying is that you're not the easiest of bosses. I can't picture you as the one in your family who compromises."

That bugged him, actually. He forced himself to lean back against the seat though, unwilling to let her see as much.

"My whole life, I've been the one in the middle. In age as well as temperament." He reached for her, lifting her legs and laying them across his lap so she was now sitting sideways in her corner seat. "When Quinn wants a highbrow hotel launch and Cameron thinks we could hit the youth market with a launch during Comic-Con, I'm saddled with finding the halfway point. And that's been true since the time Quinn was old enough to build a soap box derby car and spent all day painting it black with silver stripes, only to wake and find Cameron had used decoupage to paste 'artful nudes' all over the body."

She only half smothered a laugh. "I'd love to hear your compromise on that one."

"Before or after Quinn broke Cam's nose?" That had been the first of some ugly fights. They'd learned to work around each other—and respect their very different approaches—since then. But the learning curve hadn't been pretty. "I tried repainting the car, but since I was only eight at the time and had to paint over decoupage, it lacked the cool refinement of Quinn's version."

Lydia was quiet for a long moment. Feeling that he'd failed to bring the right touch of humor to the story, Ian wished he'd kept it to himself.

"Perhaps not getting your own way in the family dynamic made you all the more disposed to dictating the terms in your life." She tipped her head up to the moonlight for a moment, giving him a tempting view of her long neck and damp shoulders.

But her words had distracted him even more than her body. Did she have a point?

He filed the notion away, unwilling to lose this time with her by getting caught up in their differences.

"What about you?" He turned the tables, only because it was the first conversational tidbit that occurred to him and he didn't want to start analyzing his own situation. "No one defaces your prized possessions when you're an only child."

She tensed, a reaction he felt where he stroked her calves under the water.

"I wasn't, though." She straightened in the tub, but didn't turn away from him or move her feet off his lap. "My mother made sure I was very aware that I had half siblings and that my father treated them very differently from how he behaved with me."

"Damn. I'm sorry, Lydia." He sure as hell hadn't meant to stir up old hurts.

"No." She shook her head and waved a hand as if she could brush aside his concern. "Don't be. I think she hoped throughout my entire childhood that Dad would swoop in and raise me for her, but that never happened. Once she realized that she was going to have to be my mother—well, I was mostly grown by then. But we got along better once I stopped expecting her to be a mom and started enjoying her as a friend."

"Yeah?" He massaged her feet, hoping to ease away the tension that had crept into her body since he started this conversation. He hated to think she'd never been her parents' number one priority. "Maybe I ought to try that approach with Liam. He was the nonparent in my youth. But at least I had my mother and grandfather."

"Although you were the one standing between your siblings when they came to blows." Her green eyes pinned his for a moment before shifting lower. "Maybe that's why you and I ended up getting along so well. For a few incredibly memorable weeks, we put one another first."

Until they didn't.

He wondered if that realization echoed through her with the same dull ache that it did for him. But Lydia was already shifting closer, her naked thighs straddling his on the hot tub seat and making it impossible to think about anything but her. Them.

This moment.

* * *

Lydia needed to lose herself in Ian.

She didn't want to think about how much it had hurt when he put his family before her. When he'd refused to see how painful it might be for her that he'd allowed his grandfather to collect potential bride prospects for Ian when she thought she'd been the most important woman in his life.

All he had to do was deny it. Or explain it. But he'd done neither, drawing a line with her that she had been too hurt and angry to cross.

But even though a year apart had done little to soothe the raw, empty gap he'd left in her life, she was able to breathe all that hurt away enough to kiss his damp shoulder. To plaster her hands to his bare chest and absorb the hard warmth of his strong body. Selfish?

Maybe.

Or maybe there was a tenderness underneath that cold control of his. And maybe she'd kiss her way to it this time.

She could feel the moment when the fire that burned her caught him, too. His body came alive beneath her. His fingers flexed against her lower back, hands palming her spine and drawing her hips closer to his. Her thigh grazed the thick length of his erection, the contact making him groan with a hunger that reverberated through her, too.

"I want you." He said the words even though she understood as much from every single touch on her body.

"Not in here," she cautioned, her too-brief pregnancy coming to mind and causing a fresh pang in her chest.

"Too risky." He spoke into her ear, his hands wrapping around her waist and lifting her higher against him. "I know."

In a flash, he had her on her feet, with him following her. A moment later, he stepped out of the tub and opened the warming drawer full of fresh towels, a billow of dry heat spilling out along with the scent of detergent and lavender. He turned back to her before she'd even stepped all the way out of the spa and extended a towel for her to wrap herself in.

Rather, he wrapped her in the towel and his arms, too. He already had one around his waist and one on the deck where they stood. She couldn't touch him back since her arms were pinned to her sides in the towel, but she arched her neck for his kiss, getting lost in the man and the moment.

Just the way she'd wanted. And better.

"Where should I take you?" He asked the question against her cheek as he trailed kisses there, down her jaw, and onto her neck.

Her whole body came alive for him, like it always had when he touched her. Every single time.

"Anywhere," she murmured, not caring as long as he kept touching her.

When he stopped kissing her, she opened her eyes a moment to see him gather up a stack of more towels before he took her hand and tugged her out on the deck toward a teak porch swing covered in gold-and-turquoise cushions. Gossamer-light mosquito netting was draped over it and there was a table full of hurricane lamps to one side of the swing, which looked like a pasha's bed. Ian paused to light two of the lamps before pulling her into the netting enclosure with him. He tossed the towels into one corner of the bed, a foil packet sliding off to one side.

She smiled at his careful thought to protection, a sweet gesture that made her relax against him as he pulled her underneath him.

"I can't get enough of you." He breathed the words into her skin as he kissed his way down her body, sliding aside the towel and licking over her sensitive breasts.

His thigh pressed between hers, the welcome weight hitting the place where she craved his touch most. Her back bowed off the cushions, hips meeting his despite the lingering barrier of the thick terry cloth at his waist. She tunneled her fingers through his damp hair, holding him to her, feeling the tension build deep inside her.

Still warm from the hot tub, her skin heated to a dull sheen from the humid air. She tugged at the remnants of the towels between them, needing to get rid of all barriers to having him deep inside her.

He touched her before she could finish the job, however, his hand covering her sex and moving in a slow circle that made her head loll back against the cushions while ribbons of pleasure stroked her from the inside. Helpless at that touch, she held herself very still, not wanting to miss the slightest movement of his fingers over the slick warmth.

When he slid a finger inside her, she went mindless, boneless with a melting desire. Delicate convulsions fluttered through her, one after the other, drowning her in sweet fulfillment.

"Please," she urged him. "Please, please. Right now." She patted around the cushions in search of the condom.

Seizing upon it, she clutched it in her fist and passed it to him. But there must have been two, because he already had one in place. She'd been too intent on her own mission to notice his.

He rolled her on top of him and she forgot all about it. He thrust into her and it was all she could do to remain upright. She held very still for a long moment, getting used to the feel of him. Relishing the way they moved together.

A tightly perfect fit.

Ian gripped her hips and held her in place, moving beneath her. She met each thrust, closing her eyes to lose herself completely.

The tension built again, the rapid pace of it catching her off guard. She steadied herself against his shoulders, her hair falling forward to stroke his chest while he moved faster. Harder.

Her release blindsided her before she was ready. Before she knew it would happen. It rolled over her, through her, again and again. She collapsed against him while his climax overtook him. She kissed his shoulder. His face. Whatever she could reach as the pleasure spent itself and their heartbeats quieted.

Slowly.

For long moments she simply listened to Ian's ragged breathing, liking the way the feelings played havoc with him, too. It helped to know she wasn't alone in this. That she affected him as much as he did her.

The force of it, the raw power of the attraction and

the chemistry, was unlike anything she'd ever experienced. Unlike anything she knew could transpire between a man and a woman.

Maybe a small part of her had hoped that this marriage would show her that she'd been wrong about how monumental their relationship had been. If anything, being back together with Ian now only proved that they were more combustible than ever before.

The problem with combustible heat?

It didn't tend to burn itself out quietly.

Ten

By noon the next day, the honeymoon was over.

Ian regretted leaving Costa Rica, but Lydia kept saying she was worried about their families' reactions to the secret marriage. So, wanting to keep her happy, he'd arranged to leave, and now here they were, back on a chartered jet. It touched him that she seemed as concerned about the McNeills as she was about her own mother's response. And, of course, she had a legitimate reason to be concerned about how the tabloid media would choose to spin the story given her unique past. Whatever gossip played out online would be best quieted by a press release of their own.

So shortly after noon, they boarded the same private plane that had delivered them to Central America. The plan had been to return to Miami—and the Foxfire renovation project. But they had the aircraft at their disposal for the day and their bags packed with enough clothes for several days. So Ian needed to speak to her about a change of travel plans that he hadn't wanted to mention previously.

A change of flight plans he'd given to the pilot the night before.

He slid into the soft leather seat beside her, taking her hand before she could boot up her electronics for the trip. He understood she was anxious to check on the media reports about their marriage, but first he needed to clear a side trip with her.

No longer dressed in the honeymoon garments he liked so much—his T-shirts or the silk dress knotted at the knees for wading in the ocean—Lydia was now wearing a peach-colored linen sheath that reached her knees with an ivory jacket buttoned over it. With her dark hair pulled back in a neat ponytail and a heavy gold necklace, she had returned to work mode. His beautiful, endlessly competent wife.

"I've asked the pilot to give us a moment before takeoff." *Damn it.* Ian should have brought this up sooner. He'd been too busy enjoying what they'd shared this weekend—the connection and spark he remembered from their early days together. He'd wanted to lose himself in that when he knew damn well they would never return to the time when they offered one another a tenuous trust. Love.

Thinking about the betrayal of that trust—on both sides he could now acknowledge—still burned his gut.

"Why?" Lydia straightened in her seat, immediately alert. "Did you leave something behind?"

"No. Nothing like that." He took both her hands in his, hoping he'd earned back some small amount of her trust during this weekend together. They'd need that to make it through this marriage. "I wanted to speak to you about a possible change in our travel plans today."

She tipped her head to one side, more quizzical than upset.

"You know as well as I do the pilot has to file any alterations to the flight ahead of time—" She cut herself off, understanding lighting her features along with a new coolness. "Of course you know that. You've already changed our plans, haven't you?"

Ian could change the itinerary back again. They'd just need to wait until the plan was approved. He gripped her hands tighter, hoping she'd understand.

"Remember when I told you my brothers contacted me on the flight here yesterday?" At her nod, he continued, "They didn't check in just to let me know the news of our marriage had leaked. Apparently my grandfather has asked to see us—all of his family—as soon as possible. My brother said it wasn't cause to interrupt the honeymoon, but the sooner we could come to New York for a family meeting, the better."

"Is it his health?" The look in her green eyes was compassionate. Concerned.

Something about that quick empathy soothed the raw places inside him.

"I don't know. I would have thought I'd be able to tell by my brothers' faces if they were worried about him. But honestly? I couldn't read them. I don't know if they're putting up a brave front because we just got married." The fear had been in the back of his mind for nearly twenty-four hours and it was a relief to share it.

To feel Lydia squeeze his hands in return.

"Of course. We'll go straight to New York. There's no work in the world that's more important than a loved one's health."

Her reaction humbled him. Even as he gave the nod to the pilot and settled in for takeoff, he recognized that he'd missed out on something special with this caring woman. What might have happened if he'd swallowed his pride last spring and forced her to listen to his explanation about why his profile was circulating on a matchmaker's website even as he dated her? If he'd fought harder for her—hell, fought for her at all—could he have made her see the truth? That he hadn't given a rat's ass about anyone but her?

In all the months since their breakup, he'd been too busy blaming her for believing the worst of him. For not having any faith in him.

But maybe he'd been every bit as guilty as her. More, even.

The realization made him wonder if he could use these next months to turn this marriage into something real. Convince Lydia that they were meant to be together after all.

He was still brooding over the idea when Lydia's soft expletive hit his ears—an unlikely exclamation from the woman who had cultivated a perfect facade to keep scandal-hungry tabloid reporters at bay.

"What's wrong?" He glanced over at her as the plane began to taxi toward the runway to begin the flight.

Lydia squeezed her phone in a white-knuckle grip.

"It's my mother." She shook her head, slowly leaning back in the leather chair with a sigh that blew her dark hair from over one eye. "She's already lining up press interviews for us." Lydia turned an anguished look his way. She caught her lip between her teeth for a long moment, worrying away the slick peach lip gloss. "She wants to meet me at a network television studio in New York tomorrow for a live interview with one of the morning shows." Lydia drew in a long breath. "The host already shared her lead-in to the story." She flipped the phone so he could see a text from her mother in all capital letters.

BILLIONAIRE'S REJECTED LOVE CHILD FINALLY HITS THE JACKPOT AS A MCNEILL BRIDE!

Six hours later, seated beside Ian in a chauffeured limousine transporting them from the private New Jersey airstrip to Malcolm McNeill's residence on Park Avenue in Manhattan, Lydia talked herself through her plan for getting through this day. Ian had taken a business call to handle a few details on the Foxfire Hotel project in South Beach, leaving Lydia alone with her thoughts for their ride through the city.

For which she was grateful.

Trying to steady her trembling hands and jittery nerves, she sipped the bottled water stocked in the limousine's mini bar. The events of the last day and a half had been staggering. Her wedding. Finding out the event had been leaked to the press. The unbelievable honeymoon night in Costa Rica. An unexpected trip to New York because Ian's grandfather wanted to meet with his whole family.

Her mother's sudden interest in her life now that Lydia had tied the knot with one of the wealthiest men in the country.

Lydia's stomach churned as the limo stopped at a red light. Ian had been kind about her mother's meddling notes and eager desire for involvement in her life. He had reassured Lydia that he understood she wasn't responsible for her mother's behavior and promised her that the McNeills would deal with any media stunts her mother pulled.

In the end, Lydia had opted not to contact her mother just yet. For all that Mom knew, Lydia remained on her honeymoon for the next week or more. She had no reason to believe Lydia was back in New York and all too close to the network studio where her mother had committed to an interview.

Lydia thought she was done with this kind of thing— trying to manage her mother's need for the spotlight while staying firmly out of it herself. She hadn't factored in this kind of thing when Ian had offered his proposal for a marriage that would benefit both of them.

Sliding a sidelong glance at him now as the car turned into Central Park and headed east, Lydia braced for the swell of desire that just a simple look inspired. His dark suit was more casual today with his white dress shirt open at the neck. His legs were sprawled, one knee close to hers, his left hand resting on his navy trousers, the platinum wedding band glinting in the sunlight.

She thumbed her own ring as she watched him, her eyes greedily moving over his strong jaw and the dark hair that brushed his collar. Her heart tumbled over itself in an odd rhythm, alerting her to the presence of all the old feelings for him. The ones she wanted so desperately to ignore. The ones that tingled along her senses even now at just sitting near enough to touch him.

When he'd kissed her the night before and told her he wanted them to have a fresh start, she'd felt her defenses tremble. And today, after she'd read the texts from her mother and she'd been hurting and embarrassed on so many levels, Ian had been quick to assure her he could handle any of her mother's media antics, promising to hire a full-time publicist to manage Lydia's image and ensure that the media knew whom to contact for all stories having to do with Lydia McNeill.

It had sounded so smart and reasonable, and it probably was a very real possibility that his solution would work. It helped to have the financial resources, of course. But more than anything, the gesture had spoken of a kindness and consideration for Lydia's feelings that rocked her old perceptions of him.

Had she been too quick to judge him last year? Too insecure in herself to ever believe that Ian might have a reasonable explanation for his presence on a matchmaker's site? Her gaze returned to his platinum wedding band as he finished up his call. He might have pressured her into a marriage that would help him fulfill his grandfather's wishes, but he was helping her at the same time. She couldn't afford the scandal or the financial strain of a legal battle with Vitaly Koslov.

Another kindness Ian had done for her sake.

"I wonder what you're thinking, Mrs. McNeill." His words cut through her daze as the limo emerged on the east side of Central Park.

Startled, she sat bolt upright on her seat, her drink sloshing droplets on her arm. She set the water aside in the cup holder to give herself time to gather her thoughts. When had he finished his phone call? She needed to get her head on straight before they walked into his grandfather's house and faced the full contingent of McNeills. Ian had phoned his brothers from the plane to let them know they were flying to New York earlier than anticipated. Apprehension flitted through her, and Lydia wished she'd taken Ian up on his offer of a light lunch during their flight to New York. Maybe having something in her stomach would have helped ease her nerves.

"Just a few jitters about meeting all the McNeills at one time." She smoothed the hem of the peach-colored dress some anonymous staffer of Ian's had packed for her back in Florida before this trip. She really needed to find out more about him and the people who worked with him, who'd made this trip just a little less stressful by sending some of her own clothes with her. "I know you said that your family trusts your judgment so they will accept your choice of wife, too."

"They will see what I see. A smart, compassionate woman who's battled complicated obstacles to carve out a good career." He took her hand and lifted it to his lips, his blue eyes warm.

Would she ever get used to the way he made her pulse flutter like that?

Then she recalled the whole reason for this trip and cursed herself for becoming sidetracked by her own worries. "But I'm being selfish." She shifted to face him on the bench seat, her knee grazing his. "You have much deeper concerns than that for this visit. More than anything, I hope your grandfather is well."

"Me, too," he said simply, turning to peer out the window as the driver slowed the car. "But we'll know soon enough how he fares because we're here."

Lydia marveled as they came to a stop at the curb outside a six-story limestone building with an Italianate facade and a delicate wrought iron balcony off the second floor. Her designer's eye went to the clay-tiled mansard roof and neo-Renaissance details, but it was difficult to enjoy the beauty of one of New York's turn-of-the-century masterpieces when Ian's family was on the other side of the front door.

No matter what Ian said, she worried what his brothers would think of their unorthodox—and rushed—marriage. But right now, she needed to be there for Ian in case his grandfather's health had taken a turn for the worse.

Resisting the urge to pull a mirror out of her purse and indulge the old insecurity demon her mother had given her, Lydia took a deep breath and stepped out of the vehicle as the chauffeur opened the door. She would remain calm. Composed.

Strong.

Ian had been all of that and more for her in the face of her mother's attempted publicity stunt.

The iron gates of the foyer rolled open before Ian

announced them on the intercom. Clearly, they'd been expected.

"I texted Gramps's housekeeper," Ian explained as they strode into the house without knocking. "She must have been watching for us. She said my brothers are here. Sofia is running late because of a ballet performance earlier in the day, but she's due to arrive shortly."

He closed the door behind them and Lydia did her best not to gawk. She'd read that Malcolm McNeill was an avid art collector, but she hadn't expected to be greeted in the foyer by a Cezanne and a Manet. The pieces were hung to be enjoyed, with the focus on the art. The only piece of furniture was a settee in a shade of cerulean shared by both paintings. Lydia had seen the opposite approach often enough in her time as a designer—boastful collectors who were more interested in having their taste admired and envied.

"Wow." She'd been drawn to the pieces in spite of herself, only realizing after a long moment that Ian was speaking in quiet tones to someone off to one side of the hallway.

Lydia turned to join them, but the older woman in a gray uniform had already hurried away.

"Cindy tells me the family is upstairs," he informed her, pointing the way. "It's two flights to the library, though. Let's take the elevator out of deference to your shoes." He cut a quick sideways glance her way. "Though they make your already-gorgeous long legs look damn amazing."

Before she could think of a response to his outrageous compliment—that yes, she did enjoy—he was already pushing the call button, and the elevator door swished open. She followed him into the cabin. The grand staircase snaked through all six floors with a mammoth skylight at the top, and though beautifully impressive, she didn't relish the idea of testing her heels on the sleek, polished treads. Not that she planned to take them off and walk in to meet Ian's grandfather barefoot.

As the door closed behind them, whisking them upward, her apprehension grew. But Ian stepped nearer, and the warmth of his physical proximity somehow comforted her.

"Thank you for coming with me." He spoke with quiet sincerity. "I'm glad you're here."

The words so perfectly echoed what she'd been feeling at that moment, they slid right past her defenses and burrowed in her heart in a way that made her breath catch.

Before she could think what to say, Ian folded her palm in his and squeezed. "We might as well hold hands." He planted a kiss on her temple. "We're newlyweds, remember?"

The soft warmth of his lips stirred a hungry response in her as she recalled their honeymoon in vivid, passion-saturated detail. But as the full import of his words sank in, she wondered if the display of affection was for his family's sake more than anything.

The elevator cabin halted and the door slid open on a third-floor hallway flooded with light from the skylight over the central staircase. Male voices and laughter sounded from nearby. Ian led her to a partially closed door flanked by carved wood panels that were flawless reproductions in the French eighteenth-century style. Better to focus on the home design than the butterflies in her stomach.

"That's my grandfather's voice," Ian noted, walking faster. "He sounds good."

Lydia squeezed his arm, offering what comfort she could as she followed him into a library where the walls were fitted with historic Chinese lacquer panels between the windows overlooking the street. But not even the superb design details could sway her attention from the impressive men scattered around the room. Even before introductions were made, she knew she was seeing three generations of McNeills. The gray-haired eldest sat in a leather club chair in the corner. Wearing a retro red-and-black smoking jacket belted over his trousers, the patriarch of the family gripped a crystal tumbler half-full of an amber-colored drink, a forgotten copy of the *Wall Street Journal* tucked into the chair at his side. At the window stood an extremely fit man who looked to be in his late fifties. He'd shaved his head completely, and she could see a tattoo on the back of his neck. Was this Liam McNeill? His gray pants and black T-shirt combined to make him look more like hired muscle than Ian's father.

But as the middle-aged man turned toward her, she saw the same ice-blue eyes shared by every man in the room.

Ian introduced her to each member of his family in age order, ending with Quinn and Cameron, who rose from their seats on opposite ends of the room to greet her.

Quinn and Cameron, she thought, looked more alike than Ian, whose bronzed complexion favored their Brazilian mother. But Cameron was very tall, perhaps six foot five. She would have thought him a professional athlete if she'd seen him on the street.

Lydia was saved from making small talk by the arrival of an exquisitely beautiful, petite blonde, hair tightly coiled in a bun at the back of her head.

"I'm so sorry," the woman offered, rushing to Quinn's side. "I thought the train would be faster since traffic was ridiculous after the show, but there were delays." She kissed Quinn. Her eyes darted around the room and, finding Malcolm McNeill, she moved to give the older man a kiss on one cheek that coaxed a smile from him.

"Sofia, my new wife, Lydia." Ian repeated his simple introduction from earlier.

Lydia braced herself for a chilly greeting since she'd unwittingly stolen some of the woman's wedding thunder with their preemptive visit to the justice of the peace, but if Sofia Koslov resented it, she hid it well.

The ballerina winked at Lydia, although she remained at Quinn's side as he guided her to a love seat at the center of the room.

"I've been so eager to meet you." Sofia pulled a silver phone from her small leather hobo purse and waved it. "Let's exchange numbers before you leave."

"I'd like that." Lydia couldn't help smiling, feeling more at ease with another woman in the room full of accomplished, powerful men. She and Ian took a seat on the long couch opposite Quinn and Sofia.

Without preamble, Malcolm McNeill reached for his silver-topped cane and rose to his feet, every bit as tall as Ian, even with his bent knees and back. "Lydia, we're all glad to welcome you into our family." He lifted his glass in a silent toast and took a sip before returning it to the side table. "I hope you will consider a more public celebration this summer so we can show the world how pleased we are to call you a McNeill."

The old man's blue eyes pinned her, inciting gratitude for the warmth of the gesture even as she regretted deceiving him. All of them.

Ian squeezed her hand as if he guessed her thoughts.

"Thank you, sir." She ducked her head, oddly intimidated to be in the hot seat in this room full of strangers who would be her family for such a short time.

Luckily, she didn't need to worry about saying anything else, because Malcolm continued to speak.

"It's Liam who asked me to round up the whole lot of you." Malcolm looked over to his son and gestured to the room. "Go on now. Tell 'em."

"Dad wanted us all here?" Ian rose to offer his grandfather an arm while the older man lowered himself into the large club chair. "Gramps, I thought you called us together to talk about your health. How you're doing since the heart attack and the trip home from Shanghai."

"No, no." Malcolm McNeill waved aside the help and the concern. "I'm healthy as a horse."

Lydia felt the unease all around the room in the shifting of positions. Cameron sat forward in his chair, elbows on his knees.

He then scowled at his father. "Dad, what gives? Ian left his honeymoon for this. Sofia ditched her meet and greet after a ballet performance."

Liam cleared his throat. "It's not easy getting you all together at once." He strode around to the desk, staying on the perimeter of the room, rubbing a hand over his shaved head. "My apologies for the timing, but I've waited long enough to tell you about this."

Quinn spoke up. "That sounds ominous, Dad." The oldest of the McNeill sons turned in his seat to better see his father. Quinn was a hedge fund manager, Lydia knew, and had all the appearances of refinement and wealth. But then, at the end of the day, that's what he sold—access to a world of privilege by gaining the trust of the world's wealthiest investors.

Cameron sighed. "What gives?" the youngest asked again, spreading his hands wide, a note of impatience in his voice.

Ian remained silent at her side.

Then Liam McNeill stopped pacing the perimeter of the room and turned to face the rest of the family. Lydia held her breath.

Liam looked around the room at all of them before speaking. "I have another family I've never told you about. Three more sons, actually." A ghost of a smile flitted across the man's face before vanishing. "Your mother left me because she found out about them, but I could never convince Audrey—my other, er, girlfriend—to move to the States and be a permanent part of my life."

The news landed with all the force of a grenade,

sending shrapnel into the heart of every McNeill. And that was before Cameron McNeill stalked across the room and launched a fist into his father's jaw.

Eleven

Ian hauled a steaming Cameron to one side of the library while Quinn stood in front of their father, blocking further physical confrontation. They might as well be a freaking reality TV show at this rate. *McNeills Gone Mad!*

Ian couldn't believe he'd left his honeymoon and flown to New York for this news, let alone that he'd dragged Lydia into it. Lydia—a woman who had lived her life as carefully as possible to avoid big, messy scandals. He noticed that Sofia had moved to sit beside Lydia on the couch, the two of them silently on the same side without saying a word. What was it about women that they could remain civilized when all hell broke loose around them?

Even Quinn looked the worse for wear after the

dustup, with his shirttails untucked in front and jacket unbuttoned. Ian hadn't fared as well; struggling with six-foot-five inches of pissed-off muscle and impulsiveness had sent him through the wringer. While epithets flew back and forth, it became apparent that Liam had been cheating on Ian's mother for years, fathering sons with a mistress on the West Coast until the woman got fed up with his refusal to divorce his wife and left the United States the year after Cameron was born.

Private investigators had trouble finding her, but then she'd had years of McNeill money stashed to help her make the getaway. Liam had lost touch with her and his sons until a few weeks ago, when one of the old investigators snagged a lead on a McNeill family ring in a pawnshop in the US Virgin Islands. Liam thought it was just a ploy by the PI to resurrect an old job, but he'd contacted Ian's friend Bentley to track it down, and it turned out the ring was real, verified by a family jeweler. Bentley traced it to the servant of a wealthy family—named McNeill—in Martinique.

"They use our name?" Ian barked, feeling more than a little angry with his father himself.

Furious, actually.

"I don't know when the boys started using the name," his father said, hanging his head. "But their mother died long ago and they want nothing to do with us, so you don't have to worry about anyone coming in here and..."

Quinn swore. Cam accused their father of several indecent acts. Ian's eyes went to Lydia, wishing she didn't have to hear all this. She looked calm, however, if a little pale. She held her cell phone in one hand; her other was tucked under her thigh on the couch.

"Quiet down, all of you, and listen here." Gramps stood, using his cane as he moved. "These young men are your half brothers, like it or not. They are your blood. My blood. Every bit as much my grandsons as you are. That doesn't mean, however, that I plan to give them the whole kit and kaboodle of the family portfolio." He straightened as much as his bad back would allow and used the cane to point at Cameron. "I've invited them to New York and we'll take their measure when they arrive."

Ian exchanged glances with Quinn. Family was all well and good. But what did this mean for them? And for McNeill Resorts if their grandfather handed over shares to people who clearly resented them? Ian didn't give a damn about money, but the family business they'd poured their blood, sweat and soul into? That was another matter. Let his father do right by his offspring financially, sure, but protect the business.

"Gramps, that's fine," Ian said reasonably, stepping on Cam's toe to ensure his brother didn't gainsay him. "We understand you want to meet them and provide for them. But what about McNeill Resorts? You've spent our whole lives trying to impart what the company means to you and how you want it developed. You can't honestly mean to start parceling off your business to people who are complete strangers to you?"

Out of the corner of his eye, Ian noticed Lydia straighten in her seat. Belatedly, it occurred to him she might feel differently about this newly unearthed branch of the family. Hell, in her childhood, she'd been the unacknowledged heir, and it had caused pain her whole life.

"I meant it when I said they're as much my grand-sons as you are." Gramps leveled a look at each one of the brothers, a stiff set to his jaw, before he put his cane back on the floor and shuffled toward the door. "Now that we have that out of the way, I'm going to change for dinner. You're all invited, but don't stay if you can't act like grown-ups." He paused at the door, almost run-ning into Lydia, who had leaped off the couch to open it for him.

Gramps smiled at her. "You're a pretty thing, aren't you? If it gets too rough in this room, just head down to the dining room and someone will fix you up a cock-tail." He patted her arm.

"Yes, sir." She beamed.

Gramps had made one person happy today. As for the rest of the McNeills, Ian couldn't imagine what this meant for the family. He'd just gotten married to se-cure his portion of his grandfather's company because he had been under the mistaken impression it meant so much to the old man.

Now? The whole damn trust and will were almost assuredly going to be rewritten to incorporate this new branch of the family their father had never bothered to mention.

That bugged Ian on a lot of levels—mostly because he had to contend with the news that his father was a selfish, cheating bastard. Yet what bothered him more than anything was the idea that if the will was altered and it no longer included a stipulation about taking a wife to secure a portion of McNeill Resorts, would Lydia suggest they dissolve their marriage?

You can't honestly mean to start parceling off your business to people who are complete strangers to you?

Ian's words echoed in Lydia's mind long after they left his grandfather's home. They chased around her brain even now, late that night, after they'd arrived at Ian's apartment at the historic Pierre Hotel on Central Park, where both Ian and Quinn owned space. They'd opted to spend another day in New York so that he would have time to meet with his brothers and figure out what their father's news meant for the family.

Lydia hadn't argued, understanding why he would want to talk to his brothers privately. But the events had shaken her. Ian had locked himself in his library to make calls and Lydia found herself walking in aimless circles around the kitchen at midnight.

She and Ian hadn't stayed for dinner with Malcolm after the McNeill family blowup. She understood why a meal together might be uncomfortable with so much unsettled among them, but no wonder she was hungry now. She rifled through the cabinets in the sleek, caterer-friendly kitchen, searching for food.

Lydia had said good-night to Malcolm McNeill in his study while he drank his aperitif before going in to dinner. Liam had left immediately after his father walked out of the library. Quinn and Sofia had made their excuses as well, and Sofia had looked strained, although she'd taken Lydia's number and promised to call her so they could arrange a time to get to know each other.

Cameron alone had remained behind to have dinner with his grandfather. In the car afterward, on the way to Ian's apartment, Ian had sincerely apologized for the family dustup. But Lydia hadn't cared about that half as much as she cared about the fact that Ian didn't believe in welcoming half siblings into the family. He'd called those half brothers "complete strangers," implying they had no right to any McNeill inheritance.

He reacted the same way her half siblings had when they found out about her existence. It didn't matter that they all shared a father. She'd never been good enough in their eyes and it troubled her deeply to think Ian felt that way about people who shared his blood.

Peering into the huge Sub-Zero fridge, she retrieved a bottled water and sat at the breakfast nook overlooking the lights of Central Park. She'd changed into a night-gown and a white spa robe she'd found in the bathroom. Although Ian owned the Pierre apartment, apparently the whole building shared the hotel maid service and—come to think of it—Ian had told her there was twenty-four-hour room service from the kitchens downstairs. She would have phoned for something, but now, as it neared midnight, she tried to talk herself out of it.

Even all these years after that photograph of her in a magazine with a "baby bump" at sixteen, Lydia found herself careful not to overeat. Except, of course, in those weeks where she hugged the news of a real pregnancy close. Then, she'd fed herself like a queen, dreaming of the baby she'd never gotten the chance to meet.

"There you are." Ian's voice from the far side of the kitchen startled her from her thoughts.

He flipped on a pendant lamp over the black granite countertop. The backlight made it so she couldn't see out the window anymore. Instead, her own reflection stared back at her, a pale, negative image in black and white.

"Were you able to resolve anything?" she asked, careful to keep her thoughts to herself about any disappointment with Ian's reaction to his father's news.

It was possible the shock of the moment had colored his response. In time, he might feel differently about welcoming his half brothers into the family.

"Not really." He took a seat in one of the four white armchairs surrounding the polished teak table in the open-plan dining area. He set his phone on the table beside him. His shirtsleeves were rolled to expose strong forearms and he'd removed his jacket and tie. "I spoke at length to Bentley, the same friend who found you when I was looking for Mallory West. My father called him to go to Martinique two days ago and confirm the identity of my half brothers. Bentley said there's no doubt. He has photos of my father with his other family when they were young."

Ian switched the phone on and called up a photo of Liam McNeill standing with one woman and three small boys in front of the Cezanne she recognized from Malcolm McNeill's foyer. The three boys had to be Quinn, Ian and Cameron—all three of them sweet and adorable in jackets and ties, but with mischief in their matching blue eyes.

Below that photo, was another of Liam with an obviously pregnant blonde in a long, white gauzy dress. They stood on a beach at sunset, the sky purple and pink behind them, their arms around two small boys who could have been twins to the three in the photo above. Same blue eyes, same grins. The only difference was that the boys in the beach photo wore white T-shirts and cargo shorts. She wasn't sure why the third half brother wasn't in the photo.

"I can't believe that no one knew about this." Lydia ran a finger over the woman's pregnant belly in the photo. Had she known about Liam's other family when she carried those children? "I think back to all the stories that ran about me as a teen—complete fiction. And yet your father successfully hid a whole double life from the tabloids."

"My mother knew about this." Ian slid the phone from her hands and turned off the screen, setting it facedown on the table. "She just didn't want our lives to turn into a media circus so she kept quiet about it when she left my father."

"Our mothers are cut from very different cloth, aren't they?" Lydia wondered if he had any idea how much she identified with his father's *other* family. "I'm more surprised that his mistress didn't expose the truth."

Ian shook his head. "Maybe she had enough money. Bentley said the house where she raised her sons was paid for in cash."

Lydia drew a deep breath and reminded herself the shock of the news hadn't worn off yet for him. And still, she couldn't keep from pointing out, "It's not always about money. Most women want their children to have a relationship with their father. Don't you wonder why she cut off all contact and her sons never got in touch with the family either?" She turned that over in her mind. "As much as I resented the way my mother tried to get my father's attention by making us a spectacle, I wouldn't have had any relationship with him if she hadn't brought me to his attention."

And in the end, her father had been kind. He'd encouraged her desire to study art and design and introduced her to prominent people in the field in which she now worked. She'd found common ground with him and enjoyed those long, last conversations about beautiful buildings he'd seen all over the world. She treasured those memories.

"If not for that damned ring showing up, we might never have discovered them." Ian stared down at the table and she wondered if he'd heard what she'd said. "And now? Everything my grandfather worked for is going to land in the laps of people who never wanted anything to do with us."

She tried to bite her tongue. And failed.

"They're still your family," she reminded him. "That counts for something."

She wanted—*needed*—him to agree. Even when she had been pregnant with their child—a baby who would not have had the legal protection of marriage—she had thought Ian would embrace his offspring. That he would see beyond those rigid notions of what "family" meant. But if he truly believed that he could only count the legally recognized brothers as worthy of his notice...

Then she didn't know him at all. Then her marriage really was based strictly on a piece of paper and all those tender touches in Costa Rica were just a case of physical attraction.

He turned on her, blue eyes thoughtful. "How can you, of all people, believe that family trumps all? Your half siblings did everything in their power to discredit you and your mother when your mom sued your father's estate. How could you even consider them family when they've gone out of their way to hurt you like that?"

Disappointment prickled all over her, deflating the hope she'd had that Ian was a different kind of man. That they were building a tentative trust again.

"You can't pick family the way you choose your friends. But I still believe those relationships are worth investing in. If I hadn't gotten to know the Whitneys, I would have missed out on knowing my father." She stared down at the yellow diamond on her finger, more confused than ever about what it meant.

About what Ian hoped to gain by playing the part of her husband in a way that had fooled even her.

"Lydia, I'm sorry that this had to come up right now." He took her left hand and kissed the backs of her fingers. "I can see you're upset and I don't blame you. I'm going to order a tray for you from room service and have something brought up."

"There's really no need."

"I insist." The gentle concern in his eyes undid her as he stroked a thumb over the inside of her wrist, still holding her hand. "I haven't forgotten about your mother's attempts to reach you. And with your permission,

I'll invite a publicist over tomorrow and you can plan how you want to manage the news about our marriage and your public image. The woman—Jasmine—is a good friend of Sofia's. Quinn highly recommended her."

"Thank you." Lydia slid her hand away, the diamond weighing heavily on her finger. "I appreciate that. But in all the events of the evening we haven't even spoken about what this news of your father's means for your grandfather's will."

A muscle in Ian's jaw flexed as he leaned back from the breakfast table. "It means nothing."

"Ian, it's not too late to say the wedding photo was—I don't know—a prank?" She held her breath while he looked back at her with stunned eyes. "I'm not trying to add to your problems, but if it simplifies things for you to quietly annul this, we could—"

"No." He bit off the word with a fierceness echoed by the flash of emotion in his eyes. "Absolutely not." He leaned over the table and kissed her—a hard, possessive kiss. "As much as I regret that you had to witness the whole drama with my father, having you with me was the only bright spot in this day."

Her heart contracted, squeezing hopefully around those words. She took a deep breath, no closer to answers than she had been hours ago. Before she could say anything he rose to his feet.

"I'll have the kitchen bring something up and then I've got a few more calls to make." He kissed the top of her head. "If the publicist is here at ten tomorrow morning, is that too early?"

"That's fine. I'll be ready." She knew she needed help

figuring out how to manage her public image. Whether or not she stayed married to Ian for the rest of this year, she'd come to one decision tonight. She'd allowed the fear of a scandal surrounding Mallory West to send her running into his arms for protection from a lawsuit, and that problem wasn't going to go away after twelve months.

Even if Ian ensured Vitaly Koslov never sought legal retribution, there was the fact that Lydia wanted to return to matchmaking. And aside from that one small scandal that she'd never addressed, her alter ego actually had a great, lucrative reputation.

More than ever after tonight, Lydia was convinced she had a mission in life to champion single mothers. Women who were ostracized by family or lovers who refused to recognize their own children.

So, at ten the next morning, she planned to ask Jasmine the publicist how to introduce herself to the world as the mystery matchmaker, Mallory West.

As for Ian? She didn't plan to consult him about that particular decision. She had every reason to believe he wouldn't understand.

Twelve

Two hours later, Ian paced the floor of his study, a restless unease still weighing on his chest even though he was checking things off his mental to-do list with reasonable speed.

He'd exchanged emails with the site manager on the Foxfire project and gotten an update on the South Beach property, a lucky stroke since the guy was as much of a night owl as him. Ian had triple-checked the marriage paperwork to ensure it had all been filed properly, then he faxed his attorney the signed files outlining the provisions Ian was making for Lydia no matter what happened in the next twelve months. She'd made it clear she didn't want any kind of financial settlement in a year's time—an issue he'd revisit—but for now, he made sure she received all the legal and financial protections possible as his spouse.

What she'd said at the kitchen table earlier still nee-
dled his brain and he didn't understand why. He had
the impression she was unhappy with his response to
his father's bombshell about his second family, but he
couldn't quite put his finger on what he'd done wrong.

Sure, she'd made the comment that family wasn't all
about money. But she'd also seemed upset that he wasn't
welcoming the McNeill interlopers into his grandfather's company. And since Ian couldn't untangle what
bothered her, he planned to make sure she knew that
he didn't equate her position in the family with these
pseudo McNeills.

Lydia's case was different. *She* was different.

Special.

Ian made his last call of the night to Quinn, still
hoping to dispel some of the tension of the day. He
knew none of his brothers would be getting any sleep
tonight either.

"I have Jasmine confirmed for tomorrow morning,"
he informed his older brother, who was probably staring out at this exact same view of Central Park three
floors above him right now. "Thank you for the recom-
mendation. She got back to me almost immediately."

"She's a go-getter." Quinn sounded weary on the
other end of the call, but no doubt he'd been making
calls well into the night too, trying to sort through the
news of their half brothers. "Jasmine is very protective
of Sofia and her image. They're friends, of course, but
I got the impression that she's the kind of person who
invests a lot in her clients."

"That's exactly what Lydia needs. Her mother has

tried undermining Lydia's image too many times." It had upset Ian when he made a quick scan of articles about Lydia tonight—so he could give the publicist some background on the situation. "It will help her to have a go-between she trusts to manage the stories that circulate about her."

Lydia had a giving heart and a willingness to help people that was too rare in his world. She should be recognized for her efforts. Or, at the very least, not belittled by sensationalized stories that focused on her personal life.

"You'll be happy with Jasmine." Quinn paused a moment. In the background, Ian could hear the clink of ice cubes in a glass. "And I've been meaning to let you know that Sofia has told me twice to cancel any efforts to find Mallory West."

"Seriously?" Ian stopped his pacing, instantly alert.

"Yes. She mentioned it a couple of weeks ago, saying that we shouldn't hound someone who was responsible for bringing the two of us together." Quinn's tone shifted as he spoke about his fiancée. There was a lightness that had been absent in him until Sofia arrived in his life. "I thought she was just being sentimental, or... I don't know. I didn't think she was serious about it. But last week she raised the issue again, and apparently she's already spoken to her father. So definitely call off any search for the matchmaker."

That was good news for Lydia.

And Ian was happy about it, too. One less thing to worry about that could chip away at Lydia's public image during a time when they were trying to cultivate a new one.

Yet he had to wonder. Would this give Lydia all the incentive she needed to end their marriage early?

"Ian? You there?"

"Yes. Sorry. I'm just surprised. But I'll abandon that project and call in the investigator." No use telling Quinn he'd already found Mallory and that she currently slept in his bed.

"Thanks. And don't be surprised if Sofia knocks on your door tomorrow morning. She has a ballet class to teach at noon, but she mentioned wanting to personally introduce your wife to her friend Jasmine before she heads in to work."

Distracted, Ian agreed to relay the message before disconnecting the call.

His brain was still stuck on the news that the Koslovs no longer cared about finding the matchmaker who'd embarrassed them. Now Sofia had decided it was because of Mallory's matchmaking that she'd met Quinn in the first place.

Ian couldn't keep up. Shutting his phone off for the night, he padded barefoot through the apartment, heading to his bedroom. He craved Lydia's touch. Hell, she was most certainly sleeping already. Even just lying beside her would be enough to chase some of the restlessness away.

But as he stepped into the master suite, he knew right away that she wasn't there. Her suitcase had been moved from his closet where he'd set it himself earlier. His bed was still made.

Maybe she was still in the kitchen? Even as he stalked through the darkened apartment, however, he knew she wouldn't be there. When he passed the closed door to one of the guest suites, he knew she'd found an empty bed to sleep in for the night.

He placed a palm on the door, missing her. He told himself that she was probably just trying to get better sleep. This way, he wouldn't wake her when he went to bed. If that was her reasoning, he could hardly begrudge her the guest room. But the vague unease in his chest all evening took a new form. He'd been worrying about what his father's betrayal meant for the family when he should have been paying attention to Lydia.

He'd let her sleep for now. They would speak in the morning when they were both clearheaded.

Because deep in his gut he knew she hadn't sought that spare room for the sake of a good night's rest. His new wife wasn't happy with him. And more than ever, he feared that she was already dreaming up ways to end this marriage.

As Lydia prepared for her meeting with her new publicist the next morning, she nibbled on the scones that Ian had had delivered to the kitchen, along with a huge platter of other breakfast choices. If this was a real marriage, she would ask him about the possibility of rethinking some of his extravagant expenditures to help others. She could think of five struggling young mothers she helped through Moms' Connection who were probably going without breakfast today so their kids could have something nutritious. It made it hard for Lydia to enjoy the scone when so much food sat there untouched.

She hadn't seen Ian yet this morning. She'd awakened to discover he had a meeting with the McNeill family's private attorney. He had been in the study all morning.

So she prepared for her own meeting with the publicist by herself, asking the morning maid to set out the coffee and pastry treats in the living room to offer her guests. Because apparently Sofia Koslov would be joining them briefly, too, if only to make introductions. She'd texted Lydia this morning to make sure she didn't mind.

Already, Lydia had the impression she would have been truly fortunate to marry into this family for the sake of gaining a sister-in-law like Sofia. Lydia had read a great deal about the principal dancer for the New York City Ballet last winter during the awkward media coverage of Cameron's proposal to her. How would Sofia react one day when she learned that Lydia was actually Mallory West? The possibility of being rejected that way—by someone so warmhearted—stirred a deep regret for how she'd handled the matchmaking mistake.

What struck Lydia now, as she finished her scone and reviewed her notes for her morning meeting, was that Sofia Koslov must share some of Lydia's desire for family. The dancer's mother had died when Sofia was a girl, and she'd never been close to her father, even though the Ukrainian-born billionaire had stepped in to claim control of her life. But as Lydia read about Sofia, she couldn't help but think they might have really enjoyed being sisters.

Too bad Lydia's temporary marriage was proving even more temporary than she'd imagined.

She heard the apartment doorbell chime and checked her watch, guessing that it was Sofia since it wasn't quite 10:00 a.m. and Sofia was scheduled to arrive a little before Jasmine. Letting the maid answer the door, Lydia took another moment to freshen her lipstick and check the fall of her bright green summer dress with big purple flowers embroidered at the hem. She wore a thin yellow sweater around her shoulders to cover up the dress's square halter neck.

When she got to the living room, Sofia darted off the couch. Dressed in slouchy pants and a leotard with a hoodie thrown over it, she could have been a nineteen-year-old college student with her clean scrubbed face and glowing skin. Her still-damp hair was piled on her head in a bun with a braid wrapped around it. She moved gracefully toward Lydia, meeting her in the center of the room.

"You look so pretty!" Sofia exclaimed, taking in the embroidered hem of Lydia's dress. "You already dress like a publicist's dream. Jasmine is going to love working with you."

They made small talk for a few minutes, comparing notes on clothes, but before Lydia could offer her guest a seat, the door to Ian's study opened down the hall. The voices of Ian, Quinn, Cameron and a stranger echoed off the Italian marble floor.

"I forgot Quinn was coming down here for the meeting with their attorney." Sofia's smile was infectious, the grin of a woman in love. "He worked so late last night, and then was up at the crack of dawn. Not that I'm supposed to know that since I'm technically living in my own apartment until my wedding." She made a good-natured eye roll. "But how could I leave Quinn alone last night after what they had to deal with yesterday?"

Lydia felt a pang of guilt at Sofia's empathetic words. Should Lydia have kept more of her opinions to herself last night?

Her eyes went straight to Ian as the men walked into the living area, close to the private elevator. Their business conversation must be done, as they joked about their golf handicaps and a charity fund-raiser at a popular course in Long Island the following weekend.

Cameron checked out of the guy talk early, his eyes landing on the plate full of pastries on the coffee table. He made a beeline for it as his brothers said goodbye to the attorney.

Cameron gave Lydia a thumbs-up before speaking around a mouthful of jelly doughnut. "This must be your doing. Ian never has food in this place. Good job."

"I'm glad someone is enjoying it." She smiled in spite of the tension knotting her shoulders at Ian's arrival in the room. Something had shifted between them last night and made her uneasy today. She had slept in another room, but he hadn't spoken to her about it— last night or this morning. Had he thought it peculiar? Or were they back to being strangers with a contractual marriage?

Quinn and Ian joined them in the living area. Sofia and Quinn drew together like magnets, each pulled toward the other irresistibly, splitting the distance between them to meet in the middle. It was beautiful—and painful—to see, making Lydia realize all that she'd sacrificed in tying herself to a man who didn't think in terms of love and family, but business and legal obligations.

Sofia tucked her head to Quinn's chest. "Quinn, did you tell your brothers that we don't want to pursue any investigation into Mallory West?"

Lydia gasped. She covered it with a cough and a murmured, "Excuse me."

She was careful to avoid Ian's gaze, although she felt it on her.

Thankfully, Cameron McNeill spoke over her gaffe. "Are you kidding me? I thought we were going to sue her for all she's worth and donate the money to one of Sofia's favorite charities?" He leaned down to the coffee table to scoop up another pastry and a napkin. "I thought it was a great plan."

Ian was suddenly standing by Lydia's side, his arm sliding beneath her lightweight sweater to palm her back. "Quinn told me you no longer wish to pursue the matchmaker. I've called off the investigator."

When? And had he planned on telling her that the Koslovs no longer cared to sue Lydia's alter ego? She tensed beneath Ian's touch, anger tightening every muscle.

"May I ask why?" Lydia asked, not caring if they all thought her rude to question them about a piece of private family business.

She needed to know. Why had Ian let her think that the lawsuit from Sofia's father was still very much a possibility? Had he been that intent on marrying her to fulfill his grandfather's will? Her chest burned with frustration and her stomach rebelled at the scone she'd eaten earlier.

Sofia smiled warmly. "Of course. I was never upset with Ms. West after I discovered it was my father's matchmaker who truly caused all the trouble with me getting paired with Cameron." She gave a sisterly elbow to Cameron's stomach as he stood beside her. "But I made a point of speaking to my father about it last month and convinced him that there was no need to scare a good matchmaker out of practicing her skills in New York. I mean, thanks to her—and Olga, the matchmaker my dad hired—I found Quinn."

How kind of Ian to let me know.

Lydia felt breathless and immobile, kind of like she'd had the wind knocked out of her. Behind her, she felt Ian's grip tighten on her waist, but she knew that as soon as his family left, she would tell him what she'd known yesterday and hadn't wanted to admit to herself.

She could not possibly stay married to him.

Thirteen

From a leather slipper chair in the corner of the spare bedroom, Ian watched—stunned—as Lydia packed her few things an hour after Jasmine left the apartment following a tense meeting. He'd only stayed for a portion of it, sensing he was the one causing the tension for Lydia. But he'd been able to see for himself that Jasmine had things well in hand for managing Lydia's public presence, making smart suggestions for how to handle Lydia's mother all the while maintaining control of all publicity.

He hoped she was simply preparing for their flight to Miami to return to work on the Foxfire. He feared it was more than that since their plane wasn't scheduled to take off for nine more hours.

Lydia folded a white silk nightgown with unsteady

hands, her focus overly careful. "How long have you known that the Koslovs didn't plan to sue me?"

Her words hung in the air. She smoothed the neatly folded garment on the bed, then tucked it into the small travel bag she'd set on a nearby luggage valet. Her face was still averted. She looked too pretty in her bright dress, and he wished he could twirl her around the room and make her smile the way they had in Costa Rica.

And before that, in Rangiroa.

What was it about their relationship that it only seemed to thrive in vacation mode? He should've never returned to New York with her so soon.

"Quinn told me to call off the investigator last night in a phone call after you'd gone to bed." It was the honest truth.

But it wouldn't be the first time she'd ignored the truth to draw her own conclusions.

She gave a vague nod, hearing his words, but never slowing her pace as she moved to the closet and found the next item of clothing to fold—the sheath dress she'd worn yesterday.

"You didn't have any inkling that your family no longer cared about uncovering Mallory West's identity?" She glanced his way, her green eyes huge and rimmed with red, before she returned to her task. "I asked Jasmine about my double identity in confidence, and she said—if I want her to—she would speak to Sofia about having us reveal the truth together and turn it into a story of happily-ever-afters." Lydia's voice hitched on the phrase and she stopped. She swiped an impatient hand across her cheek as she refolded the dress that wasn't cooperating. "She said it could be the perfect publicity spark to relaunch Mallory's matchmaking career, especially if Sofia were to get behind the Moms' Connection charity."

Ian hated to see Lydia hurt and upset. He wanted to wrap his arms around her and comfort her. Remind her that she knew him better than that.

But she'd never had faith in him, assuming the worst of him when his profile had landed on a matchmaker's site last summer. Assuming the worst of him now, even though he'd told her the truth. That's why he'd kept this marriage agreement *flexible*.

Smart of him, right?

So why did he feel as though her leaving was driving a knife through his chest?

"I had no idea that Sofia had talked her father into giving up the search for Mallory West," he reiterated, hoping if she heard it clearly, a second time, the words might mean more to her. "Lydia, I will tell you honestly that I was confident once I spoke to Vitaly Koslov and told him I knew Mallory's identity and that she meant no harm, he would forget about pursuing legal action."

"Yet you used the threat of a lawsuit to maneuver me into a marriage that would secure your share of McNeill Resorts." She straightened from folding the clothes and faced him. "That in itself seems…disingenuous."

"Perhaps," he conceded. "But don't forget that when I came to Miami to speak to you, I thought you'd been playing revenge games with me by matching me up with inappropriate people through your matchmaking service." He cut her off before she could argue.

"Only you weren't. I jumped to that conclusion about you, not realizing you'd just lost our child and were hurting desperately. And I am sorrier for that than I can ever say."

He rose from the chair, needing to hold her. Hoping she would let him.

"It seems we are both at fault for misjudging each other," she admitted, her voice thin and her expression unhappy. "But I was in the same apartment as you last night when you found out that your family had forgiven me for the matchmaking mistake. You could have told me then, or this morning."

"It would have been easy to do if you'd been in my bed, where I thought you'd be." He wondered why he hadn't knocked on the door to the guest room last night. Asked her what was wrong and shared that good news with her.

Maybe he really hadn't wanted to know that she sided with his new half siblings over him. That once again, he didn't come first with someone he loved—

Loved?

He let the word settle in his head, into his heart. And yes, hell, yes, he realized he loved her.

That's why his chest hurt as though it wanted to bleed out on the floor at her feet. He loved Lydia. And she was already looking for a way out of his life. Again.

"I wasn't half a globe away, Ian. I lay wide-awake in a bed one hundred feet from yours," she reminded him, tears gathering in her green eyes. "I guess I thought after the way our honeymoon went, maybe you wouldn't always have to put the McNeills before me."

He reached out to her, clasping her shoulders in his hands.

"You are a McNeill, damn it." He'd spent half the evening making sure she was legally protected in every way.

But Lydia was already tugging off her wedding ring. She held it out to him, the yellow diamond winking in the afternoon sunlight slanting in through the curtains.

"Not for much longer, Ian." She dropped it into his hand, and it was only then, when he held the cold stone in his palm, that he realized his hands had fallen from her shoulders.

"We still have months together," he informed her, his tone fiercer than he intended.

How could he convince her to make this a real marriage unless she stayed with him?

"It's not too late to admit we made a mistake." She turned her back on him, her green dress swishing as she moved around the room, taunting him somehow. "I thought I could pretend with you for twelve months and somehow survive the emotional fallout, but after how close we got in Costa Rica, I know I can't do that. I can't pretend when it hurts this much."

"And you're not worried about a scandal now, when a divorce after a three-day marriage will put you in the headlines for the rest of the year?" He hated himself for saying it.

Especially right on the heels of realizing he loved this woman. He should let her go with some dignity, damn it. Except he'd tried that once before and it hadn't made him any happier.

"I've realized a scandal is far less painful than a broken heart." She snapped the suitcase closed. "I called for a car, Ian. I'm going to stay at my place and see Kinley before I return to South Beach. I'll send someone up for my bag."

She picked up her purse and walked out of the guest room while Ian scraped his heart off the floor.

Wait a minute.

Why would *her* heart be broken?

He tried to put the pieces together and figure out what she meant. Why she was so upset.

Bloody hell.

Just as the elevator doors shut behind the woman he loved, he realized the truth that should have been obvious ever since they'd peeled each other's clothes off in Costa Rica.

She loved him, too.

By some kind of miracle, Lydia rode the elevator all the way down to the first floor without crying.

She hadn't wanted to walk through the busy lobby past the concierge desk with tears streaming down her face. She'd spent too much of her life trying to avoid making a scene to let herself fall apart publicly.

She hadn't called for a car. That had been total fiction she'd made up for Ian. And she didn't send someone up for her bag the way she'd told Ian she would. The tears behind her eyes were burning, burning, burning, so she blindly hurried out of the Pierre and rushed toward the closest traffic light so she could cross Fifth Avenue and lose herself in Central Park. A sea of tourists crowded the Grand Army Plaza, but she bypassed all of them, feeling the tears already plunking from her eyelashes to her cheeks.

Hugging her purse tighter, she squeezed through a line of city visitors waiting to ride the Big Bus. Couples and families milled around the food vendors, some checking street maps and others negotiating prices with the hansom cab drivers.

Lydia's shoes clicked along the pavement and onto the shady road leading into the park down to the pond. She found an empty bench near Gapstow Bridge, close enough for her to enjoy the view as well as some privacy. Only then did she give in to the crushing feeling in her chest, letting loose a soft wail of sadness that only constricted her lungs more.

Damn him.

She rummaged for tissue in her purse and came up with an antique handkerchief she'd purchased in a vintage shop a year ago. She'd washed it and tucked the linen in her bag, but hadn't found reason to sob her heart out in public until now.

She just couldn't see any reason to remain in a marriage with a man who freely admitted he only wanted to wed her to legally protect his share of a family business. But now, with the news of his half siblings and his grandfather's need to rewrite his legal documents to include the rest of the family, Ian didn't need her to serve that role anymore. Plus, she didn't need Ian's protection from a lawsuit since that wouldn't be happening either.

They'd been hasty. And she'd been too entranced by his kisses to see what a bad idea it was to play house with a man who held your heart in his hands. She'd been foolish.

She'd loved Ian McNeill ever since that first night together in Rangiroa.

"Is this seat taken?" The familiar masculine voice came from over her left shoulder.

She debated her options for running and hiding. She did not want Ian to see her like this. Sniffling loudly behind her handkerchief, she gave an inelegant shrug and tried to collect herself.

"Lydia, I need to talk to you." He lowered himself to the bench beside her.

She felt the warmth of his knee graze hers, but he didn't touch her otherwise. She ducked her head, unwilling to meet his eyes. How on earth had he found her? He must have followed her.

"I feel like you had your say back in the apartment, but I didn't really get to make my case." He draped a hand along the back of the metal bench, but didn't touch her. "I'd like a chance to tell you a few things before you follow through with…whatever you decide to do."

She was going to have their marriage annulled. That was her plan. But she hadn't recovered her voice yet from the crying. And she couldn't deny she was curious.

"I have not been myself for the last twenty hours— ever since I learned about the way my father betrayed my mother. Let me just start by saying that much. I know that I upset you last night, but I was too caught up in the family drama to chase down why, and I regret that. Deeply." He moved closer. "There is no McNeill more important to me than you. Not my brothers. Not my half brothers. And yes—there will be a difference for me until I meet the McNeill doppelgängers in person and decide what I think about them."

She heard a big group of people coming down the path near the bench and wiped her eyes on the handkerchief, not wanting to look like a basket case. But her ears were closely attuned to what Ian was saying. She was surprised he'd come after her at all.

"I swear to you, I didn't know Vitaly Koslov was going to drop the idea of a lawsuit when I proposed to you. I may have hit that angle hard to convince you to marry me, but I genuinely believed he would sue you. Cameron is working closely with Sofia on a new ballet video game, and he's mentioned more than once that bit about suing Mallory West so Sofia could use the proceeds for a charity that helps bring art and dance to underfunded school systems." Ian drew a breath, pausing as the large group of tourists walked past, led by a private tour guide still giving statistics about the Gapstow Bridge's reconstruction.

The pause gave Lydia time to process. Sofia and Cameron were making a video game? Not for the first time, she wished she could have been a part of the family. A real part.

She'd never had that, always on the outside looking in.

"Anyhow, I had every reason to think Sofia's father would make good on that threat until Quinn told me otherwise last night." Beside her, Ian traced a flower on the hem of her dress where the fabric lay between them on the bench. That part of the full skirt didn't touch her body, but still…

The small action felt intimate.

Her heart ached.

"I believe you," she blurted before she'd even planned to speak. "That is, I already regret the way I didn't hear you out about why you were on a matchmaking website last year. I was hasty and misjudged you then, and I'm not making that same mistake again." If only that was the extent of their problems. She shifted beside him, finally daring to turn and face him. "But, Ian, you can't deny that you deliberately put a time limit on our relationship. That you tied up our relationship with a contract because you had no interest in a real marriage."

"A fail-safe," he said simply. "I fell in love in Rangiroa, Lydia. I wanted you to marry me then and bought this ring a whole year ago." He produced the yellow diamond from his pocket. "When you said you never wanted to see me again…it crushed me. But not so much that I pawned the ring."

Her heart tripped over itself, and then lodged somewhere in her throat. She swallowed hard, her smile wobbly with love. And hope.

"You've had the ring—all that time?" It didn't compute. Even when she'd been miscarrying alone? Even when he'd found her in Miami and maneuvered her into a fake marriage?

"Yes, although I have to confess, I couldn't look at it for months." He held it up to the sunlight and the smaller stones ringing the yellow diamond refracted light in a dazzling pattern. "But when I went to South Beach—a job I took specifically because I knew you were working there—I brought the ring with me and thought I'd see what happened."

"But you wanted a contract. You said it was only temporary." She thought back to that day on the rooftop of the Setai when it felt as if she had no options but to say yes to him.

"How many times could I risk breaking my heart on one woman? Or at least, that was the logic I used then." He took her left hand in his and stroked over the finger where the ring once rested. "But after what we shared in Costa Rica, after having you fall asleep in my arms again, I knew that my heart is yours to break, Lydia. However many times it takes."

Emotions swelled and burst inside her. She had to clutch a hand to her chest to keep them all in. But she couldn't hold back a shocked gasp as he handed her the ring again.

And then he got down on one knee in front of the bench in Central Park for all the tourists to see.

"Will you marry me, Lydia? For real, and forever? I love you, and if you think you can love me, too, we can say our vows again in front of our family. All of them." His lips curved in a smile more compelling than that gorgeous, one-of-a-kind diamond. "Even the Caribbean McNeills, if you want."

She could sense people nearby stopping and staring. It was the first time in her life she didn't mind being a spectacle.

"Yes." A half cry, half laugh hiccupped out of her throat. She nodded fast. "Yes, Ian. I will marry you again and again. I'm far too in love with you to do anything else."

All around them, people clapped. Whistled. Cheered. The whole tour that had passed them before had stopped to watch the Central Park proposal.

Lydia let Ian slide the ring onto her finger, and then hauled him up onto the bench to kiss him, not caring who saw.

When he stopped, he whispered in her ear, "You think your publicist will mind we didn't clear this with her? I'm pretty sure there were some cameras around."

"I'm returning to matchmaking," she whispered back, her heart swelling with happiness. "I need to show I can at least get it right for myself."

Ian leaned away to look in her eyes and cupped her cheek in his hand. "You just made your first customer the luckiest man on earth. If you want, I can give you a testimonial."

She couldn't withhold a grin. She traced a finger over his mouth and watched heat flare in his blue eyes. "I'd rather have an encore."

To his credit, he didn't hesitate.

* * * * *

If you loved this story, pick up these sexy, emotional stories in THE MCNEILL MAGNATES *series from Joanne Rock!*

THE MAGNATE'S MAIL-ORDER BRIDE

and

HIS ACCIDENTAL HEIR (Available June 2017)

and then don't miss

HIS SECRETARY'S SURPRISE FIANCÉ
SECRET BABY SCANDAL

Available now from Mills & Boon Desire!

* * *

If you're on Twitter, tell us what you think of Mills & Boon Desire! #MillsandBoonDesire

MILLS & BOON®

Desire™

PASSIONATE AND DRAMATIC LOVE STORIES

A sneak peek at next month's titles...

In stores from 18th May 2017:

- **His Accidental Heir** – Joanne Rock
  and **Unbridled Billionaire** – Dani Wade

- **A Texas-Sized Secret** – Maureen Child
  and **Hollywood Baby Affair** – Anna DePalo

- **Claimed by the Rancher** – Jules Bennett
  and **Reunited...and Pregnant** – Joss Wood

Just can't wait?
Buy our books online before they hit the shops!
www.millsandboon.co.uk

Also available as eBooks.

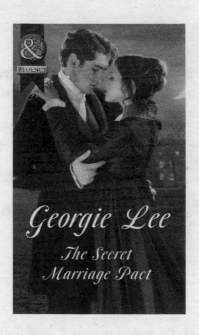